THE SISTERS
KARAMAZOV

THE SISTERS KARAMAZOV

An Autobiographical Novel

NATALIE KARAMAZOV

 ENROUTE

THE SISTERS KARAMAZOV

An Autobiographical Novel

NATALIE KARAMAZOV

ENROUTE

En Route Books & Media
5705 Rhodes Avenue, St. Louis, MO 63109
Contact us at contactus@enroutebooksandmedia.com

Cover design by TJ Burdick

Paperback ISBN: 978-1-950108-43-5
E-book ISBN: 978-1-63337-061-6

Printed in the United States of America

Introduction

"So what kind of a title is that? The Sisters Karamazov? So you think you're a female Dostoevsky? Isn't that more than a little arrogant?"

Let me explain.

The idea for writing this fictionalized account of my life came in this way:

A friend of mine once announced proudly: "I'm reading the famous *Brothers Karamazov* by Dostoevsky."

"You may not believe it, but Karamazov was my mother's maiden name!" I replied grinning.

"What? I'm studying Russian history, but I never saw that name except on the Dostoevsky's book title."

"Let me tell you how my mother got that name."

After a while I could reel off the 5 minute spiel, the 30 minute account, or the 2 hour short version of my whole life according to whether Dostoevsky's famous novel *The Brothers Karamazov* came up over coffee, lunch, or a dinner at my home.

Usually, after my explanation for my Karamazov connection, someone would say:

"Natalie, this is such a fascinating story. You ought'a write a book."

"I can't. The family would kill me," was my standard reply, rolling my eyes.

"Why don't you use a pseudonym and have the same events but with different names?"

The 10th time someone said this to me, I happened to have a free summer on my hands. So, "by popular demand" here is *The Sisters Karamazov.*

Not yet! A little more back-story about this novel. Dostoevsky manages to make many comments about his characters by having an omniscient narrator who not only sees and hears all, but also makes observations as he tells the tale. In this case, since Sisters Karamazov is autobiographical, the narrator voice is I, Natalie Karamazov. And, so, it is I who take the liberty of putting in commentary on the plot and characters as I go along. If this annoys you, just ignore those paragraphs introduced usually with the word "tangent"!

I

It started where so many stories begin, on Ellis Island, the gateway to New York City. Picture Immigration, year 1899. As the family legend goes, the translator from English into Russian and from Russian into English was explaining in English to the official: "They say that they lost their passports during a storm on the boat coming over from Bremen."

The tired forty year old male bureaucrat sighed, shrugged and muttered, "Bremen? They don't look German. They look Russian." That was because the women of the group trying to get into the United States wore babushkas – head kerchiefs tied in a knot under the chin.

The translator, a short woman in a formal blue suit relieved by the lacey lapels of a starched white blouse, nudged the father of the huddled group of seven, including a baby, to a spot in the crowded room a little out of earshot. Then she returned and explained in a loud voice to the official in English:

"They went from St. Petersburg, Russia to Finland and then from Finland to Northern Germany and took the ship from Bremen."

"What name do they call themselves?" the immigration scribe asked in a bored voice twiddling his pen.

At this, the go-between turned to my grandfather and asked in Russian, "What name do you want to be called in your new land of freedom and opportunity?"

When the translator conveyed this question in Russian, my aunt, Juliet, age 14, blurted out "Karamazov!"

Their real name, we grandchildren were always told, was Feldstein. So where did Karamazov come from?

My aunt Juliet, who invented this name for us, explained it the best to guests who visited their house in Brooklyn back in the 1900's, and also many decades later to us, her nieces:

"You have to understand that in 19th century Russia everyone in the intelligentsia read Dostoevsky's books. They were serialized in the magazines, chapter by chapter, and after the greatest novelist ever, Dostoevsky, died in 1881, people read the bound books or borrowed old magazines with the novels in them. Those readers included precocious teen-age Jewish ancestry Russians, such as, ahem, me." She would smile from ear to ear as she boasted about herself.

Now you, the reader of *The Sisters Karamazov*, might be thinking, "What you, Natalie Karamazov, have described in your book so far doesn't tally with our image of immigrant Jews!"

And I reply excitedly, eager to boast: (boasting is a prime characteristic of sisters Karamazov) "That's because most of the Jews you hear about who came to America were from Poland, not Russia. Maybe you never heard that the Czar imported doctors from Germany to St. Petersburg in the last decades of the 19th century to modernize backwards Russia. The Jews among these professionals were nothing like the peasants you see in films like *Fiddler on the Roof* with their ghetto Jewish garb and strongly traditional religious life-style.

Now I will explain about the non-Jewish religion part of our Karamazov's. Since my grandparents, the first in the United States to call themselves Karamazov, were long dead when I was a child, I never found out how far back the atheism in the Feldstein family went. I presume that my great-grandparents came out of the Enlightenment – the time when the orthodox Jews you read about in books like *Tales of Hasidim*, moved from little towns to the cities and rejected the religious practices which isolated them from their Catholic or Protestant neighbors. Many of these new-type Jews would still believe in God but, perhaps, the vague pantheistic God of Spinoza.

In any case, my mother, Elena, the babe in arms at Ellis Island, used to recount to us and our high school and college friends:

"The Feldstein's, who came to the United States in 1899, now with the name Karamazov, were atheists, left-wing atheists, part of the growing movement of social reform that would later be known as Communism."

"But we've read those books about the horrors of Communism," someone would surely pipe in. "How could anyone, anywhere, think his could be good?"

Elena, with her thin face, high cheek-bones, and sharp brown eyes, always eager to entertain others with narratives about her background, would lean forward at the table. All conversations in our house always took place over coffee and cake in the kitchen.

"Russians, in the 19th century, saw with their own eyes vast discrepancies between the wealthy and the poverty-stricken. They read about factories in France where workers endured terrible conditions while industrialists lived in luxury."

Then would come the shocker when Elena Karamazov would add: "Unlike the Polish Jews who left the old country because of anti-Semitic pogroms, the Feldstein's left Russia because the Czar was having radical atheists shot in the squares of St. Petersburg!"

Depending on how much time the guests wanted to spend listening to the details of my family's history more of the story would be narrated. What comes now is what I remember from my mother, Elena's, more fulsome tales.

Since my mother's father, Morris Karamazov was a doctor, not a philosopher, he didn't argue about religion with the Polish immigrant rabbis in their old black garments who came to his office in Brooklyn for medical treatment. He just scoffed at religious belief in the family and among his socialist friends at the rallies they joined in on, going into Manhattan across the Brooklyn Bridge in a large horse drawn carriage.

And the children, including my mother Elena, my aunt, Juliet, and the uncles, going to public school, just assumed that all religious people of any kind, Jew or Christian, were simply stupid, weak, or both.

However, the Feldstein's, now called Karamazovs, coming from the middle-class bourgeoisie of Russia brought along with them to the New World two of their Polish servants, a cook and a chamber-maid.

Tangent: I heard nothing about these women when I was a child, but they must have been Catholics since when my mother, Elena, was baptized Catholic at age 70 in 1969, she suddenly made the sign of the cross on her forehead and chest, "In the Name of the Father, the Son, and the Holy Spirit," in Polish: W imię Ojca, i Syna, i Ducha Świętego!

Well, you see, *The Sisters Karamazov* is going to be a very long story, full of unexpected events! As I write this in the year 2014, I am winking at the readers I hope to have for this novel. The wink suggests – the Sisters Karamazov will be jam-packed with religious themes, but not in so heavy a way that if you are not religious you will hate it!

II

Tangent: note to my beloved readers: 'Beloved?' Oh, you have no idea how authors love their readers! Writing is a lonely profession. We sit at a desk for hours and hours and hours with no idea if anyone will ever read our books! Then we get a letter, a phone call, or an e-mail from one of you saying how a book we wrote changed your life or, at least, delighted you. We grin from ear to ear. We get courage to write the next one. But that is not what this note started to be about. You just saw in the last little chapter that I leaped ahead from the early 1900's to 1969. Is that good for a writer to do? Probably not. But it is part of the personality of Natalie Klein (Klein is my married name), a professor, by the way, to go off on tangents. One student once told me with a smile:

"Dr. Klein, guess what? Whenever you look up from your notes, we wake up, because your tangents are much better than your ideas!"

So, I decided that instead of changing my tendency to leap ahead and then back again, you will just have to put up with it!

So, what happened after the Karamozov family settled into a house in Brooklyn? My grandfather, Morris Karamozov, a man of 5 feet 5 inches, balding but with sharp black eyes, ran his medical practice out of a large room with an entrance at the back of the house. I know that he must have been very busy and successful because my mother told me that, as the middle child, with an older sister, older brother and one younger brother, that her father, the doctor, never had time for her.

And here's another leap ahead: many years later, my mother Elena, about 5 feet 2 inches short, with a large bosom, short dark brown hair, and sharp black intelligent looking eyes, worked as a secretary for a psychoanalyst. This was back in the 1950's when the patient lay on a couch, eyes fixed on the ceiling, answering questions about his or her otherwise hidden fantasies, often about the wish to murder some antagonist or about illicit sex.

The therapist took notes, usually sitting at his desk. But this analyst contrived to sit in a chair near the sofa behind the head of his patients in a position where the client couldn't see him. This was because as well as taking notes, Dr. Eisenstat wrote out in long-hand the correspondence he laid on my mother's desk during the short break between patients! These my mother turned into perfect typed letters to be signed and mailed each day.

But sometimes Dr. E. came running out the door of this office into the reception room.

"Elena, take a break, client "x" is hysterical. Get me a glass of water. No more letters until I calm her down."

When Dr. E. had to put his whole mind on such a patient, my mother was left free to check out one of the numerous books on the psychiatrist's shelf about this fascinating new subject: psychoanalysis. It was from such readings that she gleaned how traumatic it could have been for herself just to be a middle-child ignored by a busy father!

Back to Brooklyn in the 1900's. What about our grandmother, Olivia, Elena's mother? How I wish I could have met this woman! A photo-portrait of Olivia, 8x6 inches, could be found in the old albums my mother kept until her death in 1987!

Looking at the photos I would say to Cassandra, (that is my twin sister's name), look at those beautiful, large melancholy eyes of Grandma Olivia! Look at her perfectly contoured face. Do you think we will look like her when we grow up?" My mother favored her father whose face was not beautiful at all, but typically Jewish with small inquisitive eyes and a sharp nose.

In the photo, grandmother Olivia's hair was in a fat, traditional bun, the kind worn by most women before the time of the short cut hair of the flappers. She was wearing a fancy satin dress, tightly covering the uncomfortable corsets most women wore in those times, at least on formal occasions. Maybe you, my reader, didn't know that this was why you read about Victorian women fainting so often. Those corsets hid the fat but stopped the breathing!

We grandchildren found Olivia's image fascinating. Especially her clothing interested us because our mother, Elena, was a post-suffragette, before feminism became a movement, who always wore pants; this, when all the other mothers of the children at our school wore skirts with panty-girdles underneath. So we envied the kids with the fancy mothers.

Morris Karamazov, grandfather, the doctor, died in 1930 at 50 years old, the usual age to die in those days. Olivia, his widow, immediately set sail for the Russia she had pined for all those years. That Russia was now a Communist state, called the Soviet Union, bothered her not at all since most of the Russian refugees in New York still thought of the U.S.S.R. as utopia.

Many decades later, when I was researching the family tree, a cousin produced a photograph of that same grandmother, her aunt Olivia, with the same bun but this time in a looser dress.

"She looks ecstatic," I exclaimed. This cousin remembered hearing that Aunt Olivia's joy was because she was back in her beloved Russia in St. Petersburg.

In the course of my research with relatives, a letter was found, with Russian stamps on the envelop, from Aunt Olivia to this cousin, saying how happy she was that Elena, her younger daughter, after many adventures, was now settling down and was expecting twins. That was us! We were named Natalie and Cassandra.

Olivia Karamazov died of tuberculosis in that far away land of Dostoevsky before she could see us. We also never met our aunt Juliet, Elena's sister who died suddenly of cardiac arrest in her 30's but, as you will see, we loved those names: Olivia, Juliet.

"What was public school like in Brooklyn, NY in the early 1900's?" we sometimes asked our mother.

My mother rarely talked about school since she didn't like it at all. The most she would say was that "The curriculum was not as classical as was still the case in Europe. No one expected public school kids in progressive America to learn Latin." However, the students did read sagas about the Greek and Roman gods, the great poetry and fiction of the Western world, and learned how to write in meticulous penmanship and grammatical English style. The girls also learned the new skill that would bring millions of women out of the home into the office: stenography. This education my mother put to good use in her life-long profession as an editor.

By the time Elena was a teen-ager all the girls wore short hair and it wasn't until I was a young adult that any girls went back to buns or thought that long granny dresses were cute.

III

Teachers at the public school compared Elena favorably to Stiva, her older brother, who by High School changed his name from the Russian: Stiva, to the English: Steven. Stiva, short like his father, but muscular, was what is, in our times, called a real pistol!

Without being a bad kid herself, it seemed that my mother, Elena, as a school girl nonetheless, was the start of a whole line of females in our family who hated the regimentation of classroom education. This tendency would come to include my daughters, who dropped out of High School at age fifteen and refused to take advantage of the college education they could get totally free at the university where I, their mother, was teaching. Free tuition for one's children is quite a perk for university professors.

When I was a school girl my mother, Elena, would ask, "So, you got all A's, Natalie? That's good." This she would acknowledge with no enthusiasm. You'll be like my sister Juliet who slugged away for a Ph.D. in history."

The expression "slugged away" seemed to me symbolic of the huge difference between the accolades other parents bestowed on their children at graduations and my mother's nonchalant half-pride/half-indifference to my successes.

What, then, were Elena Karamazov's interests when she was a teen in Brooklyn in the 1910's? Literature and adventure! Not the kind of adventure that boys dreamed of, involving battles or airplanes, but quite another kind. You see already, my Russian grandmother found home-making boring. Leaving cooking and cleaning to the Polish maids, Olivia spent her spare time reading Russian and French novels. Is it surprising that my mother's fictional heroines were not happy wives and mothers, but rebels such as Anna Karenina, or Madame Bovary? These proto-feminists, escaped from conventional bourgeois roles, not by seeking careers, but by means of secret, adulterous love affairs.

Years later I would reminisce with my sister about this feature of my Russian grandmother and mother's life and ask: "Cassandra, did you also idolize fictional women such as Anna Karenina and Scarlet O"Hara?"

"Never!" Cassandra replied. I idolized Pavlova and Ulanova." That was because Cassandra became a dancer.

"How come I never noticed how unhappy Anna Karenina and Scarlet O'Hara became?" I wondered much later.

Tangent: I teach Plato's Republic sometimes in courses on the Great Books. My students are astounded that this genius insisted on censorship of Greek literature and drama in his utopia. This censorship Plato thought was necessary for the sake of preserving of the morals of young people. I don't agree totally with Plato's remedy. But I do explain to my students:

"True the characters in Greek drama and present day fiction end up tragically. But unless they are counter-balanced by some saintly heroes and heroines, the young reader may easily ignore the sinfulness of the choices of the protagonists, and instead become seduced by the thrilling romantic aura of those exciting sins."

Back to Brooklyn at the end of the 1910's: thinking university might be less boring than High School, Elena enrolled at Barnard, the prestigious woman's college of New York City, next to Columbia University. That venture ended quickly because, as she would tell us on rainy Saturday evenings over dinner:

"I fell in love with a Columbia journalism student, Allen Weiner, also a left-wing Jewish background atheist. Allen was short but lean with large dark soulful eyes. When Allen was offered a job in Paris for an American newspaper he asked me if I wanted to come along. After a jiffy civil marriage, insisted on by both sets of parents, off we went, Allen and I, on an ocean-liner said good-bye to the Statue of Liberty en route to the land of Cezanne and Monet! You can't imagine how excited we were!"

Allen Weiner worked as a journalist covering Europe for the American edition of a French weekly. My mother took a secretarial job at the same newspaper. This was the one that all those expatriates from the United States bought and read regularly at the café tables. Interestingly enough she did not call herself Elena Weiner but, instead, Elena Karamazov. Probably because Weiner sounded Jewish, and there were plenty of anti-Semites in France, and Karamazov sounded Russian, of course.

"Did you eat all your meals at cafes, Mommy?" I once asked her when she was describing life in Paris.

She smiled, her wide lips in a slightly sardonic twist: "You don't suppose that a young woman like me had the slightest interest in becoming the sweet little wife, cooking for her husband, do you? Why shop and make meals when for a pittance I could immerse myself in the café-society milieu of the most exciting city in the world?"

Tangent: Now as I write the Sisters Karamazov, remembering my mother's sardonic smile is it a wonder that I found cleaning and cooking unbearably tedious when it was my turn to be a housewife?

A woman friend, who was also a Ph.D. and a university professor, told me that she was only teaching part-time because she wanted to be sure her daughters understood how beautiful being a wife and mother was by being home most of the time.

"I want them to see my joy that with just a rag and furniture oil I can turn a dusty table into a gleaming witness to the beauty of wood!"

Even though the image was kind of charming, just as I was thinking she could be right, she followed up with this heavy critique of my ways:

"Natalie, how will your daughters learn how to be happy wives and mothers if they see that you value teaching Great Books more than being a housewife?"

Even if this question would haunt me, relating the accusation of my friend to my family tree, I thought: I bet that this super-Mom's mother was a lot different from Olivia and Elena Karamazov!

If it's a no-no to put tangents from future decades into an autobiography, it is probably even worse to give away the theme in a chapter as early as the 3rd. The hidden idea behind the whole book is only supposed to become clear on page 300 earliest. But I'm too impatient for that! At least one of the themes will be how the Russian-style drama queen personality can be redeemed by Jesus.

When my mother was on the verge of baptism she once asked:

"Why do we have to be saved? What do we have to be saved from?"

"Saved from myself," was my answer then and still is.

Close of tangent.

IV

Café-society in Paris would become the hub of the American expatriates. The crowning glory of this new breed would one day be Ernest Hemingway!

After only a few months of married life, Elena became pregnant for the first time. She explained to us, her only children, that there in Paris at only 20 years old, the idea of being a mother was unbearable!

"What? Give up my interesting job and the fascinating conversations at café tables to be shut up inside an apartment feeding a baby! And, even worse, I would be trapped at home alone with a reporter-husband exploring all the cities of Europe!"

Was it surprising, really, that my mother, Elena, rushed instead, to the back alley office of an abortionist?

Tangent: Hindsight, I now would want to ask, "Why wouldn't you have considered taking a leave of absence from your job, having the baby, hiring a nanny for the infant, and then going back to your newspaper, with happy sprees in the evenings to the international conversation of your friends at the cafes?"

But such practical and ethical questions never came up from us, young teens, hearing such a story from our mother.

Of the many abortions that followed, I learned when I, myself, was not only a mother, but a pro-life Catholic activist! I think my father told me about them, but I am not even sure. Did I talk to her about them? I don't think so. Is it likely that my mother, then grandmother to my babies, still not sure if there even was a God, would want to give me the details of her tragic young adult Paris choices?

Now writing this novel I am getting in prayer that my mother, Elena, being a middle child and never being a favorite of anyone in the family, might have desperately wanted the feeling of being central in the sex act of a lover. She would want him to be forever her lover, not the father of their baby. She wouldn't have been able to predict the joy of being central to a dependent baby!

An important caveat here. My twin-sister, Cassandra, absolutely does not believe in the quantity, twelve, that I was told of, as being the number of my mother's abortions. She thinks there were abortions but that my father had a streak of mental illness in his make-up that left her, Cassandra, never sure that what he said was true about the woman, Elena, who he had grown to hate.

Maybe you do not know that in the rite of baptism of an adult convert, all the sins of the person's past life are forgiven. It was consoling to me to know that when I watched the priest pour the water over my mother's grey head so many years after those events.

Are you beginning to understand the title of this book: *The Sisters Karamazov*, in so many ways being a feminine version of the hair-raising happenings of *The Brothers Karamazov?*

Another Tangent: it occurs to me that some of you, dear readers, may not have ever read *The Brothers Karamazov*. Or, maybe you read it many years ago. It is the story of 3 Russian brothers and a fourth illegitimate brother. Their personalities are diametrically opposed. Dmitri is a wild soldier. Ivan is a skeptical intellectual. Alyosha is a saintly monk. Never mind about the 4th brother for now.

The important heroines in the book are also different. Katerina is a proud educated woman of the nobility. Grushenka is a wounded but good hearted seductive woman. The plot revolves around the murder of the father of the young men, a disgusting, lascivious, alcoholic wreck of a man.

Why would I, an American woman, identify with these characters in such a way as to entitle my novel *The Sisters Karamazov*? First there is the fact that Karamazov was our family name, as described above. But even more there is a certain rhythm to the emotions and ideas of Dostoevsky characters that I find to be very much my own.

A philosophical friend and colleague of mine in the 1980's found my anecdotes about the past, told him over lunches at the campus cafeteria, and my own personality, both intriguing and off-putting. He liked how colorful my family past was, but found the intensity of my personality somewhat alarming. Over a long vacation he decided to read 19th century Russian fiction. "No wonder you're like this, Natalie, coming out of such a background!"

Back to Elena in Paris. How about the adulterous women in novels of the 19th century? When they got pregnant did they have secret abortions? We know that in some countries it was customary for women with unwanted pregnancies to go to old crones living in the forests who performed such magic to rid mothers of the sad "baggage" of unwanted babies. Other unwed women went off for visits to far-away relatives and then left the babies behind for adoption. Poor women were known to leave the infant in a basket outside the door of the Church, praying that some merciful person would take the baby before it died of exposure.

I got quite a surprising insight into my own psyche, in relation to my mother's many abortions back in Paris, when reading an article by a medical researcher into side-effects of abortion. This doctor was compiling the results of studies of families where there was an abortion followed by live-births.

"The living children of mothers who have aborted once or more times, even when these live children were never told about past abortions, tend to have the following syndrome: insecurity to an unusual degree because they somehow pick up, in their unconscious psyches, that only perfect children have worth and that if they were not good enough in their behavior now, they could be killed by their parents!"

At first this theory seemed to me far-fetched, indeed. However, the possibility of such an extreme side-effect did provide an explanation for the incredible amount of insecurity both me and my twin-sister have always exhibited. In my case, the insecurity that I still have, takes the form of having anxiety attacks whenever I have to ask any authority figure for help, and, even more so, if I think anything I do would be judged as bad by any parental figure.

Of course, the evil of abortion itself, in arranging for the dismemberment of the innocent baby is much more important than side-effects for other children in the family! May God have mercy on all the present day millions of women who, often in a state of panic, commit such acts! Psychologists say that the mother's themselves are deeply wounded and many of them have great trouble after abortions with guilt, depression, numbness, withdrawal or substance addiction. Wonderful healing groups such as Project Rachel, help women who have aborted babies to embrace the forgiving love of Jesus for their abortions and to get healed of such side-effects in their own personalities.

I put in this tangent about insecurity of other children in the family from abortions previous to their own birth, because the present counselor that I am seeing at the age of 77, thinks that writing *The Sisters Karamazov* can be a healing for me.

My counselor claims: "Adults who have inordinate anger and anxiety need to go back to sources of pain all the way back to childhood. Allowing ourselves, in some present form, to experience the original, repressed pain again, can bring release."

So far this present psycho-therapy based on the theory of coming back to the pain of childhood has been a source of greater peace.

One healing thought I shared with my twin, Cassandra, was this: "Mommy would never have had a large family of many, many, children. Without those abortions, you and I would never have entered this world!"

V

Back to Paris in the 1920's and '30's: Most of what I know about my mother, Elena's, life in France comes from chit-chat on Saturdays when we were pre-teens. In the morning our mother forced us to help her with house-cleaning. As a reward, in the afternoon, if we didn't go to the movies, we sometimes went through old photo albums dating back to Paris café-society.

These pictures included some strange yellowed pictures of French people. Most fascinating was a portrait photo of a woman's profile pitched upward at an awkward angle. Her name was Antoinette.

I was haunted by the face in this photo for a special reason. One day I picked an old novel off my mother's shelf whose heroines were lesbians. I was astounded. How could such a thing be?

"Mommy, I am reading this novel about lesbians. I don't understand. I thought only men and women had sexual intercourse."

Using my question as an opening, she told me, in a matter-of-fact tone of voice, that she, herself, was bi-sexual! Somehow I connected this revelation with the photo of Antoinette. But I never asked if this beautiful French woman had been her lover. Maybe I didn't want to know? Did I disassociate, as psychologists call a tendency to "stuff" things we find upsetting?

Maybe I didn't ask more about Antoinette because the photos in the album of a French artist called Guy were displayed with much greater passion by my mother. When displaying the albums of the Paris time, she would stroke the photos of this man, Guy. The photos showed a tall debonair fellow with a lock of hair covering half an eyebrow. "He was the love of my life."

"Why didn't you marry him?" I remember Cassandra asking.

"Oh, he was married. He loved me more than her," she said smiling happily," but his wife was a wealthy woman who supported him in his unlucrative life as an artist."

What about Allen Weiner, Elena's journalist husband? What was he up to when she was having affairs with these women and men? It seemed that the personalities of Elena and Allen didn't match well. They divorced after only two years of life in Paris. However, he wrote an obscure novel that I found on our bookshelf in NYC in my high school years. This was the time when writers such as James Joyce created fiction so obscurantist that few readers could understand what they were about. Allen Weiner's small novel was of that type, so my desire to comb the book for glimpses of my mother's life with him was fruitless.

Long tangent: Sisters Karamazov style, later, as a senior at the university, I was gleefully telling the life-story of my family to a graduate student. What did I look like then? I was a rather slender 5 foot 4 inch girl with long brown hair and bangs. The most noticeable part of me was large teeth always showing because of a broad smile with which I greeted anything interesting anyone else said.

To continue my narrative about the grad student when I was at the university. He looked at me quizzically: "Wait a minute? Your mother was married to Allen Weiner, the writer? Why I'm a friend of his son. We studied world literature together at Harvard?"

"Was Allen's father alive?"

"Oh, no. But Michael, the son, is still at Harvard in graduate school."

Out of curiosity, I decided that I absolutely must meet this son to pump him for information about his father, my mother's first husband. My friend gave me the address of Michael Weiner in Boston. Since Harvard had one of the graduate schools in Great Books that I was applying to for a scholarship, I arranged an interview with the chairman of the department on a Friday and contacted Michael Weiner to see if I could visit him perhaps on Saturday.

The deep voice at the end of the phone said, "Oh, that weekend I'm having a house party. Why don't you come and stay over and go back to NYC on Sunday. He had plenty of room because he lived in a large old Victorian Boston mansion.

In my feverish imagination, it was going to be love at first sight, followed by elopement to Paris, where what didn't work with my mother and his father would be a spectacular success with us. Not too drama-queen that scenario!

If you happen to have read *The Brothers Karamazov* you will recognize the Russian trait of projecting fantastic illusions of total happiness with next to nothing to go on!

This "blind date" with Michael Weiner turned out to be not only disappointing but also bizarre. The parties hosted by the short, thin, unprepossessing young man, Michael Weiner, involved some kind of sado-masochism, as I was to see!

After an elaborate gourmet dinner served to some 7 Harvard students, I was dying to get Michael aside to ask my questions about his father.

"So tell me about Allen Weiner, Michael. He is like a legend to me."

"He was very reserved. I was closer to my mother, my father's second wife."

"Did he talk much about his marriage with my mother and their life in Paris?"

"No. never."

29

After a few other such unsatisfactory answers, he asked me if I would like to see the guest bedroom on the second floor. Up a spiral staircase we went into a room furnished with a four-poster bed, with travel posters hanging on the walls.

"You must be very tired from your trip. Here are some towels. See you tomorrow morning. We all generally sleep late."

Since I really was tired after the long trip on Friday from New York City on the train, followed by the interview at Harvard, I accepted this proposal even though it was only 9:30 PM, way before any student's bedtime on a weekend.

In the middle of the night, I woke up thirsty. I stumbled down the stairs to get a glass of water. There I saw Michael in striped pajamas on his way into the library wiping tears off his eyes with one hand, and with the other hand clutching a whip! I scurried upstairs so that I wouldn't interrupt anything.

On arising at 8 AM the next morning I decided not to stay in this strange house. I made a cup of coffee, wolfed down 3 croissants, wrote a thank you note, left it on the kitchen counter, and walked out the front door to hail down a taxi to the train station. I licked my wounds as I hurtled back from Boston to New York City.

Remembering this incident from time to time it occurred to me that there may have been drugs involved in this house party. But this was still in the '50's before we thought in such terms.

VI

The post-Paris photo albums in the bureau drawer of our apartment that we looked through on Saturday afternoons, provided visuals for a running commentary on our mother's life once she came back to New York City. Exactly why Elena Karamazov returned to the United States was never divulged. I am wondering now, as I write this so many decades later, whether that long love affair with the married Frenchman became too difficult.

Prominent in the New York City albums were photos of herself, and our father, Jeronimo De Toledo, sitting at large desks doing editorial work for the WPA (Writer's Project's Administration). The WPA was a huge agency of the New Deal created in 1935 to hire millions of unemployed people for all kinds of useful projects.

Enter, Jeronimo De Toledo, as major player in the drama of *The Sisters Karamazov.*

I describe Jeronimo as our father rather than as Elena's husband because Jeronimo and Elena never married legally. But they lived together for more than 8 years. They met in the Communist party.

The father of myself, Natalie, and Cassandra, my twin-sister, Jeronimo De Toledo, had one of the most unusual backgrounds imaginable even in a country where unions of men and women from diverse ancestries were and still are not uncommon.

Jeronimo's mother and our paternal grandmother, Hope Paderborn, was a Quaker farm-girl from Allentown, Pennsylvania with long blond hair and large blue eyes, innocent as a dove. His father and our grandfather, David De Toledo, was a handsome Don Juan from Colombia, South America, studying dentistry at the University of Pennsylvania. Jeronimo looked nothing like his hispanic father who was short and dark-eyed. With a long pale face Jeronimo looked like his German ancestry mother, in spite of his hispanic name. Jeronimo was 5 feet 10 inches. In those days he was considered tall. He had greenish blue eyes and reddish brown straight hair. Our daddy looked unusual mainly because of his habit of wearing dark green corduroy pants, and open shirts instead of the stiff gabardine suits and silk ties other middle-class men wore in those times.

I will write now in the more clipped sentences of my father, Jeronimo as he described his ancestral background. These histories we would hear after our parents separated when we were about 9-years old. They were told to us by Daddy on Sunday afternoons when he had his visitation rights. I associate them with sarsaparilla soft drinks at the cafeteria of the famous New York Museum of Natural History on Central Park West.

Jeronimo's manner of describing anything, in contrast to my mother's more impressionistic amused raconteur style, was always factual, and never emotional.

Here is a sample:

"David De Toledo, my father, your grandfather, was an offspring of a family of Sephardic Jews. Some Spanish Jews converted to the Catholic religion. They were suspected of being Catholics in name only, and of conniving with the Muslim invaders of Spain. Such Jews, both non-converts and converts, escaped the Inquisition in Spain by fleeing to Holland. Perhaps there was intermarriage with fair skinned Dutchmen, because my father was pale white in spite of his dark black hair and brown eyes.

"From Holland these Spanish Jews migrated to the Dutch Colombian towns in South America in the 1850's. So the extended family members on the ships to Colombia included Catholics and Jews.

Of the un-converted Jewish immigrants to the New World, some remained traditional, observing the holidays of Spanish Jews, but they were never as religious as their Jewish counterparts in Poland. This Spanish Jewish De Toledo family lived on the Island of Curacao from whence at the end of the 19th century some of the sons were sent to study to the United States.

Tangent: Way later, in the 1980's I would learn that some of these Jews were not religious Sephardic Jews at all, but part of the secret Jewish Masons! It was the branch of the secret Jewish Masons who sent some of their sons to the United States to study dentistry at the University of Pennsylvania. This profession was to be the cover for their clandestine purpose of organizing the secret Jewish Masonic temples in New York City!

To continue with the part of the story my father told us as children, which did not include the Jewish Mason part at all:

"To the dental chair of David Toledo, an intern in Philadelphia, one day appeared a Quaker young woman, Hope Paderborn, hair in a demure blond bun. In an attraction of opposites, they fell in love, married, and moved to New York City.

"David de Toledo set up practice in a posh Madison Avenue office building. To this office, besides the usual clientele, would also, from time to time, appear from the clan in Colombia, touring New York City, dark, flamboyently-dressed hispanic women who would drop in on Tio David to get their teeth taken care of. Among those members of the wider family from Colombia would also come to New York City young people from the old Catholic branch of the De Toledo's also living in Colombia, some who studied at such Catholic colleges as Marymount." These were not flashily dressed, by the way.

Daddy never told us the story of his birth on trips to the Museum. It came to light, instead, when he wrote his memoirs in his '80's. But to keep the biographical part complete I am including this information here.

According to his later autobiographical manscript:

"The first born to Hope and David De Toledo was a "monster" so disfigured that David, his father, threw the body into a large furnace in the basement of the apartment house where they lived. A year later, I, Jeronimito, came into the world as a beautiful baby, doted upon the more for the contrast with my ill-fated sibling."

[Note, this anecdote about the monster first child of our paternal grandparents is one of the other stories my twin sister denies, considering it an aberration of our slightly crazed father.]

A photo stapled onto the memoir shows Jeronimo with blondish-red hair looking so much like his mother that you would never imagine his Hispanic father had any role in his genes. Occasionally as an adult I would wonder if perhaps the marriage of Hope and David De Toledo was arranged by her Paderborn family to cover an illegitimate birth by a Pennsylvania father. But, since I, the granddaughter, resembled in some ways, not my father, but my Hispanic grandfather David, I would, eventually, dismiss this melo-dramatic Karamazov drama-queen style theory.

More photos appended to the manuscript show this little boy, Jeromino, in lacy white dresses with long hair.

"Small boys in this time, the tail end of the Victorian era," our now 80-year old father explained while sharing with us the Memoirs, "used to be dressed that way. Remember how in English novels of that time lads were "breeched" at the age of 8 years or so? It was only at that age of 7 or 8 that boys stopped wearing long dresses and were clothed in pants, the better to straddle a horse."

VII

Back to my father telling Cassandra and I his life story at the Museum when Cassandra and I were 9 years old and older in the early 1950's.

"The unwritten contract between your grandmother Hope, the Quaker, and David, the secret Jewish Mason, was that their children would be baptized and brought up Christian. My mother, Hope, would gradually make her way up the New York social ladder by becoming a Presbyterian and then an Episcopal, attending the prestigious beautiful newly-built church in the upper West-Side: St. John the Divine. Such moves were manifest visibly in the change from simple Quaker longish print dresses to silk more tailored dresses adorned by pearl necklaces.

"Your grandmother, you know, is an anti-Semite!"

"What's that?" Cassandra asked, setting down her sarsaparilla on the marble-like table of the Natural History Museum cafeteria. Cassandra was always easily shocked by whatever anyone said that sounded blunt or crass.

"People who despise Jews," confided my father, lowering his voice.

"I wanted very much to work for this very Museum but they turned me down because of my Jewish ancestry!"

Knowing how much my father disliked my grandmother, who I

loved more than I admitted, I decided not to bring up how, recently, walking with her on Broadway, a taxi-cab almost hit us making a U-turn. Little refined old lady Christian Hope shook her cane at the driver and spat out: "Dirty Jew." Since my grandfather, being a "secret" Jewish Mason never identified himself to us as Jewish, Cassandra and I missed the irony of this expletive!

David De Toledo, though accepting that his only son would be brought up Christian, was not without his own influence on Jeronimo, however. In the Memoirs, my father described a scene I have never heard of in any other autobiographies no matter how salacious. He claims that every morning early before going to school, he was made to sit on a chair in the bathroom while his father shaved. During this procedure the little fellow was told, "Remember without fail that if you visit a prostitute you must always wear a condom to avoid venereal disease."

Jeronimo De Toledo was sufficiently discrete in his 80's not to include any of the descriptions his father must have given him of the meaning of the word prostitute" or "condoms" or "VD"!

Such instruction was surely not part of the catechism of the Presbyterian Church where he was brought to Sunday School each weekend by his mother!

In fact, my father was to exhibit the effects of the huge difference in values between his parents in a split in his adult personality between a tug toward idealism, refinement and compulsive neatness with, on the other side, a pull toward sex outside of marriage.

I do not know if it was grandfather David who suggested to my father when he was a 12 year old that the God my grandmother loved with all her heart, was actually just a myth. It could have been something he picked up from an atheistic teacher in the public school.

Here is how, at the Museum cafeteria, Jeronimo De Toledo, described the turning point of his teen life:

"At the Presbyterian Church, all us boys and girls were lined up,

wearing fussy white lace gowns, for a procession. We were to kneel before the Bishop for Confirmation. As I was walking up, I proclaimed in a
loud voice: 'I don't believe in God and I cannot be confirmed.' With that I
turned on my heel never to return."

"Your grandmother, Hope, followed me out weeping bitterly all the
way home," he reported with a derisive smile.

Cassandra and I knew that grandma Hope never stopped weeping for
her beloved only son. When we became Catholics, long after her death, we
could easily imagine her thoughts at this crisis in her life: "My son rejected
Jesus? For what? To believe instead in "nothing?" She didn't live long
enough to see her only grandchildren, myself and Cassandra, baptized,
confirmed, and Christian Catholic leaders. Will she someday greet us at
'the pearly gates'? I do believe so.

Continuing the story of his youth my father reported that, "Though I
was always an exceptional student, the high-point of my youthful life was
the summer. This was because vacations meant boarding ships to South
America with my father. So much did I love the ships, the ocean, and
travel, that I was allowed to wear a sailor suit on these trips and "help" the
helmsmen steer.

"The most dramatic summer was when an expedition of zoologists
from England, verifying Darwin's evolutionary theories, went to the island of Galapagos to collect huge turtles. Apparently capturing them was
difficult for men, but easier for swift boys. I was commissioned to join the
scientists in their hunt for specimens."

There is a photo in one of the albums of my teen father lifting such a
big turtle above his head. He was rewarded with a mention of his name in
the reports of the expedition.

Tangent: Sixty years later, my sister, Cassandra Karamazov De Toledo, was touring Hawaii. Friends who had moved from California to Hawaii, took her to a zoo where there was a huge ancient turtle crawling
about on the rocks. A plaque was affixed on the cage with these words:

"Galapagos turtle, discovered by Jeronimo De Toledo in 1925." This friend had recognized that the name of Cassandra, De Toledo, was the same as the one affixed to the fence surrounding the turtle pond!

My father would tell us, "I loved animals and the sea so much that I was torn between dreams of being one day a zoologist or a seaman. My love of the study of animals was brought into play at the Writer's Project, the government started during the Depression where I compiled a book with photos and texts called *Who's Who in the Zoo!*" I did also join the Merchant Marines during World War II.

My parents didn't meet in the Writer's Project, but, earlier, when they were both in the Communist Party. You would have to have read an entire book about the rise of that party in New York City to understand the pull of this false but utopian vision on the young people of those years. All of world-wide poverty was to be eradicated by the revolution. True, at the meetings of the little groups they had to wade through the unintelligible writings of this Karl Marx person but, afterwards over coffee, they could revel in conversations where idealism was peppered with rebellious, ridiculing, hate of the evil capitalists.

VIII

More of Jeronimo's Memoirs:

"Two events coincided that would totally change the lives of Elena Karamazov, your mother, and I, Jeronimo De Toledo. After years of Communist warnings against German fascism, the Hitler/Stalin pact was signed. A temporary shrewd move from the standpoint of Stalin, the effect was electrifying for idealistic American Communists. Thousands of us dropped out of party affiliation immediately and others left gradually. Later I became an informer about the party to the investigation of the inroads of this movement in the United States."

Tangent: the most interesting book to read about this subject is *Whittaker Chambers: Witness*. Chambers was a Communist spy in the US government. Disaffected he became a Christian, and turned against the party and some of his best friends who were other spies in high places.

"At just the same time your mother found she was pregnant. It seemed she was tired of getting abortions. I, Jeronimo, a lonely only child, and lover of animals, thought having a baby might be fun, like having pets. I promised not only to support her if she kept the baby, but also to help take care of the infant, something almost unknown among men of that generation in our set. Since we didn't believe in marriage, we just moved in together to await the baby."

The baby turned out to be twins. us: Natalie and Cassandra.

"In retaliation for leaving the Party, we got an anonymous note in the mail warning that our babies would be killed in their double carriage. Fortunately, it was just a threat."

Tangent: I, Natalie Karamazov Klein, attribute my mother's full-term birth to the grace of God. I was delivered out of the womb, trailing right after my twin, Cassandra. 70 years afterwards, someone read me a passage from the journals of Saint Faustina written around the time my mother made her decision. Jesus told Sister Faustina that the nuns in the convent needed to pray for women not to have abortions!

Hurrah! We were born!

Now I will switch from my father's narratives to my own "voice."

Of course I don't remember what being born was like. But I have albums and albums of photos of us eeny-weenies. After the death of Elena and Jeronimo in the late 1980's I took for myself most of these baby picture albums. That was because in almost all of them, I am smiling and Cassandra is frowning so she didn't want these records!

Could my sister's unhappy face in the photos be related to the theory that the first twin struggles to get out of the womb? This makes that twin stronger throughout life, some think. The second twin gets a free ride which makes him or her merrier but not as strong!

An interesting feature of the photos is that never were both of us twins in the arms of our mother at the same time and there are none of her breast-feeding or bottle-feeding either of us. It was black maids who gave us our milk, the photos of whom we could see with us little babies heavily swathed in blankets in their arms.

In those days bottle-feeding was considered not only liberating for woman, since someone else could do give the bottle for her, but also more healthy. Actually already before the 20th century many upper-class women had stopped breast-feeding babies, giving out the chore to women who were called wet-nurses. This was also to keep the figures of the biological mothers more trim.

"Cassandra, did Mommy ever cook when we were little?" I asked my twin at a family reunion after our mother, Elena's, death, when I could no longer ask Elena, herself.

"No. I remember that our Daddy, always a resourceful person, figured out how to cook simple meals after work."

"So, what did our mother do all day?" I wondered.

Cassandra did remember: "She read the New York Times every single morning first page to back page and all day and evening she read the latest novels!"

I still have photos of our early lives on my screen-saver. I especially like looking at one where my mother is holding me and my father is holding Cassandra and they are smiling at each other.

Now, we all know that one could never write an accurate history of anyone based just on photos. Why not? Because we have all been taught to smile just before the camera takes the photo. So even unhappy people get to look happy in those photos!

I have no memories of Elena and Jeronimo enjoying each other at all when we were little children. Not that they had open arguments or came to blows. My mother said that they agreed that parents should not fight in front of their children. They separated when we were 8 years old. The pediatrician, who had treated the family for 3 of those years, drily observed: "Even though you didn't traumatize the twins by open fights, don't you think your children heard the silence?"

Was my father still working for the WPA when we were little children? Maybe at first, but that program ended with the full employment that was declared in 1942.

The first job my father worked at after the WPA entailed a move from Brooklyn where we had landed soon after our birth. Jeronimo De Toledo was hired to promote a new invention called micro-film. The company was based in Norwalk, Connecticut, and the job paid enough for us to live in a large house with a vegetable garden in the back and to employ a full-time black maid.

By now we were around 4-years old and I have distinct memories to match the photos. Many show us naked playing with pets, including snakes! This was a carry-over from my father's love of zoology. I just mentioned how resourceful my father was. One form this took was itemizing dogs and cats as dependent tax write-offs! Samantha De Toledo, Hans De Toledo, were a few of these doggie "sisters and brothers."

Describing the De Toledo family here, I am wondering how my father got around the fact that he and Elena were never legally married and yet she was also listed as a dependent. Maybe this was why during those years she did call herself Elena De Toledo, not Elena Karamazov.

IX

I want to tell you more about the black maid, Penny. This married woman must have weighed about 250 pounds. In my memories she totally fit the stereo-type of the black Mama, with her own toddlers, who she brought with her to our house, clinging to her skirts. She had a deep melodious laugh. I adored her. With none of the psychological complications of women Karamazov's, she was just sheer unconditional nurturing love, manifested by never-ending goodies available in the kitchen, and a smothering all enveloping embrace should we, her little charges, run in from the garden with anything from a scratch to sudden fear of a worm.

Now my mother was no sylph. Having given birth to us when she was 38 years old, she had the usual middle-age spread, large breasts, and a naturally warm body. But, even though she was a comforting person, she could never compete in this realm with Penny, whose love and merriment overflowed as from a geyser.

An even bigger reason for the contrast between my parents and Penny was that Daddy and Mommy were both editors. Without purposely doing so, their mode of relationship to us, their children, was to correct every sentence we ever uttered either for bad grammar, pronunciation, or factual errors!

Cassandra and I, this 3rd generation of Karamazov sisters, reacted quite differently to this tutelage. My twin, in any case more introvert, became wary about speech, hiding from the possibility of criticism. I never stopped talking. But as a speaker, writer and teacher, I rebelled against my parents' editorial supervision, by being gloriously careless about words. Babbling like a brook at all times, I just let others correct any egregious mistakes, without even considering thinking first before speaking or writing.

Tangent: The most amusing incident concerning this trait is that an excellent publishing house, Ignatius Press, once contracted for a manuscript of mine. The title was *How to Teach the Great Books.* The publisher liked the topic. Later, he told me:

"You know, Natalie, the editor changed every sentence in the book to make it flow better without errors!"

Even though I had looked over the corrected manuscript before final publication, I never even noticed these changes!

Back to photos of us as children: a feature of the photos of the time between 3 and 5 years old, when we lived in Connecticut, is that we were always wearing t-shirts, over-alls, and sneakers, and never the pretty little dresses worn by most girls of those decades. We never wore the shiny black pumps you see in photos of little girls of that time.

Years later working on emotional healing exercises, it surfaced that if my parents had us girls wearing clothing only boys wore in those days, and called us by boy's nicknames: Nat and Cass, that maybe they had wished for boys instead of girls! Indeed, as will be explained as I go along, I have always had ambivalence about feminine clothing. Even though I always wear dresses rather than pants, and I hate masculine clothing, the dresses I wear are often rather plain garments, and I have never worn much make-up or jewelry.

In a reaction against being "forced" to look like a boy as a child, when I became a teen I always chose to wear dresses instead of blue-jeans, and still hate sneakers. Always a Karamazov extremist, I would wear large granny dresses in the '70's even while riding a bicycle.

Two particular traumatic childhood memories date back to Connecticut. Every evening home from work after dinner my father played loud music on the phonograph. We would dance naked to these rhythms, such as the gathering crescendos of Ravel's Bolero. Once when it was time for bed, but we kept dancing. my father smacked our behinds yelling "Enough is enough." To this day Cassandra insists:

"That was the only time he ever hit her in any way."

I don't remember any other spanking either.

At the time, I was flabbergasted. Since this memory combined, 6 years later, with my father leaving us and marrying a seemingly subservient very feminine wife, I think it remained in my psyche. My reaction afterwards, took the form of often pushing myself forward in speech with men, in confrontative ways, and then being scolded by them for doing so, not in so many words but with scowls and withdrawal. From a psychological standpoint one could surmise that I have a need to be brash with men in order to test out if they only like sweet, subservient women. If that is the case, then to hell with them!

Big Tangent: Note: After writing this theory last night at age 77, with the word "hell" in the last sentence, I woke up in the night and realized that the sudden use of that word was itself extremely symbolic. The thrust is that I want to punish men, as if I were a Goddess against whom they had rebelled by refusing to love me unconditionally. Or, at least, an animus driven woman, as Jungians describe women who have too much negative masculine in them, also called, "in the vernacular" bitches!

Tangent continued: Then it seemed to me that Jesus might want me to think of it differently. He might want me to think that "You are hitting here on the extreme of a negative side that is always a temptation for a strong woman. You are not simply that, for you have been deeply permeated with My healing love, but it explodes out of you when you are in extreme stress, and this still needs more healing love, not to banish the strength part, but to blend it in as a painter would blend a little red into a dark brown on a palette."

[Note continued: I went to confession this morning about this Jezebel-like spirit of rage at men. After absolution I felt a demon leave me and emerged shaking inside.]

Back from Tangent: The other incident also involved my father. It was the weekend, so Penny was not there to make the usual blueberry pancake breakfast. My mother was not there because she had taken a train into New York City for the weekend. My father made scrambled eggs.

"I don't like eggs that way. Make them the way Penny does!" I pouted.

I refused to eat them.

"Then you get nothing for breakfast," he yelled at me, and I cried.

X

Tangent: Many years later my mother was reminiscing about the old days of Paris café-society. Talking about the French artist, Guy, she recounted how he had once visited New York City to be part of an exhibition at the Museum of Modern Art.

"I met him there, at the Museum, after all those years."

She told us how, on her way back to Connecticut in the train, she wept thinking of how colorful her life had been in Paris and how dull it was to be with Jeronimo.

"Why didn't you go back with him to Paris?" I asked.

"He was married and didn't want to lead a double-life," she replied.

I gathered that for some men having sporadic love affairs was okay, but not a steady mistress on the side.

Hearing this story, I put two and two together and guessed that this may have been the very weekend when my father, usually not angry at us at all, was so upset about the scrambled eggs! I think he always loved my mother Elena more than she loved him and was afraid she would run off with Guy back to Paris and never come back.

If this story shocks you, I need to have you keep in mind that, in the circles my father and mother frequented, there were no ethical principles concerning marriage. It was open marriage way before this became popular in the 1960's. Fidelity in relationships, such as what came to be called common-law marriages, was not only not obligatory but infidelity was not even looked down upon. Legal marriage, and even more religious weddings were considered to be ridiculous conventions of the past.

That didn't mean, however, that women and men, living together, didn't suffer from rejections, betrayals, or abandonment. They just accepted these as part of the adventure of living.

That's the word – adventure! Life was viewed not as a gift of God, destined for fulfillment in union with the Trinity for all eternity, but rather as an adventure with risks, thrills, and calamities.

Fast forward. My mother at age 87 is dying slowly of heart disease. She is staying in my house with an attendant monitoring her feeding tube. I feel nervous about asking her if she is afraid of death. Even though she became a Catholic at age 60 she is not so strong in the faith that she is necessarily hoping to leap into the arms of Jesus as soon as possible.

Cassandra comes to visit. Sitting next to mother Elena's bed, she gently queries:

"Mother, are you afraid of death?"

"No!" Elena replies with a faint smile, "I think it will be an adventure."

End of Tangent.

We were not destined to remain in that lovely house with a garden in Connecticut.

Could it have been fear that my mother might leave him that was the reason why in 1943 my father decided that we should move back to New York City where my mother would be less isolated and not totally dependent upon him for company?

We now enter into the phase of the Sisters Karamazov where Cassandra Karamazov De Toledo and I, Natalie Karamazov De Toledo, are school girls. Those middle maternal ancestry names were not in the records at the school but, became a kind of joke.

"What's your name, little girl?"

"Natalie Karamazov De Toledo!" I would boast.

Picture the family: Elena, about 5' 3" in tailored pants, with a beret on her short black hair; Jeronimo, 5' 10" thin, usually in corduroy suits without a tie with reddish brown hair; Natalie and Cassandra, 6 year old girls in denim overalls, with short, straight shoulder length brown hair cut in bangs across our foreheads.

We are living on the upper West Side of New York City in a 10-story apartment house facing the Hudson River. If you, the reader, happen to live in that city, you could even see the still standing and functioning building with 310 Riverside Drive on the canopy at the entrance.

Back when we were living there, a doorman in a uniform was always in the vestibule helping residents bring shopping carts into the elevator or allowing old ladies and even men walking with canes to hold onto his extended arm as they trundled toward the elevator after a walk in the park.

Across from Riverside Drive at 93rd St. was a statue of a soldier on a horse facing out over the narrow park that separated the drive from the rocky banks of the river. Since World War II was still being fought, we thought of this equestrian as a kind of guardian.

Having been lurched away from the countryside of Connecticut, this city was strange to us with its hundreds of paved streets each one with names not like Green Street, or Stable Street, but only numbers from west to east and then long, long, intersecting avenues with names like Amsterdam, Columbus and Central Park West.

"This morning, I took Cass and Nat to register at the public school, P.S. 93, Jeronimo," Elena announced one August evening.

"Cass and Nat," my father replied, "I went to a similar ugly brick school that looked like a prison when I was a boy. It was called P.S. 87."

But to us it didn't seem ugly. It was just different from the white New England houses we were familiar with. We never saw the public school in Norwalk, only the orange bus that picked kids up to bring them there each morning and dump them out at 3:30 exactly each afternoon. Every morning we watched the little boy and girl from 5 houses down with their satchels, waiting, boarding, then alighting in the afternoon. We were so sure that the next Fall would see us going through the same routine. But, now, here we were in NYC where everyone walks to a huge building with iron grids covering the windows.

We felt scared. As most twins do, we usually felt the same way in new situations.

My mother continued telling Daddy about her adventures with the new school:

"Well, Jeronimo, we need to discuss the policies of this PS 93."

"Oh?"

"They told me that girls have to wear dresses or skirts and blouses or sweaters. Never pants or shorts, or overalls."

My father reached into his pocket and pulled out a twenty-dollar bill. "Elena, take them to Macy's tomorrow and get them some of these silly clothes they require. We don't seem to have any choice."

XI

I don't think either Cassandra or I dared to say how excited we were to be allowed to wear dresses and look pretty the way other little girls always did. Not the same dresses, by the way. Our parents didn't believe that twins should wear identical clothing. I guess because they, themselves, were such individualists.

"School days, school days, good old golden rule days, reading and writing and 'rithmetic, taught to the tune of a hickory stick."

The "hickory stick" part of that old jingle certainly didn't apply to PS 93, less than 20 blocks from Columbia University where the education department was dominated by the John Dewey revolution.

In case the name John Dewey has only vague associations, he was the most important American philosopher after William James. His pragmatism overflowed into an educational philosophy emphasizing problem solving vs. classics; group work at tables vs. kids chained to the desk repeating exercises; teachers as facilitators vs. teachers as authority figures.

We loved all of that. What was harder for us is that because of our head start from having such literary parents, they skipped us twice so that we wound up being 2 years younger than the other children. We could keep up with the school work but we felt woefully inferior socially. Nowadays educational psychologists realize how hard this is on bright kids. They are placed in magnet classes or schools but not skipped whole grades.

Tangent: By Junior High with the others girls 13 years old and Cassandra and I only 11years old, our song was not "School days, school days," but "I must, I must, I must increase my bust." This hilarious ditty was intoned while clenching our fists in front of our chests and drawing our elbows all the way behind our backs. I am ashamed now to say that we even succumbed to buying small size bras with cotton falsies in them!

Another difference between we twins and the other girls was income. Most of those little young ladies came from what was called the gilded ghetto. That was the designation of the area of upper West Side Broadway where 9/10th of the residents of the apartment houses were upper-middle-class Jews. Their mothers stayed home and wore mink coats in the winter. Their fathers were all business men who wore dark suits even on their rare appearances at public school functions. And the daughters wore cashmere sweaters and skirts with pleats ironed by maids to razor point.

What a contrast to my mother's pants and jackets and my father's casual corduroy suits and our plain cotton skirts and blouses!

A painful memory of PS 93 was how some psychologists persuaded administrators that twins should not be in the same class. In these big elementary schools, every grade had classes that went from 5A, 5B, 5C, 5 D with "A" for the smartest and all the way down to "D" for the stupidest.

"Now, girls," our mother told us, "next year Cass will be in room 5 A and you, Nat, will be in room 5B."

The most upsetting part of this was that in 5A they were considered smart enough to learn a little French. French! The language of my mother's years of café society in Paris!

I retaliated with one of the worst deeds of my elementary school years. I took a black crayon with me into the girl's bathroom and wrote Cassandra's name on the back of the door of one of the stalls to get her into trouble. The principal of the school called us both into the office and got me to admit that I was the culprit. My mother was horrified that I could do such a thing. My sister has never really forgiven me for this betrayal even though in later years I begged her to pardon me.

"You know, Natalie, I have poisonous memories still of things you once did when we were children!" she will say nowadays a propos of nothing!

Now while Cassandra was studying French in 5 A, I had to study Spanish, the language of my much disliked grandfather.

Why disliked? There was a rift between Elena and Jeronimo, our parents, and the De Toledo grandparents. My grandmother was stricken that her only son married an atheist. Maybe she hoped against hope that he would marry a Christian who would bring up her only and beloved grand-daughters to love Jesus as she did. So we never heard this grandmother ever spoken of with love by either of our parents, but instead ridiculed as "that superstitious silly old biddy."

Just the same we felt how much grandma Hope loved us. I think we loved her back without words or gestures. We probably felt ashamed to love at all a woman so despised by our parents! Besides being despised for being religious, it also was the case that grandma Hope was somewhat mentally disturbed. She had a fetish against any sort of dirt and had hand-kerchiefs doused in eau de cologne near the phone to wipe off any germs from previous users of the telephone!

My grandfather, David De Toledo, was a dentist. Free visits to his office were our first experience of sustained physical pain, so, of course, we didn't like him. Besides that, he had a curious personality, not actu-ally typically hispanic and certainly not Jewish in the way the male de-scendants of German and Polish immigrants were – warm and funny like Tevya of *Fiddler on the Roof.* David De Toledo was very formal. From what we were told all his emotional energies were spent on lust rather than love. The beneficiaries were hispanic women we sometimes saw in his dental office and sometimes even at dinners where my grandmother was forced to tolerate them.

Years later, my father explained, "After I was born your grandmother refused to have sex with grandpa, reverting to her puritanical heritage. Grandfather David considered that it was, therefore, his right to have sex with other women."

I never knew if this was really true or an excuse my grandfather had given to his son, my father, for his blatant extra-marital sexual life.

My parents despised my grandmother Hope's piety. There must have been some scenes about this when we were much younger, because Elena and Jeronimo never visited the beautiful apartment overlooking Central Park West where we were dropped off every Friday evening for our visit with grandpa and grandma for a formal dinner cooked by a black maid. Lulu, the maid and cook, was totally different from our beloved servant, Penny, in Connecticut. Lulu was not fat, and not talkative. She may have been told that she must never talk about Jesus with us children, because I was astounded years later when I was 18, long after our grandparents' deaths, to meet Lulu at a huge Billy Graham rally at Madison Square Garden where I had been taken on a "date" by an exchange student from Germany curious about US Protestant Revival culture. Lulu, the maid, was delighted to see me there. I had never even known she was a Christian.

XII

Our visits to our De Toledo grandparents were ritualistic. Before the dinner, served on beautiful gold plated dishes with real silver-ware vs. the bright Mexican plates we used at home, my grandmother of the beautiful golden hair and silk dresses, would bring us into the bedroom. Ceremoniously she would take a tortoise shell brush and comb from a dresser drawer. Sitting on a hard-backed embroidered chair, she would begin the tortuous process of combing a week's worth of knots out of our shoulder length brown hair. The brush wasn't so bad, but the teeth of the comb fighting with the knots was misery, indeed. And yet we did feel proud of how sleek our locks looked after these ministrations.

We never questioned why our parents forced us to go on these visits. Many years later, a very simple reason came to mind. They probably thought we children might come into a sizeable inheritance one day, but not, of course, if they, Jeronimo and Elena, cut us off completely from those stuffy upper-middle class grandparents.

Tangent: Many years later, studying Great Books, I realized there was another factor in Elena and Jeronimo's ambivalence toward these grandparents. Though neither of my parents read the actual writings of philosophers, the ideas of Nietzsche permeated the world-view of intellectuals in the early 20th century. That German writer of the famous *Thus Spoke Zarathustra*, inventor of the famous motto "God is Dead" was not a morbid despairing atheist of the later type such as Sartre and Camus. He was a joyful atheist, exalting in liberation from the shackles of Christianity. He was hell-bent (pun intended) on creating an image of the strong, irrepressible, unbeliever who he named Zarathustra.

Unwilling to let fear of death check-mate his dream of the new man of the future, Nietzsche tried to prove that there could be immortality without God. This took the form of what he called eternal recurrence. When you seem to die, you really return over and over again to live the exact same life. Incidentally, Nietzsche himself, spent hideous last years of his life as a syphilitic, eventually catatonic. He didn't live to see his motto mocked in the NYC subway stations with the witty graffiti "God is Dead: Nietzsche. Nietzsche's dead: God".

Now, my parents never heard of eternal recurrence, but what they did imbibe was a disgust for anything weak or sickly. My grandmother, Hope, was both, passing away at the age of 55, 4 years before her husband, David De Toledo's death.

Now I, Natalie, at 77 years old, still have a horror, not of death, since I believe in heaven, but of being physically weak.

But, plenty of time to tell you about that when I reach the end of the saga of the Sisters Karamazov, eh?

Back to Cassandra and Natalie De Toledo's school days.

I have the most blissful memories of Riverside Drive Park on the Hudson. There we went every day after school to the playground. Maybe because of the age difference from the kids in our classes, with we younger, because we had skipped 2 grades, we didn't spend 3 – 5 PM with friends. Just the two of us went to the park each afternoon. This pattern was soon to change.

My father, still working for Microstat for Microfilm, but no longer at the headquarters in Norwalk, used to go on sales trips sometimes as far as Canada. One summer afternoon when we were 8 years old, Jeronimo returned from a trip to Toronto. Instead of unpacking, as usual, face grim and determined, he told us to follow him outside the apartment house for a walk.

With no prelude he simply announced:

"I am marrying a woman I met in Canada. Her name is Thelma. We will live in an apartment 10 blocks from here. She has a 15-year-old daughter, Julia. You and your mother will be moving to a new apartment near Central Park West. I will come to get you every Sunday afternoon at 1 PM to take you out to the Museum or other good places."

With that, he turned us around and told us to walk back to what was no longer to be his home. He walked away in the opposite direction.

Without talking about it between ourselves, we returned to our mother at the apartment on Riverside Drive. If Mommy, Elena, gave us her side of this story, I don't remember what she said.

XIII

After this life-changing announcement, everything revolved not around anyone's feelings, strange as it may seem, but around the immediate necessary moves: Jeronimo to his new place with his new wife, Thelma and new daughter, Julia; Mommy, Cassandra, and I to our new place on West 93rd Street between Columbus Avenue and Central Park.

The moving van part of this discombobulation my twin and I did not get to see because we were shunted off for a week to Grandma Hope's cottage on Fire Island. Did they think we might be in the way, or, did they want to be sure we didn't witness angry scenes between them?

Enter Jesus!

Really? How?

You'll see.

I remember our mother taking us on the ferry to Fire Island. The trip was not new to us. We often went for a few days in the summer to this famous resort to be with our De Toledo grandparents, David and Hope. Always there were flamboyant hispanic women in colorful blouses and skirts, not in the house, but in the background promenading with Grandpa David along the beach walks. One such woman friend of grandpa owned a house on Fire Island and invited her friends from New York City for long weekends during the summer.

This time, when the ferry was docked, mother told us: "Cass and Nat, I am not coming with you to the cottage this time. I will be busy with the move. But don't worry I will come to get you in a week."

Our tears didn't change my mother's mind. She gave us big tight hugs and turned us over to Grandma Hope waiting at the pier. Elena Karamazov, never more De Toledo, went back to NYC on the return trip of the same ferry.

At the grandparent's trim white beach cottage, first, of course, we endured the ritual hair combing; then a long bath. I think we always looked dirty to our grandmother who was a cleanliness freak. In those days no one realized that it was a phobia if someone was always cleaning. An extreme of Grandma Hope's compulsions was that she had to put a fancy handkerchief with eau de cologne between her mouth and the telephone receiver.

"Why are you putting the hanky on the phone, grandma?" I asked her once.

"Germs. Telephones are dirty. Anyone whose mouth was pressed to the receiver could be sick."

After the bath came the walk to the glorious beach where we swam in the shallow part of the Atlantic Ocean, and then always made sand castles.

Back, sandy and hot, to the cottage for a rinse-off and dinner.

Just before going to bed in the guest room there came something new.

Grandma, eyes gleaming through her tears over our parents' separation, but with joyful love in her voice began to sing:
"Jesus loves me this I know
For the Bible tells me so.
Jesus loves me this I know,
Yes, Jesus loves me."

Even though we didn't have a clue who Jesus was, we sensed that Grandma Hope was singing this song because it had to do with the religion our parents ridiculed and that we were witnessing some kind of rebellion against their authority on the part of our grandmother. And after 6 nights of being forced to sing the song with her, we never forgot it.

Years after her death, when I became a believer in that Christ, I realized that grandma thought that we would need Jesus even more after the break in the family. It was worth the wrath that would come down on her from our atheist parents to introduce us to her Jesus. When my grandfather died and we were going through shelves in their Central Park West apartment looking for keep-sakes we came upon an old vintage 1890 Bible with tiny print. The words written on the opening page in Grandma's large handwriting were:

"For my beloved grandchildren, in hopes that one day you will love God the way I do."

What about those promised Sunday afternoons with our Dad? And what about that wife and teen daughter? How did the third generation Sisters Karamazov get along with them?

When we first met Thelma, Dad's new wife and Julia, her daughter, the adjective I would use to describe our relationship would be "awkward." Here was the conversation with our mother after the first encounter:

Elena: So what are they like?

Cassandra: Thelma, Daddy's new wife, is pretty. She has long dark brown hair and was wearing a colorful flowery dress.

Natalie: I didn't like her, but she tried very hard to make us like her. She smiles a lot and gave us home-made cake to eat.

Elena: And the daughter?

Cassandra: Julia was out when Dad brought us to the apartment. She only came in at the end. She's not pretty but very sexy.

Natalie: I wish we had gone to the movies instead of having to spend the whole afternoon there with them. Daddy said next Sunday we could all go on a ferry ride up the Hudson to Bear Mountain.

XIV

The move from the apartment on Riverside Drive, with the beautiful view of the Hudson River, to 43 W. 93 St. was only 6 long blocks but, for us, it was like going into an entirely new world, from a beautiful apartment building, very well kept up, to one where there were cockroaches and mice!

For those of you readers who ever lived in that part of NYC you will understand how our walk from school would have been from Riverside Drive up to West End Avenue, then Broadway with all the many shops, delicatessens, restaurants and movie theatres, to P.S. 93 in the past, but now from the school to Amsterdam Avenue, Columbus Avenue and finally, just past our 6 story apartment building was Central Park West.

Now Riverside Drive and West End Avenue were gilded ghetto with a sprinkling of upper middle class Protestants. But as soon as you got to Amsterdam Avenue you were in Catholic gangland a la the famous musical *West Side Story*.

Since the public school and the Junior High School were between Broadway and Amsterdam Avenue on 93rd Street, we walked through this changed atmosphere every weekday.

However, we didn't think of the Irish ancestry kids as gang members; nor the Puerto Ricans when they came into the neighborhood in the 1950's. We just came to identify crucifixes around the neck and rosaries dangling out the pocket with tough kids, nothing like us.

The "nothing like us" thing extended way beyond Jewish vs. Catholic, because among the Jews we didn't fit in at all either. There were Orthodox Jews, the boys and men having long curls and wearing yarmulkes with the mothers of these large families looking like peasants in rough dresses. Then there were the Zionist Jews who had nothing religious about them but who spoke even in school about the return one day of all the Jews to Israel! Then there were atheist Communist Jews, who we certainly didn't fit in with since we were anti-Communists. If you recall, our parents became McCarthy informers after leaving the party. In fact, FBI agents used to visit our apartment house to ask my mother questions about her previous acquaintances in the party. I think those perfectly groomed FBI men in dark blue suits and ties were sufficiently different looking to cause suspicion in the elevator when seen by the left-wingers. The parents of such families never, ever, invited my mother into their apartments, so they must have sensed at least that she wasn't one of them.

The reform Jews or Chanukah/Yom Kippur Jews, who visited the synagogue only on such holidays and otherwise thought of themselves primarily as Americans, lived in the gilded ghetto on Central Park West.

Most of the houses on the side streets of the upper West Side were what were called brownstones. They were 2-3 stories high with steps going up from the street and people sitting on those steps up until sundown, viewing the scene. They had no elevators and were usually the abode of the poor, working class families.

In one of these houses lived Johnny, the Irish Catholic terror of the neighborhood. Although he was only 6 years old, he used to stop us 8 year old girls on the street and ram his 3 wheeler into us. He had a pug face and vicious little eyes. He threatened to beat us up if we told anyone he was bullying us. We were so scared that we started walking to 94th street and doubling around Central Park West to get to our house without having to pass Johnny.

"Mommy, we're scared to walk home from school," Cassandra told our Mommy one day.

Hearing about these incidents of bullying my mother announced boldly, "I'll leave work early and walk with you to Johnny's house and complain to his mother."

I was sure that any poor woman would be intimidated by my heroine cosmopolitan mother in the tailored suit she wore instead of pants now that she had to work to support us.

The next day, Mommy met us at school and walked us back. Sure enough there was Johnny on his trike.

"Little boy, I want to talk to your mother about how you are bullying my daughters. Would you please go upstairs and ask her to come down to the street?"

He looked a little scared but walked up the stairs in front of his house into the building. After a few minutes a window opened on the 3rd floor and a large busted woman with uncombed hair yelled down:

"My kid never touched your girls. Who da yuh think ya are to bother me? My kid don't lie."

I was sure my highly articulate mother would have a great come-back. But, instead, she just took our hands and walked down the street to our house.

However, Johnny ignored us after that.

Tangent: Have we always felt more insecure than many other people in our generation because we didn't have a father to protect us? Divorce or separation was almost unknown in those days. I think so.

Another "Catholic" memory took place when a group of five teen hoodlums encircled us on the street coming home from school. We knew somehow that kids with crucifixes on were Catholics.

"What are you? Jewish?" one asked?

"No," I replied loudly. Now you readers know we were Jewish, but we didn't know at that age that we were Jews, because it was before our father started telling us our family history.

"So are you Protestants?" another boy asked, the others smirking.

"No," Cassandra answered.

"Catholic?"

"No."

"So what are you?"

"Atheists" we both announced proudly.

Since they didn't know what that meant they let us go.

XV

Shortly afterwards we did find out we were Jewish in a fascinating way. On Jewish holidays at the public school all the Jewish children stayed out of school.

"Mommy, it's funny how at school on Jewish holidays there are only 4 of us in the whole big school. They send us to the auditorium to watch movies."

"Well, girls, you actually are Jewish, you can stay home, too."

Who were the other 2 children? One must have been a Protestant girl. The other must have been some poorer Catholic boy whose parents couldn't afford even the minor tuition charged at the Catholic school. But this boy became a messenger of grace. He was in my class. One regular day, not a Jewish holiday, at show-and-tell the boy came in wearing a long black robe with a shiny white lace garment over his chest. He joined his hands in prayer and sang the hymn: "Oh, come let us adore Thee."

I was flabbergasted. I had never seen anything so strange, or heard anything so beautiful.

So what was our new home like?

Interspersed on each block, between the brownstones, there were larger apartment houses, made of greyish white cement. 43 W. 93 was one of those. It had no steps in front. You opened a door with a key and visitors pressed a button that rang in each apartment so a buzzer would let them in. Inside was a lobby. Nothing like the grand lobbies with doormen on Riverside Drive, but still a place that was decorated with large mirrors, a few old couches, a table to rest shopping bags on, steps up the 6 floors in case the elevator wasn't working and then the elevator, manipulated by the residents not by an elevator man as in the gilded ghetto.

How the kids at 43 W. 93 St. loved that elevator! Sometimes we were in a hurry and we would just get in, press our floor button, and get out and go into our apartments. But, when not in a rush, it was our fun to press one button or the other, ride up and down laughing our heads off and finally go up to the stop at the roof.

The roof! Oh my God, what a fun place for kids. It was a tar-covered flat surface with large storage bins on top. You could see miles of Central Park from that roof. Better still, you could throw things off the roof to try to hit the passers-by on the sidewalk beneath. We felt safe from detection because after tossing the object we would lie down flat on a dirty blanket on the roof so that the victim would never see us. Dangerous for pedestrians? Not really, because what we threw down were water bombs. These were made by folding a piece of paper up in what would now be called an origami pattern, such that it wound up as a kind of edgy paper ball with a hole in the top for putting the water in.

Another feature of this apartment building that amused us no end was the dumb-waiter. On Riverside Drive garbage was placed in an incinerator on each floor from whence it fell down many feet to a dump in the basement. But in apartment houses such as ours there was a wooden box behind a door in the kitchen. Into this large receptacle we put our open large brown bags of trash upright against the sides. Then we manipulated a heavy rope which sent the box down to the basement. The janitor periodically took out the garbage and dumped it into large bins outside the building on the mornings the city trucks came for pick up.

With regard to the dumb-waiter, recently, now 70 years later, I asked my twin sister Cassandra, whether she remembered a strange habit we little girls had.

"Remember, Cassandra, how all the students as PS 93 who lived within easy walking distance of the elementary school, walked home for lunch. On arrival back home, do you recall that we would generally throw the peanut butter sandwiches we had made before leaving for school down the vertical tunnel above the dumb-waiter box that was parked in the basement during the day. Do you remember the tiny sound that announced the sandwiches' arrival on the top of the dumb-waiter box? Cassandra, I always thought we did that because we were jealous of the gilded ghetto Jewish girls from school who used to eat glorious roast beef sandwiches for lunch."

"Oh, Natalie, not really! I think it was just a rebellion because of our father leaving, and our mother not being at home at lunchtime since she was working during the day."

"Weren't we too hungry to throw away our lunch?" I asked.

"We drank half a Coca-Cola, because we were too poor to have one each, and a bag of potato chips."

A related item, I am sure happened was when I had my first summer job at age fourteen with a salary of $45 a week as a clerk stapling pictures into albums in a photo-finishing factory. As soon as I cashed the first pay check I waltzed into a fancy bakery and bought a cheese cake just for me.

Was it because we were on a side street where there were Catholic gangs, that parents of other Jewish children at the school who lived in the gilded ghetto thought our house was dangerous for their children to come to? We would go to their houses in better neighborhoods but they rarely came to ours.

A sad, sad, memory involves this boycott. It was our 9th birthday. We had been to lavish parties at the houses of the wealthier kids where they got presents like Schwinn bicycles. We wanted to have a party at our house. We saved money from our 25 cents a week allowances to get the favors to give to the little girl guests as prizes for winning the games played at such parties. One of those favors was a fancy yellow cake of soap shaped like a rose. And, of course, our mother got us a birthday cake in the bakery.

2 PM was the time on the invitations we gave to 3 friends each. 2: 15 PM no one had come. 2:30 PM no one had come. They never came. Cassandra and I and Elena, our mother, ate 2 large slices of cake and I took the yellow cake of soap and put it in my bureau drawer. I don't think those girls gave us any excuse, nor did we ask why.

XVI

Until writing these memoirs, I didn't connect this memory of rejection at our birthday party with one where I victimized someone else. But now I can see how they were related. A rejected child will often want to reject someone still more "inferior."

One day there came into my classroom 6B an unusual looking girl. She was taller than the rest of us with a skirt slightly shorter, large fat legs, unkempt long hair, and a face filled with what older people would have called "angst." In her seat in the classrooms she would rock back and forth. Her eyelids fluttered faster than ours did and she hardly spoke unless called upon by a teacher. Her name was Myra.

All of us stared at her when she walked past in the outside play area of the school.

One day I heard a playmate's voice saying, "Look, look, look, Myra is lying on the pavement near the stairs." We gathered to see what was happening, keeping a wide circle to avoid having anything to do with this girl whose skirt twisted upward in such a way that we could see her panties.

Very soon playground monitors formed a small circle around her. Soon a teacher came out of the school building and lifted her up. We supposed that she was taken to a nurse.

How did some of us get it into our heads a few weeks afterwards that we would follow her after school one afternoon to see where she lived?

It was a few blocks away at a brownstone that she stopped in front or and reached into her purse for a key to the front door. Two others girls and I circled her and starting hitting her. She wailed and cried out "Daddy, Daddy, help me."

No one came down, but we felt scared and ran away.

After that, I never made eye contact with Myra. She must have moved out of the neighborhood for we never saw her at the local Junior High School.

The memory of this horrible deed on my part haunted me. Especially when I became a Catholic and developed a much more finely tuned sense of right and wrong, I thought this was the worst sin I had ever committed aside from young adult college age sexual sins.

Tangent: Once, 10 years later, I was on an escalator going down to the subway tracks in NYC. On the up-escalator I suddenly saw the face of a young woman who looked like Myra. I raised my hand in greeting and she waved back. I will never know if it was really her, or just someone who figured she must know me if I waved to her.

In the last chapter I told you about how alienated we were from the other people in the neighborhood. You would think we didn't have any friends at all. Not true, because there was one girl on our floor, Carol Rosen, who was also different. That was because her parents were not card-carrying Communist Jews, but more part of a middle-class group whose philosophy of life was based on trying to fit in with everyone by not looking or acting in any way Jewish or in any way radical, as if they had been dropped from the sky into 43 W. 93rd Street.

Carol became our closest friend. Carol was 2 years older than us, but she loved becoming our "older sister," leading us in games and other adventures in the park and on the streets. In those days an older girl would never play with younger children, unless they had to as part of a large family. But Carol did play with us because she was very, very, lonely.

When we met her, Carol was living with an old father, a much younger mother, and a teen-age brother. Her father was dying slowly. All I remember was that he was a professional man, maybe a former doctor. We sometimes saw him walking from the bedroom to the kitchen with a cane but we never talked to him. I think we found him scary because we had never seen such an old person in close. He was even older than grandma Hope. Carol's father died shortly after we moved into our apartment next door to hers on the 4th floor. I will always remember shortly after his death seeing a large box outside Carol's door with his cane sticking mournfully out of the top.

Even though Carol was only 10-years old when we started spending our after school time between 3:30 PM and 5:30 PM with her, she always acted older than her age. I think this was because she was 7 years younger than her brother, who we rarely saw since he went to an out-of-town college. As a result Carol had to play by herself a lot. This was especially the case because her mother, after becoming a widow, was working late at night as a receptionist at a popular New York City nightclub. This mother dressed in the gilded ghetto style with lots of jewelry, a mink coat, and an elegant up-sweep blond hair-do. She definitely didn't look like the lower and middle-middle class Jewish women in the rest of the apartment building. At a reunion with Carol many years after this period in our lives the following conversation ensued:

"Carol, how come your mother dressed so rich but you lived in our apartment house which was lower middle-class?"

"Oh, Natalie and Cassandra," Carol replied, "I never told you that she was what was called 'a kept woman' Her lover was married to another woman. They had children, but he kept Carol's mother in a suite near the night club he had rented so as to have sex with her whenever he wanted it. She would come home to the apartment after he left for the night to go back to his wife as his own home." This explanation accounted for that mink coat and jewelry.

Back to the life of Elena Karamazov, now that my mother was working as an editor at a downtown publishing house, she wore suits instead of slacks during the week, but this still compared most unfavorably to the garb of Carol Rosen's mother.

Even as a high school girl, Carol did not dress in any kind of flashy manner, but all her clothing was still much better than our mostly thrift shop attire. We looked up to her as a model of what a teen-age life could bring. We thought of her as very sophisticated. Thinking about it now, sophistication is a quality not that easy to explain. Carol was not especially pretty. She was a short girl with mousy colored hair always in a pony-tail but with a maturely rounded bust. Nowadays she would be called "cool," or "bad." She gave off an aura of total self-confidence, although she was really extremely insecure. This was because of being almost an only child with a father dying and then a mother not home in the evenings. In terror of the early night-time alone, she sometimes would barricade herself in her bedroom by moving bookcases to block the door from the inside. Her hope was that any marauders who broke into the apartment would by-pass that room.

Carol's way of speaking and moving were the exact opposite of our gauche manners, understandable because we were skipped 2 years, but also coming from having a mother who only valued intellect and creativity and despised conventional ways of "fitting in." To say we envied her would be an understatement!

Tangent: I wonder how it is that I didn't realize that my daughters, also twins, with a professor mother and a dramatist father, would have the same problem one day fitting in at school in Los Angeles among normal middle-class conventional children usually in business or aero-space,

XVII

Every school day afternoon, Carol led us in endless games of double-solitaire squatting on the beautiful wall to wall carpet on her living room floor, so different from our bare wooden floors graced only with occasional thrift shop throw rugs. Of course, she usually won at card games, but we were equals for monopoly. At Carol's house we were introduced to *I Love Lucy* on TV and also to fancy chocolates in gold paper covered boxes – presents from her mother's invisible male companion?

She also introduced us to a game she made up called "Prostitute!" She explained the name this way: "Cassandra, you pretend to be a woman this man brings to his apartment. Natalie and I will be two men friends. We will pretend we don't see you while we sit here at the table playing cards. Cassandra, you say that you want to leave. Then we jump up and force you to the floor and lift your skirt, pull down your panties, and stroke your bottom. We'll take turns for the roles."

We only played this new game a few times, and it only lasted ten minutes or so, but of course, it was an introduction to an area of touch we had never even known existed.

Nowadays some theorists claim that even such a mild experience comes under sexual abuse. It seems to me it is so completely different from youngsters who were raped once or sometimes every day by relatives or friends of the family, that it is in a different category, but I could be wrong.

Carol also taught us the thrill of petty theft. Back from school to 43 W. 93 St., after our snacks, the 3 of us would walk into the corner candy-store. While 1 of us made a purchase, distracting the owner of the store, the other 2 would swipe a candy-bar each, which we would tuck into the small purses all school girls carried. We never got caught at the candy-store.

However, we did get caught at another place. This was an exciting store where you could buy magic. The paraphernalia for the tricks ranged from highly expensive juggling balls and silky tall hats to playing cards with special pictures. An item that we actually bought was a tiny little plaster pooch into whose rear-end would be inserted tiny pellets. Lit by a match the pellets would dissolve into a liquid that resembled "s____!"

Most of the items were on display for any window-shopping kids to examine at their leisure, but there was a special shelf near to the cashier's post with tiny glass animals. Mesmerized we would stare at and ask to hold in our hands tiny orange giraffes, little black monkey figurines, white glass poodles.

One afternoon, Carol whispered in my ear: "Natalie, take that green horsey." I grabbed it and hid it in my purse. On the way out the owner asked us:

"Goodbye, girls. By the way, which school do you go to?"

"Joan of Arc Junior High School," Cassandra replied.

"Let me have your phone number."

Cassandra, always obedient, gave him the number: AC 2- 3456.

Back at Carol's apartment we hid the beautiful little green horse on a high shelf in her bedroom.

When we came back to our apartment after watching *I Love Lucy* and sat down at the table in the kitchen where we always ate, instead of serving us dinner, our mother looked at us with a serious look.

"Go get Carol and have her come over here right away."

Seated all 3 at the table, my mother explained: "I just got a phone call from the owner of the Magic Shop. He says that one of you stole a glass animal this afternoon. Is that true?"

"No," Carol immediately insisted. "But I saw a teen-age boy steal it."

"Go back home right now, Carol. Have your mother call me when she gets home."

Alone with her own daughters, she questioned us again. She knew we were lying since the owner of the Magic Shop distinctly said it was a girl who stole and Carol pretended it was a boy.

"I did take it, Mommy," I admitted.

My mother's brown eyes, before angry and quizzical, now looked very sad.

"I have long thought that Carol is too old for you two. You would never have done this without her egging you on."

Dinner was very quiet.

While we were doing our homework, Elena Karamazov left for Carol's house. When she returned she told us to sit down right in front of her at the table to make sure her announcement would be as formal as possible.

"You are never going to Carol's house again."

Cassandra's lips trembled. "But, she's our best friend."

"I can't go to work to support us if I think you will get in trouble."

I cried even more than my sister, but nothing would sway my mother about this matter.

We never found out if Carol's mother made her return the green glass horsey to the Magic Shop and we certainly never went there again!

A few years later when all 3 of us were in High School we were allowed to be friends with Carol again, but it was never that close because, by then, Carol had a steady boyfriend.

Many years after all of us had left 43 W. 93St. and all 3 of us were married, I looked Carol up and found out that she had made use of her unhappy childhood in a helping role as a High School counselor.

XVIII

With all this sad or grim stuff in the last chapter you might think that we had more trauma than fun as kids. That was not so at all!

What happy memories I have of those card games at Carol's house but also of Central Park where we met friends from school to amuse ourselves in the playground. And, a little older, fun with baseball when there were enough of us school girls together at the park to make 2 small teams, or renting bikes to ride around the reservoir.

The baseball thing has quite a moral. I think I always had bad eye/hand coordination. That label was unknown in those days of the late 1940's. I was always picked last for teams because I could neither hit well or catch a ball. I would say I was able to bunt 1 time out of 5, and run to first base 1 time out of 10, and get to home-plate maybe 1 time out of 50! Of course, the pitching wasn't that great on a team of pre-teen girls, so I often got to walk to first base. Balls hit way out in left field would be far out of range for a catch, but if I did run after the ball in time to throw it to a someone on my team guarding a base, I could rarely throw it anywhere near enough for an out.

But, just the same, I loved, loved, loved playing this game whether our team won or lost. Actually the only game I was ever good at was scrabble, word-monger, I. But I have always loved playing all other games even though I almost always lose.

Tangent: Memories of baseball came back to me when my son started going to Little League games. Having heard horrid reports of the vicious attitudes of parents with kids in Little League, I only agreed to take my 7 year old Dmitri (did you catch the Karamazov allusion?) after much begging on his part. Whereas his older twin-sisters were middling to good at sports, he wasn't. A culminating proof was the first time he went up to bat. To my shame the voice of the amiable dad-sport's announcer's coming through the megaphone filled the stadium: "Dmitri Klein is feeling very strong today, he doesn't even need his bat."

But Dmitri tossed off this humiliation without a blush. He went on to a record of hits and catches very similar to that of his mom, but still loved Little League.

The moral I take from this memory is that playing games with others provides a delightful comraderie apart from competition, maybe more so even for females than most males who are more competitive by nature?

Next best to baseball was sledding in the snow on the little hills in Central Park. Photos show Cassandra and I bundled up in ugly second hand leggings, rubber boots, tight wool hats, and long coats, the rope to the old wooden sled in a hand of each.

Ah, the thrill of plummeting down those snowy hills!

Tangent: "How about you?" Cassandra asked me once recently. "Do you find yourself living in the past too much?"

"I do live a lot in the past, Cassandra, but I have a different attitude toward that syndrome than when I was middle-aged. I believe that when we were younger we were too busy flitting from pleasure to pleasure to really savor each good thing. Part of healing of memories for old folks is escaping from the aches and pains into memories of those so sensory joys."

A more complicated experience that was supposed to be a treat for us was going to camp. After my father left us, one of the jobs my mother took was as a stenographer at the Child Study Association in mid-town New York. They had a scholarship fund for poor kids to go for 2 weeks in the summer to fancy camps in New England.

Come the week after July 4th, the summer after the move to 43 W. 93 St., we twins gathered with 50 other noisy kids at Grand Central Station for the trip to Lake Winnipesaukee. Every camper had to have a metal trunk for our clothing and sundries (as soap and tooth brushes were quaintly called in those days).

There we lived in log cabins, 6 to a house in bunk beds. To make it rustic there were no toilets in those days, only a large trailer type metal out-house building with seats over an open pool of s____! I was so disgusted that I managed to avoid going #2 for the whole 14 days! #1 was quicker!

The high point was swimming in the lake. My experience of this wonderful sport had only been dog-paddling near the shore of the ocean at Fire Island at our grandmother's cottage or at Coney Island. But camp swimming was organized to the nth degree. Sleek 14 year old girl counselors had us regimented into groups from beginner to proficient. Being forced to dive off a board was scary, but it worked. To this day it is the only sport I am at all good at, and you might see me at 77 in someone's swimming pool nostalgically performing the butterfly side stroke!

Canoeing was a different story. The combination of the heat, the strain on the muscles rowing, and the bugs at the overnight camping spots never seemed worth that little badge to sew on my T-shirt.

Campfires and songs, however, I loved. At the university where I teach many of the older faculty sit together – precisely for the joy of shared memories, and we will of a sudden, at some special celebration, lift high a glass of beer and intone "99 bottles of beer on the wall, 99 bottles of beer! If one of those bottles should happen to fall there'd be 98 bottles of beer on the wall." This song went all the way from 99 bottles to 1 bottle on the wall.

Even in paradise there is sin, especially venial ones. For a bribe, counselors would bring back, from night excursions to the nearest town, huge vats of ice-cream for the girls in their cabins to gobble up. To avoid detection we used flash-lights instead of the easy to see from a mile around ceiling lights.

That summer at camp was the continuation of my "post-parents-separation-acting- out" phase. I became the "idea girl" for mischief-making such as crawling out on the grass at midnight and ringing the large bronze bell rung during the day to summon campers for activities, scurrying back to the cabin before we could be identified. Other tricks would be stealing all the forks from the dining room and hiding them in the crafts room.

I wasn't caught. That delight in mischief has followed me through the decades of my life, not in the form of action but more in a kind of zany humor that will burst out inappropriately. For example, as a professor nowadays at age 77, I surprise my students by asking them such silly questions as "Why don't we take a little trip to the beach instead of taking this exam?" They love the relief of humor as a break from the intensity of the analysis of Great Books.

XIX

Before telling you about the High School days of the Sisters Karamazov De Toledo: Natalie and Cassandra, I want to recount some highlights from Junior High School.

Joan of Arc Junior High School was on the very same street, 93rd, of the elementary school, just before you would hit Amsterdam Avenue if you were on the way from Broadway on the way to Central Park. Catholics thought it might be a religious school because of St. Joan of Arc, but it was a totally non-religious institution whose name was chosen with the idea that she was some kind of feminist radical!

The education at Joan of Arc was totally influenced by John Dewey's revolution, and even though I would reject the ideas taught in the classrooms, I copied the methods hook line and sinker when I became a Catholic professor! The whole emphasis was on liberating the minds of the students from conventionality to creativity for the sake of progress. All but one of my teachers in grades 9-11 despised the past. They taught us to follow them in this with methods such as this:

"Who was the greatest artist ever in the history of mankind?" The teacher asked solemnly.

No one had an answer.

"Picasso, of course, because he liberated art from the compulsion of being realistic as it was in the Dark Ages."

It turned out that, according to such teachers, the Dark Ages included Greek statuary all the way up to Picasso!

This part of progressive education I later regretted since I learned nothing about the classics, the middle ages or the Renaissance.

But here was the good part of progressive education for me. Instead of trying to write or paint or act in plays perfectly according to a fixed model, I was encouraged to simply "express myself." I love to shock my traditional-minded Catholic colleagues by pointing out that:

"Catholic school children of that time who learned about all the good in the past were, nevertheless, mostly so frightened of making grammatical and spelling mistakes that they could never bring themselves in adult years to even write a paragraph for the parish bulletin. I, though, with my progressive education, I wrote 65 books with verve and ease simply because I had a lot to say. I let the editors at the publishing houses fix up the grammar I missed at Joan of Arc!"

Literally "God writes straight with crooked lines"?

The most successful piece of writing I did at Joan of Arc was to follow me in a positive way toward my ultimate conversion to the Catholic faith.

"Write a page composition here in class today about what you want to do when you grow up," my favorite English teacher announced.

Here is what I wrote as the first line: "How can I know what I want to be when I grow up if I don't know the meaning of life?"

I never forgot the A plus on the top of that paper.

Little did I know that my first sentence on that Junior High School essay presaged a lifetime in the field of philosophy! And that I would never settle for less as the meaning of life than the absolute truth, namely, God!

Could the real Joan of Arc have been helping me?

Another semi-religious moment happened at that school with the one teacher who wasn't a progressive. Miss Clancy was a tiny little middle-aged woman who taught singing. She put together a musical for us to present in the assembly. The theme was traditional life of the Indian tribes – native American or indigenous we would call it now. The choral climax was a chant to the Great Spirit.

"Great Spirit, fire on high…" our mixed choir would belt out.

What caught my attention was that when Miss Clancy came to the words "Great Spirit" her face was lifted toward the ceiling and her eyes seemed focused on something beyond our world.

Again, it was only when I became a Catholic that it occurred to me: "Clancy? Irish Catholic! She was thinking of the Holy Spirit and, probably, trying to help those mostly Jewish kids to glimpse something beyond their watered down remnant of reform Judaism."

Now this period of time 1947-1950 was just when the United Nations was founded. I have never met anyone in the 21st century who thinks, as we all did in 1950, that the UN would save the world from war.

In New York City, to celebrate the inception of the UN, we had an assembly program for the whole school representing every national group we learned about in class. Each class performed a dance based on the customs of one nation.

A humorous feature of the performance was the contribution of the newly-arrived Puerto Rican students. Some administrator apparently got the bright idea to let these new-comers rehearse their own dance without supervision. On the day of the United Nations gala celebration our gauche pre-teen anglos did our own sweet ethnic dances. Then out came the Puerto Ricans. The teen girls, much older, but in Junior High to learn English, came out in flamboyant costumes, the girls with much visible of their large bosoms, shaking up a storm to wild piped in hispanic music!

What else was going on for Cassandra and myself in those years?

Because Cassandra was 2 inches taller than me when we were at

Joan of Arc I mostly wore her hand-me-downs. It is both amusing and poignant to me to remember how I would drool over her clothing hanging in her part of our closet. Of these dresses, skirts and blouses the one I loved the best was a black and white longitudinally stripped heavy linen dress with a flair skirt. The deal was that I couldn't wear it until she outgrew it or got tired of it. So every few weeks I would ask:

"Cassandra, you're sick of that striped dress by now, yes? It's really too tight on you."

"Yes, but I love it so much, I don't mind."

"Oh."

XX

While in Junior High School, I started a little group of 3 girlfriends. Both of the others were gilded ghetto Jews but they liked me anyhow, maybe because I was mischievous! We would play together at their beautiful apartments where their mothers kept the good furniture in the living room swathed in plastic wrapping to protect it from kids. The afternoon snacks were whole bottles of Coca Cola, one each, instead of the half glass we had at our house, and glorious cupcakes, even 2 if someone wanted more. I invited Cassandra to join our little group, but by then she was on a completely different tack.

Dance! Cassandra had always loved to dance freely to any kind of music playing on our old '78 turntable. At the Junior High someone told us about a modern dance class right in the neighborhood, not too expensive. Cassandra was dying to go.

Tangent: On a visit recently, with us now 77 years old, she told me that when she was 13 she was too afraid to go to this dance studio alone, but that I pushed her and walked with her the 3 blocks it took to get there. As a result she claims that she owes her 65-year career as a dancer to her "little sister's" love.

During that time my mother's job as an editor at a big press in lower

Manhattan paid about $50 a week. Since she had never cooked, she did it the simplest way – everything on top of the stove with a weekly menu that went like this: Monday, minute steaks (this were little cube steaks, very cheap) with home fried potatoes and salad; Tuesday, thin pork chops with minute rice and canned little peas; Wednesday, meatloaf made of hamburger meat mixed with tomato sauce and salad; Thursday, lamb chops with elbow noodles and salad; Friday, to our grandfather's apartment for a big dinner or, after he died, small pieces of fish, usually cod, with a can of Spanish rice, and salad; Saturday, a roast chicken from the deli where my grandfather had an account and paid for this big treat for us; Sunday, Dinty Moore beef stew in a large can. It was our job to take turns doing dishes each night and, of course, put the brown shopping bags of garbage in that famous dumb-waiter.

This diet began to change when a woman of about fifty and her husband, who had moved to NYC from the South, rented an apartment on our floor. I guess she missed her adult children because she got friendly with us.

"Janet, what are you cooking tonight?" Cassandra asked the round smiling happy housewife. Oh, I am preparing this chicken. In a few minutes I will put it in the oven.

"My mother's has never used our oven," I said.

"What? Well, maybe she's too busy working outside the house. Do you'all want to learn how to really cook?"

Soon we were begging our Mom to let us cook dinners.

Since we, Natalie and Cassandra Karamazov De Toledo, were 2 years younger than many other students, we were only 13 ½ when we entered High School. And what an academy was the Bronx High School of Science, filled as it was with high I.Q. young people, many of whom had 170 scores on that famous test!

So how did we, the Karamazov De Toledo's with I.Q.'s in the 130's, get into this prodigious public high school? In an interesting way. Elena

Karamazov was by then working as a secretary to a psychologist. This man happened to be a consultant on problem students to all the public schools in New York City. As a perk for his so efficient secretary, Elena, he persuaded the Bronx High School of Science to take us in, even though we were so young and way less smart than their average students.

Sigh!

"We wanted to go to Hunter College in Manhattan, Mommy, with our friends! Why do we have to go to that far away borough of the Bronx where we don't know anyone? It's a long, long, subway ride," I objected.

"It's considered the best High School in New York City. You're going."

So once, again, we got to feel what is now called alienated. Physically and socially we were way behind the other girls. And we couldn't compete with the braininess of the genius boys.

Although I loved math and science in elementary school and Jr. High School, at Bronx Science the teachers pitched their explanations of these subjects to the highest denominator. Soon I was lost, and the only way I could even get what was considered the low grade of 85% was by memorizing review books. Even in English classes we were inferior because whereas we had been reading contemporary stuff our mother and our progressive teachers loved, these geniuses had been studying the classics.

"What? Your mother's maiden name is Karamazov, and you've never even read Dostoevsky?" one young man in the English club asked me?

To prove I was worthy of this young man's friendship I decided to read *The Brothers Karamazov* the summer after starting High School. Of course it was way over my head but I did pick up that the relationship between adult women and men was thrilling but not at all happy; that Russia in the 19th century, was extremely different from America in the 20th century; and that there were people who thought that ideas were more important than fitting in or being popular.

Many of the girls in our classes were dating boys, usually the juniors and seniors. They spent lots of time in the bathroom fixing themselves up with lipstick, powder, and even eye-liner.

Since my mother's job paid a little more than the previous one, our allowance was increased to $2 a week, giving us money for subway fare 15 cents a ride, and a little over which we used to buy lipstick. One Sunday I decided to show off a little by putting on bright red lipstick and wearing a tight skirt, stockings and heels instead of the usual A-line plaid skirt and bobby socks we usually wore to school and on weekends. My father met us for his usual Sunday visitation downstairs at 43 W. 93 St. He had stopped coming upstairs to get us in order to avoid arguments with my mother. Half way between Columbus and Central Park my dad exploded.

"Natalie, you look like a whore. Go back and change your clothes right away."

"But, but…Daddy, Julia, Thelma's daughter, wears lipstick and tight skirts and heels and you let her."

"She's 16, and her mother decides those things," he replied, annoyed that I was balking his authority. I ran back upstairs and changed into my usual clothing.

XXI

Before any high school boy asked me for a date, Cassandra and I starting going to square and folk dance evenings on Saturday nights at a Unitarian Church basement in lower Manhattan. Cassandra found out about these gatherings at her modern dance class.

The first part of every Saturday evening dance we all sat on the floor in a circle surrounding a folk-song group led by guitarists. The girls wore what were called circle skirts – they were mostly one color cotton garments that swirled. Underneath we wore crinoline petticoats to enhance the width of the hem. The boys wore jeans and woolen shirts not tucked in. But, the square and folk dancers were not all teens! No, there were some very old people, even some with grey hair, and these were among the most proficient dancers.

Tangent: Even now at 77 I sometimes get older people at conferences to get up and dance to music such as "When the Saints Go Marching In" and, as I laughingly lead them , I remember those old people dancing even better than the young ones. I bet they had even more fun than the teens because they weren't worrying about looking cool!

Back to the early 1950's at the Unitarian Church. This was way before performers such as the Beatles or Elvis changed the entire mood of the Western world. The songs they taught us in the half hour warm up before the square dancing started, were from many different countries, along the lines of the Australian "Walzing Matilda" or the Spanish revolutionary song "Viva La Quince Brigada."

Then the guitarists made way for the fiddlers. When these started up the square dance melodies, the boys would choose female partners. Since there were usually quite a few more girls than boys, the leftover girls repaired to the Ladies' Room, ostensibly to use the facilities, but really to hide their shame at not having been picked.

Cassandra was almost never a left-over girl because she was such a good dancer. I spent about 1 out of 3 dances in the bathroom. But I loved to see the dancing too much to sequester myself there for long. I could enjoy watching the others from a chair along the wall. Were those seats near the wall the origin of the word wall-flower?

How different was the wholesome atmosphere of square dancing from that of the nightclubs where the feeling of sexy romance predominated. I guess square-dancing was the rustic milieu for courting beginning in farm communities, contrasting not only with city night clubs but with the beautiful but more luxuriant atmosphere of European balls with their glorious waltzes.

Even more wonderful were the folk-dances that followed the square dances. These had quite intricate steps that Cassandra mastered quickly. I loved especially the Sicilian Tarantella and the Russian Troika and, of course, the Israeli hora.

We didn't think of these Saturday nights as places to meet boys we might date. It was just wonderful fun. Looking back I wonder that, in those days, parents of teens still thought it was safe enough for young people to ride the subways at 10 PM. It probably wasn't safe, but it wasn't so unsafe that everyone knew it.

As a matter of fact, young teen girls did experience something sexual and illegal in the subways. This was called indecent exposure. But it didn't just happen on lonely subway platforms. It could happen at any time, even riding home from school in the Bronx back to Manhattan.

"Mommy," the strangest thing happened on the subway this afternoon."

"What, Natalie?"

"Well, across from where we were sitting there was a man with a newspaper in his hands covering most of him, but then suddenly he lifted the newspaper and he was fooling around with his penis and this yucky stuff was coming out."

"And he was grinning at us," Cassandra added face contorted with disgust.

"If that ever happens again, you get up right away and walk through the subway to the conductor and tell him."

It did happen again, and we reported it. As a result two plain clothes policemen were assigned to occasionally ride in the same subway car with us on the D train from the Bronx to Manhattan. They would be sitting at the other end of the car waiting for something to happen.

Nothing happened when they were with us. The last time we saw them however one of them puzzled us by saying as his goodbye:

"You know, girlies, you don't have to wait for those guys, one of us can do it for you."

We didn't really get the full implication of that offer, but it gave me an odd feeling, a sort of mix between cynicism and wariness.

XII

Jeronimo De Toledo goes national! The year 1952 saw publicity for our father. Not good publicity either. Let me tell you about this turning point in the lives of our family.

When our father was a member of the Communist party he attended various gatherings on the fringe of the official meetings. The people who attended such events were sometimes called fellow-travelers. At one such meeting my father was introduced to a woman with the name of Martha Blumberg.

Imagine his surprise some fifteen years later to find that Martha Blumberg had become the executive secretary of a prominent government official. Since he was in touch with the FBI in any case for questioning about party members he knew in the past, he brought this encounter with Martha Blumberg to the attention of the investigators. Up the ladder this information went, eventually to lead to a full-scale inquiry conducted by Senator Joseph McCarthy, head of the House Un-American Activities Committee in Washington, D.C.

Before my father's connection with the Martha Blumberg case became a news item, we knew about it because my father had informed the committee that our mother, Elena, would back him up on this memory.

The problem was that Elena, called also to DC to testify, wouldn't swear to having met Martha Blumberg at the gathering in question. She claimed that she had never been at this event, and that probably Jeronimo was confusing her with his first wife who had also been a Communist.

The news story that hit the first page of the New York Daily News with a photo of Jeronimo De Toledo ran like this:

"Crack-pot Jeronimo De Toledo, at the McCarthy hearings, wrongfully accused Martha Blumberg, secretary of the US Defense Department of being a Communist."

In those days at the high school, Bronx Science, news headlines were broadcast on megaphones in each home room before the daily classes began. Cassandra was so humiliated by this open ridicule of our father that she ducked under her desk and pretended to be tying her shoe-laces.

My reaction was the opposite. I totally bought into my father's claim that he was right and that the left-wing of the government was vilifying him to avoid having to fire Martha Blumberg. I proudly asserted this to my teachers.

To understand the story here, you have to know that at Bronx Science almost all the professors were left-wingers. This became clear in the presidential election in 1953 that brought Eisenhower in. I was the only student in the whole school who sported an "I Like Ike" button!

Now, to complicate the matter, McCarthy had succeeded in persuading employers throughout the US to put into all application for work, the question:

"Are you now or have you ever been a member of the Communist party?"

The plan was that loyal Americans would never hire anyone who answered "Yes."

So, even though my father was an anti-Communist informer, he was fired from his job because he had been a Communist!

The fact that my mother refused to back him up at the hearing, convinced Jeronimo that she had never really left her Communist tendencies.

One Sunday afternoon on the way to the movies my daddy stopped our walk to the theatre with this announcement:

"I've been fired from my job because of this Blumberg case. I am leaving New York City with Thelma to look for work in another State. Julia is going back to Canada to live with her grandparents. Your mother is probably a crypto-Communist. I will pay for your tickets to the movie and then leave. When the movie is over, come to my place. Let me know if you want to leave NYC with us or go back home."

In shock we sat through the movie. We walked out of the theatre and without even discussing it simply went home to our mother.

"If your father thinks I am still a Communist, this is just another proof that he is crazy," was Elena's response.

We didn't know what to think. It was clear to us that our mother couldn't be a Communist since she espoused Republican ideas, even if not with the vehemence our father did.

After he left New York, the small checks my father used to contribute to our support stopped coming. Once I wrote at the end of a post-card from summer camp "Did you get a job yet?" Later, I felt ashamed of that manipulative question. I guess I picked up my mother's feeling of insecurity about having less money to support us. We did eventually get occasional postcards from different places sent to us c/o our grandfather. The most exotic card was from Del Rio, Texas where Jeronimo was working at PR for getting Americans to go to bull-fights across the border in Mexico. The last one was from San Diego where he landed a great job in technical writing at Convair, the aerospace giant.

Tangent: Thirty-five years later when we were re-united, my father explained that he didn't feel obliged to help us financially because he was never sure we were even his children! He explained that Elena and he used to go to orgies when they were lovers! Who knows which sperm reached my mother's eggs? Given the fact that Cassandra looked just like him, this excuse didn't seem too cogent.

Back to life without Daddy: after my father left town and stopped any support my mother got a higher paying job working as an editor in a publishing company and we started working in the summer.

Another tangent: We could have tried to write to our father through Grandpa David de Toledo, who was still alive and who we still visited Friday nights and for dental work, but we felt too loyal to our mother to pursue that.

I figured that when I was 21 and officially an adult, I would try to make contact with him again. And at 21 I did make an attempt. Before trying to find him in San Diego through the telephone directory information, I decided to look up the Martha Blumberg case to see for myself whether he was right about her.

It was possible to read the documentation through a Library of Congress system linked to the library of the graduate school where I was studying. Reading many pages from the transcriptions of the hearing, I came to the conclusion that he was absolutely sincere in his convictions but that he had been unable to prove them.

Cassandra, on the contrary, has always believed that he really had a screw loose. Comparing notes at age 77 on this, she came up with this theory:

"Because I was closer to him and you felt rejected, you tried to get him to love you more by sticking up for him and also by becoming a Catholic fanatic the way he was an anti-Communist fanatic!"

"Maybe so, Cassandra, but I think that he was a good American and that I am a good Catholic. I think that you, who felt rejected by our mother, tried to get her to love you by agreeing with her dissenting left-wing Catholic ideas!"

More about these sisters Karamazov polarities in future chapters.

XXIII

Those of you who have read *The Brothers Karamazov* might be wondering if Natalie Karamazov De Toledo's first boyfriend was more like Dmitri, the wild soldier; Ivan, the intellectual; or Alyosha, the mystic. Naturally you wouldn't think I would have been attracted to the illegitimate brother and murderer, Smerdyakov?

Most like Ivan of those famous Karamazov brothers was Abe Schweitzer, the young man I fell in love with. He was a tall, very thin fellow, with dark hair, a thin mouth, and thoughtful inquisitive brown eyes. He was a senior when I was a junior, and best of all he was a member of the Bronx Science High School Literature Club.

What did he see when he looked at me? I was 5'4," 110 lbs., with long brown hair in a ponytail, merry brown eyes when talking, but then serious and kind of sad eyes when not talking.

Even though most of my friends thought I was cute, like most females, we focus on what we don't like about our looks, in my case my smallish bust and big, big, slightly protruding teeth!

Abe started sitting at the table in the cafeteria where I sat with my girlfriends. He was interesting to me because he liked to analyze life and so did I. He especially liked talking about our teachers.

"That biology teacher, Mr. Gold, I saw him at a shoe-store working as a salesman last Saturday. He seemed like a totally different person on that stage-set, glibly flattering the customers, not like when he's out on a field trip in the park talking about trees, where he is so absorbed in getting us to see how different each species of tree is from another tree."

"Oh, yes. I bet you're right, Abe. I'll check out the store after school and see if I agree."

Then one day he stopped me in the corridor, "Natalie, there's a great movie near where you live in Manhattan this weekend…it's at the Thalia theatre. Want to go with me on Saturday night?"

I was stunned. This was…oh, a date!

"I'd love to, Abe. I know that theatre. My father used to take us there to see these foreign films with English titles. I'll check the time." I got out a piece of paper and wrote down my address and phone number.

I handed it to him saying, "So you can pick me up?"

"Well," with a shy smile, "I don't really have enough money to buy your ticket. Do you still want to go?"

"Of course, Abe. Dutch treat."

On the long ride home I told Cassandra. "So, pretty please, can I wear your white and black striped dress?"

"Okay… In exchange, maybe you can clean my part of the room Saturday morning. I have a special dance rehearsal."

We spent the rest of the ride home analyzing the pros and cons of Abe.

"He's certainly not handsome, but he's not ugly either, don't you think Cassandra?"

"He seems kinda shy, like me, Natalie, but he's friendly, not like some of those stuck up snobbish geniuses."

"Oh, he boasts of his 98 average, so he probably is a genius."

When I told Mother Elena about my first date she insisted, "Tell him to come an hour early to get you, Natalie, so I can meet him."

On Saturday, to celebrate, I bought a small round compact with pressed powder in it for my shiny face and applied the red lipstick twice.

At 6:30 PM I had my hand on the buzzer in the kitchen waiting to press it. I pictured Abe searching for the name on the list outside the door to 43 W. 93 St. that included Karamazov-De Toledo next to 4 B. To get in, a visitor had to say the name in the receiver and then open the heavy door quickly after a resident pressed the button that made entry possible.

"Bzzzzz."

"It's Abe Schweitzer coming to see Natalie Karamazov," came the deep voice I was expecting.

That was the beginning of the ritual for Saturday nights for the next 9 months. Always Abe followed me into the kitchen where my mother would be sitting, always smoking a Chesterfield cigarette, in a holder for style.

"So, Abe, what are you reading outside of school assignments?" Elena Karamazov would inquire.

Obediently Abe would talk about the book he was reading that week with my mother interrupting every other sentence to make some sophisticated or witty remark. I could never get a word in edgewise. Abe told me that he hated those conversations. He wanted to talk to me, not Elena, but he was too polite to object. I was surprised at this attitude. I adored my mother and regarded her as the most intelligent and insightful person in the world. How could Abe, so brilliant himself, not prefer to talk to her than to 130 I.Q. me!

After a half hour of this I would proclaim, "We'll be late if we don't leave now, Abe." He would grin with relief.

"Goodbye Mrs. De Toledo," Abe would say, purposely ignoring Elena's request to be called by her first name.

We only went to the movies once a month because Abe came from a family relatively poor. The other Saturday evenings in winter we sat for hours at a cafeteria nursing cups of coffee and one donut each. In spring or summer we would sit on a park bench on Riverside Drive, followed by an ice cream cone at the drug store.

XXIV

Abe's parents were Polish Jewish refugees. His father worked in a jewelry shop as a clerk. His mother spoke with a heavy Yiddish accent. They had the highest aspirations for their only son. Abe already had a full scholarship for Boston Law School.

Abe told me that his mother was very worried about his having a girlfriend so young.

"Abele, look, who is this girl? Is she Jewish? De Toledo isn't a Jewish name."

"She says she comes from a Jewish background."

"De Toledo sounds Spanish Catholic…be careful. I don't trust you to be good. If she gets pregnant you could be forced to marry her and never become a lawyer."

"Don't worry. You know how much I want to be a lawyer. Nothing's going to happen."

This was the era when many teen boys played it safe by getting girlfriends to indulge with them in heavy petting. The boy would soon get an erection and take care of that himself by masturbation, meanwhile rewarding his partner by telling her how much he loved her, how beautiful she was, and how happy she made him.

In spite of the promiscuous sexual lives of both my parents, I actually knew almost nothing about sex. Until Abe, I had never even seen a male organ. The penises of the men on the subways exposing themselves I hardly saw since they were covered by their hands! I found these activities on dates in the spring and summer performed under the bushes in the park, exciting and pleasurable, but I couldn't quite understand why they were the climax of the evening for Abe. For me what counted most was that this genius liked to talk to me in spite of my inferior mind and simply that a male was looking at me with delight. It never even occurred to me that he might like me because I contributed to his achieving sexual release.

Tangent: Now, writing about these encounters of so many years ago, I realize that they illustrate perfectly St. John Paul II's concept of "use vs. love." As a professor of ethics in Poland before he became Pope, he wrote a book later translated into English with the title: *Love and Responsibility*. In it he claims that the temptation for men is typically to substitute lust for authentic love of women, but for women it is to substitute romantic feelings, the enjoyment of being in love, for authentic love of a man.

That Abe's motive in dating me was probably to have sex with me, certainly occurred to my mother. Even though she had no moral principles about sex before marriage, she certainly didn't want her daughter to become pregnant. Thinking perhaps that I was infatuated and submissive to this male because of the trauma of the loss of my father, she decided I needed to go for psychological counseling. To conceal her hope that I might break up with Abe if properly cured, she persuaded Cassandra to go with me. Then it would look as if both of us needed routine therapy for children of divorced parents.

"Psychologists say that children where a parent separates from the family often have syndromes they don't realize come from that. I'd like you to try a little counseling." Mother Elena's face radiated an enthusiasm for new ideas that we always found persuasive.

The counselor she picked was a man by the name of Finkelstein.

One Thursday after school at 5 PM we walked 7 blocks to the office of the counselor, a tall thirty- year old handsome man with an inviting smile.

"So, do you like Finkelstein?" Mother wanted to know the minute we came back.

"I don't know," Cassandra replied.

"He's okay, I suppose," I decided.

He started us off with the usual tests. The first one was the famous Rorschach test, also called the ink-blot test. The facilitator shows the client a picture in black and white. The viewer has to say what he or she sees in that drawing. For example, there is a pistol on a table. Some say that a hunter left it there. Others say there obviously was a murder in that room. The second answer is supposed to show that this client might not just have fantasies of violence but also act them out!

Apparently many viewers see about 5 things in each of the pictures. But both Cassandra and I came up without about 50 possibilities for each one, with many the same.

The diagnosis was that we were very twin-like in our personalities. No surprise. And that we were also both severe obsessive compulsives! In fact we both have been what is now called work-aholics all of our lives, with anxiety of ridiculous proportions should we fail to complete the smallest tasks!

After a few months of joint sessions, Dr. Finkelstein suggested we come to a group therapy session. Instead of going to the office, we met in his living room. I recall feeling uncomfortable with the others who were much older, particularly a man who described himself as homosexual.

At the second group session, apropos of nothing, Dr. Finkelstein asked me what I would do if he kissed me. He got up and started walking toward me and I jumped up and ran toward the window.

Later, when psychoanalysis and counseling became more popular, there were clear rules about unprofessional behavior. If there were in the '50's we certainly didn't know about it, but after reporting this incident to my mother, she told us that we didn't have to go any more!

What happened with Abe? He left for Boston Law School as planned. At first he wrote me passionate letters once a week. Then they started trickling off – once every 3 weeks. I missed him terribly. I decided to save money and visit him in Boston for a weekend. I was to stay with a married couple he had made friends with.

The first evening was idyllic. We went to an on campus concert of Beethoven's Ninth Symphony. Now I had been brought up on the classical music that my father loved. However, in High School I rebelled and immersed myself in the popular music of the day. Always an extremist I made it a must to listen each week to the Hit Parade on the radio, making a chart of each song with its fluctuations up and down from first to tenth. Pretty compulsive, eh? I especially loved jazz, playing certain 78 records over and over again.

Nonetheless, sitting next to Abe, after the long separation, I had some kind of mystical experience of exaltation listening to Beethoven. Even though he loved 9th Symphony, Abe's mind was on something else.

Afterwards over coffee he opened up with, "You know, Natalie, there's a new thing. It's a pill a woman can take so she can have full sexual intercourse and not get pregnant."

"I wouldn't want to try such a thing. Suppose it didn't work?"

"The couple you are staying with use it. They can tell you all about it."

When I failed to accept their advice, Abe was disappointed. He didn't pressure me then and there but he stopped writing me letters.

After a month I bumped into a friend of Abe's still studying at Bronx Science.

"Paul, what's happening with Abe, I haven't heard from him."

"Oh, he wrote me that he is going with a law student named Nellie."

I was amused that she had almost the same name as mine, but very hurt that he dropped me without even an explanation. I figured she was more adventuresome about trying the new pill.

Tangent: The reader might be wondering how come I describe the faults of Abe so well, but say little about mine? I think it takes a long while to realize what our own faults are, partly because most people are loath to tell us what they are! How so? Because if they tell us our faults in ruthless detail, we might tell them theirs in ruthless detail.

One way I have found out what boyfriends and then men lovers didn't like about me, sometimes, was meeting the woman they did marry. The most obvious thing is that no matter how much a man might enjoy talking to a bright, witty, woman, all men are looking even more for motherly qualities such as self-sacrificial helpfulness! And being a Sister Karamazov, self-sacrificial helpfulness is my least developed quality, except when it comes to helping men by cooking. Duh!

Years later I bumped into a friend of Abe's in the subway.

"I'll get off at your stop and let's have a cup of coffee together," Paul suggested.

Once seated he shocked me by informing me, "Sorry to be the one to tell you, Natalie, because I know you and he were very close in High School, but Abe is dead."

"What? I can't believe it. He couldn't be more than thirty!"

"Well, as a side line to his law practice he started buying up slum brownstones as an investment. It seems he was at one of these in lower Manhattan. He was collecting rent and some hoodlum shot him dead."

"How do you know all this?"

"After Abe came back from Boston Law with his wife, Nellie, I was friends with the family. They had 2 kids. They lived in the Bronx in the old neighborhood near Bronx Science. So when Diane called me about the murder, I have been keeping up with her to be a kinda second father to the boys."

"If you don't mind, Paul, I'd like to know what Nellie was like. I never really understood," I giggled, "why he left me for her?"

"Oh, she was nothing like you…well, I mean she was smart, like you, but she was a tall round woman, very maternal. She always talks about how even though she was in law school she hated studying and loved being a housewife."

XXV

The summer before graduating from Bronx Science, where I had managed to move up from an 87 average to 94, I decided to take a course in stenography. This was not because I fancied office work but because I didn't want to be a camp counselor in the summer, not really liking children. Cassandra loved kids and always took summer jobs as a counselor. Ironically, it was I who one day raised 3 children and she who didn't conceive, though she wished she could.

The course I took was a jiffy 6 week affair in a method different from the standard shorthand of the day. And in the course of 60 years I only met one person who took that same course and could read the notations in this code that I still use today even when writing a shopping list! I guess the new method never took off. It stood me in good stead, first of all in working my way through college and graduate school as a part-time secretary, and also in taking down everything the professor said in classes up through the PhD!

After completion of the steno classes I filled out an application for an Office Temporary service and began to work summer fill-in jobs as substitute for employees on vacation or sickness leave at places as different as a girdle factory to a newspaper office. I enjoyed the slice of life aspect of these places more than the actual work which was extremely boring. Not only boring, but also frustrating, because this was before computers or even erasure fluid. If you made one mistake you had to type the whole letter over again!

In my senior year at Bronx Science I wasn't really sure about college. I found High School very difficult, primarily because I was 2 years younger than the other students, but also because many of the classes at that famous academy were really college level or higher. I happened to have read the novel "The Great Gatsby," now famous for a re-make movie in the 21st century True to form I failed to notice how tragic most of the characters were because I was so fascinated with this life-style of the advertising world, just beginning to become a popular profession. I thought, "Why not go right from High School into a glamorous business career?"

But Cassandra applied to CCNY – City College of New York - one of the free universities established in each borough of New York City - and I was too much under the sway of her dominance to make a decision on my own. As it turned out I loved university studies, but she didn't like them at all. After 2 years she transferred from CCNY to the famous Juilliard. That music academy had just opened a program in dance: ballet, modern, and show-dancing.

CCNY was then and still is an enormous university. I didn't like seeing thousands of people around me instead of the hundreds of High School students whose faces I was at least familiar with. At orientation we were warned that registration was going to be traumatic. Unlike High School where our programs were designed by the administration without any say on our parts, at CCNY freshman were herded into a large auditorium with forms in our hands. On a huge bulletin board were the names and times of classes in all subjects from A-Z. We were to pick out of the hundreds of lower level introductory classes whatever we wished. How grand, I thought. The negative was that after selecting one's 5 courses, as you walked up to enter them with the clerk, any one of them might close at the number 40 and then you had to go back and start again! This back and forth could go on for hours before you managed to keep the courses you selected. Since I had no idea what I really wanted to study I picked out: English Composition I, World History I, Business Administration I, Government I, and Psychology I.

And this is where nature, or the Holy Spirit, of whom I had never heard, entered in. In each and every class, eager beaver Natalie Karamazov De Toledo, would always be the first to raise her hand. But her questions would never be about what was being taught but about something underlying, something the professor hadn't the slightest desire to get into.

"So, you are listing all these types of government, Dr. X, but why should there be government at all?"

"You are giving us statistics about psychological types, Dr. Y, that is interesting, but aren't people really individuals more than types?"

"We are reading these short stories, Dr. Z, but why write anything ever?"

Time to enroll in classes for the Spring, explaining this propensity to my advisor, she scratched her head,

"Why don't you try Introduction to Philosophy? That's what it sounds like you are really interested in."

"Okay. What's philosophy?"

"Oh, it's about, you know, the meaning of life."

"Really? When I was in Junior High School I wrote an essay that started with 'How can I know what I want to be when I grow up if I don't know the meaning of life?'"

Now dear readers, don't get too excited. Do you think that in a school with mostly atheist professors studying philosophy leads to finding the meaning of life?

At first I thought so. Even though the Greek names were strange like Empedocles, Socrates, Plato and Aristotle, the writings delighted me no end. Here, instead of dull facts, we could read what the great minds questioned and debated. In logic one could actually figure out what arguments were valid and which ones only sounded good but were full of holes.

What is more I fell in love with Professor Orabi. This beautiful look-ing middle-aged scholar with a high forehead and burning black eyes was an Arabic man who had studied in England. He had passion yet also the inner serenity of some kind of exotic guru. But really he was the opposite of a guru because his only belief was in radical scepticism. Instead of teaching us the meaning of life, he taught us how to use our minds like knives to cut to pieces all the claims to truth of the great philosophers of Western philosophy!

When after two years of philosophical studies I asked him:

"What do you think the meaning of life is, Professor Orabi?" he re-plied with a sardonic but slightly wistful expression in his eyes:

"That's more of a religious than a philosophical question, isn't it?"

Not finding truth in philosophy and not being interested in the least in religion, I switched to a new program for studying the Great Books.

Meanwhile, Cassandra and I continued our Saturday night square and folk dance evenings. Neither these gatherings or the occasional par-ties we went to at CCNY yielded either of us a single date.

XXVI

Now 18 years old without a boyfriend, I was frantic to find one as intense of Abe Schweitzer. I thought of a plan. As had most of us teens, I had read novels about young women at out-of-town colleges. How exciting was the social life at such universities with the young people finally free of parental supervision.

Since I had a NY State scholarship, it would have to be one not too far off. It happened a friend of my mother had gone to the University of Syracuse where she had studied art and sculpture. They also had a Great Books Program. When I wrote to get an application they suggested I come and see first.

Since the train ride took 8 hours, it was suggested I take a plane. With my savings from working as a secretary in summers this was a possibility. In those days room and board for a year only cost $1,500. The tuition was paid by the State Scholarship. Surely I could use some of my savings for an air ticket. Oh how scared and adventuresome I felt on that first trip out of LaGuardia. In those days everyone dressed to the nines for such transport. There I was in a tight suit and high, high, heels, with a little suitcase. Not even world-traveler Elena Karamazov had ever flown in a plane!

The University of Syracuse had a lovely campus, lots of greenery and old-fashioned domed buildings. I was told that since I had already quite a few philosophy classes with A's in all of them, and wanted to en-roll in the Great Books program, I could be enrolled in honor's seminars consisting of some 10 students to a professor with no exams but instead readings of the Great Books and papers by each student to which the oth-ers would respond orally once a week at a round table.

"Like Plato's academy, Professor "B?" I asked the Chairman of the Department.

He smiled. He seemed to like my enthusiasm. It wasn't until I be-came a university teacher myself that I could appreciate what it means when one is mostly teaching reluctant students required courses to talk to an eager major. Of course the professors in the Great Books Program who I met over lunch were delighted with my literary name: Natalie Karama-zov De Toledo!

The cheerful administrator assigned to possible applicants said with an inviting smile, "If you decide to enroll, Natalie, we think you would like to be on the dorm wing where most of the young women from New York City live." How portentous that choice turned out to be! At a univer-sity where most of the students came from traditional Christian families who worked farms, that wing of New York City gals turned out to be a hot-bed of mischief and rebellion.

My trip that August with my furnishings for my dorm room at Uni-versity of Syracuse was much more dramatic.

You need the back story. When in my sophomore year at CCNY, I got a part time job working as a steno at a mid-town travel bureau. Every weekday afternoon I would take the subway from City College in upper Manhattan to work as the secretary of the agent handling travel to the Mid-dle East. That could sound fascinating but, of course, I was not going to the Middle East, I was just helping my boss write cover letters for tickets of travelers to those countries.

I was too naïve to pick up that the ostensible travel bureau was really a front for smuggling all kinds of cargo on planes and ships all over the world! The receptionist, and the women travel agents were dressed in colorful suits with lots of cosmetics and jewelry. Between customers they would pull up a chair next to one of the other agents and gossip for ours about their evenings at night clubs. Years after I had left this job I met one of them on the street. She took me for a cup of coffee.

"Natalie, wasn't that something working at _____ Travel?"

"Oh, yes, it was my first long-term job. I thought it was fascinating."

"Really? Well, Natalie the whole outfit was a Mafia scam. Most of the women agents were call girls doing tickets on the side as a cover!

Can you picture me in my thrift shop clothing, with unravelling sweaters, little silk scarves around my neck, lipstick only, still in bobby socks, sitting diligently taking dictation and trying to "fit in"!

If this was not bizarre enough, my boss was a Turkish man, very short and unattractive, undergoing a mid-life crisis. Mr. L. was about fifty years old when I started working for him. One afternoon when most of the other agents were out meeting a ship from Italy, he stopped dictation and told me more about his life. Mr. L. claimed that he had married his wife in Turkey because she slipped out of a boat and this accident broke her hymen.

Leaning over the desk confidentially, he whispered "In this mid-east country, Turkey, such a woman can never marry if her hymen is broken since she would not be deemed a virgin."

"Really?" By now I was hooked on hearing the whole story.

"Out of chivalry I agreed to marry her even though I never loved her at all. So, even though we had 3 children and we are living together out in Queens in a Turkish enclave, I obviously have a right to seek more voluntary female company, n'c'est pas? Mr. L. had studied philosophy in Paris so he liked to throw into little French phrases in conversation.

One day after this confession, Mr. L. invited me to a soiree at the

Turkish embassy. Even though I didn't like him, I thought it would exciting to go to such an event. I wore a red a-line woolen dress and stockings and high heels for the occasion. On the drive from the travel bureau at a long traffic light he told me:

"Because I studied philosophy before my marriage in Turkey I can appreciate your mind. But I have been waiting to be alone with you cher Natalie, to tell you that "Je t'aime.""

I said nothing.

"Every evening, I play the rapturous La Mer of Debussy on the phonograph and dream of getting plus intime avec vous, Natalie."

I had taken only a semester of French at CCNY and I was not very good, but I had enough to get the implications of his confession.

I was embarrassed. Not because he was a married man, since I had no morals whatsoever, but because I found him physically repulsive. Next time we were alone in the office I tried to steer the conversation to philosophical matters.

XXVII

When I told this Turk that I was quitting the travel bureau to go to an out of town college he was heart-broken, even though nothing had followed from his attempt to interest me in affording him a double-life.

"How are you getting to Syracuse Natalie?"

"I'm taking the train and sending boxes with my stuff for my dorm room."

"What a coincidence? It happens I have a business deal coming up in Syracuse. Let me drive you there."

"It couldn't just happen to be at the same time could it? August 25?" I asked greatly surprised.

"Oh, I can do it any time in the next few weeks."

"Won't it look strange to arrive at the university in the car of a man who isn't related to me?"

"No problem. I will drive off the minute I take your things out of the car at the dorm. You don't have to introduce me to anyone." Mr. L. added in French, "et nous pouvons parler tout le voyage."

What in in the world made me think that this would be a good idea? Partly I suppose it was the miserliness I inherited from my mother, strapped as she was as a single-parent. I could save, what, maybe $100 by taking up his offer. But, I suppose, also there was an underlying father complex such that I liked having an older man take so much interest in me.

My mother and sister Cassandra were too stricken at the idea of losing me to this far away university to pay much attention to the get-away details.

August 25th arrived. For the first few hours in Mr. L.'s car I chatted away about my dreams of independence. Returning to the automobile after lunch, however, before starting the engine, he leaned over and kissed me on the mouth and started fondling my bosom.

I pushed him away.

For a while he pouted, but then became formal and acted as if nothing had happened. On arriving, after taking out my boxes and putting them at the curb of the pavement around the dorm, I shook his hand and thanked him.

Needless to say, the young women who arrived at the dorm that day were much too busy unpacking their own stuff to notice a middle-aged man with a foreign look taking out my baggage.

The startling aftermath of the trip was a long letter in handwriting in French which came a week later. Translating the key paragraph to one of my new girlfriends, giggling, I read:

"I think that you must be a frigid woman not to have responded to my kiss and caresses. You should think about finding a psychoanalyst about this delicate matter which could deprive you of so much joy in the rest of your life."

Most of the girls on the dorm wing from New York City were Jewish. Not religious, more like our neighbor friend, Carol, wanting to fit in more than to flaunt any ethnic traits. Just the same they were surprised that I had over my bed on the wall a poster of Dali's Crucifixion.

"Are you Catholic, Natalie? We thought you seemed Jewish."

"Oh, no! I come from a Jewish but atheistic background."

"So why that picture?"

"I don't really know. I was looking for cheap reproductions to put on my dorm room wall and I passed this poster in a thrift shop. It drew me to itself in a strange way."

What else did I bring? Well, the circle skirts I made by hand for square and folk dancing, a little typewriter, photos of Mother Elena and Cassandra in cheap frames and books, books, books.

I loved those Great Books seminars with classics such as Shakespeare's Tragedies, Faust, and, eventually by the last semester of my senior year: The Brothers Karamazov! On the first day we were assigned one of the books out of 12 to become experts on. The product of our studies would be a 10 pages paper run off on a stencil in purple for each of the other participants in the class. When it was our turn the others had to be prepared to challenge every line and we to defend our conclusions.

In these seminars there was an older looking male student, tall and slightly overweight, with a face like none I had ever seen. It seemed carved in stone, with high cheekbones. His eyes looked dreamy, not in a luminous way, but more in a sophisticated, bored, and disillusioned way. John turned out to be of Russian ancestry! Soloviev was his last name. A Karamazov under the skin????

Each of the honor's students had a cubbyhole in the library to store books, briefcases and typewriters. There I would hover over John's desk between classes asking him questions about the readings.

Whereas most of the students found every excuse to escape from homework to sporting events in the city or to funky diners, we honors' students pretty much stayed in the library except for meals in the cafeteria or snacks at the campus coffee shop after the library closed at night. A generation later we would have been dubbed either egg-heads or nerds.

John and I were always at the same table in the popular campus coffee shop. He seemed to find me amusing, but he made no sign that he wanted us to become a couple. I couldn't stand this nonchalance. Was I in love with him? Not exactly the way I felt about Abe, but certainly attracted. I have always especially liked tall men. Probably the difference in size reminds me of being a child to my father before he left us.

Tangent: This attraction to large, heavy-set men was also related to the presence around our apartment of the man my mother took as a lover after my father left us. He was a Greenwich Village artist. In the part of the lower West Side of NYC called Greenwich Village from April to November there was an art show every weekend in a small park. The artists whose work was shown in the uptown galleries would never deign to sit with their work at an art show selling their painting like products! The painters and other craftsmen who displayed their work for sale in Washington Square in the Village usually lived in the area and made a living turning out copies of whatever the public liked the most – mostly landscapes or pictures of New York City scenes.

One of these, Phil, became friendly with Elena Karamazov and used to visit her every Saturday night after dusk when the passersby left the art show for the many Greenwich Village bistros. It was only much later that it occurred to us that this friend was a lover, taking advantage of the fact that 3rd generation Sisters Karamazov, Cassandra and Natalie, would be without fail at the square dance on Saturday nights. Phil was a huge fat man, warm as toast, full of fun, who loved children. His whole personality was in startling contrast to our dad who was thin, emotionally repressed, and pedantic. I think he was a healing surrogate father to us.

Since there were no fat men in my family, I think that it was contact with Phil's girth that left me with an abiding attraction to large fat men.

XXVIII

Now what follows in many of these chapters about my life up to age twenty one includes immoral sexual activity. A question for me now at 77, as a Catholic writer, is how much to include of this in *The Sisters Karamazov*. Most worldly autobiographies in the 20th century not only mention immoral sexual experience, but include even graphic, sometimes pornographic descriptions of such acts. Some Catholic fiction writers also include such narratives, not with a view to promoting immorality, but simply as realism vs. what could be thought of as puritanical hiding of such realities.

I think I fall somewhere in between. I want to put in enough of sexual immorality to be truthful about my life before my conversion. At the same time I will be adding comments about the bad side of such life-styles and the disastrous outcomes as seen from my later Catholic perspectives.

To proceed, years of tales of my mother's escape from NYC to Paris left me with a feeling that now that I was free of the oversight of my mother at this out of town university, I had to get rid of my virginity as soon as possible. Who better than a Russian ancestry man to do the job? When hinting around didn't work, I left a note on Phil's desk one afternoon.

"When? Natalie"

That evening, after the other regulars of our philosophy group finished their beverages and crullers at the coffee shop and walked away, John leaned over and said in the most unromantic tone, "Let's take a ride in my car and get this over with."

He drove to the empty parking lot of an outdoor movie.

What a horrible experience! The back seat of John's car was not large. De-virginizing a young woman is more like work than bliss. Amidst Phil's sporadic curses, I laughed. That was because I thought: "It's over. Disappointing but probably there is better to come." John didn't laugh. He dropped me off at the woman's dorm without a word.

The next day I didn't go over to his library stall and he sat at another table in the coffee shop. We just acted as if it never happened.

Except…in November John started dating a tall, sexy brainless freshman student named Cecilia. Seeing them walking around with him kissing her and she with her arms around his waist, I felt wild with jealousy.

But, by the Spring Semester it was okay. I had found a man I really loved.

"Oh Carter, you were so wonderful!" I always think it myself when I remember that man.

Here is how I met Carter.

Only about a 15 minute walk away from University of Syracuse was a Medical School. My best girlfriend loved classical music.

"They're having a concert of Handel's Messiah at the Med School tomorrow night, Natalie. Let's go." suggested Barbara.

Even though it was snowing we walked on a path through a foresty area to get there.

"Full!" announced the guy selling tickets in the lobby.

"But we walked through the snow all the way from U. of Syracuse!" I gave him a pitiful look of disappointment.

"Tell you what, after the opening chorus, I'll get you in behind stage and you can sit there." He pointed to a door that would lead through a hall to the back of the auditorium.

"If anyone stops you, say Carter told you to go there."

"Thank you so, so, much."

We loved the Messiah and walked home in the snow glowing with exaltation.

"The songs seemed familiar, but who is the Messiah, anyhow?" I asked Barbara.

"Jews like me don't believe in that supposed Jesus, but that doesn't stop us from loving the music people wrote about him," she replied.

A week later, on my way back to NYC for Christmas break, I was walking down the aisle of the train from the dining car when who do I see sitting in a window seat reading a book but Carter.

"Hello, Carter," I called out. He looked up surprised and then grinned from ear to ear.

"Sit down…eh, what was your name? The guy in the seat next to me just left for lunch."

"Natalie Karamazov De Toledo."

"That's quite a name. Did your Russian grandfather stop to see El Greco in Spain on his way to the United States half a century ago?"

What an opening!

Carter was a young medical student from the Mid-West. He was conventionally dressed in a tweed suit, white shirt, open at the top with a tie askew on his neck. He had a symmetrical ordinary-looking face, but his hazel eyes were unusual because they seemed to dance with humor as he listened to my story about the original sisters Karamazov at Ellis Island.

"How about a drink, Natalie?" Carter asked when he spied the waiter coming down the aisle.

"Why, thanks. What are you having?"

"Sweet Vermouth."

I had never heard of sweet vermouth. We didn't drink at 43 W. 93 unless someone happened to bring a bottle of wine on a visit to our mother.

"Sweet Vermouth, then, for me, too."

For the 55 years since that train ride, I never order Sweet Vermouth without thinking of Carter and wishing it had worked out.

Alas, Carter's med school buddy returned from lunch and I had to vacate the seat next to my new friend.

Carter seemed disappointed also.

"Natalie, how about giving me your phone number in New York. Maybe we can get together during the break."

XXIX

A week later, not on New Year's Eve, but the day before, Carter called and invited me to a concert of Bach Cantatas that Saturday evening.

Donning a bright red A-line dress, I took the 7th Avenue subway to St. John the Divine, the huge neo-Gothic Episcopal cathedral where I met Carter at the ticket table.

I had never heard Bach before. At the intermission, sipping Sweet Vermouth, I exclaimed enthusiastically "nothing like Ravel's Bolero or Berlioz' Symphonie Fantastique! That's the kind of music my father used to play when he lived with us. Did you listen to Bach records when you were a kid, Carter?"

"Oh, no. We were farm kids. I got into choral music at Harvard when I was pre-med there."

I looked down at the lines in the program for the Cantatas that were coming up. Sure enough they were all about that Jesus fellow.

In the middle of one of the chorales I suddenly found tears running down my cheeks!

"Carter, why would an atheist like me start to cry listening to Christian music?" I asked him on the way to the subway.

"I was brought up Episcopal. Sometime during college I started doubting, but then, especially listening to that kind of sacred music, I get a catch in my throat also."

Carter, always polite, accompanied me in the subway and dropped me off outside 43 W. 93 St. Humorously he bowed deeply and kissed my hand.

"See you back in Syracuse maybe?"

"Oh, I'd love it. Let me give you my phone number at the dorm."

"Mommy, Mommy, Mommy, Cassandra, Cassandra, Cassandra, he's terrific" I woke them up yelling down the hall.

The Saturday afternoon I got back to the university Carter called me up.

"If you're free tonight, I love to cook. Would you mind sampling a home-made dinner?"

Carter's roommate in his small apartment near the med-school was out on a date.

All my girlfriends managed to be sitting on the sofas in the dorm lobby to check him out.

When we got to Carter's place I was led to book-lined dining room. There was a table with a lace cloth on it and fancy gold rimmed plates. He lit two long candles, poured out the Sweet Vermouth, and started serving a magnificent gourmet dinner with veal picatta, linguini, Caesar salad and a dessert of syrup over ice-cream.

"Can I help with the dishes?"

"Of course not. You're my guest, Natalie."

"I'll clear the table, while you listen to this recording I just bought."

The music was Wagner's Tristan and Isolde. Romantic to the hilt!

Carter sat down next to me. "Natalie, you are the most beautiful girl I've ever met. If I kissed you would you scream?"

The next date repeated the same scenario with a different fancy dinner, but after the kiss, he gently led me into his bedroom.

Because I truly loved this young man's personality and, maybe, because he was so refined, this encounter felt totally different than the ones with Abe in the park or, of course, the rough episode with the Russian philosophy student.

Totally in love, I starting living for Saturday night.

How would I live without him all summer? I was going to New York to work as an office temporary and he was going to Boston to stay with friends and work as an intern at a hospital.

I wrote humorous letters describing daily life in the city. He called from time to time but not often.

Then one evening Carter called, "Natalie, I'm coming into NYC just for the day. Can I take you to lunch at the Harvard Club?"

In spite of my anti-snobbish disdain for formal things, I couldn't help but feeling special being ushered into a dining room of the Harvard Club with mostly white haired men in expensive suits and ties at the tables.

After they drifted off, Carter looked at me with a look of sadness. "Natalie, I have something to tell you. Remember how I mentioned this Jewish girl I knew at Harvard whose father was a doctor? I broke up with her, but I got back with her this summer and we are engaged to be married."

Tears came immediately into my eyes. "But, I thought you loved me. How could you do such a thing?"

"I do love you, Natalie." Carter sighed. "I know you won't understand. I came to Harvard off the farm. A med student needs contacts to get started. Marcia's father said he would take me into his practice as soon as I get that M.D."

I wiped away the tears, got up and just said, "Never mind walking me out, Carter."

As soon as I got in the door of apartment 4 B at 43 W. 93rd Street, I let it all out, crying and crying and crying.

XXX

What was my life like at University of Syracuse my senior year?

In the study of the Great Books I excelled, but still hadn't found a scrap of truth on which to base the meaning of life. A little glimmer of light came from reading in the Great Books the American Writer William James, author of Varieties of Religious Experience. William James, part of the famous family that included Henry James the novelist, had been the first modern psychologist of the 19th century. This was experimental psychology. But, he had fallen into a deep despair and come out of it through mystical experiences of a type then called transcendental.

He decided that science could not consider itself open-minded when it excluded religious experience, especially experiences which liberated people from terrible addictions and despair.

Even though reading his famous book *Varieties of Religious Experience* didn't bring me to belief in God, it did open me to considering the possibility that there was such a being.

I had two very close girlfriends on my floor on the NYC wing of the dormitory. One was Barbara, the Jewish girl. She was not religious, but not an atheist either. More an agnostic. Barbara was a music major. Like me she came eager to get rid of her virginity. In her case, the man she fell in love with was extremely handsome, dark haired and Jewish in the same vague way she was. He seemed to love her very much but he was so depressed that he was always off and on with her and this made her nervous and miserable.

You might wonder whether neither of us worried about pregnancy. Simple, for whatever reason neither of us happened to get pregnant. Probably Carter used a condom surreptiously. Maybe Barbara's boyfriend did also. I think our generation was the last carry-over of the Victorian era in that we never talked about sex with our partners, only with other women! It would have seemed coldly technical to raise such a factual issue as contraception in the midst of an embrace. Among college students, sex was always performed in the dark – more romantic!

The other girlfriend of Barbara and myself, Sylvia, got drunk at a party at the off-campus apartment of a graduate student and never came back to the university! One day the dorm administrator came up with a shopping cart and took everything out of her room.

"Where's Sylvia?" Barbara and I asked simultaneously.

"She dropped out of school," was the tight-lipped answer.

Where all the girls at that University involved in sexual immorality? Not at all! Most of the young women were Christians. They were saving themselves for marriage. We libertines considered them to be repressed idiots. After becoming a Catholic I looked back in shame at how we emancipated ones tried to talk these nice girls into exploring sex before marriage.

Enter Karl Kemper!

One day I walked into our seminar room where we were studying epistemology (theory of knowledge) and there, sitting amongst all the familiar Great Books majors, was a large overweight man with a round face and a pipe in his mouth. Large and fat, the type I always felt drawn to.

Dr. B. announced: "We are happy to have with us a Fulbright student from Germany who is on a year's fellowship. Please welcome Karl

Kemper."

Taking the pipe from his mouth, Karl greeted us with "Good day, my friends." He had a heavy accent but we found that he spoke English distinctly and perfectly.

"I want you to know that I was first in my class in English literature. I will have no trouble communicating with you. I am here because I am writing a thesis on Herman Melville's Concept of Fate in Moby Dick. I will be auditing Great Books seminars…and leading the one about Moby Dick."

He listened attentively to the paper that was being delivered and to our comments.

After class was over I introduced myself:

"Hello, Mr. Kemper, I am Natalie Karamazov De Toledo. Can I offer you a cup of coffee at our campus café?"

"Ja, sehr gut, Fraulein Karamazov De Toledo," he said with a wink.

Once seated at a table in a corner by ourselves, I studied his person more carefully. Even though his greenish-grey eyes had a youthful look, he had very little hair. It was light brown but just a circled fringe around his massive head and some heavy strands across the top. A person of substance was the physical and psychological impression.

Karl took over the conversation.

"So you must be someone of a Russian and Spanish background?"

"Yes, let me tell you about …"

Before I could finish the sentence he was off on a long story of all the Russian novels he had read and then a little about Don Quixote to complete what seemed more like a lecture than a conversation.

"Miss Natalie Karamazov De Toledo, I don't have a car yet. Perhaps you know of some gracious person who might take me into town to get some supplies for that tiny place they call my room in the dormitory."

"Oh, very few of us have cars, Mr. Kemper. But I can show you where the bus stop is if you like."

Later that evening I saw our new foreign student getting out of a car driven by one of the professors.

"Here's a man knows what he wants when he wants it," I joked to myself.

Very soon all of the Great Books majors, including myself, were sitting at Karl's table lunch and dinner to soak in his thoughts and stories about that awful country, Germany. Yes, Germany had lost the War, but its culture, before the Nazis took over, was so much richer in literature, music, and philosophy than ours, as he never ceased to instruct us.

"My father was anti-Nazi from the first. As a matter of fact he shot himself when he heard the Gestapo was coming!"

XXXI

The first weekend after his arrival, I found Karl alone in the coffee shop. Peremptorily he waved me over to his table.

"So, I hear you are Jewish. We called you beakies in Germany.

"Beakies?"

He touched his round nose and then reached over and touched mine. "You see my nose is like a ball and yours is like a beak." he chortled.

"Well, I am only sort of Jewish. I was brought up as a total atheist." I responded a little defensively.

"An atheist! That's terrible."

"I was brought up Lutheran in Northern Germany, Natalie. But when I went to the Gymnasium (the name for German High Schools where students went from 16-20 years old) I lost my faith. During the War I met a Catholic priest. He was truly a holy man, you know, like Alyosha Karamazov." Gustav winked.

"Most of my friends became Catholics because Father Dieter loved us so much and we loved him. He ran an underground study circle in the basement of his parish church."

"I love Beethoven and Bach," I mentioned timidly. I had a 78 phonograph in my room and played Beethoven's Ninth Symphony and Bach

Cantatas over and over again because of those unusual experiences with Carter at the live performances.

"Someday I will become a Catholic. I can't do it now because I am still such a big sinner, but someday it is the only thing that could ever save me." Karl explained, but this time with no winking. Instead he leaned over and brought his face up close to mine and repeated "Someday it will be the only thing that can save me."

I was impressed.

Karl hated dorm life. In short order he made friends with a graduate student who lived in an apartment in town and moved in with him. Very soon the apartment became redolent of Europe. On the walls were posters, cheap from the local travel bureau. A charming Bavarian Village with wooden houses and grazing cows greeted the eyes of visitors such as myself on one wall. On another was a typical scene of Paris. On another a fjord of Norway.

The flat was permeated with the smoke of the French brand Gitanes cigarettes Karl found in a shop in central Syracuse, and the odor of the tobacco he was always tamping down in his white carved Meerschaum pipe.

As our relationship progressed from attracted acquaintances to intimacy we settled into a routine where I would take the bus from the university to Karl's place and spend the weekend there. This was contrary to the rules of the university dormitory system.

"Mrs. Webster, I need to sign out on the weekends because my dear friend Paula Mason, a single mother, has to work out of town on Saturday and Sunday and I promised I would babysit her kids," I lied.

I don't think Mrs. Webster, the dorm mother, believed a word of it, but this was a transitional time between the '50's when most Americans thought pre-marital sex was a sin, to the hippie revolution in the 60's where all rules went down the tubes, culminating by the year 2000 where universities would have mixed sex dorm floors with sex on demand on every date becoming almost the norm.

How different Karl was from any American boyfriend! His youth was spent in war-torn Germany, and his young adulthood spent studying at a university where the intellectual atmosphere was dominated by the philosophy of atheistic or agnostic existentialism. Yet, here was this German man in his twenties torn between decadent sensuality and dreams of Catholic holiness!

Such conflict exhibited itself in alternate expressions of cynical amusement or profound absorption in the beauty of music or staring into my eyes as if hoping that beneath my naïve, timid, American optimism could be found authentic love for him.

Thus during a typical weekend he might play Bertold Brecht's Three Penny Opera on his little turntable, with its words in German that I read in translation on the record cover, full of strident rebellion against all convention, accompanied by glasses of cognac.

Then in the night would be a love-making that was both powerful and gently warm.

Then Saturday morning each of us would apply ourselves to our studies, me to the articles I had to read for the Great Books seminars of the next week, and he to compiling notes for his thesis about Melville.

In the afternoon he would go shopping and bring back exotic treats for dinner – artichoke hearts in garlic sauce, berries, fresh rye bread from a Jewish bakery. Then in the evening he would slowly read me favorite poems of his, the English translations of which he had found in the library during the week, followed by listening to classical music, not as background the way I usually would listen, but in total silence, that its beauty might transport us into the transcendent.

On such evenings I felt myself wafted into a world both higher and deeper than I had known. I certainly loved Karl more than any other man I had met so far. On the other hand, when he would talk about a possible marriage in Germany, I couldn't even take in the idea.

Was I too parochially American to think of living in Europe? More,

I think I was brought up so much to think of women as individuals, as my single mother became, that the idea of subordinating myself as the wife of a University professor in Germany, had no appeal.

This came to a head when I missed my period. My first thought was that I would have to go somewhere far away and have an abortion. To my amazement, Karl was horrified by such an idea.

"We can get married, Natalie, and have the baby."

But I didn't want to be a wife and mother. I wanted just to be close to Karl for the expansion of consciousness he brought with him and the warmth of his love.

Happily it didn't come to a choice, because two weeks later my menstrual flow resumed.

I started applying for scholarships to graduate schools in the United States to continue my philosophical studies. To hedge my bets I put in an application also for a Fulbright to study in Germany where Karl would be returning at the end of my senior spring semester.

XXXII

Even though in the previous chapters of Sisters Karamazov an astute reader can easily see that Natalie Karamazov De Toledo was not exactly a happy person, it is only in this chapter that you will see me totally conscious of being unhappy.

That unhappy feeling might have begun with the University of Syracuse department for future alumni suggesting that seniors take vocational planning tests. Now you have to realize that Great Books is a major that has the absolutely least carry over to life outside academe. Yes, some law students take that or a philosophy major but very few. Most of us aspire to get Ph.D.'s and become professors.

"What graduate schools have you applied to, Natalie?" asked Professor Stern, the head of the Great Books department.

"Harvard, Johns Hopkins, Yale."

"And you plan to become a professor some day?"

"Hmmmm. I don't know. I don't really want to be a professor."

"Why not?"

"Well, the way I figure it, Dr. Stern, is that I have always been a kind of aggressive student, you know, raising my hand constantly to contradict the professor...I am not sure I want to be at the other end of that."

"You don't have to decide now. You applied for the Fulbright and the Woodrow Wilson Fellowship and you are graduating magna cum laude, so just take your best option and wait and see. You could also be a teacher's aid of some professor you like in grad school and get your feet wet."

Since I was so un-enthusiastic about the only profession in my major, the idea of taking a test for vocational aptitude seemed like a good idea. It was a long, long, test with maybe 500 questions. After a week, the woman administering the test called me in to talk to me about the results.

"Natalie, you test out as being a person who would make a good small-animal farmer."

"What?" I exclaimed. "I've never even seen a farm. I like books."

Perplexed the tester looked through the answers again. "Didn't you notice that every question where it asked whether you preferred being with people or with animals, you checked animals?"

"Oh, that's because I hate people, not because I love animals that much!"

Of course this dialogue remained in my head for a long time even if it yielded no good advice.

It happened that I didn't get a scholarship to Harvard but I did get a full tuition Woodrow Wilson fellowship to Johns Hopkins in Baltimore, Maryland, mostly because Dr. Stern was an alumnus and he recommended me so highly.

An unexpected happening the summer before leaving for Maryland seems important to describe here. Karl had already returned to Germany. I got a phone call in New York City where I was spending the summer at home with Elena and Cassandra at 43 W. 93rd St.

"Hello, Natalie. Remember me, Todd?"

"Sure! Hi, Todd. How could I forget Karl's roommate in Syracuse who was never in the apartment when I was!"

He laughed. "I had a job you know. I didn't just leave the flat so you and Karl could have privacy! ...I happen to be in NYC for a few days. I thought maybe we could go out somewhere."

"Why not?" I asked trying to remember whether I liked or disliked this almost stranger who sometimes came to the apartment early on Sunday before I took the bus back to the University.

At 6 PM that Saturday night the buzzer rang and I went downstairs to meet Todd outside the building. By this time Elena no longer thought she had to meet any passing boyfriends.

"Let's go visit the Cloisters. They are having a concert tonight."

We took the subway up to that magnificent medieval tourist attraction, transported stone by stone from France. On the way I remember that I didn't like this character particularly. He looked good enough, middle-sized, dark haired, but his eyes were cold, uncommunicative and he didn't seem to have much to talk about except how glad he was to have finished University of Syracuse with an M.A. in history and didn't know what he wanted to do next.

The concert was glorious – Pergolesi. Instead of returning by the same streets to the subway, Todd suddenly grabbed my arm and led me to a bench in a dark part of the garden surrounding the Cloister. Then he leaned over and tried to kiss me.

I pushed him away. "What are you doing? I hardly know you."

"Come on, sweetie," he replied with a smirk. "You don't think I don't know that karl had sex with you whenever he wanted to."

I jumped up and started walking quickly toward the subway.

Todd caught up to me. "Why are you angry?"

"I guess you think I'm just a slut, Todd. Well, I don't think sex before marriage is wrong or anything, but that doesn't mean I want it with anyone who just happens to be horny."

He shrugged and walked in the opposite direction.

Tangent: Later on, when I became a chaste Catholic the incident helped me understand the difference between "isolated sex" (where there is no love at all, only lust) sex in a love affair, and married sex.

XXXIII

Even though Karl and I kept up a correspondence, I had pretty much decided I would not go to Germany to pursue our relationship. It was with a sense of adventure, Elena Karamazov style?, that I boarded the train for Maryland to rent an apartment near Johns Hopkins to begin my graduate studies.

Somehow, still, in the back of my mind, I thought that maybe one couldn't find truth in college but that it had to be available in graduate school. At the last minute I tucked *The Brothers Karamazov* into my suitcase to read on the long trip.

This time around, probably because of Karl's insistence that the Catholic Church was the only answer to the enigma of life, I paid more attention to the story of Alyosha, the brother who was a holy monk. I really didn't get it. How could anyone base his life on a God who didn't exist to get to a place, heaven, that was just a fairy tale?

The Great Books classes at Johns Hopkins were quite different from those at the University of Syracuse. In the undergrad seminars I attended in Syracuse for 2 years, we dealt mostly with the ideas, characters, and plots of the books. But at Hopkins, famous for history of philosophy, the truth about the ideas in the classics wasn't even raised. The purpose of the study was to become an expert on what different themes predominated at different points in the history of the Western world.

"So, Professor Glass, do you think Aristotle was right?" I might ask.

"You don't seem to understand, Natalie, we want to see how his ideas prepared the way for the Stoics."

Over coffee in the huge cafeteria, I would ask my fellow students similar questions. They had a different answer. "Too bad Dr. Phillips is on sabbatical, Natalie, you will love him. He is an expert on contemporary issues."

The small apartment I could afford on my fellowship was about 20 minutes by bus from the campus in a lower class neighborhood. It was in a brownstone, not unlike the ones on 93rd street where the Catholic gang kids lived. A trip to the second-hand store for $100 afforded me a bunch of old used furniture, plates and cutlery.

Since I had never lived alone, at first this seemed exciting, but very quickly I became desperately lonely. I was too spacey-intellectual to even realize that eating mostly canned foods, by myself, could be part of my unusually depressed mood.

Most of the Great Books grad students were men, and the most interesting were married with children. The only other female student in the department was Eva, who was a Jewish child who had been hidden during the war and then joined up with her parents to immigrate to the United States. Even though she applied cosmetics every morning to her rather dismal, tense face, with the sharp typically Jewish nose, she never looked pretty. Perhaps because of her traumatic youth, she avoided questions about the meaning of life and instead saturated herself in historical studies. I found every excuse to visit her in the graduate dorm rather than be alone in my apartment.

That first semester at Johns Hopkins, Eva was leaving for Thanksgiving to be with her family in DC.

"I've never seen Washington, D.C., Eva? Could I come with you?"

"I don't think you understand how different my family is from Jewish families in New York, Natalie. They are still frightened and don't like to meet anyone. But let's cut out early on Wednesday morning on the train, and you and I can see the Smithsonian Museum and then you can go on to NYC that evening?"

"Could I still get a train for New York City that night?"

"I'll check."

Enter Jesus again!

Even though I loved the Museum of Natural History with all the animal diaramas, and the wonderful snacks afterwards with my father on Sundays, I didn't like art museums that much. But I wanted to be with Eva as much as possible. Twins of the Sisters Karamazov clan are always looking for substitute twins to be with 24/7.

It is important to tell you this because it will prove that the experience I had with Dali's Last Supper had nothing to do with aesthetics. I was bored stiff walking around the museum where Eva would stop in front of the plaques next to famous paintings to read about the historical circumstances of the era of their composition.

Eventually we hit the Modern Art floor. There was the large original canvas of Dali's painting of Jesus at the Last Supper. You remember that I had a cheap print of Dali's Crucifixion on my wall at the University of Syracuse.

Looking at this painting, suddenly my body went numb and I couldn't move. I just stared at Jesus in a kind of trance.

"What's the matter, Natalie?" Eva eventually asked.

When I didn't answer she said in a soft voice, "I'll be back in a little while," and walked off to look at other paintings in the large room.

On her return, Eva asked, "Are you okay?" We better leave and get to the station, get you some dinner, so you can get to New York before midnight."

I followed her dumbly out of the building. Unlike the usual chatter-box me, I said nothing about the incident. I have never forgotten it, as you can tell from reading this account.

That Thanksgiving would be a huge turning point in the life of Natalie Karamazov De Toledo. All the way on the train to New York I thought about this question:

"If there is no such thing as truth or love, why should anyone want to live? Just to suffer?"

I didn't exactly plan to commit suicide, but in the back of my mind it certainly seemed like a possibility.

XXXIV

Of course my mother, Elena, and my twin-sister, Cassandra, were de-lighted to see me again and especially eager to know what Johns Hopkins was like, face to face instead of in letters (this was before long-distance phone calls were cheap).

"I'm not very happy there, actually," I started telling them over breakfast on Thanksgiving Day.

The same anxious expression came into each of their faces as I told them:

"The courses – well, I'm doing fine on papers and mid-terms, etc., but I'm not finding any truth at that University."

"You mention this friend, Eva. Do you still like her so much?" Cassandra asked.

"Oh, yes, but, you know, I haven't found an American form of Karl!"

"Well, we're glad not to hear about that Hun anymore," my mother stated emphatically.

Karl had come for a few day's visit to me in NYC at the beginning of the summer before leaving for Germany. The impression he made on my little family was not positive. They didn't like the contrasts he made so often between European culture and American superficiality. And, especially, they didn't like the idea that he hoped someday their daughter and sister might move to Germany to marry him.

Back to New York City where I came from Hopkins for the holiday. Instead of making a traditional Thanksgiving dinner, Elena and Cassandra chipped in for a deli chicken such as we used to have on Sunday nights.

The event of that 4 day holiday weekend that changed my life enfolded in this manner:

Saturday, as usual, was house-cleaning day. In the afternoon I was sitting in the living room catching up on a novel I chose from a pile Elena had saved for my return.

Although my mother never, ever, turned on the TV in the afternoon, this Saturday she did. I heard voices from some talk show in the distance.

"Natalie, Natalie, come here right away."

I walked into the bedroom to see what she wanted.

"There are two philosophers on this show. Come see!"

There on the TV I saw a man in his 60's with a long face, white hair, and intense brown eyes sitting in a chair so that he was facing the camera. There was a placard in front of him with the name Dietrich Von Hildebrand, Philosophy Professor, Fordham University.

In another chair there was a youngish woman with a very European looking face speaking with a French accent. Her name was Dr. Alice Jourdain. On the cloth over the table where they were sitting were the words "The Catholic Hour." A male interviewer sat at the head of the table.

"We cannot talk only about opinions," the man was stating. "Truth is what is important."

I started listening intently.

The woman, with an intense look at the interviewer, stated "You know, my students at Hunter College, think that love has nothing to do with truth, that love is blind, but it is only the loving heart that can know the truth about the value of another human being."

By now Elena, my mother, stopped dusting the bureau, and sat down to watch.

When the program ended, I said,

"Mommy, you know, in the Great Books program I have been study-ing philosophers such as Plato, Aristotle, Descartes, Kant... now for 4 years and I never heard any teacher talk about truth or love as if they were real. But these professors seem to think they are real."

That night impulsively I looked up the address of the TV Station in the phone book and wrote to these speakers c/o of the Catholic Hour.

Dear Dr. Von Hildebrand and Dr. Jourdain,

"I have been searching for truth as a student for many years now..." I summarized my experience at City College, the University of Syracuse and Johns Hopkins.

"Can you help me?" I ended the letter, giving them my address as 43 W. 93 St. where I would be for Christmas break.

Back from the final weeks of my first semester at Johns Hopkins, awaiting me there was an envelope with my name and address in a for-eign-looking handwriting.

"Dear Natalie Karamazov De Toledo,

I found your letter so interesting. Why don't you call me up and come and see me? It happens I live very near to you on West 95th Street.

Sincerely yours, Dr. Alice Jourdain."

I will never forget that first meeting that was to change my life so completely.

With a radiant but delicate smile on her thin lips, this woman in her thirties with a simple shoulder length-hair-do, dressed in a formal blouse and tailored skirt, ushered me into her bedroom. The room was full of books with a desk over-flowing with papers and with many religious paint-ings on the walls.

What struck me most of all was the way Dr. Alice kept her eyes fixed on mine as if to take in not only what I might say but also to seek my in-nermost person.

In some ways this was like the searching look of Karl trying to penetrate beneath my chatter to see my soul, except that whereas his glance always seemed disappointed, hers was full of loving compassion.

"All I have learned in 4 years from studying Great Books is skepticism!" I expostulated.

After listening for a long time to my woes, this woman philosophy professor made a surprising proposition:

"I feel as if you have been sent to us. I studied many years with Von Hildebrand as a graduate student." Her eyes were shining.

"I think you would love his classes. A young man who studies at Fordham now, could escort you to the Bronx to listen to him lecture. Perhaps it might be possible for you to transfer your Woodrow Wilson Fellowship to Fordham and study with Von Hildebrand and other wonderful professors."

XXXV

Luck, or God's Providence, the Fall semester at Johns Hopkins ended Dec. 5 and there were still 2 weeks left of classes at Fordham.

So, one day after returning from Maryland I got a call:

"Hello, is this Natalie Karamazov De Toledo?"

"Yes."

"This is Sebastian Adenauer. Dr. Alice Von Hildebrand asked me to escort you to Fordham University sometime. I have a class tomorrow at 4 PM. I live not far from you. I could meet you at your house at 2:30 PM if that is good for you?"

"Yes, yes, yes. You can't imagine how eager I am to visit there. I am at 43 W. 93 St. Just buzz and I'll come running down."

The next day I found Sebastian Adenauer walking toward the entrance to our apartment house at exactly 2:30 PM sharp. I didn't wait for the buzz but stood outside waiting for him.

Sebastian was a tall thin young man with non-descript light brown hair, light brown eyes, with an unbuttoned woolen overcoat showing a white shirt with no tie, and brown pants. The only unusual thing about him was an eager, naïve-looking joy in his countenance.

Tangent: Years later teaching seminarians I would sometimes be able to pick out the virginal males by that naïve, eager, pure look.

On the way to the subway, Sebastian told me about his family background.

"My father, Dr. Friedrich Adenauer, also teaches philosophy at Fordham. My parents came over to the United States from Germany toward the end of World War II." He lowered his voice and added, "They fled from the Nazis. I was just a little boy when we hid from the invading Germans in Southern France."

I wondered if Dr. Alice Jourdain had picked up that I had a Jewish background. If so, maybe Sebastian thought I would like to hear about Germans who were anti-Nazi.

What class are you going to this afternoon, Sebastian?" I asked.

"It's a course on philosophy of love that Von Hildebrand teaches."

"Fascinating!" I looked up at him from my 5 foot 4 inches. "I have been studying Great Books for 4 years and except for Plato's Symposium I can't remember ever hearing or seeing the word "love.""

Something about the innocent look on Sebastian's face made me want to shock him. "In fact, I was thinking of committing suicide because I can't find love."

"What?" he stopped walking, grabbed my arm and turned me toward himself.

"Well, I was kind of joking," I said in embarrassment.

"Even if human love is sometimes disappointing, there is always God's love." And then he added to my great surprise "If you ever feel like doing such a terrible thing, call me and I will come and stop you no matter what else I am doing."

I giggled nervously and fished in my pocket book for my subway token.

Maybe Sebastian was also surprised by the vehemence of his outburst, because once seated in the subway he started talking about the thesis he was writing.

"The topic is 'The Concept of Depth.'"

"Really? Tell me about it."

"There are many meanings of the word 'depth' in ordinary language, of course. Depth can refer to something of great importance, something not superficial, such as deep grief, or deep wisdom or deep love, of course the word 'depth' in these cases is an analogy to the spatial sense of deep vs. shallow." When he talked about his ideas Sebastian's face lost that eager look and became dead serious with his eyes looking upward, focused on the distance, as if he were lecturing in a hall full of students.

"You'll be a good philosophy professor one day, Sebastian," I remarked. "See, you've already caught my interest in a subject I never thought about before."

Tangent: In fact the reality of depth would play a big part in the conversion not just of my soul but also of my mind. It contrasted with the way we argued about ideas in the Karamazov family, more like a game than a deep search for truth.

At 125th St. we changed from the "C" train to the "D" train, all the way up to the Bronx.

"I went to the Bronx High School of Science on this same train, Sebastian."

"Oh! That's supposed to be the best High School in New York City. You must be very smart, Natalie." He smiled. "I went to a Catholic Prep School in Rhode Island."

From the "D" train stop at the Grand Concourse, we walked rapidly toward Fordham, passing the entrance to the zoo on the way.

Fordham University looked very different from the University of Syracuse or Johns Hopkins. It had many old-fashioned stone buildings. The one we entered had in front a statue of a woman in a gown with hands outstretched and a halo on her head. Under the statue were the words "Seat of Wisdom."

"Who is that?" I asked.

"That's Mary, the Mother of God," Sebastian replied.

"What does a woman in a flowing gown have to do with academe and wisdom, so that her statue is planted in front of a university building?" I wondered, but decided not to say anything.

XXXVI

Soon we were seated in a classroom of some 25 students mostly men in their twenties, but with a few older women there also. There was 10 minutes to go before the class would start.

And there was the man from the Catholic Hour, Dietrich Von Hildebrand, rummaging with his lecture notes at a lectern.

Sebastian brought me right up to introduce me. Immediately the old professor's long, serious face, lit up with joy as he grabbed both my hands and said in a faintly German accent, "You are the one who saw Alice and I on the Catholic Hour. I am so, so, glad you came. Afterwards, ja, you have time for coffee together? And I will ride back with you on the subway?

"I am very happy to meet you, Dr. Von Hildebrand." I replied stunned by the joy of his greeting.

The class took 2 hours. It was about how when we love the unique preciousness of the other we are glimpsing what God created in him or her and how this is real in spite of all the flaws of personality also in the same person.

I linked this philosophical concept up with the particular way Dr. Alice Jourdain looked at me; at the way Sebastian Adenauer looked at me; at the way Dr. Von Hildebrand himself looked at me.

And there was something about that look that reminded me of the feeling of listening to the Bach Cantatas with Carter and with the way Karl looked at me when we were listening to classical music.

On the long subway ride home with Dr. Von Hildebrand and Sebastian, my attention was riveted on the professor. So engaging was his personality that I would find later that in any setting he was always center-stage. He looked at me with his dark eyes with an expression of intense interest, yet he was so overpowering I didn't even feel like telling him my usual drama-queen Karamazov stories.

Tangent: In general, I have found throughout my life that if everyone else around is either shy, quiet, or just not willing to talk in depth, then I take over with my "drama-queen" stories. But if someone is truly great, I am happy to sit still and listen.

"Those universities such as Hopkins, did you say, that do history of thought, you realize..." he grabbed my arm as he continued "that is just nonsense. The philosophers didn't spend their lives thinking in order to be in a history book. They were searching for truth, and so must we, always, always!"

At the 125th St. station, Sebastian asked me about my Woodrow Wilson fellowship at Johns Hopkins.

"It could be transferable, if you might want to study here instead of there."

"Oh, I am sure they wouldn't transfer it. And my background is in Great Books, but, there was lots of philosophy in it...Well, I could always move back to New York City and work as a secretary to pay my tuition," I speculated vaguely.

Back home with my mother and Cassandra, I mused,

"You know, I really don't like it at all at Hopkins. The professors are such dessicated academics, and that professor, here in New York, Von Hildebrand, even though he is older seemed so full of enthusiasm and conviction."

"You would lose your fellowship, though, wouldn't you?" my mother asked brow furrowing. "Of course, we would love to have you back living with us."

The next day I got a call from the head of the philosophy department at Fordham.

"Is this Natalie De Toledo?"

"Yes."

"I am Father John Spinley from Fordham. Dr. Von Hildebrand called me about you. If you were interested, it just so happens that my secretary is having a baby next month. I could use a part-time typist and steno and that would pretty well cover your tuition if you wanted to come this spring to study here."

"I would love to, I guess, I think…" I answered torn between excitement and surprise.

As it happened the Woodrow Wilson people did transfer the grant, just for a year.

I begged my friend Eva to pack up my stuff and mail it back to me cash on delivery.

Oh, those classes at Fordham, how I loved them. That spring of 1958 I took 3 classes, Von Hildebrand on Ethics, Friedrich Adenauer (Sebastian's father) on Ancient Philosophy, and Fr. Donceel on Philosophy of Man. All these courses were taught in the afternoon at 4 PM because most of the students worked as teachers in High Schools and could only break away from their jobs in the late afternoon.

What a difference it seemed to make in the atmosphere of the classes that the professors and students here actually believed in truth! Even though the main immediate goal was to write down the gist of what the professor was saying, there was such a sense of eager absorption in their faces as they listened to the lectures.

I came every morning at around 10 AM to my secretarial job at the Philosophy Department office. I was much impressed by the low-key but genial character of Fr. Spinley. I never saw in him the slightest sign of irritation with the many students coming in and out, often making excuses for missing classes. Mildness is a quality rarely manifested in Jewish personalities so that even being in close quarters with a peaceful person I find astounding!

What startled me the most was that these Catholics philosophy teachers could refute in a few sentences theories I thought were impregnable such as skepticism and relativism.

"There is no way to know that anything is absolutely true," says the sceptic. Fr. Donceel, a Jesuit priest philosopher, wrote the sentence in chalk on the blackboard.

THERE IS NO TRUTH.

"So, is that statement supposed to be true?" If so, then we can know a truth. If not, then there also must be truth, that there is no truth."

"Huh?" I thought. "He's right. But I thought all religious people were stupid or weak or both, and this philosopher is certainly not stupid, and he doesn't seem weak either."

XXXVII

So, back in New York City, besides studying at Fordham, what was Natalie Karamazov De Toledo doing for a male companion?

Sigh! What a peculiar experience came along then. Or, someone might call it a reduction ad absurdum. That's a classy Latin phrase in philosophy which means that something is reduced to absurdity.

"Natalie, are you up for a blind date? The other editor, Janet, at Advantage Press, where my mother worked, told me about a young man she knew, a newspaper reporter, who studied philosophy at college and didn't have a girlfriend, very intellectual. He sounded interesting.

"So Elena," my mother began the conversation at dinner one night.

"Do you want to meet this young man Janet told me about, Natalie?"

"Sure, why not?" I replied.

Rich O'Connor called and asked if I could meet him at a bar one evening in downtown New York near the Daily Journal newspaper office. When I walked in the door of the bar that Friday evening at 7 PM, a thin guy with glasses, waved me over to his end of the counter. I figured my mother had described me to her friend and she, then, described me to Rich. I suppose Janet said I was a short girl with brown, long straight hair, big teeth, a bigger grin.

Rich O'Connor had large blue eyes, flat blondish hair, and an amused smirk on his wide lips.

"It's not often I get to meet a woman philosopher, Natalie Karamazov De Toledo!" he began provocatively.

"Hmmmm," I answered, a bit embarrassed. "Well, you know you don't get to be a philosopher vs. a philosophy student until you're at least 50 and maybe with a beard!"

He laughed. "So where are you studying?"

"Fordham."

"The Catholic University! I was brought up Catholic actually, Natalie, but you know after my studies in philosophy at City College I started thinking more like Ivan Karamazov than Alyosha."

"City College! I went there for 2 years. Did you study with Dr. Orabi?"

"Yes. He's the one that really got me to be a sceptic about truth and, of course, if there's no truth, there wouldn't be a God either." He picked a cigarette out of the package of Camels on the counter of the bar next to his glass of beer.

"Do you smoke?"

"Oh, yes, but I smoke Gitanes," I said pulling one out of the flat cardboard box I always carried around with me even though I didn't inhale and only smoked about 5 a day. They were expensive.

"Forgive me, Natalie, I didn't offer you a glass of beer. And me a reporter and you probably a poor grad student."

I didn't like beer but I liked being in synch with whoever I was with. The twin thing?

That set the tone of our dates which were once a week on Friday night after the Saturday news was in the press, at the same bar, with the same beers, and exciting conversations, always about philosophical topics. He wasn't the least interested in politics, as it turned out. He worked on the stories in the paper devoted to travel.

To my surprise, unlike most intellectuals, he didn't go in for classical music, but instead liked funky juke-box songs. The one that he always played when we were at the bar was "Kisses Sweeter than Wine." Those of you who dated in the late '50's probably remember it.

And, did we kiss? It took longer to reach that point than I expected given that he was an ex-Catholic atheist and I still had no morals. You would think that taking ethics at the Catholic University I would by then have had some morals. My deficiency came from the fact that Von Hildebrand's course was about ethical principles and theories and not about issues.

After about 2 months at his bar, one evening he suggested that I come to his apartment and he would make me dinner.

I won't forget that occasion soon. Rich O'Connor was a total bachelor's bachelor. His apartment, 3 flights up in a brownstone with no elevator, was just one room with an unmade bed in it, books strewn around the floor, a ratty old table, and a bathroom outside in the corridor.

"I don't like washing up, Natalie, but you're a kinda off-beat gal, so I'm sure you won't mind that my dinners consist in taking slabs of steak or chops, sticking an iron fork into them, and grilling them directly over the flames on the top of the stove."

Such he proceeded to do with 4 lamb chops while I roared with laughter at all the blood dripping onto the burner, and the smoke filling the room. Of course, besides the meat there was also beer.

No dishes! We bit pieces off each chop right off the two long iron forks.

I loved the way Rich kissed. It was very warm and passionate. It felt kind of nice that he didn't go further the first time.

There was a reason for that I only discovered three such bloody dinners later. The poor man was impotent. I won't go into the details except to say that I didn't want to drop him on that account because I loved our conversations. For me love was not sex but talk. "Reductio ad absurdum"?

The split really came because I was becoming more and more influenced by Catholic philosophy. In the class on the nature of the human person I learned about the immateriality of the soul. But Rich didn't believe in souls.

"Look Rich," I would argue, "How can you say that you love me, if I don't have a soul? You mean you only love a hunk of matter with a label Natalie on it?"

"Shut up and let me kiss you," he would change the subject.

XXXVIII

In the meantime Dr. Adenauer started inviting me to family dinners after his class on Ancient Philosophy on Thursday evenings. We would ride on the subway together with his son, Sebastian, who was working on his comprehensive M.A. examination in the library during the same afternoon I was attending our class.

What great conversations we three would have on that long ride on the "D" train and then the "C" train to 105th St. near their apartment house!

"So you think Plato is still relevant today, really?" I might ask.

"Certainly. Truth is not bound by time, Natalie."

Dr. Adenauer had been a student of Von Hildebrand in Germany before the Nazi time. It was because of Von Hildebrand's influence that Adenauer was hired at Fordham after his frightening time in German-occupied France.

Where Von Hildebrand was extremely extrovert, getting to know anyone around, talking even to strangers in the subway, Adenauer was a quiet, mild man, but full of humor and kindliness. He was terrific at languages and enjoyed making puns in English. A pun I never forgot was this:

"When you get to our place, Natalie, you can use the restroom. There you will find 'The Digester's Reader' in the magazine rack."

"What?" I asked puzzled.

Chuckling Dr. Adenauer explained. "You know they call it the Reader's Digest, but since it is mostly read in that room I call it the Digester's Reader."

Before we got to the apartment house where they lived, Sebastian told me, "I think you will love my mother. Her background isn't so different from your mother's. Her father was an atheist Jewish doctor in Munich. She was brought up with no belief in God, but she became a Catholic through my father."

The Catholic part didn't interest me, but the Jewish atheist part did. "Oh, I didn't realize there were other Jewish atheists in Germany at the same time when my grandfather emigrated from Germany to Russia."

Lise Adenauer was a short round woman whose embrace of greeting was as warm and all-encompassing as that wonderful black maid, Penny, we had when we were little children in Connecticut. When I first met Lise, a year before she would become my godmother in 1959, she was only sixty, but she seemed even older because her face was deeply lined and her hair had been prematurely white. She spoke English well but with a thick German accent.

"Ah," she said after releasing me from her unexpected long hug, "so you are this wunderbar new friend of Sebastian and student of my husband!"

"Wunderbar?"

"Wonderful," Sebastian translated. Why wonderful? I questioned silently. What could be wonderful about me, of the lower I.Q. than those Bronx High School of Science students, and the turbulent, rattled emotions?

"They saw my soul!" I would realize gradually, the more I came to believe that there was such an entity. They saw my yearning for truth. They saw my yearning for real love.

The Adenauers lived in a small apartment with windows facing Central Park West. Unlike the Karamazov place at 43 W. 93 there were no canvas sling chairs, and certainly no huge Picasso prints on the wall. Instead the furnishings were conventional and all the pictures on the wall were copies of religious paintings of the great masters.

Yet the atmosphere was not simply bourgeois in the way my grandparent De Toledo's apartment was. Probably because the living room, dining room, and bedroom I saw on the way to the bathroom with the "Digester's Reader" in it, were full of books, mostly with German or French titles.

Pretty soon the dinner invitations became a Thursday evening tradition.

Did the Adenauer's try to convert me?

Becoming a Catholic was something so far from my own mind that I think it never occurred to me to interpret the philosophical conversations about the human person, love, or truth as part of a strategy.

What I felt most was love; a different type of love from the romantic passion of Russian, French, or American novels. And this love drew me to them like a magnet.

What were Elena and Cassandra Karamazov making of all this? They first met the Von Hildebrand, Adenauer, Alice Jourdain group at a dance recital at Juilliard. Hearing that Cassandra was studying modern dance, Von Hildebrand wanted to see what it was. In Europe there was ballet and the waltz and, of course, also jazz-dancing. There was modern dance, but it was not known at the time Von Hildebrand was still in Germany. It became more known in cultured circles after the War when he had already come to the United States.

It happened that the modern dance performance at Juilliard on upper Broadway was given by the students of a choreographer and teacher called Jose Limon. Cassandra was not a member of his company but a student of his. She adored him and his way of dancing.

This very virile looking handsome middle-aged dancer, originally from Spain, had created a dance about the Mass. He danced the role of

Jesus. Von Hildebrand watched with great attention. He was impressed, of course, with the theme, but also by the new mode of dance.

Over coffee in a nearby cafeteria we all sat together. I noticed that most of them seemed more polite about the dance than enthusiastic. Alice Jourdain, with her usual intense look of empathy in her large eyes, asked Cassandra questions about what she loved about dance itself. Dietrich Von Hildebrand immediately got into a long conversation with Elena about her career in publishing.

"You didn't really like modern dance?" I asked the Adenauer's over coffee since they were so unusually silent.

"I think it is something I would have to experience more of to be able to understand it," Friedrich Adenauer remarked in his mild way. "In Europe, before we left, ballet was all the rage and that seemed the model of what dance should be. This is more angular, more expressive of jangled contemporary emotions, maybe?"

XXXIX

I now come to the graces that would change Natalie Karamazov from an atheist, free love type young woman into an ardent Catholic.

"No summer school in the M.A. program in the summer, Fr. Spinley?" I asked one day at the philosophy department office.

The handsome middle-aged priest smiled. "Natalie, I know you think this place is paradise, but most of us can't wait for the summer to do something different!"

"Different? What does a priest do that's different?" I asked with a note of coyness.

"Oh, we visit our folks, we go on pilgrimages, and sometimes we write books."

"Oh!" Suddenly I realized how bleak it would be all summer with no classes and only my boyfriend, Rich, at the bar once a week.

After the usual Thursday dinner at the Adenauer apartment, when I told Lise of my sadness at the thought of the long summer, she smiled as if she were just waiting for me to say it.

"Natalielein ("lein" is a diminutive used in German) "I was waiting to tell you about something else you might do with us!"

"You know most of those in our circle left Germany fleeing to escape the Nazis, but our way of having enough money to get back and see the parts of our families that stayed in Europe is to lead Catholic Art Tours for Americans. In exchange for Friedrich or Dietrich running the pilgrimages, they go for free, and me, too! Maybe you would like to go with us."

"Of course, I would like to go to Europe, Lise, but how could I? I don't have any extra money." I didn't say so, but I thought – I hate old-fashioned art and I have no interest in Catholic stuff, so why would I even think of such a thing.

"There's a scholarship for the tour, Natalielein, that you could apply for."

Only years later did I figure out that there was no regular scholarship and this plan was devised by a wealthy member of the circle who thought that seeing the beautiful Catholic cathedrals and paintings in Europe would lead me into the Church.

Even though the idea of going to Europe for a whole month was exciting, what really convinced me was that if I went on this tour I could be every day with Lise and Friedrich. Sebastian wasn't going. He was doing translation work for money in preparation for settling into Graduate School at Yale in the Fall.

On the large airplane I was seated on the aisle with Lise and Friedrich in the middle and window seat for the long flight to Paris. Also on the plane were some 40 Catholic women and men members of our pilgrimage group including a tall robed Benedictine monk, Fr. Ambrose.

Gay Paree! Finally I would see this famed city that had played such a large role in the young womanhood of Elena Karamazov! Most of the people on the pilgrimage were married couples or single women and men, or Sisters and so they were doubled up in the rooms we stayed in. I was the odd gal out and was booked throughout the tour in a cheap room of my own.

Upon arrival in Paris, after a hurried but delicious dinner at the hotel dining room my sixty-year old plus Adenauer's couldn't wait to get to bed. But I, not yet 21 years old, why not take a little walk before going to sleep. On the boulevard where the big hotel was located, there they were - the fabled cafés! I sat down at a table and ordered a glass of wine and a croissant.

After only 5 minutes a handsome young Frenchman made a gesture that seemed to be asking if he could sit at my table.

Tangent: Looking back more than 55 years later, I am appalled that a serious aspiring woman philosophy graduate student would play into so ridiculous a role as I wound up acting out. To revert to blunt slang, I was no better than those silly American tourists looking to get laid on quicky weekend tours to Mexican beach towns! Sigh! I guess I can forgive myself on the basis that having heard so many tales of Paris from my mother all those formative years it was not so surprising that I wanted on that first night not to be identified with Catholic nuns. But, as you will see, somehow this one-night stand with a stranger, the only such banal sin in all my life, left me crying instead of laughing. The devil trying his last shot to keep me from the miracles to come? The pull of grace?

The next day, right after petite dejeuner (breakfast), our whole group piled into the tour bus that we take us around throughout the whole month of excursions. Our first stop was the Cathedrale de Notre Dame where our monk would say Mass for us in a side chapel.

The first miracle came when I saw Notre Dame Cathedral in France. Before even entering inside, surrounded by our pilgrims with their cameras on the ready, I looked at the amazing shape of that Church and I started to cry with awe at its beauty. The line from Keats: "Beauty is truth, truth is beauty," came to mind and I asked myself, "How could this be so beautiful if there is no truth to it, just medieval ignorance?"

Wasn't that you, God of Beauty, calling me by name?

XL

The pilgrims on the Catholic Art Tour all went to daily Mass. I had never been to this strange ritual, but since the whole group was settling into pews at a side chapel I decided to join them out of curiosity.

Seeing my noble wise philosophy professor Adenauer on his knees astounded and disgusted me. I wanted to jerk him up and say no man should kneel. "You are the captain of your soul, you are the master of your fate." Of course I admired and loved him so much I wouldn't consider upbraiding anything he chose to do.

I loved the high, high, high, Gothic arches and the colorful stained glass windows. At the gift shop, a fixture, of course, at all pilgrimage places, Lise Adenauer asked me, "Natalielein, have you ever read the New Testament?"

"No, actually. I've never read any part of the Bible."

Since Lise had been marooned in France during the War, she had no trouble asking the clerk in French for an English New Testament. This she bought and gave to me with a solemn look in her small eyes.

Second miracle: on the tour bus on our way south toward Chartres, reading the Gospels without understanding much, I fell asleep. I had a dream. There was a large room with tables. Jesus and Mary were sitting backs to the wall. Mary beckoned me and said in Hebrew "Come sit with us." (I don't know Hebrew but in the dream I did.)

Wasn't that you, Blessed Lady of Zion, calling me by name?

Third miracle: Some nights later, I got the impulse to kneel on the floor of the hotel in Southern France and say a skeptic's prayer I thought Friedrich (Dr. Adenauer now allowed me to call him by his first name) had told me as a joke:

"God, if there is a God, save my soul, if I have a soul."

The next day we hit Lourdes. After we left this famous Shrine Friedrich told me that they were praying that I would not be put off by the rows of trinket vendors. I laughed when he confessed this saying, "I'm used to 42nd St. in New York City so nothing bothers me."

Fourth miracle: I was touched to the core by the Immaculate Mary hymn of the pilgrims at Lourdes, sung in candlelight procession in many languages.

Wasn't that you, dear Immaculate Mother, calling me by name?

Fifth miracle: The classical art I thought I hated, was used by God to reach me. In a museum in Florence I saw Da Vinci's unfinished Nativity. I looked at the Virgin Mary, so simple, pure, and sweet and I wept.

She had something I would never have: purity! For the first time I thought of myself as a sinner. I felt impelled to tell my mentors, sure they would banish me. Of course, they didn't. Jesus came to save sinners.

Wasn't that you, Our Lady, who called me by name?

Sixth miracle: The face of Christ in a tapestry of Raphael in the Vatican Museum came alive, not for the others, but just for me!

Wasn't that you, my Jesus, calling me by name?

Seventh miracle: the tour included viewing Pope Pius XII at St. Peter's. I had dreaded being bored at museums, but having to be in a crowd watching the Pope, who I thought of vaguely as dressed up in the gold that belonged to the poor, was more than I could stand. I would go shopping instead. Mild Friedrich Adenauer insisted I go!

So I went. At the end of the ceremony the Pope was blessing the disabled and sick. It was hard to see him because of the crowd. Old, not very strong, Friedrich grabbed me around the waist and lifted me up so I could see the charity in the face of the Holy Father. Pope Pius XII had exactly the same expression in his eyes, as the living face of Jesus from the tapestry.

Dear Holy Spirit, was that not you prompting my god-father to be? Was that not you, calling me by name?

Stunned by this profusion of supernatural happenings, but too much a thinker to proceed on that basis only, I studied books like C. S. Lewis' *Mere Christianity*. Lewis' famous challenge was an intellectual turning point. He shows that it is no good fence-sitting by deciding Jesus was just a wonderful man or a prophet. When a man claims to be divine he is either really God, insane or a liar? Since no one thinks Jesus was insane or a liar, he must have been divine. Reading books of Chesterton and Cardinal Newman made becoming a Catholic seem inevitable.

Wasn't that you, dear Holy Trinity, Mother Mary, Guardian Angel, all you saints, calling me by name?

January 4, 1959, at age 21, I, Natalie Karamazov De Toledo, was baptized a Catholic.

Tangent: There has never been a moment in my life when I have regretted being a Catholic. As you will see as you read on, later my twin-sister, Cassandra, my mother Elena, and my husband Reuben, became Catholics, making us into a Hebrew-Catholic family.

Tangent: Many Jews who become Catholic or non-Catholic Christian want to hide their Jewish identity for various reasons. Others, such as myself, feel proud of being Jewish, even if brought up atheist. One way of manifesting this choice is to call oneself a Hebrew-Catholic. To learn more, google Association of Hebrew Catholics.

XLI

Did Natalie Karamazov De Toledo live happily ever after? Fat chance, as we used to say in NYC.

"Did you think that after you were baptized you would become a little saint?" my godfather, Friedrich Adenauer once asked me with his mild, sweet smile.

I guess I did. But it didn't take long for me to see that a Sister Karamazov is rarely very happy or a saint.

At first I was very happy, though. Here is what my life was like right after that time of extraordinary graces leading up to my baptism.

I was still living at 43 W. 93 St. Every morning I got up early to walk to the large stone neo-Gothic Holy Name Catholic Church on 96th St. and Amsterdam Avenue where I joined Alice Jourdain, Dietrich Von Hildebrand, Friedrich and Lise, my godparents, and other members of the clan for daily Mass. This was 1959, pre-Vatican II, and the Mass was in Latin. I carried with me every day a fake leather bound book called the Missal which had Latin on one side and English on the other for each day's readings.

When one entered a Catholic Church in those days there was total silence within. Everyone genuflected before the tabernacle to Christ within, sometimes described in a somewhat sentimental but nonetheless poignant manner as the prisoner of the tabernacle! The image was designed to encourage Catholics to visit the Church to keep Jesus company at other times than during Mass.

The congregation at this 8 AM Mass was about 75 people strong, mostly women of all ages, but quite a number of men. This was because most of the men would be on their way to work at that hour. Seating was by choice. Generally Catholics going to daily Mass, rather than only the always crowded Sunday Masses, would sit close to their favorite stained glass images of events in the life of Jesus, Mary, Joseph and the saints. But the Von Hildebrand circle always sat in the first and second row of pews to the left of the altar.

So unusual was it to find a group of people sitting together at daily Mass that we were conspicuous. Years later I bumped into someone from that Church who surprised me by saying that she thought Von Hildebrand was inappropriately dramatic in the way he paraded into the Church, making a deeper genuflection than others did, and grinning broadly at each one of his entourage who entered one of the pews!

You see, in those days, friendliness before, during, or after the Mass was considered irreverent. The ideal was to kneel or sit in absolute stillness. If you happen upon what is now called the Extraordinary Form of the Latin Mass, you will see the same ideal manifested.

I found stillness and solemnity very difficult. After all, I was brought up in the Jewish cultural mode of incessant conversation in my family. In addition, the bohemian unconventional casualness my mother picked up in Paris, was expressed in sitting in any position most comfortable on the floor, or lounging on couches.

Desperately eager to belong to my new Catholic family, I forced myself to keep my mouth shut and my torso still. However, when charismatic renewal hit the Church in the 70's, with congregations clapping their hands in praise, and running around the Church hugging brothers and sisters, I felt liberated.

And even though Dietrich Von Hildebrand was a champion of the retention of the perennial Latin Tridentine Mass, he, himself, could never sit absolutely still at Mass because he had such a need to show his love to family and friends in the congregation by radiant smiles.

Tangent: Since some readers may be followers of Von Hildebrand, I want to explain. Von Hildebrand was born into a German family of artists in Munich. His mind was utterly systematic. But for long summers the family went to a villa they owned in Florence and there little Dietrich gravitated to the spontaneous, emotionally expressive Italian life-style.

After Mass, whoever had no morning appointments would gather in a cafeteria on Broadway near Holy Name Church to converse about whatever had happened to each one since the morning before. After this Catholic version of café-society, I would leave for Fordham during the week for my little secretarial job at the Philosophy Department office, and then for classes in the late afternoon and the return subway ride with Friedrich or Dietrich (always called by his nickname Gogo) back to 93rd Street.

On occasion there would be gatherings at the Adenauer apartment. Always there would be a time for all to listen together to sacred music. To this day whenever I read the words in the liturgy of the hours "Praise the Lord, all you nations" I sing to myself the melody of Mozart's Laudate Dominum. When Gogo first played the recording of this famous short Mozart piece, to make sure that I appreciated it, he grabbed my arm and waved it around to the music! It was almost as if he hypnotized me into loving what he loved.

Interestingly enough, for the first time in the 12 years I had lived at 43 W. 93 St., one of the orthodox Jewish men living in that building smiled at me pointing to my large crucifix. Since he only spoke Yiddish, I couldn't ask him why the smile. But I surmised that now he thought that this cute young woman was not a renegade left-wing Jew but had always been a Catholic!

Back in the Karamazov apartment in the evening back from Fordham, I would eat a portion saved from the dinner my mother and Cassandra had eaten earlier. Always my mother would interrupt evening reading to sit with me while I ate and exchange news.

Here would be a good place to write about how Elena and Cassandra reacted to my new life as a Catholic. Since we were atheist not religious Jews, their objections to Catholicism were not because of any historic Catholic anti-Semitism, but just because it involved centering one's life around a non-existent being: God! As well, with my mother, who had always been so close to me, there was now this barrier that I was living in a different world: the Catholic world!

"Professor P. gave this terrific lecture today about how Augustine saw reason and faith as mediated by experience!"

"Oh," Elena might respond hoping to change the subject. What could such ideas possibly mean to an atheist?

The first breakthrough came one evening at the kitchen table when Elena was watching the news on television and Cassandra was keeping me company.

Cassandra: "Natalie, from studying modern dance with Jose Limon, I see that he is very religious. What is it all about?"

There was a look of sincere puzzlement in her beautiful soft eyes.

Natalie: "It has to do with God. It has to do with the soul."

Cassandra: "The soul?"

Tangent: Religious people are so used to talking about the soul, that it is almost impossible to fathom how atheists simply think we are just hunks of matter with a brain at the top.

Natalie: "The soul is that part of you that thinks and chooses and loves."

Suddenly Cassandra looked straight ahead at me with total intensity.

"What's the matter," I asked.

Cassandra: "Something very strange happened. When you talked about the soul, I saw your soul and it left your body and came toward me.!'"

This was the beginning of the conversion of my dear twin, later expanded through listening to sacred music, especially Verdi's Requiem.

Tangent: I have a theory that among converts, a person is drawn to the faith through what is hers or his highest value. After the miracles in Europe, I was converted through truth, reading books of apologetics. Cassandra, my twin, was converted through beauty. Elena, my mother, would be converted through friendship. My husband, Reuben, would be converted through love of life, seeing eternal life as the only alternative to grim death.

XLII

And what about men?

In the story of the Catholic Art pilgrimage, I didn't mention the part about Assisi. In that Italian town, when I heard the story of St. Francis and then viewed the frescoes of his life, I fell in love with him.

My fantasy was: "Now that I am a Catholic I want to marry a man who is just like St. Francis."

Tangent: In witness talks about the story of my life I like to joke, "It didn't occur to me that men who want to be like St. Francis become celibate Franciscans."

The nearest I could find, not in looks, because he was tall instead of short, and light haired and complexioned instead of dark and Italian, was Sebastian Adenauer, back for the summer from Yale where he was getting a Ph.D. in philosophy.

This complicated relationship caused both of us much pain. At first it seemed like a no-brainer. Marry the son of my beloved god-parents and I will live happily ever after! On his side, it was more genuine. He saw me as this delightful new Catholic, beloved by his parents, a philosophy student like himself, who would make a wonderful professor's wife some-day - his wife.

Tangent: Now falling in love is different from loving someone's real or seeming good qualities. I like to prove this to my students in this way:

"How many of you have ever fallen in love?"

Only 2 students in my whole 45 year teaching career have failed to raise their hands. One was going for the priesthood and the other was just too emotionally repressed to fall in love.

"Now, at the time you fell in love there were probably 5 other people of the opposite sex with similar qualities: sincere, intelligent, attractive, deep, with a good sense of humor, etc. But you didn't fall in love with any of them. You only fell in love, at that time, with that one particular unique person. So falling in love is a response to a unique person, not to qualities."

To this theory, greatly influenced by Dietrich Von Hildebrand's courses and books, he usually adds that when you fall in love with someone you join the stream of the love God had when He created that person.

So, I think that Sebastian fell in love with me, but that I fell in love with the dream of being part of the Adenauer family through someday being his wife.

A factor in our growing relationship that surprised me and horrified Sebastian was that being with someone so good brought out the bad in me! Sebastian was and still is one of the most virtuous people I have ever met. Most people agree with that assessment. He is absolutely sincere, unpretentious, truth-loving, eager to love God and neighbor, kindly, and sweet.

So, what's not to like? What I missed in him were qualities in my father and in my previous boyfriends such as eccentricity, complexity, elusiveness.

We did become engaged after a few months. When explaining the failure of this bond to last, I give this one example and everyone understands immediately.

We were on the way to his house after Sunday Mass.

Natalie: "The Russian ballet is in town. Let's get tickets to Swan

Lake with Ulanova, the famous star."

Sebastian: "I am not sure ballet is the same depth of an art as music, painting, or architecture. Let's discuss it."

Natalie: "Because Cassandra is a dancer I used to go with her to the ballet. We were poor, so we waited for intermission and then snuck in and hid in the balcony."

Sebastian: "But that's a form of stealing, isn't it?"

Natalie: "Of course, you're right. Now that I am a Catholic I wouldn't do that. Now I have money to buy a ticket. Come on. You've never been to a ballet, you might love it!"

Sebastian: "I'll pray about it and see if it seems to be God's will to go with you."

Not to leave you with the impression that Sebastian was always this "straight-laced." He taught me to love his favorite piece of music: Bach's St. Matthew Passion. He sat me down one Good Friday to listen to the entire choral recording, and I have ever since listened to parts of it during Holy Week.

The breaking point was trying to imagine what it would be like to stop my own studies at Fordham and become "just a housewife" living with Sebastian near Yale.

Underlying my rejection of Sebastian, however, was something deeper. And this reason only surfaced to consciousness 50 years later when Sebastian, long happily married to a wonderful maternal woman totally different in character from me, was giving a lecture at the seminary where I taught. Over dinner at a restaurant he admitted:

"Natalie, I never have been able to figure out why you rejected me so many years ago. I loved you so much. We had so much in common. You seemed to love me and you are still one of my closest friends in the world. But suddenly you broke it off. I felt so hurt for years. And the man you chose to marry wasn't even a Catholic. Why?"

Spontaneously, I uttered this explanation which had truly never come into my mind before:

"Sebastian. I did love you. But I wasn't looking for a husband. I was looking for a father!"

The same summer of my relationship to Sebastian, did witness two marriages in the Von Hildebrand circle. One was that of Alice Jourdain and Dietrich. He had been a widower just before I became his student in 1957. Alice was his disciple and collaborator. They got married that summer in Florence. He was more than 30 years older than she.

Another marriage was between two people who were to become famous after Vatican II for starting the lay organization Catholics United for the Faith: Madeleine and Lyman Stebbins.

XLIII

A propos of looking for a father, what happened to Geronimo De Toledo all this time? I told you that after he left New York City with his wife Thelma, they moved from place to place across the United States ending up in San Diego where Geronimo got a good position teaching technical writing at a huge Aero-space Company.

We kept in touch indirectly through Grandfather David. He would send postcards to us c/o of David De Toledo on Central Park West. An intriguing feature of that connection was that the last Sunday we visited Grandpa before his sudden death of a heart attack, he asked us:

"Cassandra? Natalie? What do they teach you about God at those colleges you go to?"

"Nothing." was our response.

Geronimo did not return for the Masonic funeral.

Still living with our mother, neither Cassandra or I thought we needed to try to stay in contact with our father since he didn't seem to want to be in contact with us.

But now, a new Catholic, I realized I did want to see him again. At 21 I was my own adult person. I found his telephone number in San Diego by dialing 411. My father seemed very happy I had initiated contact. We planned a visit for a week at the end of that summer after my conversion.

Not wanting to shock him and be trapped in his rejection, I wrote him beforehand about becoming a Catholic and some intellectual reasons. He wrote back:

"Natalie, you know I am still an atheist. But this is a free country."

So, August 15 of 1959 saw me getting off the plane in the airport of San Diego being greeted with a big hug by my much older looking and heavier tall reddish-grey-haired father. Thelma, considerately letting this reunion take place without any distractions, stayed away from the first moments of meeting, but after 10 minutes emerged from the ladies room. Thelma was also older than when I knew her in NYC, but she was still pretty with long hair and a long colored Mexican skirt.

Along with them was a man of about 35, a friend of theirs, an artist. Since he came around often during the visit I began to think it was a set-up. I didn't particularly like him, but I liked the idea that my father would be so eager to have me live near him someday that he was plotting to build up attractions for me in San Diego!

My father had taken time off from work so he could be with me during the week and take me sight-seeing. After I went to daily Mass in a lovely Spanish-style white stucco Church, we would drive along the coast enjoying the Pacific Ocean, and eating at Mexican restaurants when Thelma didn't feel like cooking.

In the evening Geronimo would play favorite recordings of the same program- music type as when we were children, such as Grieg, and Dvorak and opera as well. They had a beautiful Spanish style home with balconies and verandas. On the walls were large prints of sea-scenes, and huge wall-to-wall maps of the whole world. We avoided the subject of the Catholic Church, except that he mentioned humorously that he once saw a performance of Verdi's Requiem and that if they handed out applications to join the Catholic Church that night he would have signed in.

I had such a good time there that I wrote a letter to Cassandra urging her to make plans to visit, also.

Now comes the bad part. By "accident" Cassandra, on her trip to San Diego, she used the letter I wrote to her about my visit to enfold a cake of soap she packed in her suitcase. Thelma happened by "accident" to go into the guest room and saw this letter. This is what it said:

"Dear Cassandra,

You really must visit Daddy. It has been wonderful to be here. You are probably hesitant wondering what Thelma is like and whether she will be friendly when you come. She will be friendly. You need to bear in mind, however, that unlike our mother she is not very bright so you have to simplify conversation. She prides herself most on her cooking. It is not very good, but it's not too bad either."

At the airport coming back from San Diego to New York, Cassandra, finally free to call on a pay-phone with no one around, called me up in tears.

"Thelma read your letter, by accident, the one where you said she was stupid and not a good cook. She was devastated. She showed it to Dad and made him insist that we never darken their door again if he truly loved her. She said you were a snake in the grass."

My father wrote me a letter roundly scolding me for being such a hypocrite as to seem to be so friendly to Thelma but, then, ridiculing her to Cassandra and that

"Under these circumstances, I don't want to hear from you ever again."

Apparently he included Cassandra under the same ban, even though she really hadn't done anything bad. She wrote to him on and off but didn't see him again for many decades. Of course I often wondered about the unconscious motivation of my sister in happening, just by accident, to wrap a bar of soap in such a letter!

I felt awful about the incident. What did I need to bring to confession? That I had said bad things about my father's wife to my sister? Was that a mortal sin? Clearly not, but…shame is not always related to clear sin. It seemed like a scene out of a Dostoevsky novel for subtle crimes and rigorous punishment.

It was 25 years before I saw the De Toledo's of San Diego again.

XLIV

Enter Reuben Klein:

Elena Karamozov was still working at head editor at a publishing company called Advantage Press in Midtown Manhattan. The sales manager of the same company was a man called Reuben Klein. At that time Elena was 60 years old and Reuben was 40. They struck up a great friendship mostly over lunch at a diner down the street.

One Friday evening in the Fall, after my conversion, our mother invited Reuben for dinner at 43 W. 93 St. to meet her daughters. At that time he had just become divorced from his wife. He was of medium height, sturdy looking, with a round merry face, and big blue eyes full of humor and a Marlboro cigarette always in his mouth. I still smoked Gitanes, but only about 12 a day whereas he was a 3 pack a day man.

After a short time of small talk, Reuben wanted to know all about my conversion.

"I assume, Reuben, with that name that you are Jewish," I began.

"I was brought up Orthodox Jewish in the Lower East Side…but then as a teen-ager I became an atheist. However, I have always been interested in Jesus." Reuben explained.

"Interested in Jesus? How so?" I felt my face flushing with joy at the name of my Savior.

"I lived in the Jewish ghetto. I thought the whole world was Jewish. Then one day I drifted out of my neighborhood and hit the public library. I started borrowing books from A-Z. Eventually I hit "J" and read a book about Jesus. I loved this prophet. Of course, when I was a boy the rabbis didn't talk about him."

"So, now, if you are an atheist, what do you make of him?" I asked eagerly hoping to work into the C.S. Lewis argument that if Jesus claimed to be God then either he was really God or he was a liar or insane, not a wonderful prophet.

"I don't know what to make of Jesus, Natalie. So when Elena, your mother, started telling me about your conversion, I wanted to meet you and learn more."

While Cassandra did the dishes, I took Reuben into the living room and told him the gist of my story of how I became a Catholic. I noticed that while reading her novel my mother seemed to be listening, too, having never really heard the whole story as a sequence.

Years later, Reuben said that what impressed him most that first evening was that the dinner was so meager. My mother liked us to make fish on Friday because it would be fresh. On Reuben's plate he saw a 4 inch by 1-inch bland piece of codfish, ten green beans, and two tablespoons of Minute rice!

I thought Reuben was an interesting man but he was 20 years older than me, so I put him way outside my range.

Six months later, after the break up with Sebastian, one day I was at a Thrift Shop called The Opportunity Shop in midtown Manhattan looking for cheap clothes. In walked Reuben!

"Hello, Natalie Karamazov De Toledo!" he smiled and gave me a hug.

"I'm on my lunch hour. Want to join me? I'll take you to lunch."

"Well, Reuben. That's nice of you but I brought a peanut butter sandwich with me, so I can't bring that with me to a restaurant."

"Suppose you throw out that sandwich and enjoy something much better on me."

Tangent: That conversation set the tone for our relationship for the next 35 years!

It was one thing to enjoy a delicious expensive dinner including a glass of wine and cigarettes with this sophisticated friend of my mother, but it was another much more seemingly dangerous thing to accept Reuben's invitation to come in the evening to the coffee shop in Greenwich Village he had just partnered into.

Better ask my godfather first. On the next subway ride back from class I popped the question:

"Friedrich, is it okay to go to a coffee shop that a divorced man owns where the atmosphere is not at all Catholic?"

"Who is this man?"

"Well, he's a friend of my mother's from Advantage Press. He seems very nice. He was brought up Orthodox Jewish but became an atheist. He came to dinner once and said he was trying to find Christ. Maybe God wants me to befriend him. Maybe he'll become a Catholic someday."

"Why don't you bring Cassandra with you the first time to see what it's like in that café?"

Now this was the very beginning of the hippie era, before we knew that such cafes were often covers for drug dealing.

Cassandra and I took the subway down to Greenwich Village to Reuben's coffee shop called the Fragrant Cup. "Peter, Paul and Mary Singing Tonight" read the sign taped at a diagonal on the large picture window.

Reuben knew we were coming but not exactly when. The moment he saw us walk in, he rushed over and hugged us and seated us right near the stage. Peter, Paul and Mary, not yet famous, sang doleful passionate songs, not too different from the kind we used to hear at the Unitarian folk/square dances when we were High School students.

At about 10:30 PM when I thanked him and told him we were leaving, he insisted in driving us home in his Mercedes Benz.

XLV

Even though Reuben seemed so warm, interesting, and harmless, I had this anxious feeling when I thought about him the next morning. I tried to trace it. Did it start when he gave Cassandra and me each a hug when dropping us off at 43 W. 93rd St.? Or was it when Reuben turned to me while Cassandra was opening the door to the building and said, "I'd love to see you again. I'll call."

"On the subway going to Fordham with my godfather, Friedrich Adenauer, I told him about the pleasant and innocuous visit to Rueben's coffee house.

"It looked as if he wanted to ask me for a date? I feel anxious. As a Catholic, I can't go out with the divorced atheist, can I?

Friedrich looked at me in that thoughtful way I liked so much and said, "Why don't we invite him for dinner at our house?"

I was delighted with that possibility. I was sure they would think that he was an evil rogue and that I should get rid of him as soon as possible and then I could resume my search for a husband who would be like St. Francis of Assisi!

So, the next Saturday night, Reuben came to get me at 43 W. 93 St. and we drove in his expensive car the 12 blocks to the apartment house on

Central Park where Lise and Friedrich lived.

My godmother opened the door and offered Reuben a warm hug before he had even entered the little book-lined hall that led to the dining room. Then came the more formal Friedrich shaking Reuben's hand with both of his, European style.

I was unusually quiet as I marveled at this "love at first sight" rapport between these totally Catholic people and this atheist playboy.

What did they have in common? Well, love of classical music, with a Brahm's Quintet played on 78 discs after dinner. Love of European literature – Goethe's Faust, which I had never read, was the topic.

"Do you see how even though Goethe was not a Catholic, he felt impelled to end Faust with a traditional redemptive ending replete with angels?" Friedrich eagerly explained.

"Yes, as in Gustav Mahler's 8th Symphony, based on the last scenes of Faust," chimed in Reuben, puffing away at the pipe he alternated with cigarettes on social occasions.

"You don't know Mahler's 8th Symphony?" Reuben asked. I would love to play it for you. Perhaps you would honor me with a visit sometime to my place in Greenwich Village? I was planning on playing it for Natalie sometime."

So, no veto from the godparents of this older suitor!

The next subway ride to Fordham, Friedrich explained:

"Now, before this relationship might develop from friendship into courtship, we would have to help you look into the canonical status of his former marriage. He told you it was a civil marriage in Mexico and didn't last even a year? Probably they believed in divorce as a possibility if the marriage didn't work out?"

I hadn't ever heard the word "courtship" in a living voice, but only seen the word in Victorian novels!

"Something like that. I've never met any atheists who believed in marriage as permanent and divorce as a sin."

Even though I felt a strong attraction to Reuben, this was matched with a greater fear of sin. Although on our dates to the theater he always gave me a hug goodbye, he had not so much as kissed me on the mouth. But since I had those love affairs before my conversion, I was keenly aware with what swiftness things could move from friendly hugs to total physical union, especially since after a few dates he now wanted me to come to his apartment alone, without the Adenauer's, to listen to his favorite classical music recordings.

Romantically enough, our first kiss took place in his apartment to the strains of Berlioz' Romeo and Juliet.

A student of Von Hildebrand's Ethics, I was well aware that full sexual expression was only for those whose love was a total self-donation in marriage. About other smaller manifestations of attraction nothing was said in his book.

The key issue for me was whether I was in love with Reuben or not.

Over a glass of expensive wine with Beethoven's Pastoral Symphony as background, after the first kiss, Reuben smiled,

"Do you know that a few years ago at a graduation party your mother gave for you, my first wife came with me. She told me 'Reuben, someday that girl, Natalie, is going to be your second wife!"

"What?" I exclaimed.

"I love you so much already, Natalie, that I could believe she was right," Reuben said in a soft voice, his large blue eyes full of mirth.

"I hardly know you, Reuben," I muttered.

"Sometimes the timing is wrong, Natalie. Would you rather not see me again?"

There was a look of vulnerability in those eyes as he gave me an out.

"That's when I fell in love with him, Cassandra," I confided in my sister later that night.

"Love is a response to the unique preciousness of the other," Von Hildebrand taught, and that vulnerable look was the moment I saw what I would lose if I dismissed Reuben to resume my hunt for the perfect Catholic beau.

Then, of course, I remembered that Catholics can't marry divorced people, and that Friedrich had told me something about canon lawyers.

The next week at lunch in their apartment, I told Lise and Friedrich about my feelings for Reuben. In an unusually solemn voice, Friedrich told me, "Even if you are not sure yet if you want to be married to Reuben, Natalie, it would be good to have a preliminary appointment with the canon lawyer in the Chancery Office of the NYC diocese to look into it. As your godfather I can set up an appointment for you. Probably Reuben should go also since he knows more about the details of his former marriage than you do."

XLVI

A few weeks later during one of Reuben's long lunch hours, we walked into the stone 4 story gothic building with the large sign over the heavy wooden doors: Chancery Office of the Roman Catholic Diocese of New York.

I purchased at the secondhand shop a trim dark blue suit and Reuben wore a tweed jacket and dark brown pants with a white shirt and brown tie. A receptionist sent us up to the 4th floor to look for the office of a Fr. Adrian Coyne.

The priest who stood up and walked around his desk to greet us was younger than I expected; about 45 maybe, with blond hair, grey eyes, looking very formal in his black clerical suit and white priest's collar.

"Mr. Klein and Natalie De Toledo, Dr. Adenauer informed me that you are considering marriage. As you know, Mr. Klein, the Church cannot allow a Catholic to marry someone who we believe to be already married in the eyes of God, even in the case of a previous marriage conducted in a civil procedure."

Reuben smiled in the genial way I now associated in my mind with his being a salesman by profession. "Of course, Fr. Coyne, you need to know that I have not the slightest intention of harming this wonderful

young woman by any action contrary to her conscience…Do you mind if
I smoke?"

Fr. Coyne nodded, and flipping a large yellow pad to a fresh sheet,
prepared to compile answers to his preliminary questions.

After noting the dates of birth of Reuben and his former wife, he
asked a question that surprised me. "Were either you or your wife baptized Christian?"

"I am Jewish by birth, though I left the practice of my family's religion as a teen-ager," replied Reuben. "I think my ex-wife Anne, though,
was baptized Lutheran."

The priest sighed deeply. "Most Lutherans believe that marriage is
permanent and make a vow to that effect."

"Reuben, did you and your wife, Anne, have any children."

To my surprise, my hopefully future fiancé replied, "No. Tragically
my wife chose abortion instead!"

The priest's countenance changed from bland non-descript to alert,
his eyes narrowing in an inquisitive stare.

At that point I started to worry that maybe there was a problem.
Could it be that I might have to someday choose between the Church that
I knew to be my salvation, and the man I was beginning to think would
make me happy on earth?

"Let me try to explain, Reuben," Fr. Coyne took up the conversation
again. "The Church can't be in a position of insisting that a Christian, who
married a Jew, wouldn't have pledged that bond forever."

Tangent: Nowadays there is much talk about canon-law marriage
procedures being too long drawn out and insensitive. This narration could
seem to bear that out, but over time I came to see it differently. It happened
that one summer many decades after this meeting I had occasion to spend
a month giving a course at an Institute where there was a canon law division of studies. Over meals I got to see how devoted and conscientious
these lawyers, some priests and others, Sisters or lay people, really are

concerning the people seeking annulments and dispensations. There is so much to be weighed between the rights of the husbands, wives and families in the original marriage and the hopes for another new bond based on the conviction that the original one was flawed.

At the time Reuben and I applied for such a procedure, the only grounds for annulling or dispensing from a previous Catholic marriage were such impediments as bigamy (where one spouse concealed a previous legal or Church marriage), never consummating the marriage sexually, or extreme mental illness. Over time, due to greater knowledge of psychology, it was recognized that some people, however sincerely eager to marry, simply lack the mental health to be married. An example would be someone so withdrawn as to be unwilling to relate to wife and children in any normal manner. In such cases, after investigation, the tribunal may conclude that the original marriage did not exist as a reality, even though it was performed publically in a civil court or in a church. In such cases, then, the spouse who had given up on the non-marriage, was free to enter into a valid Catholic marriage with a second spouse.

Later I would realize that in the background of this conversation there was a totally different issue: the so-called Pauline privilege. In the early Church it was not infrequent that a Jew who became a Christian was married to a Jew who shunned him or her because of the conversion to an alien belief and way of life. In certain circumstances, the Jewish marriage was dispensed so that the Christian member of the couple could live in faith together with another Christian. This privilege is still a possibility. But Fr. Coyne didn't want to even seem to be coercing Reuben into pretending he wanted to become a Catholic just to marry me. I would realize later that probably my godfather, Friedrich, had a deep spiritual sense that, under my influence and that of the Von Hildebrand circle, Reuben would become a Catholic also, so that this privilege could come into play.

Back to our meeting with Fr. Coyne concerning whether Lutheran-baptized Anne would have thought her marriage to Reuben binding: "I don't understand," I exclaimed. "Anne was not a Christian believer at all. She was an agnostic at best. She certainly thought divorce was a possibility if that civil marriage didn't work out."

"That is the sort of thing we have to investigate." He turned his gaze away from me to face Reuben exclusively and asked solemnly: "You, of course, are not under Catholic jurisdiction. Are you willing to give us written information so that we can follow up on this? We are responsible that a Catholic, Natalie, doesn't think that she can be married in the Church to someone who is already married in the eyes of God even if there was a civil divorce."

I suddenly had the feeling that Fr. Coyne hoped Reuben would refuse to cooperate!

But he didn't. With the same genial salesman-like smile Reuben agreed to fill out a long questionnaire including contact information for himself, Anne, and friends who knew them at the time of the marriage.

After shaking hands formally with Fr. Coyne, we proceeded to the elevator. Once out the door of the fortress like stone building, Reuben winked at me. "Don't you think I love you enough to go through a little paper work to get you, Natalie?"

Six months later, however, I received a letter on heavy white paper from The Archdiocese of New York Tribunal.

Dear Miss Natalie De Toledo,

We are sorry to inform you that your petition to seek a dispensation from the previous civil marriage of Reuben Klein with a view to marriage to him in the Catholic Church has not been approved.

Should you wish to contest this decision, you can fill out the enclosed document which will be forwarded to Rome as an appeal.

Sincerely in Christ,

Rev. Adrian Coyne

Canon Law Division

Archdiocese of New York

I ran upstairs from the mailboxes of 43 W. 93 St. to the apartment and called Reuben. He was not at his desk so I had to leave a message. Then I called my godmother, Lise Adenauer.

"Ach wo, dearest Natalie. Friedrich will be home soon from Fordham. Why don't you come over and talk to him?"

XLVII

I walked quickly the 10 blocks or so from my apartment house to theirs.

Friedrich was just taking off his coat and hat. He motioned me into his office-den and looked gravely into my eyes.

"Lise told me the bad news." His large blue eyes were full of compassion.

"First, always prayer. Closing his eyes he prayed softly, "Christ, savior of mankind, and savior of Natalie, help us to consider this development. We know that your plans are plans of love for us. Send the Holy Spirit to help us."

I just looked at him, waiting for the ax to fall, sure he would say, "This shows that it is not the will of God for you to continue to be close to Reuben anymore."

After a few moments of silence, Friedrich asked me: "Let me look at the letter from the Tribunal."

He read it slowly.

"Natalie, it is important that you tell me whether you think that you love Reuben more than those other men in your life you were in love with."

I thought for a few minutes. Then I smiled. "I thought I loved those others, but it was nothing like what I feel about Reuben. With him I feel that I can see into the depth of his soul in some mysterious way. When he looks at me with love I feel safe."

Then Friedrich surprised me. "Is there a way that Reuben could do book sales with a European base city?"

By what we thought was the providence of God, it turned out that just a week before the letter came from Fr. Coyne, Reuben had been of-fered a job from Dell, one of the largest publishers of cheap paper-backs. The job would involve world-wide sales of these books on kiosks in the hotels frequented most by English-speaking and reading tourists in Europe and the Mid-East. He could choose the European city that would be his base, coming back to NYC once a year. Of course, when he accepted this well-paying sales position, Reuben chose Rome as his base.

Since I couldn't stand the idea of being parted from him for most of what could be a whole year, I took a leave from my graduate studies at Fordham with a view to traveling to Rome for perhaps 6 months to help Reuben assemble our case with the Roman Tribunal for annulment or dis-pensation appeals from Catholic courts in other dioceses.

Reuben would go first to get settled in an apartment and then, if things looked good for the job, he would rent me a room near the Vatican. Reuben agreed to respect my Catholic moral convictions and not to make any attempt to get closer to me by sinful overtures.

Convinced that if Friedrich thought we should appeal to Rome this would be a shoo-in, we proceeded with our plan.

In those days before cheap international phone calls and decades be-fore e-mail, it was dramatic to go each day to the mail-box looking for letters from Italy. These love-letters I propped up next to a large portrait style photo of Reuben, while I prayed for the success of his work and our hopes to one day be married in the Church. In the background I listened rapturously to Puccini's Le Boheme on the 78 rpm discs we still played in those days in the 1960's. That lush Italian opera had become "our song" after seeing a charming production of it in Greenwich Village, NYC just before Reuben left for Europe.

Sisters Karamazov Italian style?

"Natalie, how can you plan to go to Italy without knowing a word of Italian?" Cassandra asked me the day I bought my air ticket to Rome leaving December 21, 1960 after Fordham's Fall semester was over.

We were, as usual, having coffee after dinner around the kitchen table.

"I guess I'll buy a dictionary before I leave."

Tangent: Looking back at this trip to Rome and Reuben I marvel that at the age of only twenty-two I had the daring to fly to a foreign place into the hands of a man I loved but really didn't know very well. On the positive side, you might think I had the courage because I knew Rome to be the center of my Church. Certainly, part of it. On the negative side, I know, hindsight, as a typical "Karamazov" belief that romantic love trumps all common sense!

The day I left them at the LaGuardia airport shuttle on 42nd Street was the first time I noticed how sad my mother Elena and my sister Cassandra looked standing at the curb waving. A third of this trio was taking off for a place they could not imagine. They had none of my bravado. Resignation was the look in their dark Jewish eyes.

And then, not so long afterwards, there I was waving and blowing kisses to my Reuben, my jaunty older possible fiancé, with his laughing eyes and beaming smile and tight, tight hug.

I had seen Rome before, of course, during that Catholic art tour that brought me into the Church 2 summers previous. But now I was not the youngest of a group led by experienced guides: Friedrich and Lise Adenauer. I was, instead, a wide-eyed adventurer into the unknown of the Roman Tribunal and Reuben's world of Dell paperback sales contacts!

First stop in the Opal convertible Dell had given Reuben to drive in

Europe, was a small hotel near the Tiber, right next to a parish Church. Reuben picked it out with the thought that this would give me a sense of security since, to my alarm he told me, "Natalie, unfortunately, I have to go to Naples tomorrow morning for 2 days on a sales trip."

"What?" But, can't I go with you?"

"Not this time. But you'll be fine. Here is a map of Rome. I checked, there is Mass tomorrow at the parish at 8 AM, and I've marked the map so you can see the bus that leaves for St. Peter's Basilica, and, there is a lovely restaurant at the hotel, and before you know it, I'll be back in time to go with you to mid-night Christmas Mass."

Too tired from the long trip to protest, I set my alarm for 7 AM, and slept for 10 hours. With the help of the Italian/English Dell pocket dictionary Reuben gave me, and a little High School Spanish I was able to manage well enough.

XLVIII

Christmas to New Year Reuben and I spent touring St. Peter's Church, the Vatican Museum, and eating at wonderful little Italian restaurants. We figured that by January 2nd the Tribunal would be in business and we could check out how our appeal was proceeding. In New York Fr. Coyne had provided me with an introductory letter to bring to an American priest stationed at the Vatican.

When we arrived at the address on that letter an Italian official dressed in a formal black suit, white shirt, and black tie, looked at the name on the letter. Then he ushered us into a large waiting room. We soon realized that the Vatican is nothing like the United States Church. No fixed appointments, for example, at this location. There were seated about ten people, mostly middle-aged women and men sitting solemnly, seemingly waiting, first come first served, to be called to enter some inner sanctum. Most of the men were smoking, and so were we.

After about forty minutes, a young American looking priest with a crew-cut, a clerical black shirt with a priestly collar but no jacket, came into the waiting room, smiling cheerfully as he walked up to us, shook hands, and introduced himself:

"I am Father George Maloney."

"Buon giorno, Io sono Reuben Klein" said my "fiancé" with a smile.

"Glad to meet you," responded the priest. "No need to try to speak Italian, Mr. Klein.

"That's a relief," I said, putting the dictionary back into my denim tote bag.

"I just got here from the United States a week ago, Fr. Maloney. It is already 3 months since our documents were sent from New York City, so I suppose you have news for us."

Fr. Maloney chuckled. "Oh Miss De Toledo, it will take you awhile to get used to Roman time. A year would be quick on a case like yours!"

I was shocked.

"Where are you staying?"

"At the Tevere hotel, Father. But I certainly can't stay there for a year!"

"Don't worry. Fr. Coyne mentioned in his letter that you are a graduate student of philosophy. There is an international student residence you could stay at if you wish. Not far from St. Peter's." The priest reached into his desk, took out a phone directory, and copied out the address of the hostel for students.

"And you, Mr. Klein, where are you staying."

"As a Dell book sales representative I have a large allowance for expenses. I got here a few months ago and rented an apartment on San Gregorio Settimo. I am often away on sales trips."

"I tell you what," Fr. Maloney continued with a pleasant smile. "Suppose you post me your address and phone number when you are settled, Miss Klein, and then I can contact you if there are any developments or questions we have for you."

With that we were ushered out.

Seated in one of the many cafes, called bars, near the Tribunal office, I wailed, "A year minimum! I love being in Italy, but what will I do with myself when you are off on sales trips to Switzerland, France, England, or as far off as Israel? Why a week from now you're scheduled to drive off with your book catalogues as far away as Paris!"

"Let's find this student place and see if you like it and want to move in, and then talk about how you could come on some of these trips with me maybe." Reuben assumed his usual take charge attitude.

Tangent: Such contrasts between near panic on my part and take charge problem solving on Reuben's would follow us to 35 years! Does every Karamazov need a businessman as a manager?

I liked the Casa Internazionale. It was in an old building 4 stories high with about 10 rooms on a floor, the floors divided between ones for men and others for women. It also had a large cafeteria on the first floor. It was pretty cheap. About $200 a month for the room with meal ticket options monthly or daily. Reuben's salary and commissions could easily take care of such a small rent for me and, except for breakfast, our meals would be together at restaurants. Best of all, I could go to Mass every morning at any of the many altars of St. Peter's basilica itself!

When we returned with my suitcase, it was about 3 PM. The mingled voices in the coffee shop part of the cafeteria sounded French, German, and British English with a comingling of African languages.

The next morning Reuben arranged with the management that for a small fee they would check the phone in my room for messages from the Tribunal if I happened to be out of town. I could call in long distance every few days in case Fr. Maloney called to summon me. I could rush back on a train or plane from wherever in Europe Reuben was selling books to distributors.

And so a week later off I was packed into Reuben's sleek black Opal on the way to Paris!

I bet you readers have started wondering many pages earlier than this one what kind of physical romance was going on between Natalie Karamazov De Toledo, strict Catholic convert, and Reuben Klein, divorced former playboy!

"Just because you're determined to keep our relationship chaste, dear Natalie, that doesn't mean you have to sit as close to the car door as possible. You could be a little closer and sometimes kiss my hand on the wheel, no?"

"I guess so." Kissing, often long, was the very most that I allowed.

For Reuben, as a sophisticated man, it was embarrassing on these sales trips to pull up to a motel or hotel with me by his side.

"Do you have 2 separate rooms free for me and my friend?"

Wink, wink, wink from the receptionist. "I can give you one room, mister."

"No, I have to have 2 separate rooms for myself and my friend and, where is the nearest Catholic Church? My friend wants to go to Mass early in the morning."

Oh the joy of Mass at small and large Churches throughout Europe! Some baroque, some neo-Gothic, some even Romanesque. The Mass was still in Latin in those days so there was no problem following it.

"Natalie, you act as if every Catholic Church in the world belongs to you, personally," Reuben once remarked.

"They do belong to me and to every Catholic." Usually Reuben would walk around the Church while I was attending Mass. He loved the aesthetics of it. But he didn't really pay much attention to all the lectures I gave him on those long drives about why everyone should be Catholic.

"I'd become a Catholic the next day if I could believe in God," was his way of checkmating my evangelizing attempts.

I have to relate a funny incident on our first trip to Paris. Reuben was looking forward to promenading with me down the famous Champs Elysee.

"Let's celebrate our first big trip together, Natalie, by you picking out a beautiful new dress from Paris!

"Okay." It sounded good to me. But the attempt to find me a fancy dress became a foretaste of all the conflicts about values that haunted the rest of our lives!

"Reuben, I haven't found anything I especially like. Why don't you leave me at the hotel. I can take a nap and then read more Thomas Aquinas."

"Don't be ridiculous. Aren't you a normal woman? Any woman would be thrilled to be picking out a dress in a Paris boutique."

"I'm not any woman, Reuben. I'm a philosophy student."

It took Reuben about 30 years to resign himself that whenever we travelled he would walk around for hours sight-seeing and I would be holed up in a Church praying and reading.

XLIX

So what did Natalie Karamazov De Toledo do while Reuben was visiting book distributors in the cities of Europe or, when in Rome, he was assembling book orders?

For the first 4 months I spent such time studying. I brought along a two volume set of the writings of St. Thomas Aquinas. I also tried to learn Italian at the classes provided at the Casa Internazionale.

Friends? I soon got acquainted with other students in residence. These were mostly people getting degrees in theology at the famous institutes such as the Gregorian or Regina Caeli, where programs had been opened up not only for priests, seminarians and Sisters, but also for lay students. Most of them knew English fairly well and with my smattering of French and German from classes in the United States we could converse well enough.

After 3 months of such exciting trips and absorbing studies, I finally got that phone call from Fr. Maloney I was waiting for so impatiently.

"Miss Klein, this is Fr. Maloney from the Tribunal," came the always amiable voice of the priest.

"Yes, yes! News for us?" I responded breathlessly?

"I want to give you the phone number of the canon lawyer we have assigned to your appeal. His name is Msgr. Gosner. He is a German Benedictine who lives at the monastery of San Anselmo."

"Oh, yes, we've been to visit that monastery. The whole group surrounding Von Hildebrand who brought me into the Church are Benedictine Oblates."

Tangent: When the great orders of the Catholic Church were founded, such as the Benedictines, Franciscans, and Dominicans, they were joined by men and women with vows of chastity, poverty, and obedience – brothers, nuns and priests. However, most of them were surrounded by groups of lay people who participated in the many religious services of the monastery or friary and also helped support the monks, friars, or nuns. The first order of the group were the brothers and priests; the second were the nuns or Sisters; and the lay people were called Third Order or, in the case of Benedictines, Oblates.

"Does Fr. Gosner speak English?" I asked.

"Perfectly. Msgr. Gosner taught liturgy for years at St. Meinrad's Abbey in the United States."

An appointment was agreed upon the following Saturday morning after the elaborate 9 AM Mass at the venerable medieval Abbey of San Anselmo.

Msgr. Gosner, dressed in the traditional black long habit of his order, explained in his soft voice after ushering us into seats at a remote table in a an old-fashioned high ceilinged library.

"I was assigned to you both specifically because of your connection to Dietrich Von Hildebrand," Msgr. Gosner began.

I was immediately turned off by this monk. Everything about him bespoke moderation, a quality anathema to Karamazov types like me. He seemed about 55 years old, late middle-age, medium height, with blue eyes mild and lacking in animation.

I was happy when Reuben took the lead. "Ah, sie sind Deutsch, Vater Gosner."

"Ja, Bavarian," replied the monk with interest.

"You are Jewish I read in the documents, but not believing, nicht wahr?"

Msgr. Gosner ignored my presence as he continued to interview Reuben. Upset but happy that Msgr. Gosner seemed to like Reuben, at least, my eyes wandered to the heavy wooden bookcases with all hard-cover books, not a trace of a vulgar paper-back, of course.

After asking Reuben many of the same questions that Fr. Coyne had assembled answers to, Msgr. Gosner surprised us:

"Herr Klein, I happen to be making a visitation of the famous monastery of Subiaco, the one St. Benedict himself founded in the 4th century next Wednesday. Perhaps you would like to come with me to see it."

I was pleased but flustered. Reuben failed to ask the obvious question, "You mean myself and Miss De Toledo?"

Tangent: It was only many decades later that I realized two reasons for this seeming insulting behavior. First of all, in case the appeal was lost, he didn't want us to see ourselves already as an engaged couple. Quite a number of people who apply for annulments or dispensations, are already living together sexually or in civil marriages. I realized later how anxious the Adenauer's and Dietrich Von Hildebrand were about us, especially with me far from their direct face to face influence. Secondly, he was hoping that by making a personal friend of Reuben he could help bring him to the faith. If Reuben became a Catholic, then that Pauline privilege would apply!

A Related Tangent: It is hard for Christians to understand the degree of horror many Jews feel about any family member becoming a Christian or, even worse, a Catholic. The Jewish people survived throughout the ages partly by God's grace, but also, from an anthropological point of view, because of intense bonding within the tribe. Converting to another religion, especially one with a history of persecuting Jews, is usually considered a total betrayal not of Judaism as a religion so much as of the

Jewish people. Looking backwards, I now realize that it was not primarily because Reuben was an atheist that he didn't want to publically become a Catholic, but probably because of this huge taboo. Among orthodox Jews if a family member becomes a Christian or, sometimes, just that he or she marries a Christian instead of a Jew, the family enacts the same mourning ceremony in the home as they would when a member died! It is called "sitting shiva." Sometimes conservative or reformed Jews, without going through such a ceremony might still shun the convert. With all this in mind, even though Reuben seemed like a totally emancipated contemporary non-religious person, there would have been a deep dislike of breaking with his Jewish background. His parents were orthodox Jews; his sister a conservative Jew, and his brother an agnostic, but nevertheless very anti-Christian.

Since we had not been told much about the Pauline privilege, we both assumed that the appeal would be based not on Reuben becoming a Catholic, but on the atheism of Reuben and Anne at the time of the marriage. Certainly they both considered divorce to be a legitimate option should their hopes for the marriage to work out be disappointed.

L

"Natalie, do tell. If it's not too personal, how can you and Reuben stand waiting for a dispensation that might never come?" asked my new friend from the Casa Internationale, Eileen Casey.

Eileen was an American of Irish Catholic background who was studying theology as a lay student at the Gregorian, where previously only seminarians studied. She was a pretty tall young woman in her thirties with blond curly hair. We were having coffee in her tiny room one Sunday. Reuben was off to Israel on a sales trip.

Delighted to have found a woman friend to talk to in English, I was happy to explain.

"You see, Eileen," I began, as usual twisting a cotton handkerchief in my fingers as I talked, "even though I am intensely attracted to Reuben sexually and he to me, having had all those miserable love-affairs before I became a Catholic, I don't want to risk mortal sin now."

"But isn't it difficult going on these trips with him where no one would ever know?" Eileen, who I knew to be a virgin, asked.

"God would know, Eileen. I can't risk all that I have found of truth and hope in being a Catholic for an act of love that might never be fulfilled in marriage. Since you have made the same choice, you have to understand."

"I suppose so," Eileen got a far-away look in her eyes. "Of all the men I have dated so far, the one I was most tempted to have sex with was an ex-seminarian. He was from Ireland. I met him in class at the Gregorian when he was still a seminarian. I think I would have fallen except that he was too pure to let us go further than long kisses."

"So what happened to you, two?" I questioned Eileen, eager to get even closer to her by learning more about her life.

Eileen smiled ruefully. "Well, I sure was glad we never went further since a year after we started dating he become a Cistercian monk! Would it have been fun to be the single mother of a baby whose father was enclosed in a monastery?"

"I keep hoping to hear from Fr. Maloney about our marriage case," I sighed.

"Oh, Natalie. I keep forgetting to tell you. In my class on canon-law, the professor was talking about marriage cases. He does canon-law in Milan. I was telling him about your case and he said that he would talk to you if you wished."

"Please arrange it," I insisted.

Padre Luigi ushered me toward table in a far corner of the dining room of the Gregorian.

With a heavy Italian accent he asked me to outline for him my story. When I finished he sighed.

"Non e bene, signorina. Quasi imposibile."

On the bus back to the Casa with Eileen I cried on her shoulder. "Almost impossible! Oh, Eileen, what will I do if they turn us down? I love him so much. I can't bear the thought of losing him."

After dinner, I went into the chapel at the Casa. It was dark with only candle-light on the altar and the red perpetual lamp by the tabernacle signaling the real presence of Jesus in the Eucharist.

"Christ, I beg you to find a way to give us the dispensation. But if it is not your will, I surrender my earthly happiness to fidelity to Your

Church."

As the tears flowed, I sensed a lightness coming into my heart.

The following week, the day before Reuben was due to return from Israel, I found a heavy white envelope in my box at the Casa with the name Rev. George Maloney, Tribunale on the left corner.

I tore it open.

Dear Miss De Toledo,

I am happy to inform you that the Tribunale has granted you the Petrine Privilege. Please come to our office for the documents you can give to a Church of your choice to arrange your marriage to Reuben Klein.

Sincerely in Christ,

Rev. George Maloney, Canon Lawyer

I jumped for joy and started telling everyone at the Casa I knew. Eileen and I celebrated with wine and spaghetti at a local trattoria.

I had never heard of the Petrine privilege. When I went with Reuben to pick up the documents at the Tribunal, Fr. Maloney explained: "You have probably heard of the Pauline Privilege. The Petrine (based on the keys to the kingdom given to St. Peter) privilege was put into place centuries ago to cover cases where the previous marriage of the man or woman seeking to marry in the Church is deemed not to be what the Church would consider a full marriage and where no one will be harmed by a the marriage to be contracted in the Church, such as any children. Reuben and his former wife didn't have any children.

Seeing our beaming faces, the priest was quick to add, "Now, since Reuben is not a Catholic, this marriage is not a sacrament, but will be valid for you Miss De Toledo. Should he later become a Catholic it will be a sacramental marriage."

"Where do you suggest we get married, Father?"

"You can go back to the United States of course, to the parish you used to attend or you can go to either of two Churches here that are staffed by American priests."

The most famous of these was Santa Susanna, a Baroque Church attended by most American Catholics who lived in Rome. But the other was an old monastic Church, San Onofreo, with cloister paths and medieval frescoes that happened to be staffed by American monks.

Can you guess which one we chose?

Tangent: Many non-Catholics and even Catholics think that people looking into annulments or dispensation have to pay large fees. We were charged nothing in New York or in Rome. I believe that after that time there is a fee for all the paper work and salaries of canon-lawyers, probably because more of them are lay persons who, after all, need to have a decent salary. But I have never heard of anyone turned down for not having money for any fees.

LI

Natalie Karamazov De Toledo, soon to be Natalie Karamazov Klein, certainly preferred that old monastic Church. More romantic. There was even a fountain of perpetually spouting water near the Church doors.

The American monks at San Onofreo were happy to have Msgr. Gosner preside at our July 9th wedding. My mother, Elena Karamazov, and my twin sister Cassandra Karamazov were coming from New York. My godfather, Friedrich Adenauer and my godmother, Lise, would be coming from their usual summer-time vacation in Germany. The other guests were all from my friends and acquaintances at the Casa Internazionale.

A small wedding with only some 15 guests, but still I managed to be the nervous bride-to-be fussing about the arrangements. A symptom was going up to a pack a day on the cigarettes. Not yet committed to the simplicity of life that would become a later passion of mine, just out of miserliness I had no intention of getting a wedding gown that cost more than $100. Since I could find nothing I liked for that price, my friend Eileen brought me to a dress-maker who, for $65 made me a simple long A-line satin dress. The veil cost only $15. Of course this was back in 1961. For my honeymoon garment I had made a bright yellow silk Chinese style dress. That was another $25. Reuben planned our honeymoon for Greece where he had business connections. They found us a nice hotel in Athens and a little cruise to the islands.

The Casa Internazionale agreed to host the reception for free if we paid for the food.

Even though I was ecstatic to be marrying my dearly-beloved Reuben, I must still have been nervous because the photos of me waiting to enter the Church include the cigarettes I was chain smoking! Reuben also is shown smoking. This was, of course, long before anyone thought smoking was bad for the health.

In the photos of us seated in chairs in front of the altar I am smiling at Msgr. Gosner. By now, I no longer resented his previous cold way of treating me.

By evening Reuben and I were off on the train to Brindisi on the coast of Italy where we would spend the first night and then depart by boat for Athens the next morning. I remember the thrill when for the first time, introducing ourselves to a family on the train, Reuben described me as Signora (Mrs.) Natalie Klein!

Back in Rome, the Adenauer's showed Elena and Cassandra around Rome the next day after the wedding. Then they returned to Germany and my mother and sister took a train to Paris, which Elena had not seen for some thirty years.

Ah, that wedding night! I truly believe that the first total union, physical, emotional and spiritual of a couple, that has not consummated their love before the wedding day, has a different feeling to it. Some religious couples actually experience the presence of God their creator at that moment. That was not my experience, but there was certainly a mystical sense of complete self-donation I had never known in the love affairs of the past. At the Masses I went to each day after the wedding, I was full of thanksgiving to God for the joy and peace that the fulfillment of all my hopes had brought us. Possibly our twins were conceived that first night. We couldn't know. But the due date of the one baby we knew about beforehand was 9 months to the dot.

Athens was disappointing. Somehow we hadn't thought about how Greece in the summer months is torrid and crowded. The Greeks deal with this by doing business in the early morning, then having a 4-hour siesta, followed by a slow dinner and work again in the evening.

With only 2 days in Athens we were certainly not going to "do as the Greeks do," so we trotted around viewing all the famous monuments. A highlight was seeing the play Medea of Euripedes at an amphitheater near Athens constructed centuries before the birth of Christ.

Pleasanter was the little cruise to famed islands such as Corfu and Mykonos, where I have a photo of myself riding a donkey, something I would never had done had I known how prone I would be to miscarriage.

Back in Rome we moved into a charming apartment in the section called the Gianicolo in the hills above St. Peter's Basilica. Reuben had scheduled all his sales trips for Europe so that I could easily come with him.

Once diagnosed as pregnant, we decided that it would be good to return to New York a month before the baby was coming. That way I could stay in mother Elena's apartment and then return to Rome a month after the birth.

Elena had lined up a young doctor for us who worked out of a hospital near the apartment she lived in to be close to her job at Advantage Press on 31st. Dr. Blake, a short, thin very young man turned out to be one of the very first who pushed the use of natural methods of birth, then called Lamaze, where the husband could be present at the delivery coaching his wife through her labor pains.

What I remember the most about going to the lessons on Lamaze was that I was the fattest woman in the group of 15! I carried all in the front, but still…Two weeks before the due date, Reuben decided to make a quick trip to visit his mother, sister and niece and nephew in Washington, D.C.

But my water broke a day after he left, and included blood. Dr. Blake ordered me to get right to the hospital. There he called my husband in DC who managed to get to the airport and to NYC and the hospital within 5 hours. This was very good, because my procedure was much quicker than most first births. All during the initial contractions Dr. Blake was bringing other obstetricians to check me out. Never good at pain, and becoming anxious about this unexpected attention, I remember calling out: "If it's a choice between me and the baby, save the baby."

The pain was much worse than I had been told it would be, but finally there was Reuben with me in the delivery room. After the last push and the birth of the baby girl, we had agreed would be called Olivia after my grandmother on my mother, Elena's side, Reuben removed the mask he had been given. He was grinning from ear to ear.

"Put back that mask, Reuben Klein," Dr. Blake insisted. "There's another baby coming in a few more minutes."

What a shock. It turned out that these were Dr. Blake's first twins. Not hearing a second heart beat every time he checked me out, he was worried that the second baby could be dead. He decided that he could avoid disappointing us, should that be the case, by not even mentioning the twin. That was why he had these other doctors listening for heart-beats.

Another horrible series of acute pains and out came Olivia's twin. We quickly decided to name her Juliet, as a sort of fantasy that Olivia and Juliet Klein would be as wonderful as all the previous sisters Karamazov, from Olivia, my grandmother and her sister back in Russia, to Elena and my aunt Juliet, to my sister Cassandra and me, Natalie Karamazov, now back to another Olivia and Juliet.

Incestuous ego-centric maniacs, or…how about redeemed Sisters Karamazov's!

LII

Oh, my how we loved those little babies!

Like most first time parents, we had no idea beforehand the intensity of that love. For Reuben it was also a religious experience.

"Natalie, I think I have more of an inkling about how God, if there is a God, would love us as His children, now that I am a father."

We stayed for 6 weeks at my mother, Elena's, apartment before returning to Rome.

It was too bad that mothers weren't taught how to breastfeed in those days since feeding twins, one at each breast, is a lot easier than bottle feeding one twin for ½ hour in one's arms, and then feeding the other twin for ½ hour, then sleeping for an hour and then another hour of feeding round the clock 24 hours a day! Eventually Reuben would take a turn now and then, but while we were in New York City he was most of the day at Dell working on his sales trips for the following year.

Of course Elena and Cassandra and Reuben's family, who came for a visit from DC, were delighted with Olivia and Juliet. His folks even more so since they had almost given up on any babies coming from his loins after the disappointments with Anne, his first wife, not wanting any.

Eileen, my friend in Rome from the Casa Internazionale, lined up a live-in maid/nanny for us to help with the twins on our return. After the long, cumbersome airplane ride from New York it was a relief to hand Olivia to Eileen and Juliet to Maria, the helper, for the ride back from the airport to our apartment.

What I liked best about motherhood was looking into their eyes as they gulped down their milk. Though identical twins, the eyes, windows of the soul, were quite different in expression. Olivia's eyes were always more serious; Juliet's more laughing. Years later Juliet invented these nicknames: Olivia's name was cautious doom and Juliet's was delicious cheer. By that time, however, I was seeing Olivia as more like myself in her serious sincerity, and Juliet more like her life-loving funny father, Reuben.

Perhaps only another woman philosophy student can imagine how radical would be the change from spending all day thinking about concepts to immersion in the sensory details of motherhood of one baby, no less twins. Feedings, baths, diapers, a seemingly endless cycle of such nitty-gritty activities! How I loved rushing out of the apartment, leaving the gemelli (Italian for twins) in the care of Maria, to go to daily Mass at the parish Church 5 blocks away.

Then came the loneliness when Reuben went off on 2-months' travels to sell Dell paperbacks to distributors. Those middle-men would put the books on kiosks for the reading joy of American tourists all over the world, now including Asian countries as well as cities in Europe and the Mid-East.

Maria, my helper, was a charming young Italian woman, but only 18 years old, and absolutely uninterested in talking about philosophy or literature. She was a Catholic, so I could practice my meagre Italian talking to her about the Church and the saints. What Maria wanted to talk about most was her boyfriend, Guido, a short, handsome, ex-soldier, presently unemployed. This swain arrived on Maria's day off to accompany her to the house of her parents in the suburbs of Rome.

"He is so jealous Signora Klein! When I go out to do your shopping, I see him spying on me from the window of his parents' little car. He thinks that maybe I am not going to the grocery store but to meet some other man!"

Eager to get out of the apartment house which was just a half hour from St. Peter's Square, Maria and I, with the gemelli in a double stroller, happened upon a dramatic incident. John XXIII in 1963 was dying slowly in his chambers at the Vatican. The large space between the famous columns in front of the Church was filled with people praying. Into our midst came a procession of Italians from the Pope's home town, carrying on their shoulders a huge wooden cross. They had travelled on foot, praying for him, for many days. How moving!

After John XXIII's death, during the conclave that voted in Pope Paul VI it happened that we were also in the Square when the white smoke issued forth declaring "Habemus Papam".

How happy I was when Reuben returned from his first trip to Japan and the Philippines. And how he adored our little ones. I used to affectionately call them squigglepusses because they were such fun to squeeze and tickle. Very soon Reuben began the tradition of holding them one on each knee and telling them stories. Always, viewing their progress, from only milk say, to spoon feeding of baby foods, he would exclaim eyes wide with joy, "Aren't they incredible!"

But after a month back at his base in Rome, Reuben was planning to go off on another 2 month-trip, this time to the Mid-East.

Olivia and Juliet in their cribs for the night, Reuben would play music on the phonograph for an hour and then was the time for us to talk.

"I can't stand it that you are leaving again! I can pray and go to Mass and study Italian and read, and sometimes Eileen and other old friends from the Casa come over, but that's not having you with me."

"It's part of my job to travel, Natalie. And we love being in Rome. We wouldn't like to go back to the rat-race of the publishing business in

NYC, would we?" Reuben would repeat again and again each evening, eyes sad and perplexed.

When he saw that I was even more miserable after his second two month trip away, he came up with a solution.

"Suppose we buy a camper and you and the babies come with me whenever I am traveling in Europe?"

"What? Cooped up with crying and crawling babies all day in a camper with no Maria to help? Maria would never leave Guido, now her official fiancé, for two months long."

After the next trip, Reuben announced with a tragic look in his eyes,

"Natalie, the only thing I can think is that we need to go back to New York. I looked into a job for another publisher where I can be mostly in the office in the US and make short trips to other countries of just a week. That way you can have your mother and twin-sister for company. It will be better all around."

I was stunned. "But Reuben, you love living in Rome. You hate the New York business world! How will you stand it?"

As you will see in the next chapter, he couldn't stand it.

LIII

A day in the life of the Klein family in NYC living in a brownstone apartment building on 3rd Avenue and 16th Street:

7 AM – The wails of Olivia and Juliet awaken Natalie who changes their diapers, puts them in their matching hi-chairs and feeds them baby-food alternating with milk in their plastic cups and then inserts them into their playpen.

8 AM – Reuben leaves for work at Fawcett Books in mid-town, every other day carrying out a large bag of diapers to leave at the Laundromat.

9 AM – Natalie drags the double-stroller down 2 flights of stairs to set it outside. Then she climbs up the stairs and brings Olivia and Juliet, one at a time, down the stairs, and inserts them into the stroller.

9:30 AM – Natalie strolls the twins into the Church near the time of the Consecration; wheels them out, walks around the block and returns for Holy Communion. This is because the twins make too much noise if she tries to stay for the whole half hour service.

10:00 AM – Natalie and babies are at the playground together. This area is about one square block and consists of benches where mommies and, on the weekend, daddies, sit watching the children who are in the sandbox or on slides and swings. The pavement is embellished by the liter such as beer cans and cigarette butts, of street people who camp out there. "Delicious Cheer" Juliet, now a year old, likes to pick up the butts and offer them to the street people as gifts.

(Tangent: Decades later, herself a chain-smoker, Juliet likes to shock street people who ask for a cigarette by reaching into her tote bag and taking out a whole pack and giving it to them.)

12 Noon - Natalie strolls the twins back to the house. She brings up one child in her arms at a time up the two flights of stairs, then lifts the stroller up to the apartment.

Next comes lunch for all and a nap for Olivia and Juliet with Natalie taking her own nap.

2 PM – 5:30 PM is play time. The twins run around the apartment with Mommy following them, with a book in hand to read between breaking up fights or changing diapers. The most alarming fight came when little Olivia beat out her identical twin sister by standing up first in the playpen. Enraged at all the praiseful attention going to her twin, Juliet sat watching and trying over and over again to stand without success. She finally was able to stand, of course, but in the interim pulled out all of Olivia's hair!

(Tangent: Since at the time I was rereading the Brothers Karamazov once again, this envious incident reminded me a little of the famous scene where Grushenka devastates Katerina over their rivalry for the love of Dmitri.

5:45 PM - Daddy comes home! Alleluia. Natalie makes dinner while Reuben plays with the twins.

7 PM - After dinner comes the usual hour of classical music, Olivia and Juliet playing in the living room, while Natalie does the dishes.

8 PM - The twins sit on Daddy's lap listening to stories.

8:30 PM Mommy sings hymns and prayers with the twins in their cribs.

9- 10 PM - Natalie and Reuben talk together and go to bed.

On weekends Elena and Cassandra would come to visit. Sometimes we would pack the babies into our car and drive to New Rochelle where members of the Von Hildebrand circle, including the Adenauer's, had relocated.

The first totally unforeseen, dramatic incident in this routine was the miscarriage of my next pregnancy. Only 2 months after conception patches of blood in the panties; examination; short visit to the hospital; and great sadness.

The hospital chaplain came by and blessed me. "Think of the baby as like a little angel in heaven."

We were bewildered.

"Did I do anything wrong, Dr. Blake?" I asked plaintively.

"Oh, no. Miscarriages are very common. No reason to worry," the gyn/ob doctor replied as if it were nothing.

Reuben was especially crushed.

"I feel as if my womb is a tomb!" I wailed.

Much worse was the next miscarriage six months later. Reuben was on a 2-week trip for Fawcett in South America. When I called to find out how to reach him to come home quickly, his boss manipulated me into not making a fuss. "That airfare is huge, Mrs. Klein. I'm sure your mother and sister can take care of you and the twins without him coming home. He'll be back in 10 days anyhow."

This time Dr. Blake took the miscarriage more seriously.

"Natalie, it would be good to avoid pregnancy for at least a year. I will prescribe a contraceptive pill for you."

"Oh, Dr. Blake. I couldn't do that. Catholics don't accept contraception."

"Don't be so sure. I've heard things are changing in the Catholic church. Check it out before you say you can't."

Now this was back in 1966. I consulted two priests, both of whom I admired.

"Fr. 'X,' what do you think about the pill? Is it the same as condoms and diaphrams and, so, forbidden?"

"Absolutely. Don't use it."

"But, a whole year without sex? Reuben isn't a Catholic, as you know."

He wouldn't budge. So I consulted another priest.

"Fr. 'Y,' what do you think about the pill? Is it the same as condoms and diaphrams?"

"Natalie, this is a matter presently being discussed in the highest Church circles. If you want my opinion, I think you could use the pill."

I took his advice. Reuben was greatly relieved.

(Tangent: Two years later Pope Paul VI wrote an encyclical, Humanae Vitae, to the whole Church explaining, among other things, why any kind of contraception was wrong, including the pill. This caused an uproar among moral theologians, priests, and lay people, because most of them were sure the pill would be considered an exception. This is not the place to explain why the Pope was right. I will go into it when I describe teaching ethics myself some years later. Shortly afterwards Fr. "Y" left the priesthood, married a divorced woman, and they eventually left the Catholic Church. Dietrich Von Hildebrand wrote a short book called *Humanae Vitae: Sign of Contradiction* not only showing why contraception was so wrong, but also why it was so easy for people in our times to be value-blind to that wrongness. You can find used copies on Amazon if you are interested.)

LIV

That year on the East Side of NYC saw 2 very life-changing happenings in the life of the Sisters Karamazov.

The first was Cassandra's redemptive drama-queen scenario. After Cassandra's becoming a Catholic she went to daily Mass in a Church in Greenwich Village near her small apartment. She worked part time as a registrar at Julliard, took modern dance classes with the famous Valerie Bettis, and became part of a small dance company. All this was okay but nothing so satisfying and exalting as what would occur due to a providential encounter on the street.

"Hello," a thin, bearded, long, light-brown-haired young man greeted Cassandra one day on a street in the Village. In his arms were a stack of newspapers. The banner read *The Catholic Worker – 1 cent a copy.*

"Oh, I've heard of that paper," Cassandra replied, smiling. "Sure, I'd like one. That's the paper Dorothy Day edits, isn't it?"

"Right." He pocketed the penny Cassandra extended to him and added unexpectantly, "Philip O'Malley's" my name, what's yours?

"Cassandra De Toledo...but I like to stick in my mother's name: Karamazov, just to interest people." Cassandra smiled shyly.

"I recently became part of the Catholic Worker Movement. I feel called to reach out to the poor," Philip explained.

"I am a modern dancer, Philip, but I also want to help the poor. I'm not yet sure how exactly."

"How exciting! It happens I have been wishing I could dance to the Gospels. But I don't know how to dance. Could you teach me?"

"Dance the gospels? I never thought of that. Where would you dance the gospels? At the Catholic Worker House?"

"Why not right on the steps of the Church we are talking in front of?"

That evening Cassandra came to visit us for dinner at the Karamazov/De Toledo/Klein apartment.

"You're glowing with joy, Cassandra, what in the world happened to you?" Natalie asked after the hugs all around.

"Dance with us, dance with us, Cassandra," Juiliet and Olivia pulled on their aunt's long-striped hippie skirt.

"Give me 10 minutes with your Mommy, and then we will dance," Cassandra said waving them off.

"You won't believe what I am going to do! Dance to the Gospels on the steps of St. James Church in the Village! And…"

Of course, I was much more interested in hearing about this Philip man than about the plan to dance on the steps of any Church. Could he be the perfect Catholic husband for my dear twin?

At dinner Reuben suggested protectively that Cassandra bring this gypsy around.

Whether because he was so poor he would accept any invitation to eat, or because he was really interested in Cassandra was not clear, but a few days later there he was knocking at the door with my twin.

"Are you Jesus?" little Juliet asked staring at his long hair and beard?

Nothing daunted Philip swung her around and questioned my little 2 1/2 year old in return, "Are you like Jesus?"

"No, silly, I'm a little girl," Juliet replied.

"Philip means that we are all supposed to be like Jesus, Juliet," Cassandra put in solemnly.

During the spaghetti dinner I prepared, Reuben inveigled Philip into telling us about his background on a farm in the Midwest, and how he left college after a year to find out what his vocation might be.

"I live at the Catholic Worker House with the street people Dorothy takes in, helping at the soup kitchen and selling the paper."

Evaluating the visit after they left I figured that Philip realized that, as a businessman, Reuben was trying to make sure his sister-in-law wasn't being exploited by some ne'er do well.

But this was the surprising way Philip handled the tension he couldn't help feeling. When we were sitting in the living room, the twins playing at our feet, Philip suddenly asked Cassandra to find a basin and fill it with water and also bring a towel.

These Philip brought to the floor in front of Reuben. "Do you mind if I wash your feet, Mr. Klein?"

Startled, Reuben looked at him as if he were crazy, but decided quickly to let him do his thing.

"Jesus said we should copy him in this, Reuben…to be humble."

We all stared fascinated as Philip lowered his head and gently untied Reuben's shoe laces, and took off his socks. After washing the feet, he dried them and looked up at my husband with a beatific smile.

Later Reuben's comment to me was, "I think he's crazy but probably harmless!"

The following Sunday I took Juliet and Olivia in their stroller in the subway to the Church where Cassandra and Philip planned to dance out the parable of the return of the Prodigal Son. Philip was the sinful son, Cassandra was his mother, and they persuaded other people hanging around to dance other roles.

Then, after this ground-breaking innovation, Cassandra invited all the on-lookers to do a spontaneous circle dance to a simple old Quaker song, "It's a joy to be simple, it's a joy to be free."

Of course Juliet and Olivia loved dancing with the grown-ups. I did, too. I was amazed that my shy twin could pull off such a thing.

A most spectacular occasion I witnessed of Cassandra and Philip leading sacred dance was one Easter Sunday in a park in a large square in lower Manhattan. It turned out that the place was invisibly sectioned off with different ethnic groups "owning" park benches surrounding a central area with statues. There were the Puerto Ricans, the Slavs, Blacks and Irish gang teens. They were all in their usual turfs after Easter Sunday dinner.

Enter Cassandra, dressed in a long white modern dance dress with her long hair, thin and ethereal face and Philip with his long hair, beard, and a large cassette player with Christian folk music to play. In an unusually loud voice for him, he stood in the middle of the square and announced:

"We are here to celebrate the Resurrected Lord by dancing with joy. Forget any bad feelings you have for different groups here, and praise the Lord by dancing with us."

A few mothers and children got up when the music started and joined Philip and me and Olivia and Juliet. My twin, Cassandra, went around waving the others into the circle.

What a happening! I was stunned.

And what was the second momentous event of that year? Check out the next chapter.

LV

"Natalie, I have a possible full time job for you at Hunter College in the Great Books Department!" It was Alice Von Hildebrand with her beautiful Belgian accent.

"I couldn't even consider such a thing, Lily." (Lily was the nickname of my dear woman philosophy professor friend who helped bring me into the Church.) I have 2 little toddlers and Reuben is either at work most of the day or on trips out of the country. Besides, don't you think that mothers of small children should be home with them?"

"I thought you told me that you found it almost unbearable to be with children all day. Well, even if not now with the job, why don't you finish up your Ph.D. at Fordham so that when the children are in school you could teach, as least part-time?"

"It would cost a lot of money to finish that Ph.D. And maybe I will keep the next pregnancy."

"Oh, dear one, I pray and hope so, but in case you miscarry again, I saw an announcement on our bulletin board at Hunter about a special scholarship for women who had left graduate school to get married and have families. It pays for all expenses so mothers of children can finish their degrees. If you get that scholarship you could get a nanny a few afternoons a week so you could go to Fordham."

To my surprise, Reuben thought it was a great idea. I won one of the scholarships and the next Fall found me Tuesday and Thursday afternoons on that D Train up to the Bronx once more. I found a wonderful round black woman, like the one who took care of Cassandra and myself when we were little, to take care of Olivia and Juliet just those 2 afternoons until Reuben came home and through the evening when he was off on foreign sales trips.

By that time Dietrich Von Hildebrand was retired from teaching at Fordham and I had taken all Friedrich Adenauer's classes, so I took other courses from Jesuit priests and studied for the big comprehensive exam. Compared to teaching kiddies how to tie shoes this was all duck soup for highly intellectual me! Soon I was working on my thesis about the Christian philosophy of the Danish existentialist, Kierkegaard.

In the meantime many of the parents of the children in the park each afternoon were coming to a different conclusion. Why live in filthy noisy NYC paying rent when one could buy a house in the suburbs and have the children enjoying gardens and pets? Commuting was hard on the hubbies, but seemed worth it to the wives.

For Reuben, coming from such a poor Jewish ghetto childhood, owning a house in the suburbs was a sign of affluent success. A reasonable and beautiful house we chose to buy for some $100,000 in Spring Valley, N.Y. across the Hudson River. It had a half acre of birch trees and many rooms. The people in the nearby Catholic Church seemed very friendly. Reuben car-pooled with other management level men every morning during the week and didn't seem to mind the commute. Olivia and Juliet loved playing in that garden.

The first few months seemed idyllic with Reuben's classical music records flooding the house with beauty every evening and my more-balanced life working on my thesis each evening after the twins went to sleep.

And then "all hell broke loose" in many ways. It started with Reuben getting attacks of coughing and wheezing in the night. Terrified I watched him trying desperately to breath. Once we had to call the ambulance. Late onset asthma was diagnosed as the cause.

Even though Reuben was very frightened of this chronic disease he decided to go on a long planned sales trip for 2 weeks to Japan. On his return he told us about the wonderful 7 course dinners he was treated to in Tokyo and also about beautiful geisha girls.

In a moment I became absolutely sure that my beloved husband had betrayed me with one of those girls. After praying with the twins in their cribs as I did every night, I confronted him tearfully:

"You slept with one of those girls, didn't you?"

With an angry look on his face, Reuben shrugged, "I won't even answer such a silly question."

But he didn't deny it.

Now, I am actually not the kind of jealous woman who imagines that every woman is after her husband or that he is after every pretty woman. Occasionally I have intuitions, but mostly I like to prove things philosophically.

I walked out of the living room and went to my desk and worked on my thesis.

It would be more than twenty years before the subject ever came up between us.

But I was devastated. Even though I knew that as a Christian I had to forgive him, and I attempted to do that, at least in my head, in my heart our marriage was over. Gone was the illusion that our love was so beautiful that such an act on his part would be inconceivable.

Since, as a Catholic, I didn't believe in divorce, instead I threw myself into the arms of Christ, and he threw his arms around our adorable little princesses.

Long Tangent: How often I have mulled over this incident in my mind, conflicting theories vying to become paramount. For example, ten years later I was chosen to be one of the professors who would judge applications for the same scholarship I got myself to return to graduate studies. We are all at a hotel in a big city interviewing the competing women. At the end of the sessions there turned out to be a free night before we would all be taken to the airport to fly back to our own cities. We went to a movie and I stopped in the diner of the large hotel for a cup of tea. It was crowded. I was ushered to a spot where there was a handsome middle-aged man among the 4 seated at the table. Desultory conversation drifted along about why each of us was "doing business" in that city. The other 2 strangers left to go to their rooms.

"So, Ms. Natalie nee Karamazov, would you like to have a drink on me?"

I looked into his inviting eyes. "No, thank you very much. I am exhausted and we have to get up early. Good night."

I realized at that moment just how easy it would be in a strange city among strangers to fall into temptation. A tiny particle of understanding? Would it have meant that I didn't love my husband if I had fallen that evening? And, if not, why was I so sure that his perhaps only one-time fall meant he didn't love me?

Had I not been a Karamazov drama-queen, on Reuben's return from Japan, might I have just suggested that we needed marriage counseling? And if we had gone for that option might Reuben have admitted his sin and begged for forgiveness?

I will never know. However, twenty years after his death Juliet told me casually,

"Once when I was very unhappy in my marriage I was dallying with the idea of having an affair with someone else. I asked Dad. He said, "Juliet, don't do it. You could hurt the one you love best in the world in a way that you could never make up for."

Another Tangent: I rarely give talks about marriage, but when I hit upon the subject with audiences who are usually full of very, very, spiritual women, I warn against the path I took those many years ago. I describe it this way:

"You could start with your husband being an idol; then go to he is a fallen idol. But couples who forgive each other and are reconciled through Marriage Encounter or counseling or other graces come to see each other as neither idols or fallen idols but funny little creatures! Instead of hating each other's faults, they just laugh at them!"

Church teaching is not to love God most and your spouse with patient agapic love but no delight or good erotic love. As the Von Hildebrand's taught so well (See Dietrich Von Hildebrand's classic *Marriage*), we are to love the spouse in Christ, see their flaws as their own enemies. If we forgive totally, with the grace of God, then we can delight in their virtues and be happy to be one with them in sexual union.

In my marriage, even though I fled to the arms of Christ after feeling so betrayed, we still had much joy in each other and the children. Our sexual life became less and less frequent not because of this crisis so much as that Reuben's asthma attacks made him terrified of such acute physical exertion.

LVI

Enter Charles Rich. Shortly after becoming a Catholic, people started asking me if I met a famous NYC Jewish convert, Charles Rich. This man would play a large role in my first years as a Catholic, a greater role after my crisis with Reuben, and a still greater role when I was in my 40's and 50's.

Born in a village like those in *Fiddler on the Roof* in the mountains of Hungary, then Chaskal Reich, even as a boy evidenced pronounced mystical tendencies. Noticing that he spent hours in the forest praying to God, the rabbis slated him to become a Yeshiva student. But instead the family moved to NYC. Here the young man, now with the Americanized name of Charles Rich, lost his faith, as did so many orthodox Jews in NYC. At age 33 he found Jesus in the Catholic Church and became a lay contemplative, devoting his time to holy Mass, prayer, and the spiritual mentoring of many other passionately religious Catholics. His life story you can find in a biography called *Hungry for Heaven*.

"Natalie Karamazov De Toledo! What an interesting name? You will tell me about it, but we won't become friends unless you want to become a saint, because I don't waste time talking to anyone I won't know for all eternity!" That was the opening salvo of a small man with blazing black eyes, a strong Yiddish accent, then in his sixties who I was introduced to at a conference in downtown Manhattan.

Whereas I mostly read Catholic philosophy books, Charlie Rich interested me in reading the mystical saints. Ten minutes a night, anyhow. But, after becoming disillusioned in marriage, he suggested I should try delving more heavily into the writings of the great mystics such as St. Teresa of Avila and St. John of the Cross. "God alone is enough," is a motto that could appeal to someone who no longer thought marriage would bring the total bliss she expected.

Tangent: It has taken me many decades to sort out the wisdom of this sea-change in my interior life. On the one hand, I did become closer to God because of the prayer-life that comes with the spirituality of the mystics. (Sometimes I jokingly say that I am an uneasy mix of Barbra Streisand of Funny Girl and Teresa of Avila). On the other hand, this change also deflected me from trying to improve my marriage and my motherhood. Not that I didn't try to be a good wife and mother, but not with the energy I might have put into it had I been reading books about Catholic family life instead of treatises by Carmelite celibates!

Looking back, I think of Catholic families I knew where the parents were as devout as I was, but they saw their life with each other and the family as the way to live out love of God.

Another change for the Sisters Karamazov the same year was that Cassandra joined Philip on a walking pilgrimage first on the East Coast and then in Puerto Rico. They danced the Gospels everywhere.

The premise of the partnership was not romance between the two, but love of Jesus and the people they evangelized in their unique manner. Before leaving on the trip Philip insisted that Cassandra needed to bring nothing but a backpack for absolute necessities: absolutely no money. The people they met would put them up and feed them.

Since this was in the 60's, but before wandering young people were called hippies and were rejected as druggies, they actually were housed and fed by amazed family people who thought they might be Jesus and Mary in modern disguise!

The adventure only lasted 8 months. On their return, Philip moved back to the Catholic Worker, and Cassandra to a small cheap apartment. They managed to convince me that the middle-class life-style Reuben and I and our darling kiddies, Juliet and Olivia, were pursuing in the suburbs was not the Christian ideal. Not that they thought we needed to live in total simplicity as they did, but that buying lots of unnecessary luxuries wasn't right either.

Tangent: You will see how this issue will color our whole lives.

Much more significant still, however, is that Reuben's asthma attacks became increasingly alarming. Night after night would see him unable to sleep because of wheezing.

"Mr. Klein, if you want to survive this, I suggest you move out of cold, often wet, New York, to Arizona," the doctor insisted.

Now Reuben was an intensely citified human being. Rome, Paris, Frankfurt, London, fine, but the deserts of Arizona?

"Listen Reuben," his younger brother, Jacob, told him, "Why don't you think about moving to Southern California near our family?"

A quick trip to look into it yielded pessimistic results from Jacob's doctor. "Smog is the worst possible environment for an asthmatic, Mr. Klein."

"Guess, what Natalie, honey?" Reuben called long distance to tell me: "I am setting up a one-man office on the coast further south from Los Angeles in Orange County. From that place I can go off on sales trips for Dell and avoid not only the cold winters in NYC but also all the crap at the NYC office of Dell!"

"Really? So would we live in Laguna Beach near the office?"

"Better, Natalie, you'll love it. I found a beautiful Spanish style cheap condo complex in San Juan Capistrano nearby. It's cheap and within walking distance of this beautiful old Church."

So, 1968 saw the Karamazov/De Toledo Klein family en route to California. And, since I had gotten that Ph.D., I would be looking into teaching a course now and then at some small college.

LVII

The selling of the house in Spring Valley, N.Y, went easily enough by a fluke. The real estate agent was having trouble selling because of the bad condition of our home. Because I came from such a bohemian atmosphere and also loved spontaneity above order in child-raising I was delighted when little Olivia and Juliet decided to use the walls of the family room on which to practice painting! With large brush strokes they "frescoed" their versions of fairy tales with amusing giants and dwarfs. Since we were planning to live there forever, Reuben didn't care. Another feature of our mansion was a bucket in the living was placed under a hole in the ceiling to catch rain water.

But after only a month on the market a couple came by who bought it in spite of these defects. The wife hated the place, but the husband was a radio buff who jumped on it because it was on top of a hill and, therefore, great for antennas.

Because Dell had scheduled Reuben for a trip to Canada just before the move, a week before the new buyers took residence, repainting the family room, of course, I left on a plane with Juliet and Olivia. On his return Reuben would drive with a U-Haul. That gave us a week with a rent-car to acclimatize ourselves to our new life.

The condo was in a charming little village of apartments with balconies and a common swimming pool, all set among the umbrella pine trees and small hills. It was a 15-minute walk to the Old Mission Church with Mass each day still in Latin with Spanish hymns to Mary at the end. "Oh Maria, madre mia, o Consuelo del mortal…" and the congregation in the long narrow Church replete with statues of saints roughly made by Franciscans of the past with strands of straw hair on their heads.

As is the case with all the Missions built in the 18th century, the Mission Church was now a historic tourist attraction surrounded by the hut-like buildings used for farming or storage by the Native American converts.

Tangent: Some descendants of these early evangelized Natives, act as if the missionaries had the same greedy motives as most of the colonialists. I read a book by a Franciscan missionary, Palou, translated from Spanish to English describing in 500 pages the indefatigable work of priests such as St. Junipero Serra, in bringing to these people not only the faith but a simple and beautiful life of farming. Certainly, some exploitative colonialists enslaved the peoples of the countries they came to govern.

The missionaries had motives of love and often castigated the colonialists for their greed and cruelty.

I started off with mixed feelings about Southern California. After all we had spent years in Italy with its thousand year old Churches, and had visited European cities steeped in Catholic culture. By contrast, except for the old Mission Church California seemed ersatz. Where the tops of old cypress trees in Rome waved gently in the wind, in Laguna Beach they were clipped at the tops to fit under the eaves extending toward the streets from the floors of apartment buildings.

Now, the condo we had bought had all the necessary appliances but, as yet, no furniture. What an adventure to live for a week out of sleeping bags and a few pots and pans picked up at local stores! With my simplicity of life leanings taken from the other Sister Karamazov, Cassandra, I exulted in seeing how little we needed to survive. The only luxury was a trip to Disneyland, only a half hour away.

In this case, I thought Disneyland would disgust me. The publicity around it made it sound to me like a contrived idiotic fake place. What a surprise! I found the exhibits not only tasteful but ingenious replicas of past life-styles and wonderful futuristic rides. We especially liked the Pirate ride and the famous "It's A Small World" musical treat. There was a glimpse at the future where you could see an actual live person at the other end of a phone. This invention, of course, pre-figured our Skype by some 45 years!

In general, I find God likes to surprise me. Things I think I will hate I love and sometimes things I think I will love are tiring.

What joy for the twins and myself, hanging off our balcony in expectation, when finally Reuben's car and the U-Haul arrived all the way from NY!

By the fall, Olivia and Juliet, now 5 years old, where enrolled at the Mission kindergarten. Reuben went every day for a few hours to his office up the coast to plan his out-of-country sales trips.

I heard that the El Toro Marine base offered college courses to the military. I was accepted to teach once a week an introduction to philosophy to these men in uniform. A unique feature was that on the long table that served as the professor's desk was a huge machine gun, evidently for demonstrations for quite different purposes than proving logical syllogisms!

I was a little nervous teaching older men for the first time. They behaved themselves with refined propriety. One reason, I eventually learned, was because one of their Majors was also in that classroom.

One of the first requirements imposed upon Reuben by his new California doctor was that he give up smoking.

"Okay, Mr. Klein, you gotta bite the bullet. Either you stop cold-turkey or I won't treat you. Why bother with a guy who will be dead in 6 months?"

Out of loyalty I agreed to also stop. It was damned hard. We would throw out our cigarettes only to sneak butts out of ashtrays at markets. This was before smoking was outlawed in public places.

St. John of the Cross came to my rescue. I was pouring over the Ascent of Mt. Carmel, when I came upon this line:

"If a bird is tied by a chain or by a thread, it still can't fly."

For me, the cigarettes were this thread, and I got the grace to suddenly lose all desire for them. From one moment to the next I went from craving them to looking at them with indifference and I have never smoked a cigarette since.

For Reuben, though, it was torture.

Since he continued to wheeze in the nights, and sometimes had to be taken by me to the emergency room of the Laguna hospital, his doctor suggested a more drastic remedy.

"Ever hear of the Jewish Lung Hospital in Denver, Colorado, Mr. Klein? They bring in severe asthmatics and by doing surgery on their sinuses, the patients get considerable relief and can live many years afterwards. But you have to go for 4 months. It could save your life, think about it hard. "

"I would have to drop my job. I dunno, but I will think about it." Reuben replied.

"If the surgery doesn't succeed I could get you on disability."

LVIII

That first May in California, Reuben was trying to make his big decision about giving up his job, with all the delightful travel to foreign lands, in order to try the Colorado sinus surgery. Just then it was suggested I apply for an opening for a full time Great Books professor at St. Ignatius University in Los Angeles.

"If I succeed in getting the job, Reuben, it would be more than an hour commute each way. And who would take care of the kids after school if you were in Colorado for 4 months?"

"How about your friend, Marie? You could pay her $10 an hour to get them from school and take care of them until you got back from Los Angeles. She needs money, doesn't she?"

The interview at St. Ignatius University seemed providential. On the door of the office of the chairman, Dr. Murphy, was a picture of Edith Stein, the famous Jewish convert phenomenologist who died as a martyr in Auschwitz.

Dr. Murphy flipped through my Curriculum Vitae.

"You studied with Dietrich Von Hildebrand? Like Edith Stein, my favorite woman philosopher, he was also a disciple of the famous founder of phenomenology: Husserl....You could be our Edith Stein!"

Later, I realized that even though what was then called Women's Lib, and later became the feminist movement, was not yet fully blossoming, already men in administration got the idea that it would look good in an all-male Great Books department to have at least one woman professor. In fact, almost all the jobs I got subsequently were based on this need to look as if women professionals were respected.

Tangent: After years of teaching full-time to supplement Reuben's disability payments or lack of any income when Governor Reagan cut down on welfare, I would often wonder about this decision to teach full-time. Sure I was only 29 when I started, with plenty of energy, but working full time and raising children and keeping house is really much too much. Especially it was exhausting because I was often up in the night commiserating with Reuben in his asthma attacks, ever at the ready to take him to emergency.

I would sometimes think about what would have happened if we lived more simply in a welfare apartment house with me working part-time. But in those days no middle-class people thought that if a wife could earn a living when her husband was disabled they should go on welfare instead.

Once I was teaching Great Books full time, I gradually morphed into a Catholic whose passion was teaching. The exhaustion of teaching full time and also caring for the family became a problem. This was true even though I adored the individual personalities of each of my children.

There were many other factors contributing to this problem in the life of Natalie Karamazov De Toledo Klein, as you will see as you read on, but I put this tangent here because I want to warn women like me to be aware of the pitfalls of being a career Mom. Curious? Well, here are a few of these observations. Highly intellectual women and men are often impatient with daily life with children. Probably some upper middle-class women in previous eras who felt this way, hired nannies for the children not just because it was the custom but also because they preferred other activities to child-raising! Even if such a career Mom is scrupulous about spending lots of quality time with her husband and children and taking care of all the necessities of household work, she can easily burn out or … read on to see what else.

The autumn when Reuben went to Colorado and I started commuting to St. Ignatius University began with a totally unexpected change in my spiritual life that came to be called "receiving the charismatic gifts of the Holy Spirit." A little background before I describe this change.

Following in line with the Von Hildebrand circle, I always went to daily Mass and recited what is called the liturgy of the hours for evening prayer and night prayer. I also tried to get in about 10 minutes of quiet heart to heart prayer with Jesus. My new friend, Marie, got me into praying the rosary also.

"You don't pray the rosary, Natalie?"

"No. I was never told it was obligatory."

"Let me tell you why I do," Marie told me enthusiastically. "I wanted my Protestant husband to come into the Catholic Church. So I made a vow that I would pray the rosary every day if he converted. The next day after I started praying the rosary, he said he wanted to be a Catholic!"

"Wow! That's terrific, but….Marie, isn't the rosary kind of long and boring?"

"Oh, no! You can pray it while your husband is filling the car with gas."

This was, of course, before the elaborate Scriptural rosary with passages from the New Testament for every decade became popular.

I decided that since I desperately wanted Reuben to become a Catholic I would try the same vow. He didn't become a Catholic for another 10 years, but I grew to love this traditional prayer. I came to see it as a kind of umbilical cord to my Mother in heaven. If you, the reader, are thinking that Marian prayer is not Scriptural, be sure to google something like Catholic Answers and you will probably change your mind quickly.

However, even though praying a rosary to being Reuben into the Church, didn't work soon, he did get much closer to Jesus in an awful but very moving way. After the sinus surgery at the hospital in Colorado, he had awful pain in his throat. He identified this with the pain of Jesus in the crucifixion. But, when questioned by my many friends who were trying to bring him into the Church as to why he didn't want to make this decision, he would still say, "If there is a God I would be a Catholic. But since I am at best an agnostic, I can't be in any religion."

Back to the big change in my spiritual life, Cassandra came for a visit to California to see us in our new place. Reuben had just left for Colorado. So, one evening, just after Olivia and Juliet were in their beds, Cassandra started telling me about this new Pentecostal movement in the Church.

"People in New York are praying in tongues and healings are happening."

Since she couldn't explain this in philosophical terms, I didn't believe her.

"So, what is your relationship to the Holy Spirit, Natalie?" my twin asked in her peaceful, non-confrontational way.

That was the first time in our entire relationship where I didn't have an answer to any questions she asked about something religious. I changed the subject as soon as possible.

"Cassandra, let's listen to music instead of talking about this crazy topic."

I happened to play a recording of Bach's B-Minor Mass. This is a long choral work. In the middle of the Gloria, there is a trumpet blast that comes with the words about the Holy Spirit (cum Sancto Spiritu).

Suddenly Cassandra's face turned into the face of Jesus.

"Do with me what you want, Cassandra," I shocked her by insisting right in the middle of the rest of the music.

Cassandra laid hands on my head and prayed in tongues, which I had never heard before.

Immediately I started praying in strange words.

Shortly after we went to bed. I woke the next morning not only with the strange words but with a soul on fire.

Whereas previously I could have characterized my prayer life as being, as it were, on tippy-toes, trying to reach the transcendent God, after this experience I always found God right in my own heart waiting for me!

Cassandra sent me a book about Catholic Pentecostals. I read it without much understanding. What really got me involved in this dynamic prayer style which was sweeping not only the Catholic Church but also many main-line Protestant Churches, was that when I started teaching at St. Ignatius University, one of my students approached me:

"Dr. Klein, we have a little prayer group where we develop the gifts of the Holy Spirit. Would you like to come one evening?"

I begged my friend Marie to take the twins longer one night so that I could see what this group was doing.

LIX

Let me tell you about my first day as a full-time Great Books professor at St. Ignatius University.

First Juliet and Olivia and I went to Holy Mass at the Old Mission Church. Then I walked them to their classroom.

"Now little squiggles, remember Marie will be picking you up at 3 o'clock and bringing you to her house until I get you before dinner."

"Will Buster be there?" Juliet asked.

"Of course. Buster is always there." Buster was Marie's cocker spaniel.

"And, will she give us cupcakes?" Olivia asked.

"Of course, she always gives you cupcakes."

Next came the 1 hour and a little more drive from Capistrano to Los Angeles. On the way I prayed my rosary, then tuned into the classical music station and heard all of Tchaikovsky's Swan Lake. 10 minutes before leaving the freeway I prayed in tongues. By now I had received what is called the gift of interpretation so that I had a pretty good idea what the strange words meant, allegedly from the Holy Spirit: "My daughter, do not fear. I am with you. My truth will flow through your words. Be at peace."

My first class was at 11 AM teaching Plato's Republic and Aristotle's

Ethics. I picked up the roster in my mail slot. There at the desk in my tiny office I saw the names of 40 students.

Refreshed by coffee and donuts at the café in the building where we professors had our quarters, I was off to my first class.

What a contrast to classes at Fordham in NYC. Instead of suits and ties and dresses the young men were in shorts and T-shirts. The young women were also in shorts and T-shirts! Casual to the nth degree. I felt a bit awkward in the tailored suit and white blouse, with small heeled black shoes I had selected for my entre into the new world of California college students.

Will you guess that a year into this life I would be wearing Mexican Moo-Moos, cherise, bright green, or yellow, and Berkenstocks? Often with classes held on the lawn!

After starting with an Our Father, Hail Mary, and Glory Be, and introducing myself, I handed out the elaborate syllabus including books I had read in graduate school. Then I proceeded to read aloud from my lecture notes.

"Dr. Klein, do you mind if I talk to you?" a handsome young Philippino ancestry student asked.

"Of course not. Come along to the cafeteria. We can have lunch together."

Once at a table in this large room seating 200 students at a time, he smiled and confronted me. "You're not going to read us lecture notes you prepared long before you even got to know us are you?"

"Of course! Philosophy is universal. Everything true applies to all human beings…your name was what?"

"Alfredo….yeah, sure, but, I mean don't you want to know what we think about life?"

After 15 minutes of telling me his favorite ideas such as how the search for truth is more important than finding truth, he took off.

I cried all the way home to Capistrano thinking "I am finished already. I can't just ask them questions. All I have prepared is my lecture notes. Suppose they won't listen?"

As you can surely guess, this was not the end of my teaching career. That young student's question forced me to gradually revise my entire trajectory away from conveying to them only what Von Hildebrand and others had taught me. Instead I developed a method in all my classes of going back and forth between the absolute truths in the Great Books and the application of these truths to the daily life of the students.

By next semester's registration Alfredo was walking up and down the line and urging the students in a loud voice to "Take Dr. Klein's classes. They're terrific."

When Reuben came back from Colorado he had stopped smoking and was on heavy cortisone treatments. This did not stop the asthma attacks but would give him another 20 years of life.

"Natalie, sweetie, sit down and listen to me," Reuben announced portentously one evening after his return from the hospital.

"If I'm too sick to work at sales any more, the last place I want to live is this little Spanish town."

"But I need my job at St. Ignatius U to support us, Reuben. I can't suddenly move some place else."

"Let's move near your work in Los Angeles."

"What about the smog? Remember your brother Jacob's doc said it would kill you?"

"Well, it will kill me worse to be bored to death here. Los Angeles is an exciting city… You wouldn't have that long drive back and forth to teach." He turned out to be right. In spite of the bad air, he was much happier and not better but not worse either health-wise for the move.

It was sad to leave the charming old Mission Church to go to Los Angeles. The house near the university we found to buy was walking distance to St. Ignatius U. It was white stucco and much larger. Our house was across the street from a public elementary school. The parish church,

St. Michael's, was packed with families some of them of the professors I knew from the university.

And joy of joys I became pregnant once more.

I had hardly figured out how to get a substitute for the due date of the baby or babies (twins?), when another early miscarriage put an end to that dream.

I was too busy with my hectic life-style to pine over another baby I wouldn't see on this earth, but Reuben was deeply grieved. If his wife's womb was going to be a tomb why even enter it, he seemed to decide. Years later when Olivia and Juliet were mothers, they told me that they were grieved also but didn't have words to speak of their feelings.

LX

Enter: John Finney.

The second semester of teaching at St. Ignatius U, I was teaching Tolstoy's War and Peace and Dostoevsky's Brothers Karamazov. My goal was to introduce some of these not very literary surfer-type students to the great masterpieces and also to themes such as types of love, positive and negative masculine and feminine traits, trust in God in the midst of tragic sufferings, etc. I was given a seminar room, not unlike the one where I was an honor's student at University of Syracuse so many years ago.

On the first day of class in walked a slightly older male student, John Finney. He was about 6' 2 inches tall, with long dark brown hair, a long unkempt beard, and large brown eyes intensely focused and luminous.

John Finney sprawled down in a chair next to a lovely young woman with straight blond hair all the way down past her waist, who I knew from my Plato and Aristotle class. Their smiles and interlocking glances betokened familiarity at the least.

As I had the 14 students take turns introducing themselves not just by name but by answers to such directives as:

"Each one tell the class about the most dramatic incident of your life."

Victoria, my former student, the blond beauty, told about her joy in watching the birth of her baby sister. John Finney spoke slowly with eyes focusing alternately on each of the students around the table, ending with me:

"I was in the battle field in Viet Nam. We Marines were trying to charge a hill... I was the last to climb it...On the top I found all of my buddies splayed out dead... After that I stopped believing in God."

"Oh, John, how horrible," I blurted out. "But, listen, this is exactly the kind of experience you will find in some of these readings, especially the Brothers Karamazov."

For my most dramatic experience I told them about my conversion from atheism to the Catholic Church.

Each Tuesday afternoon the students brought to the 3-hour seminar on philosophy in literature their responses to the questions I devised about how themes in the Russian novels fit in with contemporary relationships to other humans and to their feelings about God.

Soon Victoria and John started coming to our house to listen to Reuben's record collection and rap about whatever was on their minds. Like most of the St. Ignatius U students they had no knowledge of classical music being, instead, enamored of the Beatles and other songsters Reuben detested.

Reuben enjoyed being an informal mentor to this couple and the others who began to flock to this professor's house where they could deepen their knowledge of the great masterpieces of music and art.

Juliet and Olivia, now almost 7 years old, fell in love with my students. As soon as any of them came in the door they would be forced to admire the frescoes and writings of my twins. During the music-listening times each girl would take over the lap of one or another of the male students and stare into their eyes with fascination.

Tangent: 12 years later each of those daughters managed to find one of these favorites and date them for a few months before the magic wore off on both sides.

In spite of the evident affinity between Victoria and John, they never became either lovers or fiances. Each drifted off to other partners. It was at this point that my relationship to John became closer and more problematic.

John would be the first of a long line of what later I would see as fitting in with what has been labeled as co-dependence. This syndrome, now in the 21st century called an addiction, consists in any relationship where the need for the other becomes extreme. Mild symptoms would be wanting to spend lots of daily time with another person even to the neglect of family, work, or other friends. More extreme would be feeling insanely jealous of any other friends of one's idol.

As a teacher, nowadays, I sometimes warn those I think are becoming too co-dependent, with this question: "How will you feel when this person you think of as just a nice friend tells you that unless you leave your wife and marry her she's going to commit suicide?"

The reason for the "co" at the beginning of the word "co-dependency" signifies that it takes both people to keep such a relationship going. One may seem the needier of the two, but the other one gets much pleasure or satisfaction about being admired and idolized by the weaker one. So such reasons keeps the stronger- seeming one allowing an unhealthy attachment to keep growing.

It began with John Finney approaching me one day on the campus this way:

"Dr. Klein…or can I call you Natalie, I know you are very busy, but I would appreciate it very much if you had time to advise me about my future."

"Oh, of course, John."

"How about now at the student coffee shop?"

That conversation lasted 2 hours and ranged all the way from John's concerns about future graduate study to his deep philosophical questions.

Because John was such a deep and intelligent student, I found that meeting and the others to come moving and stimulating. To my surprise, I began to have fantasies about this man who was then 25 years old to my 30 years and Reuben's 50 years.

At first I was sure that these dreams about how it might be if Reuben died of an asthma attack and I was free to re-marry, and how John would be such a wonderful second husband, were just harmless reveries, anyone might be tempted with.

When I brought this problem to confession the priest didn't seem concerned. He suggested just that I avoid any near occasions of sin and never talk about my feelings for the man.

A different take on the situation arose when one of the other young women in our Great Books class confided in me that she was very attracted to John and that they were going to a party that weekend. Immediately I felt jealous.

LXI

The next class after the weekend, I noticed that John and this other female student had changed seats to be closer to each other.

Happily it was the night of the charismatic prayer group. This had grown from 7 students to hundreds of Catholics from the neighborhood. The format was to have praise and worship music, then praying in tongues, then interpretation of those tongues, then prophecies, and then individuals being prayed over for healing, physical and emotional, by the leaders.

Tangent: There is a difference between people praying and singing in tongues alone or in a group, and a proclamation for the whole group in a tongue. The later is what has to be followed by an interpretation.

One of the things I loved about charismatic meetings was that at the parish we would all try to look our best and seem peaceful, here it was taken for granted that we all had problems and needed help.

So, at the time of individual prayer I got my favorite leaders to stand over me with their hands on my head and shoulders:

"What do you want prayer for, Natalie?"

"I think I am over-attached to one of my students. Please pray that Jesus will take away obsessive longings."

At the next coffee conversation with John, he led me to a remote table and handed me a letter he had written with no names on it, not his or mine. After he walked out I read the letter:

"I will never forget all the caring love you have shown me. When I first met you I was still broken from my war-time experiences. Your classes gave me hope. I came to identify not with Dmitri the soldier brother, or with Ivan the despairing atheist, but more with Alyosha, the saintly monk. I am not sure about going to Church yet, but I feel God's love when I walk alone on the beach. But you need to know that I have a strong sense of how important marriage is and I would never want to be part of breaking one up, so I am going to distance myself from you. Please don't feel hurt."

"Hurt" would be a mild word for the feelings that tore me to pieces. I was forced to realize that I had truly invested in the fantasies of something working out between myself and this younger male student. The Russian novel that came to mind for me was not so much *War and Peace* as Tolstoy's *Anna Karenina*, depicting a woman unhappily married to an older man who falls in love with a dashing handsome young soldier and eventually throws herself under the wheels of a train because she is afraid to lose him.

I rushed from the coffee shop to a small student chapel. It happened that some students were rehearsing songs for the evening Mass. "Day by day, day by day, O dear Lord, 3 things I pray. To love you more dearly, follow you more nearly…" Suddenly I seemed to see in my imagination the stricken face of Jesus with the crown of thorns on His head. And the words He spoke in my heart were these:

"The way you feel rejected by John, dear Natalie, is the way I feel rejected by you when instead of bringing your lonely heart to Me, you chase after other loves, in this case a love I have not willed for you."

Happily the semester was almost over and John was graduating so I would not have to see him much after this dramatic end to our friendship.

You may be wondering, what was happening during this time between Reuben and me? Earlier in this book, *The Sisters Karamazov*, I told you how I doubted Reuben's fidelity because of the incident on his sales trip with the Japanese geisha woman, which he never denied or asked forgiveness for. And then, as I told you, I turned to Jesus, and he turned to Juliet and Olivia for the love we withheld from each other out of my non-forgiveness and his denial.

By 3 years later, now in our new circumstances, here is how I felt. Reuben's sufferings with his asthma attacks moved me to compassionate love, for sure. It seemed to me that he was too anxious and exhausted to expend any energy on improving our marriage. We never talked about how infrequently we made love. I attributed this always to his fear of over-exertion that could impede his breathing. Just the same, I felt unattractive and rejected.

As well, I came to see as hard to overcome a tension within Reuben of two opposite values concerning women. On the one hand, he loved creative intellectual women such as his first wife, my mother, and myself. On the other he craved the warmth that a woman could give who was a wife and mother of children with no other interests. It seemed as if even though I was working full-time to support him and the family, he took my interest in this work to be a fault. For example, he wanted me to put lots of time into cooking delicious meals, whereas I, tired after a day of teaching, was eager to cook tasty but minimally exciting dinners. He chided me for not being good at child-raising.

I brought these feelings about the relationship with John, and my feelings of rejection from Reuben to my godfather, Friedrich Adenauer, when he and my godmother, Lise, came for a visit that summer after the experience of John.

"I am terribly sorry about this, dear Natalie. You are in a precarious position now, after this ambiguous friendship. You must be very careful to avoid anything like this. I will try to talk to Reuben about the faith. If he became a Catholic he might be healed not only physically but also have the sins of his past removed so that he could approach all of life and you, as well, differently."

Whatever took place between Friedrich and Reuben, I saw no sign of change. In the meantime quite a different crisis emerged at St. Ignatius University.

In connection with my first miscarriage and the ob/gyn suggesting I use contraceptives for a year afterwards, I briefly mentioned the conflict that arose later in the Church over Pope Paul VI's encyclical Humanae Vitae forbidding contraception. Largely because of the influence of Von Hildebrand, I was convinced that the Pope was right and that those who dissented from that teaching were in error. The philosophy and theology faculty at St. Ignatius U were sharply divided about this issue.

Even though I was teaching Great Books, I would put in lots about ethics and conscience into my lectures wherever I could. Soon I became ipso facto the enemy not only of dissenting faculty but also of the Jesuit priests who were teaching that contraceptives were okay in many circumstances.

Some of the faculty members who most disputed the teaching of the Pope on this subject were among my closest friends. And some of these close friends were also the close friends of my mother, Elena, who had moved to Los Angeles in her retirement to be close to our family. She lived in an apartment near us and the University.

Earlier, in a tangent, I told you about Elena Karamozov's baptism into the Catholic Church. This took place when she was already in her sixties and, according to her, could only have taken place because she could identify with the dissenting lay people and priests in the Church, not only on contraception but also on abortion and pre-marital sex.

So you can imagine the arguments that took place when I found that my mother liked to spend time in the cafeteria and coffee shop backing up the views of students who refused to accept the truths I was teaching them in my classes.

More about this in the next little chapter!

LXII

Something very wonderful that changes the grim picture I painted of the life of the Karamazov/De Toledo/Klein clan in the last few chapters concerned Reuben's 3rd vocation. If you recall he was first a seaman, then a book salesman, but now, disabled, he became what he always wanted to be most, a writer!

Every evening after the table was cleared we sat in the living room and listened to whatever Reuben wrote of his latest masterpiece. This was always a combination from me of oh's and ah's of delight at his great narrative skills, but impatience with a need he had to write sentences no one could understand. Well, not no one! By the time Olivia and Juliet became teens they understood every word he wrote. But, then, they understood Shakespeare when they were 10 years old, and I still, at 78-years old, only understand the plots and the soliloquies of those famous plays! But that's not because I am stupid. I understand every word, after all, of *The Brothers Karamazov*. It's just that I don't get poetic language.

The first book Rebuen wrote was a novel about Judas Iscariot. The theme was that Judas couldn't possibly have been so close to Jesus and then betrayed him just for the money. What Reuben tried to show, instead, was that Judas couldn't bear the suspense of waiting for the great triumphal scene where Jesus would defeat the leaders who opposed him and the Romans next. Therefore he organized the showdown. When he saw Jesus trapped by his enemies he realized he was wrong and then committed suicide out of shame.

More about the other books Reuben wrote as we go along with the adventures of the Sisters Karamazov.

What was a typical day in the life of our family in Los Angeles:

7 AM The alarms go off. I rush downstairs to make breakfast.

7:30 AM Reuben strolls in to the dining room for breakfast with the daily newspaper. He is always grumpy. I have, by now, become a thoroughly morning person and am full of chat which he ignores as much as possible.

8:00 AM Juliet and Olivia eat breakfast, pack their lunches and leave for school which is right across the street.

8:30 AM I leave for St. Ignatius U which is an 8-block walk in the usual sunny clime of Los Angeles.

9:00 AM Reuben starts writing his book.

10 AM I teach my first philosophy class.

12 noon I go to the University Mass and then eat lunch. Reuben, at home, makes his own lunch of Top Ramen soup.

1 PM I teach another class. Reuben takes off in his car to wander about downtown Los Angeles, checking out bargains and buying stuff. Sometimes he drops in on his brother Jacob's used bookstore.

2:30 PM I come home and take a short nap.

3 PM Olivia and Juliet come home and play.

4:30 PM I make dinner. The girls watch TV.

5:30 PM Reuben comes home and we all have dinner together.

6:30 PM Reuben reads his manuscripts to us.

7:30 PM Reuben selects recordings to play from his huge collection. The music booms through the house on his stack speakers. I sit next to him marking student papers or preparing classes. Juliet and Olivia do their homework and play games when they finish.

8:30 PM – 10 Reuben watches TV. He wants me to sit next to him even though he often dozes off. I continue my work unless I love the show. The best is Masterpiece Theatre, but another favorite is All in the Family. Olivia and Juliet also always watch All in the Family because the 3 of us females think that lots of the awful and funny traits of Archie Bunker are shared by our Reuben Klein. He doesn't see any resemblance at all.

9:30 The girls go to bed and I pray with them free style from the heart ending with the old Latin Marian hymn, the Salve Regina.

10 PM Reuben and I read in bed. I like to joke that the dual control electric blanket saved our marriage because warm-blooded Reuben would set it at 1 and I would set it at 10. Reuben takes his last cortisone pills, and blows on his inhaler and hopes to sleep through the night. This rarely happens. He awakens at least once and I sit by him as he tries to overcome the wheezing in his lungs.

Friday evenings this routine changes because I go to the big charismatic prayer-meeting. I love the loud praise music and come home brimming over with joy.

Saturdays sometimes we have guests for dinner. Reuben likes to check out yard-sales. The girls and I clean house Saturday morning. Sundays after the 10 AM Mass at the University, Elena Karamazov, my mother, comes home from the service with Juliet, Oliva, and myself for a large lunch.

The Mass at the University is celebrated in the new fashion that became popular after Vatican II. No more Latin. No more organ music. No more silent times. The kids of the professors and other children from the neighborhood, process in to the Church with banners. Music ministry people stand in front near the altar singing songs to guitar such as "It's a Brand New Day, everything is fine…."

Here is a typical conversation at lunch Sunday:

Reuben: So, how was the sermon, Elena?

Elena: Very good. My favorite Jesuit gave it. He emphasized how we need to get over harsh judgements of people of other religions and emphasize what we have in common.

Myself, Natalie: Oh, sure. Other Christian Churches where they refer their people for abortions!

Tangent: 1973 saw the famous Roe vs. Wade decision legalizing abortions. Even those professors at St. Ignatius U who thought contraception was okay, were anti-abortion. I soon joined a group of us who stood in front of abortion clinics Saturday mornings, trying to counsel women about alternatives to abortion and praying the rosary. Elena, with her long history of abortions knew I was doing this but never talked to me about it. When I brought up abortion, she would change the subject, with a look of tight toleration of my fanatical splutterings.

LXIII

1969: First Moon Landing and Visit to David and Thelma De Toledo in San Diego!

Most Americans of my generation will never forget what it felt like watching that moment!

It happened that, when we were kids, our Dad had always said he hoped he would be on the first trip to the moon. I decided to 'take my life into my hands' and give him a call to remind him of this.

Now, if you recall, our relationship had been completely cut off 12 years ago because of that painful incident about the letter I had written to Cassandra describing Dad's wife that was found by Thelma.

I found David De Toledo from 911 from the phone directory.

"This is your long-lost daughter, Natalie, Dad," I began.

My father's voice sounded distant and strained as he responded with a wary "Yes?"

"I'm calling you because we are watching the moon landing and I remembered that you always wished you would be on that flight."

"It's a tremendous event."

"But also…um…I thought in spite of that awful incident in the past which I have always been so sorry about, maybe you might want to meet your grandchildren?"

In a choked up voice, he replied, "Every day since Cassandra told me about your twins I've wanted to see them but could never figure out how to overcome the breach."

The next weekend found the Karamazov/Klein family on Pacific Coast Highway on our way to San Diego. At that time, Olivia and Juliet were 7 years old. Dressed in casual but pretty flowered sun dresses with hair combed at every rest-stop on the way, we arrived at the main entrance to the famous Zoo at exactly 2 PM as arranged.

There was my father still tall but heavier in his usual casual shirt and corduroy's but with greying hair. After all, he was now in his late 60's. As he walked slowly toward us, we could see Thelma sitting on a bench in the distance.

Quick introduction of the granddaughters, big hug for me, warm handshake for Reuben who he had never met before. Then he led us toward Thelma, still looking beautiful and youngish in her late 40's with long black curly hair and dressed in a long colorful Mexican skirt and white blouse open in an oval shape.

When her eyes met mine she just winked.

What a relief! Evidently she had decided that it was the right thing to do to help her husband through this awkward reunion.

That first meeting at the Zoo was so successful that it led to weekend visits to the De Toledo house every few months.

"What a house!" I exclaimed on first viewing.

The De Toledo's lived in the old Spanish quarter of San Diego called Old Town. Their house was made of old stucco with red tiles on the roof. Inside the 2-story home were all the usual De Toledo style furnishings, huge maps on the wall, many shelves of musical records, with pride of place for the large stereo area for playing them. There was a small office where my father, now retired from his job as technical writing teacher at the big aerospace lab, spends his time compiling encyclopedia like volumes.

From Cassandra they knew how Catholic I was. With a sardonic smile he took out of the shelf his most well-known book.

"Famous Atheists of American History" is the title you see. You can look at it later, after lunch.

My Dad, always extremely organized, had our visits follow a schedule:

12 noon arrival after our 2 ½ hour drive from Los Angeles.

12: 15 PM dining together at an outdoor restaurant near the boardwalk of the San Diego beach.

1:30 PM Visit to some tourist attraction that girls would like such as the amusement park.

4 PM Reuben, Dad, and I listening to music in the living room while Thelma either took Olivia and Juliet downstairs to a family room to play games or let them enjoy baking cookies with her in the kitchen.

6 PM light evening snacks and goodies. The girls were brought downstairs again to watch some comedy TV show with Thelma, while we had long discussions about ideas.

David: Natalie, you know that all the US Presidents were atheists, don't you?

Natalie: Actually, Dad, they were Deists most of them. That is men who believed there was a God but didn't like Church.

Reuben: Even though I can't bring myself to believe in God, I have a great yearning for something higher than us, David.

David: Let's look at these old photo albums of you and Cassandra...

The next morning Reuben drove me to the nearest Church for Mass. He left me there while he perused the swap meet tables of Old Town's Plazas.

By 11 AM Sunday we would be off on our return trip.

Even though I couldn't find a way to talk about my own interests in philosophy and religion, I always felt warmly healed by these visits.

Five years later, David and Thelma took a train up to Los Angeles to visit us. When we met them at the station, Thelma looked at me and laughed.

"There's the little bastard!"

I was too shocked to realize that this was the new uninhibited Thelma at the very beginning of the Alzheimer's disease which took ten more years to kill her!

LXIV

Enter Dmitri Klein!

After a year of living in Los Angeles, when Juliet and Olivia were 8 years old, I got pregnant.

"Some more spotting," I told Reuben after 6 weeks.

Sorrow filled his eyes. "Should you check with the doctor about another miscarriage?"

I prayed a lot. I hopefully thought of names for a girl, a boy, twin girls, twin boys. I didn't lift heavy things.

This time, in spite of some spotting the baby didn't miscarry.

"Mommy, why don't you iron your stomach, it is so lumpy looking?" Juliet asked.

A month earlier than the due date, the water broke. Elena rushed over to take care of the girls while Reuben drove me to the hospital.

The labor and delivery went very quickly. The pain escalated from bearable to excruciating within 2 hours.

"It's a boy," I heard Reuben call out.

A few hours after the birth the doctor came into my room with Reuben.

"Where's my little baby?" I asked.

"Don't be alarmed, Mrs. Klein. The baby will be okay, but he is so small, only 4 lbs.8 ounces, that he needs to be in an incubator for a while. You might have to leave him here for a week.

"But I want to breast-feed him. Can't I stay and do that?"

"We can try, but when they are so small they often can't suckle enough. The bottle is easier."

For a few days I stayed in the maternity ward. Every few hours the nurses led me into the room where the newborns lay in their little cribs. They put my beautiful little baby into my arms and tried to coach him to suckle but he couldn't do it.

So, they sent me home.

Next day by 9 AM I insisted:

"I'm going to the hospital to try to feed my little Dmitri."

"Why not wait until maternity calls us?"

"No, I'm taking the car and going right now."

After a week little Dmitri figured out how to suckle and we were told we could bring him home.

"Now, Natalie, it is only natural that Olivia and Juliet will be a little jealous. Just be sure to spend a lot of time with them," my mother Elena had warned.

Easier said than done. Breast feeding takes more of the Mommy's time than bottle feeding. Since Reuben was home so much, he would certainly have been able to take turns with Dmitri. But I had been introduced to the blessings of breast-feeding by the then just becoming popular La Leche league.

Happily this was just the era when it was considered "cool" for women professors to bring little newborn babies to school. The plan was that after my 2 week maternity leave from the University where the students did readings on their own, I would return to classes.

I fed little Dmitri just before my first class in my office. Reuben came during my 10 o'clock class and wheeled the baby in a carriage around the campus. I would go to Mass at noon and then feed him in the cafeteria during my lunch. Then Reuben took little Dmitri home, and I would feed him again on returning home. If Dmitri got hungry when I was teaching, Reuben would give him enough of a bottle of my pumped out breast milk to quiet him.

"Olivia and Juliet stop playing that game and change the baby." I could hear these demands as I tried to get in a nap.

It soon became too complicated. I was exhausted from night feedings. Reuben missed his afternoon walks. Between breast-feeding and teaching, I had little time for other tasks. Very soon Reuben convinced Olivia that she should cook dinner and Juliet should wash dishes.

"I guess we're Cinderella now and little Dmitri is the prince," I once heard Juliet complain to Olivia.

"There's a very sweet, competent, woman, just down the block from where you live who takes into her home babies of working mothers," the wife of a philosophy professor told me. "Why don't you visit with Dmitri and see if you like her?"

So, by the time Dmitri was 2 months old he was adjusting himself to one-half Mommy's breast and ½ bottle milk from the hands of Mrs. Bartolli down the street.

It happened that Juliet and Olivia had just been reading the famous story of Tolkien, The Hobbit. One Sunday morning they came into our bedroom with Dmitri dragged between them.

"Dmitri isn't a horrible little brother. Dmitri is a hobbit."

From that time on they did seem to like him better.

Tangent: From a psychological point of view I could see, hindsight, that the coming of Le Petit Prince, Dmitri, was the beginning of those little princesses feeling displaced. Reuben loved having a son onto whom he could project all his dreams. Dmitri would be slowly formed into another Gustav Mahler, Reuben's favorite composer. And I, Natalie Karamazov, felt very differently about a son than about rival princess daughters. I would try to bring him up to be another St. Francis of Assisi. In ten-year's time, Sisters Karamazov style, Juliet would come to resemble the charming, seductive Grushenka and Olivia the proud beauty, Katerina.

LXV

Meanwhile, how was teaching at Ignatius U. developing? Besides the wonderful themes of the Great Books, I found that the Holy Spirit was inspiring me to reach out to the students in their doubts about the Catholic faith. Most of these young people were Catholics by birth and training but on the cusp of dropping out now that they were living away from parental supervision.

Since my class technique was informal with lots of time for free discussion, there was room for lots of tangents. A student might ask,

"Why go to Church every Sunday? You can pray to God anywhere. The beach is a much nicer place to pray than the parish."

"Hmmm!" I might respond, "What would you think if your boyfriend never wanted to see you Saturday night? You might think he had another girlfriend for big date night...after all, Saturday night is the traditional time for dating...Now, consider that we have Sunday off from work or household chores because it is the Lord's day."

"But I don't get anything out of the Mass!"

"What would you think of a man who liked to talk to his wife but never come into her body? If Jesus wants to leap down from heaven to be inside you, shouldn't you be there to receive Him?"

Of course, the missing element is faith. Sometimes just seeing my joy in the faith would help them to go deeper into asking Jesus to show them personally how His love was coming through the centuries-old rites of the Church.

With big ethical issues such as why not pre-marital sex, after the usual points about how bodily union with the souls and hearts not united is sinful, they would always come up with but "if we really love each other."

"So breaking off with a girlfriend or boyfriend or even breaking an engagement to be married is a sin?" If not, then such closeness isn't really a full commitment, is it?

Concerning the raging debate about contraception, the Holy Spirit gave me provocative analogies about why postponing a baby using natural family planning is different from using contraceptives.

"The Mass is the peak experience of the priest, as conception as the highest metaphysical fulfillment of the married couple. Now, imagine a priest incarcerated in a Communist prison, subjected to unbelievable physical and psychological torture. On Christmas Day he begs to be allowed to say Mass. Permission is given. With awe and bliss he intones the words of the liturgy—but, horror of horrors, at the moment of the Consecration when he is about to say the holy words, the torturers gag him and shout, "This is not my body; this is not my blood!" What a diabolic desecration!"

This got the attention of the students, but where is this leading, they would wonder. And I would proceed:

"Now, here is the comparison: It is the fertile time. There is the couple joined in sexual union: a new life can enter the world! But no! Instead, the life-giving sperm is contained in a little rubber bag, later to be discarded. Or, perhaps even more grotesque, the woman has taken a pill which prevents conception by causing a simulated pregnant state—mocking, betraying the natural state and making real conception and child-bearing impossible. What a desecration!"

Or, still more far-out, if you will, but equally memorable, was this analogy:

"I was delighted when black Americans stopped trying to look like white people by flattening out their hair and sometimes wearing lightening make-up to look more like 'whitey.' I thought it grand when black people started wearing African hair-dos and beautiful African clothing, with the slogan: Black is Beautiful."

"Yeah, so?" a student would grumble.

"Here's the comparison. Instead of a woman thinking of her fertile time as the "bad time," and wishing that, like a man, she could have sex without conceiving a baby in her own body, wouldn't it be wonderful if she boasted of her "miracle, glow, fertile time"?

I guess some students were paying attention, because one time a young man who was not one of my students came to my office with this complaint:

"I want to meet you, Dr. Klein, because in the clinch, when I was about to make the big move, my girlfriend said "I can't do that because I am a disciple of Natalie Klein!"

You may be wondering whether my problem with getting too close to men other than my husband disappeared. No, it didn't. A faculty member in a different department of studies became more and more friendly, liking to spend his spare time in my office chatting. He was a married man of 60 at the time and I was 37, so it just seemed like a wonderful fun friendship.

Since charismatics used to hug each other at prayer-meetings, this man giving me an occasional hug as he left the office didn't seem like anything problematic. But, then, slowly I began to think that I loved this warm, humorous, brilliant man much more than I loved my so sick and, by now, depressed, husband.

The male professor came down with a deadly cancer. We all prayed for him. I found that I felt terrible grief at the idea of losing him. One day he came into my office and shut the door.

"Natalie, which priest do you think is the best for confession?"

"Oh, Father "X" for sure. Why do you ask?"

"I haven't gone to confession for 30 years, so I want a priest who will have time for me."

I was stunned. This man was a daily Mass Catholic. Only then did I notice that since he always served the Masses at the university, I never noticed if he went to Holy Communion or not. It turned out that he didn't.

After his long delayed confession there was a change. Besides going to Holy Communion, he started looking at people directly, eye to eye!

After he died I realized that this relationship with me could have developed into a sinful bond and that, possibly, other such "friendships" of his in the past could have been the reason he didn't receive Communion.

Tangent: For any readers who are not Catholics, it is the teaching of the Church, based on passages from the Old Testament and the New, that we cannot approach God intimately if we are committed to unrepented serious sins.

Another Tangent: Looking back I realize that there was a reason many husbands didn't want their wives to work outside the home. I think most of us females have a certain weakness. We want to lean on strong men. This is good if he is our father, brother, or husband, but not so good in other situations. I have had women admit to me that they felt more secure at their jobs if they knew the boss was attracted to them and was having fantasies about sex with them. Some even fulfilled those fantasies, partly for the romantic intrique, but partly just to keep their jobs.

LXVI

Much worse was the next co-dependent friendship with a man. It began with working together on a university committee. We disagreed about a portentous decision. I got others in the prayer group to join me in storming heaven. I won the battle, but in the course of arguing with him, we became real friends.

Hindsight I would realize how dangerous can be close friendships between a man and a woman both of whom are having difficulties in their marriages.

"Fr. 'X,' I am getting scared," I told my priest spiritual director. I have such a strong attachment to this professor. Even though we only talk about philosophy and theology, when we meet I get a feeling of great anxiety. I have fantasies of running away with him."

"Don't worry about it, Natalie," the priest advised. Just stay away from near occasions of sin. Never go anywhere with him except your offices."

"But what about those fantasies?"

"Everyone has fantasies, Natalie. When they come just pray for him and take care of the family and do your work."

Things got more frightening when my man friend told me one day,

"You, know, Natalie. I think we should avoid seeing each other so much. I am going to start going to counseling with my wife to see what we can do to improve our marriage."

In a way, I was relieved. I missed the frequent office conversations, but my anxiety level decreased. I certainly was "in love," but how deep was this love, I wondered.

Then, one evening, we were both at a large gathering where everyone was drinking. When it broke up, walking together to the faculty parking lot, we both at once felt a tremendous urge to consummate this attraction. A deserted beach was not so far away…

On the way back home I was horrified. This was mortal sin. In the morning I called up a different priest from off campus and begged him to hear my confession. I thought he would look at me with disgust, but instead with eyes full of compassion, he told me about an Egyptian woman prostitute who repented of her sins and afterwards became a saint.

When I called up my consort in sin, he immediately said,

"I went to a priest for confession and he told me I must never talk to you again or see you except in passing on university business. I am sorry. I know this will hurt you."

What I felt was not just hurt but total despair.

"Jesus, help me," I prayed. "I feel as if I can't bear to live without him. I am sure you don't want me to commit suicide. What should I do?"

God's answer surprised me, but it didn't surprise Reuben.

This is what happened. The next day after that desperate prayer, a woman professor passed me in the corridor of the classroom building.

"Natalie, I have this great friend, Dr. Anna Dvorak. She's a counselor. Some student of yours told her about you and your ideas and she wants to meet you."

"How about right away?" I blurted out.

"Oh, sure. I happen to be meeting her for lunch tomorrow. Why don't you come along?"

Dr. Anna turned out to be originally from Czechoslovakia. When she was in her thirties, her husband took a job in California. Here she studied Jungian psychology. She was presently working at a Catholic counseling institute with private patients.

After telling Reuben about this fascinating Czech psycho-therapist I had just met, I gingerly asked him:

"Reuben, I'm in a kind of crisis. What would you think of my going for some sessions to this Dr. Anna?"

He looked at me with grave attention and sighed. "I think it would be a wonderful idea. I have been worrying about you for a long time, Natalie."

This would be the beginning of healing of many of my underlying problems.

At the first session, Dr. Anna asked me whether the man I was so attracted to was more handsome than Reuben. No, I said immediately. I love Reuben's full beard! This man was very ordinary looking.

During our weekly meetings, what Dr. Anna to persuade me to work on was how to improve my life at home.

"Since you are so over-extended, why is it you who makes breakfast for everyone each day during week days?"

"Oh, Reuben comes from a background where men don't cook."

"So, let him make cold cereal."

"Well, Olivia and Juliet, could certainly make bacon and eggs, probably better than I do, but what about Dmitri?"

Dr. Anna smiled in her knowing way, "I never met any little boys who would care a lot if their bacon and eggs came from the hands of their older sisters or their mother!"

In general, she thought I had a habit not unusual among very devout Catholics.

"You project what you think a saint would do in your situation and then you try to do it, right?"

"Of course. We are all called to be saints!" I replied, shocked.

"Suppose you started instead with 'since I am not yet a saint, what would be a sensible solution to this or that problem?'"

As a result we insisted that Olivia and Juliet take turns making breakfast and we hired a student to come every afternoon to pick up Dmitri at his day-care and play with him. This way I could take a long nap after coming home from the university and work on dinner quietly.

It was a long time since I had a warm, intelligent, motherly woman thinking about my needs. This was healing, just in itself.

LXVII

Tangent: As a result of that one mortal sin, I got to see how any Catholic, no matter how committed to the practice of the faith, could fall into such sins. Of course, I thought about this sin all the rest of my life, especially when reading that line from the Psalms "my sin is always before me." How could I have done it? What if I had gotten pregnant with this man's child? How much I would have hurt my beloved children if I had actually gotten my fantasy of running away from my husband and home! Is it wrong to experience so much guilt over one sin? Some Catholics would think so. After all, I was forgiven by Jesus through the confessional. My philosophy professor, Von Hildebrand, explained this differently. Many sins are terrible. But what makes adultery especially terrible is that it cuts to the innermost core of our personhood breaking the bond of self-giving in the sacrament of marriage.

As you will see if you read on, I stopped teaching at St. Ignatius U. within a few years after this traumatic sin. So once I had left, I didn't have to pass my friend on campus to exchange sad, sad, hello Professor, greetings. Many years later I met him and his wife at a conference. While she was chatting with someone else, he looked at me with a penetrating glance. His only words were these:

"That was quite a learning experience back then, Natalie, wasn't it?"

A year after the sinful crisis, a great grace came to me that would change my spiritual life in a way that brought me much closer to my Savior. One morning during Christmas vacation I was at the morning parish Mass. A woman friend came up to me at the end of the recitation of the rosary:

"Natalie, I wonder if you would like to have the statue of Our Lady of Fatima in your house for a week."

"Oh, thank you, dear Peggy. What is involved?" I asked.

Eyes beaming with hope, my friend explained, "This is a replica of the statue of Our Lady at the shrine in Fatima. It goes around the world and people take her into their homes and pray for her intercession with the family. Sometimes miracles happen!"

"I don't know, Peggy. Our household isn't very pious. You know Reuben isn't a Catholic...well not yet...."

"But Natalie, it's Christmas week coming up and so far no one wants her!"

"Oh, then, of course."

I forgot all about it actually because I was busy grading papers, finishing out the Fall semester, and preparing syllabi for the Spring semester.

The phone rang. "Natalie, this is Peggy. Can we bring Our Lady to your house this afternoon?"

"Sure." I gave her the directions. It is important to tell you, my readers, that I was not in a good mood. Peggy's phone call interrupted my nap. "I guess it will only take a few minutes to let them in and take the statue, and then I can go back to sleep," I thought.

The reason this is important is that there was no way that the amazing grace that came with this visit could be explained on the basis that I had psyched myself up to have a mystical experience.

In the door came 3 ladies carrying a long wooden box. Out came a 2 foot statue of Our Lady of Fatima, the famous one with the gold crown and long white dress with gold trim. They set her on the dining room table. Then Peggy took out 4 copies of a fat booklet of prayers.

"Now we will pray the rosary together for your family and the consecration prayer to Our Lady's Immaculate Heart, dear Natalie. Are the children around?"

"No, their sitter took them with her to pick up Dmitri and go to the playground."

I couldn't refuse to say those prayers, but I certainly wasn't eager.

First we prayed the glorious mysteries of the rosary. Then came the consecration. Peggy intoned:

"Dear Immaculate Mary, take out of us our stony hearts, and put into us your Immaculate Heart."

The three of us dutifully repeated the prayer.

At that moment suddenly an incredible peace filled my heart. After my nap, I awoke with more than peace. It seemed as if the whole of heaven as Mary experienced it was open to me.

For years after, in my prayer times but also in the night, when awakening I would get beautiful illuminations of truth and interior visions of Jesus or the Trinity. Instead of my usual stream of consciousness filled with anxieties and anger mixed in with frantic prayer, my mind was full of poetic images such as this one:

> Transfiguration
> The taste of time
> cloying peach fuzz.
> A glimpse of eternity
> liberating gold white
> draining my touch of all heaviness.
> Light of Mary be my presence,
> 'Oh that I might fly on the wings of a
> dove to the place of rest."

As poetry this is not very good, but as an experience put into words, it certainly was good.

The only person I knew who I thought would understand what I was experiencing was my old mystic friend, Charlie Rich, back in NYC, now in his 80's. I wrote him about these graces. Pretty soon he was writing back every day in answer to my letters contributing accounts of his own thoughts about God and the saints to what I was "getting."

Happily I was scheduled to give a talk in NYC the following summer so we could have a joyous reunion with me, now not a troubled wife and mother asking advice, but a sort of mystical partner!

Tangent: After a few years of teaching I became a writer of books about spirituality and daily life and also a speaker because of these books. I decided not to go into this side of my life in this autobiography. After all Natalie Karamazov is a pseudonym and giving any titles of these books could steer the reader toward my real name! Smile.

LXVIII

So what were our children like – members of the Karamazov/De Toledo/Klein clan?

Someone said that twins, especially identical twins, are a gang of 2. They were always closer than Cassandra and I. As many identical twins do, they developed a language of their own, but also a male twin correlate – two young men called Reuben and Mario about whom they wove intricate story lines. At this writing when Juliet and Olivia are over fifty years old, they still have on the walls on their houses magnificent drawings of Reuben and Mario, handsome dare-devils!

From an early age Olivia developed the writing talents that would lead her eventually to become a poet. Juliet also writes poetry sometimes, but excelled in art – her style being a cross between that of Chagall and Van Gogh.

In personality Juliet was so much more extrovert that Olivia's plaintive cry was:

"When the other girls in school come up to me they only ask me where is Juliet?"

It was Juliet who first made friends at school who related to herself only, not as just part of "the twins."

"I have never forgiven her for that," Olivia sometimes says. "It was the worst pain of my life as a youth to think that Juliet could ever want to spend time with anyone more than with me!" In fact, now in their fifties Juliet is just as close to Olivia as she has always been to Juliet.

The twins went to the public school across from our house. They excelled in all subjects. I insisted that they should go to a Catholic High School. There was one a bus ride away in Santa Monica that was highly touted. It was run by an order of teaching sisters who believed in combining a classical education with Catholic teaching.

So our cute little girls in their colorful clothing were forced to wear the traditional white blouses and checked skirts of the parochial school system. Off they went on the bus each day, seemingly acquiescent enough to their new routines.

Not for long! When they were not yet sixteen, one Sunday when I came back from an out-of-town speaking engagement, Reuben met me at the baggage claim with this announcement:

"Juliet and Olivia have quit High School. They want to work selling donuts at the super-market instead."

"What?... You agreed to this?"

"Let them learn from life," Reuben responded voice bitter with disappointment. He, who had always wanted to go to college but was too poor, was seeing his brilliant daughters reject education.

I was appalled, but didn't know what to do.

"Why do you want to drop out of school, girls?" I asked them as soon as we got home from the airport.

"It's so boring. We hate it there. We want to be free...wear the clothes we like...wear make-up...meet boys."

I think both Reuben and I thought that if we let them make this choice, very soon they would hate working at the donut shop and beg to go back to school.

We were wrong. Sometimes, when they reached middle-age, they would say that if there had been home-schooling they would have pre-ferred that. They hated regimented learning unrelated to their own inter-ests.

As it was, they became self-taught, reading usually a book a night. And once they learned computers they eventually could earn $100 an hour to my $5 per hour as a university professor with a Ph.D!

And little Dmitri? What happened to him? You last heard of him be-ing dropped off at day-care. Of course, Dmitri was not a twin. In a family with 2 sets of twin Sisters Karamazov, he was the odd-ball without a twin. However, his face looked exactly like the faces of his sisters – only they had brown eyes and his were greenish grey. So, when he was older if you looked at the three of them together with the twin's hair covered by hats they would seem like triplets!

Adored by both parents and with two sisters eight years older to play with him as a Hobbit, he certainly felt appreciated and cherished. He had not the mind of a philosopher, or writer, or poet, or artist. He was a mu-sician. As soon as we tried piano and, then, cello lessons on him, he went beyond our expectations. Not ½ hour of practicing but hours absorbing the beauty of music.

In school he was always popular even though he was smaller than the other boys and less athletic. To keep a balance we enrolled him in Little League. I will never forget his first time at bat:

"Dmitri Klein is feeling very strong today," came the surprising an-nouncement on the loud-speaker, "he doesn't even need his bat!"

Somehow he managed to arrive at the batter's plate without a bat!

Even though he never did well at baseball, he loved playing on a team.

At school he always did very well and was always a good child with-out the mischievous streak of the gang of 2, his sisters.

Dmitri's mind was more intuitive than analytic. He would come out with unexpected pronouncements. One time I was feeling ugly and decided to try a permanent hair wave. Normally my hair was long and straight.

My daughters thought the perm was kind of cute looking. But , Dmitri, aged about 10 at the time, remarked:

"For other women it's okay to get a perm, but for you, Mom, it's a sin."

"Really, Dmitri," I was stunned, "why would you say such a thing?"

"I thought you loved St. Francis. He wouldn't have spent money on anything like that."

Later, when old enough to read one of my shorter books about how to be holy, he made me laugh by saying, "Gee, Mom, if you ever lived what you write about in that book you would be a saint!"

In some ways professor's kids are like preacher's kids. They see sides of the parent the public doesn't see and they like to point those out.

Before she left school, Juliet was in a graphic arts class. The assignment was to make a business card for someone.

"Mom, would you like a classy business card?"

"Oh, sure. I've never had one because I'm too miserly to pay for something like that."

A week later she showed me the draft:

"Natalie Karamazov De Toledo Klein, Ph.D.

Full-time Martyr

Part-time Saint"

It became a family joke. The next time I taught Brothers Karamazov, I used the incident to explain Ivan's confrontations with Katerina. She certainly had a martyr complex.

On a humorous note, some psychologically Catholic pundit invented what he called the Joan of Arc complex.

"You tie yourself to a stake and hand out matches to the crowd!"

LXIX

Meanwhile, what was happening to my sister Karamazov, Cassandra, the sacred dancer?

After the wonderful hippie-like Catholic worker man went on to another vocation, she had a few other boyfriends, but nothing very serious until

Enter Alan Drury:

One day Cassandra was walking her little poodle dog down the street where she lived near Riverside Drive not far from her sacred dance studio at St. John the Divine.

She bumped into an older man in his late '50's leading a German shepherd. He was tall and lean, with long grey hair, and a friendly grin.

"What's your name lovely young lady?" he saluted Cassandra.

"Cassandra De Toledo Karamazov," she responded. She liked to trot out that full name to see if her interlocutor was familiar with world literature.

"Are you kidding? I'm just plain Alan Drury, but I love Dostoevsky," he said in a soft rich voice with a twinkle in his large blue eyes.

Sixth months later:

"Natalie, what would you think of a little visit to your house in Los

Angeles, next month?"

"Delighted, of course. Is your company doing something here?"

"Actually I want you to meet a man who I'm thinking of marrying."

"That's exciting, dear Cassandra. Sure. Tell me about him." My heart beat faster with joy. I had feared that my twin would never be married or have children.

"He's a psychoanalyst, Episcopal, older, like the same difference in age as you and Reuben. He has 3 adult children, but he's divorced..."

"Divorced? Is it a marriage that could be annulled in our Church...?" I started getting worried about this match.

"Let's not talk about that now. We could visit for a week on the way to San Francisco where one of his daughters lives."

Since it was summertime when they came and I was on vacation from St. Ignatius U. we had plenty of time to get acquainted.

"Reuben, I think this Alan Drury guy Cassandra is in love with... is a very interesting, intelligent, and warm person but still not the right person for her," was my comment as soon as I could get Reuben alone in our bedroom out of earshot of our guests.

Ready to doze off Reuben muttered, "Hard to tell. Cassandra might have thought that about me and you, when we first started getting close years ago."

I lay awake, reviewing the happenings that seemed so difficult.

"How about the way he took out the one-third empty bottle of vodka out of his heavy knapsack and finished it off by the end of the evening?

"How about how he walked right into the kitchen and started pulling out condiments out of the herb shelf to transform our, what, dull as dishwater chicken dinner?, into some kind of exotic goulash?"

"How about how while Reuben was playing Cassandra's favorite Ralph Vaughn-Williams Lark Ascending, he maneuvered Juliet out onto the back porch. Was he trying to psycho-analyze the family through questioning her?"

Feeling a little threatened, Sisters Karamazov style, I decided to go on the offensive.

The next day we took a picnic lunch to the beach.

"Tell me, Alan, what school of psycho-analysis do you practice?"

"I'm eclectic, Natalie. I use whatever ideas seem they would best help my clients."

"Do you carry the bottle of vodka into the sessions?"

"Of course, not, Natalie, are you pulling my leg?" he answered laughing as he gulped down another swig of vodka neat.

Tangent: Strange as it may seem, at this time in the late '70's unless someone was passing out on the floor or the curb on the street, we didn't think they might be alcoholics. Actually toward the last decade of Alan's life, he stopped drinking so much.

Cassandra and Alan got married in an Episcopal ceremony at St. John the Divine, without benefit of any Catholic annulment of his previous marriage. The wedding was embellished by the sacred dancers from her Catholic parish and the guests clapping as they surrounded them in a circle after the marital promises.

I didn't want to go to NYC for Cassandra's wedding since I considered that she was entering into a liason that was disobedient to our Church, but Reuben, who always put family above all else, insisted we go. Elena, our mother, was pleased as could be to be surrounded by interesting Episcopals instead of up-tight Catholics like me.

After my daughter Juliet, Alan liked Elena best in the Karamazov/Klein clan.

"Elena, Elena,

Never a yentah,

Always a talk-ah,

Hurrah!"

He would greet her on family visits with a warm hug.

After some 10 years in NYC the Drury's moved to San Francisco and we saw them more often.

For the next 35 years of our visits Alan would slither around my questions, seeming to ply me with liquor so as to "relax me." Usually this worked.

Where we did get along very well was when talking about psychology. Allan was up on all the latest theories about personality types, Myers-Briggs, the 4 Temperaments, etc., and as long as I listened to his informal lectures on these, we did fine.

The 30-year marriage of Cassandra and Alan was in many ways more compatible than mine with Reuben. How so? Both of us were looking for our father, and both of our husbands were very fatherly. Even though Cassandra and Alan would have liked to have children, they didn't conceive any. Alan was close to one of his daughters from his first marriage and those grandchildren.

A big difference was that Alan was not only fatherly, but also extremely motherly. He had a deep paternal love for Cassandra. As a child his mother trained him to help her with her housework. So, while Cassandra did her beautiful sacred dance in a parish, Alan, did all the housework and cooking. He loved Cassandra's dancing and, even though not a Catholic, went to all her parish sacred dances taking care of the costumes and props. So, whereas I felt over-burdened with the combination of teaching, motherhood, and household chores, Cassandra's life became easier because of Alan.

Back to my relationship with my brother-in-law, once on a visit we made to the Drury home in San Francisco, I was with Cassandra at her parish. Reuben and Alan were walking around the city. On the drive back home to Los Angeles, Reuben casually reported:

"You know what Alan said about you, Natalie? He actually said, "You know Natalie is full of shit, but I like her anyhow because she's so lively."

This remark, of course, did nothing to improve our relationship.

LXX

What a painful chapter comes now! The 3rd generation of Sisters Karamazov, Juliet and Olivia now "went to hell in a hand-basket," as the saying goes.

3rd generation? Yes, I mean Elena and her sister – first generation sisters Karamazov; myself and Cassandra – second generation; and then Olivia and the younger Juliet – third generation.

Contrary to our expectations that they would hate working in the donut shop and beg to go back to their Catholic high school, Juliet and Olivia loved their new life. They were on the late afternoon through 9 PM shift.

"So, what do you actually do there, kiddos?" I asked.

They both giggled. "Oh, we have so much fun. The afternoon is pretty busy with guys and gals coming in after school. We give them the donuts of their choice and coffee or coke," replied Olivia.

"The cooks in the back, neat guys, ummm, around 20 years old, come out every hour with fresh trays of assorted donuts and crullers. We arrange these on the display shelves," added Juliet, smirking when mentioning the cooks.

"The easiest part of the job is after 6 PM. Most of these are regular customers, lonely older people looking for a place to eat a donut and sit at the little tables and talk to strangers.

"Best of all are the cops. We've memorized what they like to order and when we see them parking their motorcycles we have their favorite donut ready to offer them as soon as they get in the door."

"They really dig that personal touch," Juliet smiled. "They show it with nice tips. Sometimes a whole dollar bill!"

Before they dropped out of High School Olivia and Juliet still went with me to Mass on Sundays. Now that changed.

"Mommy, we're awfully tired after our late work at the shop. Can't we go to a Saturday evening Mass?"

"Sure, I'll drop you off at the parish at 5 PM and pick you up at 6 PM."

After a few weeks of this, one time I asked Olivia what the sermon was about.

"Well, uh, boring!"

A friend of mine who happened to go to that same evening Mass called me up one evening.

"Natalie, I think you should know something. You're not going to like it. I saw your girls come in a side door of the Church and go out the front door after a few minutes before the Mass started. I was sitting in a pew near that front door and they didn't come back until the Mass was almost over!"

My heart sank. They were rejecting the best thing I had ever given them!

Before the week was out I brought them to one of the priests at the university they liked. He was about 35 and very handsome.

When they came to my office after this visit to the priest, Olivia gave me the bad news.

"Mom, Father S. thinks that teens need a little freedom to make their own choices. They can't go to Mass just to please their parents. He thought we could take a little break. Tell your Mom you'll be back to Church soon on your own steam," Juliet smiled at me in her usual charming way. Reuben, not yet a Catholic, thought the priest could be onto something right from a psychological point of view.

Grief! At this writing, at age 52, the 3rd generation Sisters Karamazov/De Toledo/Kleins still don't go to Church!

6 months after this incident I came to find out that the confessor, Fr. S, left the Jesuit order and married a Hollywood actress outside the Church!

Before working at the donut shop the twins, when not at school in childish- looking uniforms, used to wear long granny dresses. Now they wore mini-skirts and tight tank-tops with plenty of cleavage showing the large bosoms they inherited from Reuben's side of the family. Their faces were covered with make-up and their finger-nails and toes bright with garish many-colored polish. They looked like contemporary versions of Grushenka and Katerina of the Brothers Karamazov.

You might wonder, why didn't Natalie Karamazov/De Toledo/Klein force them to dress modestly?

At first I think I was too stunned to figure out what to do. Soon after, however, more serious problems arose.

Both girls were a little overweight; normal in 15 year old adolescent girls, but they hated being fat. Olivia began to give excuses to skip meals.

"Forget about saving dinner, Mom, we'll buy snacks at the grocery store on the way to work."

This was before parents knew about anorexia. Without becoming full-fledged victims, Olivia was soon living on coca-cola and french-fries. Since the weight loss made her look sleek and not yet skinny, we didn't pay too much attention.

Juliet, the cheerful, friendly twin was the first to have a real boyfriend. Joe seemed like a nice enough young man.

But, then, came this never to be forgotten phone call:

"Natalie, come and bring Juliet to the hospital, she raided my pills and she is passed out!" This was my mother, Elena.

Reuben and I told Elena to call 911 and rushed to the emergency ward. After 2 hours in the waiting room in panic, the doctor emerged.

"Juliet is probably going to be all right, folks. We pumped her stomach. She can stay here watched by nurses' aides, but if you can guarantee that someone stays up all night to check her, she could go home."

Gulping down coffee to stay awake, all that night we kept Juliet between us on our bed.

"Why, dear, dear, Juliet, did you do that?"

"Joe broke up with me. He said he didn't really love me," our beautiful daughter sobbed out.

"But we love you. Olivia loves you. Dmitri loves you. Grandma Elena loves you," we insisted with me adding over and over again, "Jesus loves you, Mary loves you." It wasn't until more than 30 years later I found out that she had aborted their baby just before this suicide attempt.

Tangent: In middle-age Juliet became deeply pro-life and advises every woman thinking of an abortion never to do it. She would invite anyone considering an abortion to come and stay at her family house. And, in cases, where the friend kept the baby, she has become a second mother to those children.

LXXI

Shortly after this terrifying incident, Olivia made her big move out of the house.

"Daddy and Mommy, I have something important to tell you about," it began after dinner one evening.

"You know my boyfriend, Tom?"

"Of course, the older security guard, tall with blond hair?" I replied.

We rather liked Tom, even though we suspected that they were having sex.

You must know that I prayed hard to be able to convince the girls to be chaste before marriage. They never talked to me about that side of their friendships with boys and men. Since Reuben didn't think chastity was even possible for young people, they probably told him more about their love affairs. But he didn't tell me about these confidences.

"Well, Tom wants me to move into his apartment with him. And I'm going to do it and you can't stop me!"

Hindsight, again I wonder that we let her go. Again, I think we thought it was a phase and she'd be back soon to the home where she was surrounded by real love.

Another reason was that a boyfriend who wanted to live with one of our daughters seemed a step up from the more awful men that surrounded these flashy young Sisters Karamazov.

Here are 2 examples of these worser case scenarios:

One day Olivia came running into the house crying. She locked herself in the bathroom, ran the water in the tub, and wouldn't come out. Finally Reuben insisted she open the door. We came in to find the bath water tainted with blood and Olivia's underpants with blood on them on the floor.

This is the story that came through Olivia's tears:

"I was at the beach … not dressed up, by the way," Olivia said glaring at us.

"It was in the afternoon but suddenly there was no one around except this man in jeans and a T-shirt. He started talking to me but suddenly his eyes changed. He looked insane, I swear he did."

Choking on her tears, she continued, "then he took a long knife out of his back pocket, and threatening to kill me if I resisted, he raped me!"

"He left me on the beach. I hitch-hiked back home."

We took Olivia to the ER where they washed her properly.

You can see after reading this why Olivia living with Tom, a boyfriend who loved her and who was also a security guard, seemed like a step up!

The scary incident with Juliet was funny in its own macabre way.

Before Juliet knew she was pregnant with the baby she would keep, she came running into the house one evening in the summer when it was still light outside.

"Lock the doors, Daddy, there's a gang of boys following me."

Reuben called the police immediately.

"We'll get there as soon as we can, sir, but it might be awhile."

They didn't come for an hour!

Meanwhile, Juliet called Olivia and, within 10 minutes, she came over with Tom who sat inside the living room with a shotgun on his lap waiting for trouble.

Sure enough, five minutes later a group of rowdy young men circled the house and tried to get in the back door, calling out

"Heh, princess Juliet, come out and we'll get you some good weed."

I was in the room in the back near the door praying up a storm while Juliet tried to sweet-talk them.

Finally we heard the wail of sirens.

I whispered in Juliet's ear, "The police are almost here."

"Get out of here quick guys – the cops are coming," Juliet warned the gang of drugged up young men.

They managed to flee across a garden between the back of our house and back of the house from the next street over.

After the police took notes for their report, we asked Juliet why she had warned these dangerous guys that the police were right near.

Smiling charmingly, Juliet responded, "Mom, wouldn't St. Francis have warned them?"

We were right that Olivia living together with Tom didn't work out, but Olivia didn't move back home. Now 18-years old, she decided to get her own little apartment near the beach.

She could afford this because a half year earlier I had arranged for both girls to leave the donut shop and became trainees in a computer business run by the husband of a friend. It turned out my poet and my artist Karamazov daughters were very good at this totally opposite type of profession. I eventually came to see that because of their flamboyant drama-queen propensities, analytic computer work was a kind of balance.

So now the Sisters Karamazov each had enough of a salary to live away from home. Juliet didn't move out. She got pregnant with the baby of another young man and, this time, decided to keep the baby. Since her beau didn't want to get married, she rightly counted on us for total support with a place in our home to live in and bring up the baby.

Little Debbie became indeed a Karamazov/De Toledo/Klein, adored by all of us, but not a Sister Karamazov because she never had a sister!

During this time the life of Elena Karamazov was not static either. But this story I will tell in the next chapter.

LXXII

A big but unhappy adventure of the Sisters Karamazov came when my mother, Elena Karamazov, was in her '70's.

"My lease is up on my place near the University. I would be happy to give you $1,000 a month rent, to live in my own little apartment within your large house Reuben and Natalie," Elena, now grey haired and a little stooped, remarked at one of our Sunday after Mass luncheons.

Reuben, always eager for more income to satisfy his spend-aholic addiction, jumped on the chance.

"That would be great Elena. You can enjoy being closer to Juliet and new-born Debbie, and your grandson, Dmitri. You could put in a kitchen area for yourself so you could eat the way you like whenever you want."

As usual, Reuben didn't even ask my opinion. Actually, even though I foresaw problems, I felt so bad about how tense I was with Elena over Church matters that I was eager to have a plan of something that could make things better. Besides, since we had been so, so, close when I was a child, there was a part of me that always hoped to revive that love. She felt that, too. Whenever we met we hugged and kissed with real enthusiasm, but then lapsed into conflict by the end of the visit.

Tangent: You have probably heard the old adage "Never talk about religion or politics at dinner parties." The way I think of it is that you can describe each person as a circle. Meet another person and there is an overlap between the two circles of common ideas, likes, beliefs. If you stay in the overlap area you are happy; but the minute you stray out of that area, ka-boom!

Oh, how happy and excited Elena became as she watched the work of the construction men painting the walls and putting in a wooden floor. She would visit our house often and sit around chatting with Juliet and listening to Dmitri play his cello dreaming of this happy denouement living in our house after so many years of tension with me over Church issues.

Everything went swimmingly in the 6 months of preparation and we had a lovely open house in her new quarters with mutual friends from the university.

Very soon, however, a problem arose none of us thought of:
Noise!

Only later when I was in my 70's myself would I understand how most old people need quiet.

3:30 PM: "Bang!" went the front door as Dmitri and his friends came running through the house to the backyard after school.

3:45 PM: After their snacks, hilarious whoops and hollers as they threw the ball into the basket.

6:30 PM: Loud music from Dmitri's cello in the evening conflicting with the sound from the magna-stereo during Reuben's 2-hour nightly classical music binge.

3: AM: Crying of baby Debbie in the night.

"How about putting insulation on the walls of Elena's suite?" a friend suggested.

As this turned out to come at a price of $5,000, Elena had a different plan.

"Natalie, after school is out, why don't you have Dmitri and his friends do their basketball across the street at the elementary school playground?" Elena asked during the one shared meal on Sunday after Mass.

Looking back I think this query, which didn't sound at all outrageous to me, triggeredd some memory of Reuben from his domineering mother as she was in his childhood because, at this suggestion of Elena, he suddenly burst out with:

"Absolutely not! Dmitri, make as much noise as you want!"

Shocked, Elena walked away from the table into her suite.

"I'm moving out because Reuben is persecuting me in an attempt to get me out of there," she told all our mutual friends at the Ignatius University.

Next day I got a phone call from one of them. "Natalie, is this really true about Reuben and Elena?"

"What?.. She told your wife that Reuben was persecuting her. That's nonsense. He gets along with her much better than I do. Why does she think that?" I asked.

"She says she thinks he's a money grubber and wants her out to rent her beautiful little apartment in your house to students for 2x the price!"

"That's crazy."

"Well, in case she leaves and he wanted to rent it, my husband and I think it would be only fair for you to fix it so half the rent would go to her. That would gradually pay off her investment?"

That's what happened. Elena took out a 6 month's lease on another apartment. We rented her suite to students from Ignatius U. for $1,000 a month. We agreed to give her $500 a month as compensation for her loss of the renovation costs.

What Elena did as it came near to the end of that lease totally surprised me. "Natalie, I want you to drive me to see Pacific Retirement Colony in Santa Monica this weekend."

"Really?...Sure."

This retirement colony was a beautiful building right across from the Ocean. Every small studio apartment had a balcony with a view of the

Pacific. There were about 200 elderly people living there with a deluxe dining room and lounge. The total cost per month was $1,500.

From the Sisters Karamazov standpoint, what astounded me is that our very bohemian-looking mother, Elena, with her short straight hair, pants, brightly colored shirts, and off-beat non-stop conversations about ideas, had chosen in her old age to live among the Los Angeles version of the gilded ghetto Jews she had despised in NYC!

There, sitting at the dining room tables, were conventional old women with dyed hair, perms, and diamond rings on their fingers, who liked to play bridge and talk about their previous fancy houses, luxurious vacations, their husband's businesses and the successes of their adult children! The men ate their meals as quickly as possible to sit in a circle around the TV watching the news of the day and sports.

God took pity on my mother. He helped her find another type of retired person at Pacific Retirement Colony: bored inmates who loved to listen to Elena's juicy stories of her past Karamazov life!

LXIII

The next not only surprising but deeply moving event in the lives of the Karamazov/De Toledo/Klein clan was the baptism of Reuben into the Catholic Church!

Way back when telling you about meeting Reuben, I told you that he had been fascinated by the figure of Jesus even as a youth. Working on his novel about Judas, eventually published by a small Christian press, brought him closer and closer to belief that Jesus actually was the Jewish Messiah. Absorption in Catholic sacred music brought him closer in a wordless way.

Of course, all along, I was praying every day that Reuben would convert, since for me the whole meaning of life was to grow in love of the Trinity and of neighbor to prepare our souls for heaven and I believed the Catholic Church to be founded by God. But Reuben felt no attraction to the folksy guitar Masses post-Vatican II.

Here is how the great grace came to him.

"Reuben, get the next flight out to DC, our mother is dying," Jacob called to get his brother to join him. He had been visiting from his home in Los Angeles, when she had a heart attack."

Even though Reuben had such a complicated relationship of aversion/love for his Yiddishe Mama, the idea of her death threw him into a panic. On the plane he prayed to the God he still wasn't sure existed: "If Mama is still alive when I get there, I promise I will start looking seriously into the Catholic Church."

In this way, as it were, the Jewish side of the family finally brought Reuben to Christ. Mama was still alive when Reuben got to the hospital. She died a few months afterwards, but by then my husband was taking instructions in the faith.

When I met Reuben at the airport back from DC he announced with a sheepish grin, "Natalie, sweetheart, I promised Jesus that if Mama was still alive when I got there I would start going with you and Dmitri to Mass on Sundays."

Ecstatic with joy I looked for the most wonderful Churches I could find in the Los Angeles area, ones with organs and choirs and highly-recommended priests. But one Sunday it was raining hard and we didn't feel like driving an hour away.

"Reuben, let's go to St. Michael's, the parish nearest to us. You'll hate it, but…."

Why would I think he would hate it? Well, almost all the Ignatius U. professors hated the parish and went to Mass at the university instead. Msgr. O'Reilly was the pastor at St. Michael's. He was a short, bald, old belligerent priest. Years before I once brought little Dmitri with me to a daily Mass. Even though we were sitting way in the back of the Church far from most of the other people, Msgr. O'Reilly interrupted the ritual to yell from the altar "Get that squalling brat out of here."

I took Dmitri out for a little while, came back for Holy Communion and gingerly approached the priest:

"I am sorry my child annoyed you. It was his birthday and I wanted to bring him. If the cry-room was open I would have gone there with him."

"Do you think I'm the janitor to open doors for you?" he barked.

Tangent: Catholic parents differ on the questions of bringing children to Church on Sundays or weekdays. Some take turns with mother bringing some to one Mass and Father to another. Others sternly reprimand any children who talk or even squirm during services. Many parents come together with children of different ages, some with coloring books or candy to distract them, and if a baby or toddler gets fussy the mother or father takes that one for a little walk. By the time of Dmitri in the 1970's however, many large parishes arranged a blocked off an area in the back of the Church with a large picture window facing the altar for parents with little children.

I didn't go back to Msgr. Reilly's Masses for a long time after that unpleasant incident.

Now, on that particular rainy Sunday so many years afterwards, Reuben, myself and Dmitri entered St. Michael's. We sat in the middle of the Church. When Msgr. O'Reilly was giving his sermon, after about 10 minutes, Reuben leaned over and whispered in my ear, "Who is that old dinosaur? I love him. He's just like the old Orthodox Jewish rabbis."

After Mass I introduced Reuben to Msgr. O'Reilly. This curmudgeon, by God's grace, took an instant liking to my husband.

"Perhaps Reuben could come to you for some instructions in the faith?" I asked.

"Wonderful," came the answer.

Tangent: The tradition in the world-wide Church is that anyone seeking to become a Catholic takes lessons from a priest first. Shortly after Reuben's private instructions there was a new method devised from the rituals of the early Church where a whole group of catechumens, as they were called, studied together for at least 6-months time.

After one such private session Reuben reported:

"There's a little black book Msgr. O'Reilly refers to when I ask questions. So, today I asked him, 'What's that book that is better than all the unsatisfying answers I've ever got from those Jesuit priests who Natalie brings to our house to convert me?'"

"Oh, that's the Baltimore Catechism," replied Msgr. O'Reilly.

This was the catechism devised in the American Church of a century ago, often mocked by post-Vatican II Catholics for its method of rote memorization of questions and answers. The new idea was that, instead, those entering the Church should listen to personal witnesses of Catholics and read Scripture.

But, somehow, Reuben, with his super-deep mind, didn't need interesting answers. He needed just the truth written authoritatively.

Just before the date for the baptism, Reuben took me aside after our evening sacred music time.

"Natalie, listen closely. I want to be a Catholic, but not your kind of Catholic! I will go to Sunday Mass, and pray while listening to music, but I don't want to go to daily Mass, and I don't want to pray the rosary, and I absolutely don't want to go to charismatic prayer meetings! Do you get it?"

Of course, I accepted this declaration since I was so delighted that we would be going to Mass together even once a week and that he would be receiving Holy Communion.

Within a few months, the Karamazov/De Toledo clan (Natalie Karamazov Klein, Cassandra De Toledo who flew in from San Francisco, Elena Karamazov, Juliet and Olivia in their glamorous low cleavage dresses, and Dmitri, 10 years old in a suit and tie) were at the baptismal font with Reuben, face radiant with joy and faith. And Msgr. O'Reilly was so happy with his convert that at the communion rail after putting the host on his tongue that he actually pinched Reuben's cheek!

And since old, bald, ferocious Msgr. O'Reilly was the one to win over my Reuben to the Church, I loved him, too.

LXXIV

Enter: Ray Smith

I got off the plane from an out-of-town speaking date and there, as always, was Reuben with a big smile and hug waiting to walk me down to baggage claim. Before I could tell him a word about the ups and downs of the trip, he came out with this:

"Guess what, Natalie, honey, Olivia is engaged to be married!"

"What?... To whom?" I exclaimed not being able to guess from the bland expression on his face what kind of news this was.

"She met this guy, Ray Smith is his name, at the beach Friday. They fell in love and got engaged and told me about it just this morning."

"Ray Smith? Oh, my God. How can a young woman with the name of Olivia Karamazov De Toledo Klein take such a dull name as Smith?"

By now Reuben had an impish grin on his face. "Wanna get a drink at the bar?"

Once seated on our stools, me with a Bloody Mary and he with a Reubeni, Reuben told me the story.

"Saturday morning Olivia and Juliet were playing volleyball with some friends at the beach in front of Olivia's apartment. This new guy joined them. One thing led to another and eventually Juliet drove off to her place to let little Debbie's sitter go home, while Olivia stayed in a huddle with this large new friend."

Tangent: Juliet stayed with the baby at our house for a year, but eventually found it confining on her social life to be with us. Since she was offered a good job in the same computer company where Olivia was still working, she moved to her own place, bringing Debbie each weekday to a woman with children who took in other kids of mothers working outside the home.

Reuben continued his narrative: "Olivia called me up Saturday evening: 'Dad, I have something to tell you, but it would be better in person. Can I bring my friend around to the house tomorrow morning?'"

"So, around noon, Olivia shows up hand in hand with this big lout of a guy. 'Ray meet my Dad, Reuben Klein. My Mom's off on a trip, so you can't meet her yet.'"

"So what does this Ray do?" I asked Reuben almost thinking the whole thing was some kind of joke.

"He said he was an accountant."

"Dad, I know you're going to think this is crazy, but we've been talking for 24 hours and it's incredible all we agree on."

"Meanwhile this Ray is just sitting there in his jeans, T-shirt showing a segment of his belly, smiling from ear to ear as if he just won the lottery."

"So our daughter, Olivia, bursts out with this: 'The best of all, is we both want to have children, immediately. They are waiting for you to help with the wedding plans."

"Wedding plans? Where are they getting married? Is Olivia coming back to the sacraments?"

"I don't know. They'll be at the house when we get there. You ask."

To my surprise I liked Ray immediately. That was because I always like big, fat, warm men. Just the same we managed to persuade them to think of a wedding date at least 6 months in the future. In the meantime, Ray left his apartment up the coast and moved in with Olivia.

I will never forget those sessions with Olivia skimming together a book she took out of the library called "Planning Your Wedding." Since dealing with practical things, especially involving clothing and food has never been my long suit I just persuaded Reuben that we should just give them $2,000 and let them decide on stuff like limos for the guests, restaurant receptions, etc. We noticed a chapter at the end of the book entitled "Etiquette for Cancelling a Wedding" but we didn't even look at it.

Ray was vaguely Christian but hadn't gone to any religious services since boyhood. Olivia didn't want anything to do with St. Michael's. So they picked out an old-fashioned Presbyterian Church that looked like a Catholic Church. As near to Hollywood as we were, it was customary for many Christian Churches, especially old beautiful ones, to let couples marry in them even if they weren't part of the congregation. Sort of like a stage set! Juliet went shopping with Olivia and she got a beautiful long modest lacey bridal gown.

A month before the wedding Olivia asked me to take her to lunch.

"Mom, I have something sad to tell you. This marriage is never going to work!"

"What? Oh, that's terrible. Tell me about it."

"He's just not really right for me. He has this complex...what is it called ODC, OCD, I forget what they call it... everything has to be cleaned up all the time. He won't even let me keep a cross-word puzzle book on the dining room table between meals!"

"It's good you are finding this out, no matter how disappointing, Olivia. So, should we take that book out of the library again and look at the chapter on how to cancel a wedding?"

"Oh, no! I want to have the wedding. This is the most wonderful moment of my life. That beautiful gown!"

I thought there was an element here of Olivia liking the idea of having a big wedding before Juliet had one.

"Olivia, that's crazy. You have to cancel the wedding. How can you make that vow, "until death do us part," if you don't even think it will work?"

The petulant chin jutted out with the glaring brown eyes. "You can't tell me what to do, so don't even try, Mom."

"Reuben, I refuse to go to that wedding under these circumstances!" I told Reuben.

"Now, now, it could be just a passing phase. Olivia's so proud and always wants her own way. Let's wait a few more weeks and see what happens," Reuben decided.

The wedding, though not Catholic, was beautiful to the eye. They went off to Disneyland for their honeymoon and moved to a cheaper apartment north of Los Angeles but within commuter distance to their jobs: Ray's job in an accounting firm and Olivia's at the same job at the original computer office.

Everything seemed to be going fine until one evening at 7 PM I got a call from Ray: "Pick up your daughter immediately or I'll kill her!"

"What? I want to speak to Olivia immediately," I demanded. I remembered seeing a hunting gun leaning against a wall in their closet.

"Should I call the police?" I asked when Olivia came to the phone.

"No," came the answer in a dull sad voice, "just come get me."

I would have had Reuben drive but he was on a trip to Las Vegas with his brother. I didn't want to take any chances waiting for him to drive 5 hours.

Bad and slow a driver as I usually was, this time I made an hour's usual trip in 45 minutes. Olivia was outside the door to the apartment on the second floor of their complex sitting on her bags. She jumped in the car and cried all the way home.

The next day we saw Ray's car sitting in the parking lot of the elementary school across from our house. When Reuben went out to talk to him, Ray had tears in his eyes.

"Mr. Klein, don't to let any men come into your house to see Olivia.

I'll kill them." He pointed to a rifle in the back seat of the car.

Ray left shortly after, before we had time to deal with Olivia's insistence that Ray was just kind of over-emotional and would never hurt a fly. He got a legal annulment.

A few months later we got a call from Juliet who had moved out of our house with the baby a few months ago. "Guess what? You know how Olivia's Ray loves babies. Well, he's going to move in with me and Debbie to help pay our rent…just as a friend, of course!"

This arrangement lasted about 2 years. I decided that Ray wanted the same looks with a different personality. What better than living with the identical twin of your "ex"!

LXXV

Have you been wondering what was happening during this time to the relationship between Reuben and myself? Maybe you think it was slowly getting better or thinking it might have been slowly getting worse?

Hmmmm? From Reuben's side even though, after his sinus surgery, his medical condition was stabilized, it wasn't improving either. He was on heavy cortisone which meant putting on more weight and he was often up in the night with asthma attacks.

On the other hand, his soul was much happier. The graces of Holy Communion each Sunday and from occasional Confessions gave him a sense of greater connection with the eternal. Most of all that connection came from his work on a new book, this one not about Judas, but about Jesus and Satan in the desert during the 40 days of Temptation.

"We have those short descriptions of the 3 temptations in the New Testament, but it was 40 days. I want to dramatize what Jesus and Satan might have talked about that didn't make Scripture!" Reuben would explain to friends interested to hear what he was writing now.

As in the past, but now with only myself and Dmitri to listen, each evening after dinner Reuben read aloud from this book called *The Jesus/ Satan Dialogue*. These sessions brought his soul closer to mine because

I loved Reuben's Jesus, who combined a Jewish sense of prophetic utterance with a unique transcendent piercing of the Father's truths into the mind of the Son.

Meanwhile, for my spiritual growth, I continued my daily correspondence with Charles Rich, the Jewish convert mystic in New York City. By no means, though, had I been released from the syndrome of spiritual friendships with men that were not rightly ordered. The wonderful counselor who helped me through the crisis after my one night of adultery had died. Without feeling tempted to sin in that way, I still found myself entangled in strange obsessive co-dependent bonds, one after the other. These always collapsed finally from the strain of emotional demands on my part that the partner found burdensome and troubling.

A big breakthrough took place at a large charismatic healing service at Ignatius U.

You will not be able to understand what I next relate unless you picture clearly how I felt about my daily life.

I was now working at a teaching job that was increasingly unhappy. Why? Because more and more of the students were into parties and sports and not into learning. The eager hippie like students of the past were mostly gone, replaced by male jocks and confused young women eager to be popular. Most of the faculty and Jesuit priests dissented from some of the teachings of the Church so that I became more and more isolated in my fierce allegiance to those truths.

I felt that I had to stay at this University because of the salary needed to support Reuben and Dmitri, but I was discouraged. My traditional afternoon nap was followed by cooking and dishes and then, afterwards, the good time of music and Reuben's reading of his chapters. But then came hours of marking student papers while Reuben watched TV. Around 9 PM Reuben would always say: "How about tea and cake, Natalie?"

How I resented that nightly question! Why couldn't he have gotten up and made that tea and brought in the cake to the table in front of the

TV? Why not? Because he was a Jewish man who was brought up to be-lieve that only women go in the kitchen. So, I did my duty, marching into the kitchen to put the kettle on and bring out the cake, but with clenched teeth!

Now back to that portentous evening at the charismatic meeting. But, wait, maybe you have never been to one of those, so I will describe them first.

A large group of charismatics would assemble for either a Healing Mass or a Praise and Worship gathering. There would be lots of joyful singing. Then the person known as being graced with healing gifts would address the crowd.

"I sense that there is a woman here who has pain in her legs. She has had these difficulties for many years. If this is you, come forward."

Usually after a few minutes, 1 or more persons would come forward to the space between the altar of the Church and the rows of pews. There would be a team waiting for them. The healer and the others would lay hands on the afflicted part of the body of the suffering one and pray in tongues. The rest of the congregation would extend a hand toward the one being prayed over.

Occasionally someone would immediately witness to a healing as, going up to the microphone at the lectern and telling the rest of us some-thing like

"When they prayed over me I felt this warm heat going through my body, and the pain went away."

At this we would all raise both arms in the air and praise God.

Usually, though, the team would lead the person being prayed over back to his or her pew whispering advice about continuing to pray and not to lose heart if the healing was gradual or if God was allowing the pain to continue for His own reasons.

This particular evening, after a few such announcements by the heal-er that he thought someone was in the group in need of one or another type of relief, the priest-healer suddenly changed course.

"The Lord is telling me that I should pray for all the married couples here present. Stand up and hold hands."

With envy I looked at the numerous married people who stood up. "Oh, dear Jesus, how I wish Reuben was here. How is it that even though he became a Catholic, I am still feeling lonely, especially at such times."

I got the impulse to grab hold of my wedding ring with the fore-finger of the other hand while the priest continued his out-reach.

"Now the Lord wants you to unconditionally forgive each other for every way your spouse ever hurt you!"

The healer paused to let this challenge sink in.

In my heart I prayed along with the couples, grabbing the wedding ring even tighter, Oh Jesus, right now I totally forgive Reuben for every hurt unconditionally."

Tears came into my eyes.

At the end of the service, I staggered out to my car. I was fumbling with the key to the front door, when Reuben opened it for me. He stroked my cheek and said:

"Natalie, sweetheart, you look tired, can I make you a cup of tea?"

What I realized, remembering this moment that began the healing of our marriage, was that because of my unconditional forgiveness, probably an expression of coldness or hatred had disappeared from my eyes. Then, he could finally see the fatigue and respond to it with tenderness!

LXXVI

How did our marriage improve? Not that Reuben ever made tea for me again! Not that our sexual encounters were more frequent, since his fear of asthma attacks was unabated.

No, it was more that a wall came down from years of defensiveness so that, instead of grimacing, we could more often laugh at each other's foibles. And with this lightening up came less of a need on my part to indulge in fantasies about perfect second husbands who would first have been close spiritual friends.

When I talk to unhappy wives I like to put it this way: most of us start with making our spouse into an idol. Then he becomes a fallen idol. But if we forgive, he can become just a funny little creature of God, like ourselves.

Shortly after my charismatic healing of marriage miracle, there was another dramatic event in the lives of the Sisters Karamazov.

"Mom, stop whatever you are doing and come to my place. On the way go to any drug store and get a pregnancy test!"

"Juliet, dear. I'm busy grading papers. How about tomorrow evening?"

"Nooooooo! You have to do it immediately."

On the short trip to Juliet's apartment I wondered: "Why wouldn't she get her own pregnancy test?" Of course I prayed hard that if the test was positive she would keep the baby.

The minute Juliet opened the door, she grabbed the little drug store bag out of my hands and ran into the bathroom. While waiting, I checked out Debbie in her little bed next to Juliet's large bed and was glad to see our 4-year old was fast asleep.

Soon Juliet was sitting close as can be on the couch next to me staring at me wild-eyed.

"Positive!"

I gave her a big hug but she wiggled out of my arms and went to get the portable phone from the kitchen.

"Al, come over right away…forget about the end of the football game… I need you!"

"Tell me about Al, Juliet?" I tried to keep my voice low and calm.

"Oh, he's just this guy I met at a party a few months ago…You know it was one of those immediate attractions. I only went out with him 2x and now…Oh, my God. Mom you know I love babies, but I don't want to be a single mother again."

Knock, knock. Juliet opened the door to a 6' 5" man with huge muscles.

"Eh, Al, this is my mother, Natalie Klein…Al Dupres. He's a hardware computer man at Cal Tech."

"What's up, Juliet?" Al asked lowering his large frame onto a chair opposite to the small couch we were sitting on. His voice had a thick Southern accent I learned was typical Cajun Louisiana.

"Al, I know we hardly know each other but you are now a father!" Juliet blurted out, eyes darting about but with a tentative smile.

I was watching Al's face carefully. To my great surprise, without skipping a beat, he walked over to my Juliet, lifted her up off the couch,

326

gave her a hug and kiss and said:

"Don't worry, honeybun, don't even think of an abortion. I'll marry you!"

At this point I figured I should fade off the scene. "Bye, bye, Juliet. Call me later."

When she called the next morning early she admitted, "I made you come with the pregnancy test because I knew, Mom, that if you were there and the test was positive, I couldn't choose abortion. After all, if I went to the clinic to have one, you and your pro-life friends might be outside praying the rosary!"

To understand how quickly Ray Smith wanted to marry Olivia and Al Dupres wanted to marry Juliet, you need to understand that my Karamazov/De Toledo/Klein twins are absolutely gorgeous women. The way I describe them to people who haven't met them is that they look like a cross between Elizabeth Taylor and Ava Gardner.

Unlike their shorter, small breasted mother, they have identically large bosoms, but small waists, with curly brown shoulder length hair, brilliantly vivacious eyes and large expressive smiles.

In spite of these traits in common, most people can soon tell them apart. The reason is that Olivia holds her 5'6" body with taut dignity as if conveying, touch me if you dare. But Juliet holds herself like an inviting pillow of sensual warmth as if conveying, I'm yours for the asking.

I thought that Reuben would not like Al Dupres. Not so. Because of the trauma with Juliet's first rejecting boyfriend and her almost suicide, and the miseries with Olivia's first husband, Reuben was happy to see a man with an excellent job, who looked ready to step up to the plate.

"Up to the plate," turned out to be the problem. Al Dupres was a total baseball fanatic. Even though he was crazy about his new fiancé, our Juliet, he had little quality time for her. After work most days he either played baseball with a Cal Tech team or he met at the apartments of his sport's buddies to watch baseball, football or car racing on huge wall size

TV screens.

"Mom, I love Al, but I can't marry this man. I'm a twin! I'm used to having someone to talk to all the time. I don't want a husband who loves baseball more than me."

"I'm sorry to hear this, dear Juliet…but don't worry about the baby. You can move back home and we'll help you with Debbie and the new-born when he or she comes."

"No! No! No! I've given it a lot of thought. You pro-lifers always talk about the option of adoption. That's what I'm going to do."

"Oh, no, Juliet. We want the baby."

Juliet found a lawyer who fixed her up with a couple who would pay all her pregnancy and birthing expenses. I had not known beforehand how hard such decisions are not only for the pregnant mother and/or father but also for those in the extended family who want that baby!

But, then, Karamazov drama-queen style, but redeemed, 2 months before the due date Juliet suddenly told the lawyer she wanted the adopting parents to be Catholic.

"You never said that before, Juliet Klein. That is very unfair to the parents who have signed the contract already to adopt!"

"It's my baby!" Juliet replied stubbornly. The lawyer sucked up the loss of the final fees for his services. Juliet went to a Catholic adoption agency and this baby was given to a fine couple with several other adopted children.

Tangent: 18 years later Juliet found him on a web-site. There was a picture of this handsome lad, 6' plus tall, playing baseball!

LXXVII

Enter George McNamara:

One Friday evening into our home waltzed Olivia in a tight short black dress, face brightly made-up, with 3-inch high heels, followed by a handsome young man.

"Mom and Dad, I want you to meet my new friend, George." …

George was a pleasant looking fellow, 5' 10" or so, with curly brown hair, a slim torso and intelligent looking hazel eyes.

"I met your daughters… Olivia and Juliet Karamazov De Toledo Klein at a party a month ago," he began with a twinkle in his eyes about remembering the whole fancy name. Since I am a fan of Dostoevsky, it didn't take me long to tell Katerina/Olivia apart from Grushenka/Juliet!"

Of course, with that remark I was won over immediately. Reuben, however, was more impressed that George turned out to be a computer engineer at Cal Tech, a friend of Al Dupres, the father of Juliet's baby given for adoption. This was not a coincidence because George and Olivia met during the time when Juliet was still engaged to Al. Computer engineers make very good money, he thought happily.

George was different from Olivia's first serious boyfriend, the security guard, because he was not at all a macho type. But he was also different from her annulled first husband, Ray, because he was much more of an intellectual. A link with Reuben, the former seaman, George's favorite pastime was sailing.

After the couple left this introductory meeting with us, I called up Olivia an hour later at her apartment.

"So, Olivia, is George religious?"

"Shhhhh, Mom! He's here."

Then she whispered, "No, he's not religious. He was brought up Episcopal by his mother, but his father is an atheist and that seemed to have left a larger impression on him."

Even though Olivia still prayed, especially the rosary, she never went to Church and so George's atheism was not a big deal for her.

Just 5 months later we got a call:

"Mom, how about you and Dad meeting us at the Maritime Bistro on the shore in Playa del Rey. We're celebrating our engagement."

Olivia ordered Reuben's favorite – lobster – before we even got there.

Wariness was our mood, as you can imagine, after the fiasco of the big wedding, just a year before of Olivia and Ray that ended with the annulled marriage so soon afterwards.

Even though I was longing for my daughters to be married in the Catholic Church, it was something of a relief when Olivia announced that they decided to get married in Lake Tahoe by a roadside minister rather than plan a formal wedding. If it wasn't going to last, why go through all the fuss of a big wedding?

"We can call it an elopement because George's mother would have a fit if her side of the family weren't invited, and she would want the whole Episcopal formal ceremony for sure which George refuses to do.

The first year of the McNamara/Klein marriage went pretty well. Olivia was working at the computer company. Each evening, on weekdays, they went out to dinner somewhere and on the weekends Olivia made wonderful gourmet meals to which she often invited Reuben, myself,

Dmitri, and Juliet, Debbie and Elena. Of course, Ray, Olivia's ex, still living with Diana and Debbie, was not invited.

No sign of a baby, though. Since Olivia adored babies we were surprised.

"The Ob/Gyn I went to tells me that I will not conceive unless I have a small operation," Olivia confided to me one day.

It worked and, unlike me, with my 4 miscarriages, Olivia eventually racked up 4 sons fathered by George, and one more on her third marriage... but that comes up many chapters after this one.

The first son, Richard, soon dubbed Richy-poo, was a bouncing 7 lb. baby.

"One smile from Richy-poo," Dad and Mom, "and I knew that nothing would ever mean more to me than being a mother."

George felt the same way. He found every excuse to take Richy out of Olivia's embrace into a denim baby-carrier on his own chest. So much did George love being a father that even when he was busy with yardwork in the garden of the large house they bought in Playa Del Rey, he would carry baby Richy with him.

"Reuben, you won't believe this," I once called the new grandpa during a visit to the McNamara's. I am watching George with Richy in one arm, cutting down extra branches of a tree with the other arm and hand!"

"Make them take a photo!" Reuben insisted.

Tangent: Now, as I am writing this, when I am 78 years old, among my most precious possessions are those old photos. I find this is true of most grandparents. Their walls are filled mostly with images of former times.

Within a short time we all realized Olivia had a big problem. Probably this was because of the rape trauma or also because twins never like to be without a matching adult with them 24/7. Throughout the day, at home with the baby, Olivia would have panic attacks whenever there was some unfamiliar sound in the house.

"George, come home right away. I think there's someone trying to break through the back door!"

George would tell his boss at Cal Tech that there was a family emergency and head home early.

When this anxiety increased to one incident a day, it became clear this wasn't going to keep on. Over an invitation to a deluxe lobster dinner at the Maritime Bistro, for nostalgia, Olivia came out with the plan.

"Dad, you get kind of lonely at home when Mom teaches at the university and Dmitri is at school all day. Wouldn't it be nice for you if the Karamazov/De Toledo/Klein/McNamara clan all lived together in a big house? Between all our incomes we could easily do this. I would cook nice lunches for you. You could enjoy little Richy-poo. George wouldn't have to come home when I'm scared because you would be there to protect me. Juliet could live with us also with darling Debbie – of course, Ray would have to find his own place."

And that's exactly what we did!

LXXVIII

We found a 5 bedroom house in Playa Del Rey, white stucco, with a swimming pool. This was the time in the late '80's when, if a family had a big steady income, for very little down, you could get a big house with a mortgage of $1,500 a month. With George's salary of $3,000 a month, mine of $2,500 and Reuben's disability payments, we had more than enough and luxuries added on from Juliet's $2,000. A decade later that would be impossible! Everyone chipped in for the food bought each week by Reuben and for utilities. Olivia and Juliet took turns cooking gourmet dinners. Dmitri, now 15, put the plates into the dishwasher after dinner and took out the garbage.

Reuben absolutely loved having Olivia home with him, cooking for him. He loved playing with little Richy-poo and, in the afternoon telling stories to Juliet's daughter, Debbie, now 5 years old and in kindergarten. I especially loved weekends around the pool.

So what was happening all this time to the non-Sister Karamazov, young Dmitri Karamazov De Toledo Klein?

Unlike my dear, rebellious daughters, Dmitri chose to be the good child. He didn't seem repressed, being a joyful lad, full of fun, and a kind of leader among the kids on the block. Long past was their original jealousy of him by his sisters, since Juliet was too busy with her boyfriends and Olivia with her husband. As he grew up, the Sisters Karamazov became the unofficial mentors of their younger brother.

We used to say that Dmitri was the most loved creature on the planet. There was the love of his doting father, home most of the time when he was, rejoicing over his triumphs as a student of the cello. I loved Dmitri as a kind of soul-mate. Even though he wasn't wrapped up in the Church as I always was, he had a Franciscan kind of spirituality expressed in spontaneous friendliness with strangers, and utter disdain for any kind of ownership.

"Did you like eating the roast beef sandwich at lunch today at school?" Olivia once asked.

"Oh, thanks for saving it for me from last night, Olivia but, on the way to school, I gave it to this street person who looked hungry."

Dmitri went to High School at what was called a Magnet. These institutions grew up when skipping bright kids was totally out. Child psychologists thought that having 7 year olds with 9 years olds was crazy from a developmental point of view. Instead, when a Junior High School teacher thought one of her/his students was very bright or very creative, they suggested that the parents enroll them in a Magnet school. One such High School might be devoted to Math, another to Theatre. Dmitri went to a Music Magnet School.

Encouraged by these specialty teachers that Dmitri branched out from being a cellist in young orchestras to composing his own music. These were quartets written about themes in his favorite books such as his Aslan Suite based on Chronicles of Narnia. Oh, how Reuben and I loved going to the High School concerts.

How could we have dreamed that a few years later we would be trying to save such a son from suicide?

What was my life like at Ignatius U.? Better? Worse?

It was worse because each group of Freshman was less motivated to learn about the Great Books. More and more were mostly attending because their parents thought it was a good university for grooming their sons and daughters for successful professions in the world.

The catalogue said it all! "Our mission in to prepare your people for careers in the world. And, also to understand their Catholic heritage."

A far cry from the words of Jesus: "Seek ye first the kingdom of heaven, and all things will be added unto you!"

The good part is that teaching classes in such new subjects as Woman in the Great Books, prompted me to work out my own thoughts and have them published as well. Used to writing off traditional arguments concerning such subjects as the male priesthood or masculine language about God, they were surprised when I would come out with formulations such as these:

"Okay. You are in a parish. There is going to be a Nativity Play on the Sunday before Christmas. If he was a member of the congregation, would you choose Nick Nolte to play the part of Mary?"

"No? Then why do you think a woman, no matter how holy, should play the part of Jesus, proclaiming "This is my body, this is my blood," at the sacred drama of the Mass?

"You say since God is motherly why call God Father instead of Mother? Okay. A son says to his father, "You are such a warm, tender, man, Daddy." The father will be pleased, hopefully. Now if the son adds, "So do you mind if I call you Mommy from now on?"

I also loved teaching my Great Books course in Tolstoy and Dostoevsky. I longed for the male students to see that they wanted to be not rich Fyodor the crazed father, or Dmitri, the crazed macho man, or Ivan, the crazed intellectual, but instead to want to be close enough to Jesus to become their own version of Alyosha, the saint.

And for the female students, how I wanted them to see that the arrogant feminine pride of Katerina was hopeless for finding real love from men. And, that the seductive ways of Grushenka led to despair until she begins to want to give herself in a true love of Dmitri.

Tangent: Some students did get these messages. Now at 78-years old, living far from California, I get e-mails saying:

"You were the best teacher I ever had."

"I still read my journal responses to the books you assigned."

Thank you, Holy Spirit!

LXXIX

Re-enter: Al Dupres

In the middle of a night, about a year after we moved into the big Karamazov House, I went downstairs to the kitchen to make tea for Reuben recovering from an asthma attack.

Passing the living room on the way to the stove, I heard Juliet and Olivia in animated conversation. Here is what they were saying as I passed by:

"Guess who was at the party last night? Big Al! He was so happy to see me. He took me out to a bar after the party died down and begged me to marry him!"

"Oh, Olivia? I don't know? What do you think?"

"Juliet, dear, dear, sister. I don't know what to tell you. Has he changed or are you just hoping he'll change?"

"He swears he will spend every other evening of the week with me, not his baseball and football buddies, if only I will marry him."

A few weeks later 3 cars left the Karamazov house for Lake Tahoe and another roadside wedding. This time it was not Olivia and George but Juliet and Al. The best photo shows Debbie between the 2 of them in a frilly white dress. Juliet is wearing a lacy pink calf-length party dress with

Al in a rented tuxedo.

Not a big fan of the Karamazov clan, except for Juliet, Al insisted they move out of the family house into his condo. 9 months later little Clark Dupres came into the world. And this one never, ever, introduced himself as Clark Karamazov De Toledo Klein Dupres! Clark Dupres was his whole identity.

But another Karamazov did move into our mansion. Here's how.

"Is this Natalie Klein?"

"This is Marvin Gottleib…the administrator of Pacific Retirement Colony."

"Oh? Is my mother okay?"

"It's not an emergency but we need you to come in and talk to us as soon as possible?"

"I'm teaching a class this afternoon at 2 PM, but can I come around 4:30?...should I tell Elena, my mother, that I'm coming?"

"Better not tell her. After we meet you can certainly see her."

Of course I felt anxious driving the half hour to the luxurious residence. Was my mother sick? I wondered.

I entered the splendid lobby area and was immediately ushered into Mr. Gottleib's office behind the main desk.

The short, fat man in a business suit and tie, came around his large oval desk piled high with files, and shook my hand. Then he walked me over to a plush sofa.

"A cup of coffee, Mrs. Klein?"

"No, thank you. Look Mr. Gottleib, I am very nervous. Please get to the point." I was surprised how shaky my voice sounded.

"I'm sorry to tell you this, but your mother is showing signs of less mental acuity than when she came to us."

"What signs?"

"For example, one of our attendants was crossing the street to get to the coffee shop on the opposite corner. The light turned red, but Elena started walking just the same. A truck made a screeching halt, but it was a close call."

"Oh, that's terrible. My mother must have been terrified."

"No, she wasn't. She didn't even seem aware of the danger."

My mind started spinning. What is he going to say next?

"Something else?" I asked softly.

"Well, yes. Last night, one of the waiters who brings trays up to any guest who can't come down to the restaurant, saw your mother totally nude knocking on the door of someone else's room."

I couldn't help giggling at the image of Elena, naked, but so eager to talk to someone she didn't notice she wasn't wearing anyting.

"We think that you should look at transferring your mother to a more controlled environment."   He picked up a few brochures from the coffee table.

"How much time do I have to decide, Mr. Gottleib? I think my husband will want to discuss this with you. He is older than I am, and always knows more about possibilities.

Checking out some convalescence homes near us where the residents are not able to leave the premises unaccompanied, we didn't like what we saw. The atmosphere was drab and depressing.

After visiting the third of the facilities in the brochures, Reuben came up with this suggestion:

"Natalie, I think you told me your mother has plenty of savings in the bank. Suppose she moved into Juliet and Debbie's former room in our house?"

"How can I take care of her and also teach full-time, Reuben?" I replied glaring at him."

"Well, I can't do it. What would happen if I had a heavy asthma attack and had to go to Emergency?"

"Would Olivia want to take care of her? She's always loved her very much?"

"I couldn't be responsible," Olivia looked panicked at the very idea of it. "I have little Richy, and I don't drive very well, so if Grandma Elena needed to get to the doctor and you were both out of the house, Mom and Dad, what would happen?"

"I see," Reuben stroked his beard thoughtfully. "I have another idea. I just wanted to check these options out first. Suppose Elena hires a nurse's aide type attendant to live with her here?"

After calling Cassandra in San Franciso, to bring her up to date on the problem, which it took us a while to realize was 'dementia', I asked for her advice:

"Cassandra, what do you think of an attendant for our mother in our house?" I called to be sure there would be no "communication" problems later if my twin didn't have any say in this decision. After all, the money for the attendant would be coming out of a possible inheritance for each of us after our mother's death.

"I think it's a terrific idea. I happen to know there is an agency that sends out nursing aides to the elderly who have been trained for this by Mother Teresa's Missionaries of Charity. It's not too expensive either."

Tangent: "What an intervention of God," I thought. "A Missionary of Charity woman!" To understand my reaction you have to know more about the numerous conflicts about money between Reuben and myself. I thought that we should give any money that came in that we didn't really need to charity to help the poor or support Pro-Life help to unwed mothers who might otherwise have abortions.

Reuben's idea, enunciated to friends with literary flair, was that before he was born God saw all the fields of cattle destined by become steaks for himself some day.

"God is disappointed," he would state with a grin, "if I fail to make use of His gifts through miserliness."

Finally we came to a truce with the solution that we would tithe Mother Teresa of Calcutta's order. No chance of money being bamboozled into the pockets of administrators with them, since in India, in solidarity with the poor, the Sisters don't even have toilet paper.

Now one of Mother Teresa's favorite stories is about how on visits to the US she thought we were even poorer than the Asian Indians of Calcutta. Her two examples were that some of us are too poor to even take care of our babies but abort them instead, and that we throw our old folks into convalescent homes not having enough "wealth of the heart" to take care of them ourselves.

And now, as a kind of pay-back, after giving so much money to the starving through Mother Teresa's Sisters, I could get a nurse's aide trained by her Sisters to care for my mother in our home!

LXXX

Within 5 years the Karamazov clan saw 4 deaths.

Let me tell you first about the death of Elena, my mother, the only Karamazov left of the sisters who came to this country from Russia. I sometimes greeted her, lying in her bed most of the day, with the endearment of malinkaya, meaning little one in her long-ago mother tongue.

Even though the death of the elderly infirm is expected, bereavement ministers tell those left behind that it is still always a shock when it comes.

I told you earlier about this wonderful Mother Teresa trained nurse's aide we hired with my mother's funds. Lucia, was a middle-aged Filippino woman living in the US with her extended immigrant family. Apparently members of the Missionaries of Charity in the Philippines found young women in that country, interested in nursing but unable to pursue formal studies, and showed them how to help the sick and aged elderly, especially those close to death.

Lucia stayed on a cot with Elena night and day at our house, with a day to be with her own family on Sunday. After taking care of washing her and administering medicines for her weak heart, Lucia's favorite activity was just to sit with the Bible in her lap, reading aloud comforting passages and singing little Christian children's songs. Imagine my delight to come home from the University to find Lucia and Elena clapping their hands and singing:

"Now we're going to go, to our Father's house, where there's joy, joy, joy!"

In this way, my highly rationalistic mother, was brought in her dementia to a state of childlike trust in God. What a grace!

For me it was a healing time. Elena was too weak to argue with me. So, in role reversal, I was in charge of her, and could set the tone when I came to see her in her room. I would hold her hands affectionately and talk about good memories and pray aloud from the Psalms.

When she stopped wanting to eat, the doctor gathered the adults in the house together, including Cassandra who came down from San Francisco, to confer about a feeding tube. While my sister Karamazov twin thought our mother would probably not want such an intrusive device to extend her life, when asked Elena said simply:

"I would like to live longer if I could with the tube."

Tangent: This was before feeding tubes became a big issue in the Catholic Church. Many doctors and nurses world-wide were into a kind of passive euthanasia by simply letting sick old people die when they lost interest in food. Our Church, however, came out with a document insisting that feeding tubes did not constitute an extraordinary means of keeping people alive, but was a relatively inexpensive and not painful minimum of care.

While Cassandra was visiting, she asked our mother in a gentle voice:

"Mommy, are you afraid of death?"

"A little, but mostly I think of it as a new adventure!" was the surprising answer.

Asked if I could call a priest to hear her confession and administer the sacrament of the sick, Elena agreed.

In a way I deem typical Karamazov style, when I fished around after the priest left about whether this sacrament had been something she found comforting, she replied:

"I was struck by how hard it was for a man as ugly as that priest to lay hands on a woman during face to face confession in a home setting. I might have rejected him!"

Tangent: This sacrament used to be called the Last Rites. Since many Catholics were terrified when a priest was called to the home, because they were afraid it meant certain death, and for other Scriptural reasons, it was decided after Vatican II to call the sacrament instead "the anointing of the sick." Though administered most often when a Catholic is close to death, there are also anointing services in the Church where anyone with a serious illness can receive this sacrament.

Soon after the anointing of the sick, Elena was going into cardiac arrest every few weeks, with emergency resuscitation by para-medics rushing to the house, reviving her and taking her in an ambulance to the hospital. On the last of these incidents, at age 87, Elena Karamazov died in the hospital.

There was a beautiful funeral Mass at the chapel at Ignatius U. Cassandra invited those willing, to dance in a prayerful manner around the closed coffin. Juliet, Elena's favorite grandchild, gave a charming eulogy.

Back in the Karamazov house, however, all hell broke loose. Now, Allan Drury, Cassandra's husband, who attended the Episcopal Church but was also into New Age practices, was the initiator of this conflict. Was it an inspiration of the devil for Allan Drury, Cassandra's husband, to ask the family that evening:

"Why don't you all join me in a séance to see if Elena might have a message for us from "the other side"?

"This is my house, Allan!" roared Reuben. "I forbid you try such a thing in my house and, if you insist, I will throw you out."

Oy veh! Allan swigged a long gulp of vodka, shrugged, and led Cassandra out to the garden. When they came back 10 minutes later Cassandra, always the peace-maker, addressed the waiting Karamazov family:

"Reuben, why don't you play Elgar's Dream of Gerontius instead."

Tangent: This piece composed by the English composer to Cardinal Newman's famous poem was a favorite of ours. It sets to music parts of the Latin Mass for the dead with other lines from Newman's poem.

A year afterwards saw the death of Thelma, grandfather De Toledo's wife with Alzheimer's. There was no funeral but her daughter came down from Canada.

But a year afterwards we were called by the executor of David De Toledo's last will and testament, to tell Cassandra and myself that our father had died suddenly of cardiac arrest. Since he had left each of us as well as his step-daughter a considerable sum we should arrange to meet with him.

Arriving at the house in San Diego was a bitter-sweet experience. Sweet because I was so glad that we had become reconciled after all those years of hurt and separation. Bitter because I had so wanted to help my father find Jesus, his Savior But there was a little sign. Shortly before his death, I was reading a biography of Abraham Lincoln, my father's great hero President. In it I found all these references to how Lincoln loved God even though he didn't go to Church. I put a post-it on each reference and brought it to him. He put it on his desk, but when we came to his house after his death, I found that paperback bio of Lincoln near his pillow!

LXXXI

Exit Dmitri Karamazov/De Toledo/Klein:

As soon as I decided to write this semi-fictional autobiography I started to dread coming to these next chapters. It is about the most terrible suffering of my life and Reuben's life and possibly also, so far, in the lives of his sisters, Olivia and Juliet.

I am praying that after having told this part of our family story so many times, more catharsis and healing will come from putting it in writing.

At 18, Dmitri got a full scholarship to USC, majoring in music. He had been very popular in the Magnet High School. He had a charming Asian ancestry girlfriend. Everyone else but me knew they were having sex even though he continued to come to Church on Sundays and receive Holy Communion. Did he go up for the sacrament just to avoid having to talk to me about the sinful side of his life? Later Reuben admitted he knew about the sex but didn't try to convince him to stop.

Later on I found out that he and his closest High School friends were experimenting with drugs. Also, that he talked to his father about dropping out of Church.

"I don't get much out of it any more, Dad. Do I have to go?"

"Dmitri, wait on this decision. Your mother is about to get a masectomy. This is traumatic. Don't add to her sufferings now by dropping out of Church."

Obedient to Reuben, Dmitri continued to go with us to Mass on Sundays, but instead of sitting with us, he would crouch on the floor at the back of the Church, looking as if he was deep in prayer.

Tangent: Right after my pilgrimage to Medjugorje, I was diagnosed with breast cancer. In those days the word "cancer" seemed much more like a death sentence than now, twenty-five years later. Reuben was very sad. He was always sure he would die first. But he was very supportive of the surgery, reassuring me that he would not be disgusted to see me with one less breast!

Just before the mastectomy, I was in a Church that had a huge crucifix hanging from the ceiling above the altar. Jesus seemed to say to me: "Don't be afraid, Ronda. After the surgery you will look like me with a wound in your side!" This way of thinking about it was a great help getting through the trauma. I was even able to joke about it going around the University saying "Well, you all always thought I was too one-sided (about Catholic teaching) and now God is proving it!" A rabbi, who was teaching Jewish Roots of Christianity, told me:

"Nothing you ever told me about why you became a Catholic impressed me as much as that you are able to joke about losing a breast. Why some of the women in my congregation kill themselves rather than seem mutilated to men!"

Cassandra came for a visit to support me after the operation. She asked if she could kiss my wound. It was such a tender Sisters Karamazov moment.

Studying composition at USC was not what Dmitri thought it would be. The professors were into contemporary cacophonous music on its way to what would be called minimalism. Dmitri's work was modern in tone but much more melodious. He didn't get the praise he was used to at the

High School. He had broken up with his girlfriend, a senior at the Magnet school, who he decided was not deep enough for him. Shortly after performing for the class a piece for cello, a poignant but lyrical requiem, he surprised me one day by begging:

"Mom, I have a huge favor to ask you. Would you be willing to go with me to my favorite mountain? It's in the Malibu State Park, just 30 minutes from our house."

"Of course!"

We had a lovely day climbing the trails around this mountain.

2 weeks later, Dmitri wasn't home at the usual time of 11 PM. Always he told us if he would be out with friends overnight. I walked outside looking to see if his pick-up truck was in the driveway, or thinking any minute he would pull in. I noticed that the little flag on the mailbox was in its upright position signaling the mailman for a pick-up. When I looked in to see what was there I found a note in Dmitri's handwriting.

"I am at my mountain at Malibu State Park."

I went into an anxiety attack. Reuben called the Park. "We are closed at 9 PM every night. If you need to talk to a guard, call…….."

Reuben dialed that number. "By chance have you seen a tan pick-up truck on your grounds, or my son, a short teen, name of David Klein?"

"No! But we'll check and get back to you."

We woke up Olivia to sit by the phone while we raced toward the Park. There was quite a walk on a trail before we reached the security station. Any minute I thought Reuben would have an asthma attack, maybe even fatal, since the air at night in vegetative areas is especially toxic for asthmatics.

Praying constantly on my rosary beads, breathing heavily from the terror, I was glad to finally see a parked security car with a headlight swirling around on top.

"You must be the Klein's. We located the truck high on the mountain, but not yet your son," a man in uniform with a gun in his holster informed us.

Just then we heard the voice of Dmitri coming down a trail toward us. He rushed into our arms and after we all cried with relief, Reuben asked him:

"What was in your mind, my beloved son? Your mother and I were very frightened."

"I was going to leap off the top of a cliff, the one I took you to see, Mom, but I was too afraid. You should lock me up. I must be going crazy."

The security guard had us all go to his desk at the Station and wrote up the incident.

"Mr. and Mrs. Klein, this sort of thing is not infrequent. I could call the local police who would bring him to prison, but if you want to take him to a psychiatrist immediately tomorrow morning, instead, that would be okay."

Since we opted for the psychiatrist, he gave us the name of one in our neighborhood, near my university.

LXXXII

Reuben drove the truck back with Dmitri next to him shaking all over. I drove our car. The next day we got to Dr. Mason on an emergency basis. He talked to Dmitri alone for an hour and then to Reuben separately while I sat waiting with our son.

When they came into the waiting room the doctor repeated his advice to me:

"I recommend that you immediately bring him to a mental hospital. They can do a complete diagnosis. If he doesn't want to go, since he is under 21, you can have the police bring him in handcuffs. The point is he can't be left alone at all until he is sufficiently medicated to relieve his pain…and likely there's no way you could keep him under 24-hour surveillance. Talk it over and let me know what you decide."

It happened that one of Dmitri's favorite movies was "One Flew Over the Cuckoo's Nest," about a very dysfunctional mental asylum.

"I won't go voluntarily, Dad and Mom. I'm not going to the Cuckoo's Nest. I feel much better. I won't try this again. I promise. I think I just need a break from pressures of school."

Since so many of us lived together, it was possible to watch him all day. At night we set him up on a cot in our bedroom.

The next day we brought Dmitri to a psychological counselor at the University for crisis therapy. He got him on Prozac. Even though he seemed depressed, he also seemed peaceful. He especially enjoyed playing with his little nephew Richy-poo. Once when I was alone at home with him, I took him for a walk around the block with our dog.

"Mom, if I come out of this, I want to encourage you more. You think you are a bad Catholic because you are so angry. But I think you are a wonderful Catholic because you are so vulnerable!"

After 3 weeks of home supervision, Dmitri made a proposal:

"I know you're worried sick about me and want to watch me every minute, but this it's driving me crazy to be cooped up here. I am thinking I should change my major from music which isn't working out so well to English. I'm a pretty good writer, and that's so much part of the Karamazov heritage. It would be a breeze."

We check with the counselor who thought it would be okay to gradually let him go out alone for longer and longer times. But one day Dmitri didn't come home as scheduled.

Again the red flag on the mailbox was up even though it should have been lowered after the usual pick up time.

An envelope was addressed in large block letters: "For My Family."

Inside was a letter with these words:

"I have discovered that the fathomless currents of my soul which once overflowed within me to give me new life have now flowed past and have reached the sea, which is death. The very force within me which hitherto brought me rebirth and a glorious bubble of dreams, now turns backwards toward destruction…the only thing left is a fall toward my friend, the end….God has been good to me, for I have found the most beautiful country in all the world on which to lay my head…just North of Malibu State Park there is an arched bridge…I will be carried to the ocean if I am lucky…I am not sad that I never became a man because if I look even fleetingly at the possibility of the future I feel only dread and loathing…

"As a free spirit, wanderer and pilot of my destiny I cry to all you that I love. Farewell, Dmitri."

We called the police. They knew all about that bridge, known as a favorite place for suicides to jump to their death.

Still we hoped and prayed that he had changed his mind. We drove to the bridge to find it cordoned off by police cars. The ambulance had already carried off our son, pronounced dead, to a nearby hospital. There, after they made their medical report to the police, we were allowed to say goodbye to his corpse. He looked beautiful and at peace.

"Jesus, please. You raised Lazarus! Can't You raise my son?"

"The funeral home can call us to get the body," the ER doctor told us.

We called Olivia and Juliet with the terrible news.

I howled, shrieked and wept all the ride home. Reuben turned numb.

Before this I had never seen someone prostrate with grief. When we got home Reuben slumped down in his recliner in the family room and stared into space. Except for going to the bathroom, he stayed this way until after the funeral, with Olivia and I bringing him meals.

Little Richy-poo walked around not understanding the black aura around his home. Occasionally he would ask his grandfather:

"Where is Uncle Dmitri?"

"He left for outer space," Reuben would reply, tears streaming down his cheeks.

Although I never cried so much in my life, it was for me to arrange the funeral and welcome the many guests who streamed through the house. After Mass the next day I accosted Msgr. O'Reilly:

"Before talking to you about the funeral, please, please, tell me exactly what you think? Do we have to believe he's in hell?"

"No, Natalie. Come to my office." That priest who was so strict, but who had brought Reuben into the Church, opened the new catechism and read out to me a passage about how most suicides are so mentally ill that any guilt is mitigated and we can hope that God has mercy on their souls.

"I have something for you. This is called the mercy chaplet. Keep it on you at all times and as the waves of grief pass over your heart repeat "Lord, Jesus Christ, have mercy on Dmitri and on the whole world."

This chaplet has never left my wrist since Dmitri's death 24 years ago. At my daily Mass I always sit next to a replica of the Pieta feeling close to Mary who knew what it was to look upon a dead son's body.

LXXXIII

The Church was packed for the funeral. Besides the family, including Cassandra and Allan, and Reuben's brother, Jacob, with his wife and son, there came many from the University, and many students from Dmitri's High School, including his former girlfriend. Reuben's closest friend, a pianist, played Dmitri's last composition, prophetically called Requiem, as these mourners filled the pews.

Instead of a formal eulogy, Monsignor, contrary to his usual custom, allowed Juliet to read excerpts from Reuben's poem about Dmitri:

> Dmitri, my Dmitri,
> I heard the threatening hoofs,
> Black Rider's (a reference to the Lord of the Rings)
> behind you.
>
> I heard the music pause…stop.
> Each note wrenched out in torment
> Emptied itself in silence.
> You know I was watching
> When the dark world descended full force,

Trying to urge your soul from your body.
I looked into your mirror
As the fuzz touched your cheek
And the knowing look replaced
The innocent sparkle….
Would that I had died instead of you!
Would that you had inherited my life force…!
Had we the power of choice –
20 years of your lovable being
Ending in a constant state of loss,
Or not knowing you at all –
How gladly would we
Pay the fee.
You must know that I take the sacrament
Praying, Jesus,
Cover with Your Body and Blood
The naked soul of my son!"

That evening, Reuben sat in his recliner listening to Elgar's Dream of Gerontius. Olivia and Juliet sat at his feet. Juliet was the spokesperson for them both:

"Daddy, we're afraid you are going to die soon because of this loss. Prove that you love us just as much as you loved Dmitri by willing to live!"

And for their parts, each one conceived another baby that very month.

For my part whenever I met anyone unsure what to do when a beloved person attempted suicide but survived, I would implore them:

"Lock that person up in a mental asylum! Never think that your love will save them! Give God a way to work through the professionals!"

And from God's part, after months of misery and uncertainty, Jesus seemed to tell me: "I let him do it because I knew his pain. He had his foretastes of heaven in the joys of his youth. You will find him in My Sacred Heart."

LXXXIV

Grieving is a long, long, process. Even now, 24 years later there is a dagger in my heart when I think of the suicide of my Dmitri. At the time I found myself a crisis counselor who was an expert for a group called Survivors of Suicide designed to support the families.

"The pain diminishes but at such a slow pace that you can't easily believe it. Like, first month you can think of nothing else. Second month you sometimes think of other things. Third month you think about that death only half the day…" said the woman counselor I visited for about 6 months.

Dr. Maria Gabino gave me books to borrow about suicide. The most helpful was one called *The Enigma of Suicide*, with case studies. It showed how different the reasons for suicide are and that we in the family can never understand because those same reasons wouldn't necessarily lead us to the same deed. Going over the back-story thinking how "if I had only done this…" is futile.

A proof of this came when Msgr. O'Reilly asked if I would talk to a mother in the parish whose son committed suicide shortly before Dmitri did. "My Andy was such a gifted, talented, boy. I keep thinking if only I had been like him and understood him, but I never got past High School…"

she told me with tears in her eyes.

"Oh," I shared, "I have been berating myself for putting him in day-care while I worked and thinking, if only I had been a total stay-at-home Mom, maybe he wouldn't have been so insecure."

A thing I like to say to other survivors who are believers in God is this: "Never picture the person who died floating in space. Picture him or her in the arms of Jesus." This image came from a holy card someone gave me of Jesus holding in his arms the body of a scruffy looking dead teen-age boy.

At a Survivors of Suicide group, it helped me to reach out to a couple whose son was their only child and they with no faith in God or eternal life whatsoever: "Let me tell you my reasons for believing in the immortality of the soul...I totally believe I will see my Dmitri again."

Such witnessing reminded me of this hope again and again.

A priest told me that I would never feel reconciled until I was convinced Dmitri was in a better place. Even if that meant purgatory, I do believe that this is a better place than earth because those in this place of purification know they are saved and on the way to heaven.

C.S. Lewis' famous book *A Grief Observed* detailing how God gradually overcame his skepticism about such doctrines of the faith, after the death of his wife, was also helpful.

Reuben decided to go with me to daily Mass because it was the only at the liturgy of the Mass that he got a sense of hope to see Dmitri again.

We found it was important to anticipate how difficult holidays would be. The gap left by the missing loved one tended to overshadow everything else. It took prayer and effort not to ruin such occasions for all the others in the family. Surprisingly, we found it good to talk about the good times of Dmitri so as not to fixate on that last month as if it were his whole life.

In some situations the parents of a child who commits suicide become estranged to the point of divorce. Each one blames the other.

For a month after Dmitri's death, Reuben and I would lie in each other's arms at night crying. Reuben confided:

"You know, Natalie, I feel the closest to you since our honeymoon. Because you are so close to Jesus, it seemed to me you never came to me with your sorrow, instead rushing to him. Now you need me."

Was I really too proud before to cry on Reuben's warm shoulder? Did the pillow seem a better comforter? I have a feeling that many very religious women and men make this mistake. To be vulnerable with our Savior is easier than being vulnerable with our spouses.

Joy in the midst of suffering! Nine months after Dmitri's death:

Enter: Bob McNamara – Olivia and George's second son

and

Anthony Dupres – Juliet and Al's son.

We cherished the memory of baby Bob in Olivia's arms attending the birth, one week afterwards, of his cousin, Anthony.

And even Reuben came out of his grief to delight in these 2 new grandchildren. We have photos of him with a babe in each arm to prove it.

I don't think Reuben ever did get over the loss of Dmitri. My suicide counselor gave me a book called *The Plight of the Gifted Child.* The idea is that the parents invest enormously in such a prodigy. He or she becomes the sign of our own success. In our case, Dmitri was going to be the next Gustav Mahler for Reuben and the next St. Francis of Assisi for me! Indeed, Dmitri fit pretty well into the Jungian concept of "the eternal child syndrome." Such offspring typically come from families where they were deeply loved. They hate the idea of having to make their way in a world of strangers.

"The degree of grief is proportionate to the degree of dependency," Dr. Mason explained. One rarely feels catastrophic grief over the death of a grandparent because the dependency was minor. With the death of a child it is our dependency on this one to be our "pride and joy," validating our importance as the parents."

I sighed. That seemed pretty true.

"Heh, Natalie, look at this! Only $900 for a week's cruise to Hawaii," Reuben showed me the half page ad in the New York Times. "They fly us to Honolulu and there we get on the boat."

Usually I would reject such suggestions immediately between my miserliness and my desire to give any extra money to the starving. But this time I decided it could be good for Reuben to have a change of scene.

Enamored of the beauty of Europe, I had no great expectations of Hawaii, associated in my mind with mindless surfers and silly women swaying in grass skirts.

Surprise! We had a wonderful time. The ocean and the mountains and the waterfalls were spectacular. Reuben even overcame his fear of asthma attacks: "Maybe we can conceive Dmitri again!"

"I've been post menopausal for 3 years, Reuben!"

"Look at Abraham and Sarah, he was 99 and she 90!"

LXXXV

Exit: Reuben Klein

This is how it happened. Just before his 75th birthday, we were having a family Sunday by the pool. After dinner, suddenly Reuben keeled over. We thought it could be from a recently diagnosed hernia. 5 minutes later he started groaning loudly pointing a forefinger in the air saying "Don't you see him?" (Later with thought maybe he saw a vision of Dmitri.)

The paramedics came quickly, but he had died of cardiac arrest and no resuscitation attempted worked. He was taken anyhow to the emergency. Olivia's husband George and I drove behind the ambulance. I got to see my full-of-life Reuben now a grey corpse lying on a table.

Strangely, when we got home, I grabbed the hem of my bright yellow Hawaiian Muu-Muu and ripped a 6 inch tear. This is an old Jewish custom. Remember how the Jewish leaders ripped their garments when they thought Jesus was uttering blasphemy?

That night Olivia and Juliet slept with me holding each other and crying. The son-in-laws, after dealing with the children's bedding, sat up for awhile drinking and laughing. Remember they were old friends. I excused them in my mind because, after all, Reuben had been a pretty domineering son-in-law.

At the funeral Mass, old, old, Msgr. O'Reilly spoke about Reuben's conversion. Juliet read from a poem she had written and given to her father a few months before he died about his life from childhood onward:

"A baker's son, he smells the fresh-baked loaves,
he sees his father's eyes, tired late at night…
'My son, the one who will grow up to see great wonders
happen…'
A father lost to sea and toil, New York, the East side,
Not much time to hold a little boy…

And Reuben would go to sea,
Leaving the rich warm scent of bread behind,
He grabs at life with both hands
Clutching at the railing,
And feels the sweet, sweet breezes whistle by…
A man can read in books and find a beauty
That can cut his heart in two…
A man can try to write –
One finger poking at the keys…
A man can hear his life in music, birth to death…
And suddenly, a woman, young, naïve.
And suddenly, a light that wasn't there before.
And if you see the gap between my life and yours,
Then bridge it with a ring that screams 'Forever!'…
There are little starlings born within his heart
that take shape on this earth as little girls.
To be Daddy now is sweeter than the world
He held between his fingers not so long before…
Reuben looking at his newborn son,
Incubated, fighting for his life –

His blue eyes pierce the plastic
'You will live!'
And slowly, those unfocused eyes meet his –
a tiny hand lifts up as though to call a toast to life - ...
(and after that child's death)
 A man can look at Jesus in the face,
And lightened by a tiny glimpse of heaven,
Can hear the voice of the Father say
'You are my son, and you will see great wonders, yet,
Believe it, and hold the hands of both your son and mine.'

And so, at age 57 Natalie Karamazov De Toledo Klein, became a
widow.

LXXXVI

I'm sure with the title like the *Sisters Karamazov* you didn't think that after the death of Reuben, Natalie Karamazov just curled up in a ball and hid in the house!

Some of you readers, even widows, may be scandalized by what you read next, but I think truth is important, even if one is a little ashamed of it.

New friends certainly laugh when I tell them about my early years of widowhood.

"After trying to interest 12 different single men in becoming my second husband and being rejected 12 times, I finally decided that I would choose Jesus as my second bridegroom. One of those 'perfect second husbands, checked himself into the hospital to get away from me! I knew Jesus would never reject me!" I report with a grin.

"Actually, think about it? If you had a husband who was 20 years older than you and thought he was dying of asthma every night, wouldn't you be expecting to be a widow? Wouldn't you think about other men who might make nice second husbands?"

I go further to explain:

"There are many single devout Catholic men who don't want to be married at all, but they want some feminine warmth in their lives. They don't want to get into sin, so they like to get close to families where the wife is warm and hospitable and, above all, safe. But, then, if she becomes a widow they run like hell. After all, an unmarried single man of 70 probably didn't want to marry, not just because I was not available."

Then, to top it off, I recount how Olivia said during this time of searching for the perfect holy second husband: "Gee, Mom, we always thought that Dad was the only man in the world who could have lived with you!"

Now, 22 years a widow, I have come around to her point of view. I mean, how many men want a woman with my qualifications:

- Here is a woman who will try to refute every single thing you say she thinks is erroneous with airtight syllogisms.
- Here is a woman who will forget she is cooking burgers on the stove until they become rocks because she is busy writing a book.
- Here is a woman who will chide you for spending a cent on anything that is not absolutely necessary telling you the money belongs to Mother Teresa.
- Here is a woman who thinks a prayer meeting is more fun than a movie.
- Here is a woman who wants to nag her man to get out of denial and, to overcome his faults, to be changed every day into a holier saint.

I'm sure you get the picture. I was not exactly that warm, nurturing, help-mate depicted as the ideal wife in Holy Writ! One of these many single men who rejected me did marry at the age of 60. He married a warm, nurturing help-mate, Charlotte. We remained friends from a distance, but he once told me:

"Think about it Natalie, between you and Charlotte who would make a better wife and who a better friend?"

Among these men were some who were just vague fantasies, but there were others I truly loved. I felt very rejected by these and the hurt was real, even though later, I liked to describe the whole thing with humor.

A basic problem was, as I explained it to a therapist years afterwards:

"I have a gift to see the most wonderful part of anyone I like, men or women. I try not to see whatever would make them unsuitable to be close to me because I am desperate for love. Then I am surprised that the relationship doesn't work."

To this, the counselor responded: "Relationships don't work between a real person and the ideal they have projected onto another person. Only between 2 real persons."

"So with the ones I thought were really holy so that they could make me holier by osmosis, I was just projecting onto them my longing for them to be holy and they weren't?" I really wanted to get to the bottom of this.

"There is holiness in you and holiness in them if they are open to God's grace, but there is also the other part in both of you that is not holy and if you pretend that other bad part isn't there and don't work on that part, then eventually all the negatives clash so badly you can't stand each other."

Tangent: 30 years later I was chatting about this time in my life with a psychologist who suggested to me that I might have unconsciously not really wanted to be married again, so I picked out men to get close to who were exactly the kind that would reject me!!! When I wrote this in my journal 'dialogue' with Jesus, He seemed to say "Can't you see that I "arranged" it that these men would reject you because I wanted you for myself, as a dedicated widow who would have Me as your Second Bridegroom!"

After a year of 'making contact' with these men I thought were truly holier than me and whose companionship would make me holy by osmosis, I had this mystical experience:

I walked into a Church where there was a huge copy of El Greco's

Christ hanging on the wall, with the face El Greco imagined to be on Veronica's veil. It had always been a favorite of mine. Google El Greco - Veronica's Veil to see it for yourself.

As I was staring at the picture, I had an interior vision. That's where you don't see something outside with your eyes, but somehow inside your mind but very sharp, not like some daydream.

In the vision, the same El Greco head of Christ was on top of the rest of the body, and He was wearing a bridegroom's tuxedo. He looked at me with those beautiful huge Spanish-Jewish eyes, and He said in my heart:

"Be mine!"

Since the image of Jesus in a contemporary tuxedo was so comical, I wouldn't have paid much attention to this seeming interior vision, except that in the vestibule of the Church was a Catholic newspaper rack, and as I walked out of the chapel in a daze, I saw the title of an article "Consecrated Widowhood being Revived in the Church."

The article told about how consecrated widowhood was the first type of vow in the early Church, before even orders of nuns. Gradually this way of life morphed into religious communities of sisters. But now, some bishops were consecrating widows to serve the Church, living mostly in their families or by themselves. They made private promises not to re-marry, each with her own individually devised rule of life, devoting themselves to Catholic ministries.

After reading this article, I walked back into the church proper and sat down near the El Greco Veronica's Veil Jesus:

"Should I look into this as a way to be Your bride, my beautiful Jesus?"

"Yes," He seemed to reply.

When I asked Jesus why He wanted to appear to me in a tuxedo, he seemed to answer, "I wanted to be sure you understood that I wanted you to be My bride. Without the tuxedo you would easily have just thought that after all those rejections, I was just telling you that I loved you, not that I wanted you to enter into a new way of life in a consecrated way."

Now, today, in the present having written all this last night, I woke up thinking Jesus was telling me this:

"I didn't like so much your caricature of yourself in that writing yesterday. That is a form of sarcasm! You especially left out all the good that these same men loved about you, such as how affirming you are of the good in others, including them!

With the part about Me in that interior vision, it is hard to work with you, My children. You see me as exalted and sublime as in an icon and then you feel distanced. So I show myself more on the human side to you and then you doubt it is Me. On this book write down what you want to first and then it will be good to let Me help you edit it. I had the same problem on earth. Some were afraid to draw near because I seemed too sublime. Some leaders, on the other hand, didn't see how I could be divine if I was eating with tax-collectors and sinners."

LXXXVII

Enter: The Big Los Angeles Earthquake

It was a year after Reuben's death. In the middle of the night everyone in our house was woken up by the shaking and rumble noises of an earthquake. I bumped into 5-year old Richy in the hall leading to his parents' bedroom when another tremor coursed through the house.

We found the others huddled together with little Bobby in the arms of his father on the king-size bed and Olivia clinging to both of them.

5 more tremors later there was a pause.

"Mom, turn on the TV just in case there's already a report," George ordered me in his usual calm voice.

Contrary to our expectations, the TV was still working. "A 7-point earthquake hit the central LA area 15 minutes ago" were the words gliding across the bottom of the screen. Stay on this station for more information. Emergency hot-lines are being set up. Don't call 911. Here is the number to call if you need immediate help: 800-_____.

Another tremor and Olivia, always since the trauma of that rape subject to panic attacks, began to shake. I held her tight in my arms while George, carrying the baby, walked around the house to see about damage.

The most obvious result of the quake was kind of humorous. The day before, George decided to repaint the kitchen cabinets. He took off the large doors of these 8 storage facilities and left them on the back porch to work on the next day.

So when the quake shook the house, hundreds of cans and jars "leaped" out of the shelves onto the kitchen floor. What a mess!

The phones were also still working. When we called Juliet and Al they said damage was minimal in their more southern part of LA.

A daily communicant, in spite of the quake, I decided to go to the Church. On the way out, George handed me $10 to replenish his stock of beer at the liquor store. At the Church there were big announcements taped to all the doors:

"CHURCH CLOSED. NO MASSES UNTIL FURTHER NOTICE TO AVOID DANGERS FROM QUAKE DISASTER - BY ORDER OF THE ARCHDIOCESE."

Disappointed I drove back home. Remembering George asking me for that favor, I stopped at the liquor store. There were many cars double and triple parked in front to the store. The door was locked but employees were handing out liquor for cash through the holes in the broken front windows.

"Heh, George," I said, handing him his beer, "I guess in Los Angeles, in an emergency, booze is deemed more necessary than Holy Communion."

By the next day the Church set up outdoor Masses in parks.

None of us had ever been in a quake like this one. We certainly had no idea how frightening would be the after-shocks. Every hour or so, came a series of these, much less powerful than the first ones, but scary because our bodies were already traumatized.

After a week, Cal Tech resumed business, with employees and students required to come back.

"Don't go," screamed Olivia, when she saw George packing up his briefcase.

"I can take care of her today, George, but tomorrow I need to be back at Ignatius U." I reassured my son-in-law.

Easier said than done! Olivia brought her computer and the children into the bedroom. Whenever there was an after-shock she dragged the kiddies under a strong table. I went back and forth bringing food. But when an after-shock came along, there she was again, under the table shaking.

That evening we piled into the van for dinner at the Dupres' home. The purpose was a summit meeting:

Olivia: "I can't stand this. It's the last straw. I want to move away from this horrible city right away."

Juliet: "No, you can't leave me here. We're twins. The Sisters Karamazov have to be together forever!"

George: "Here is what I am thinking. You know I got this huge advance to write a book on computer engineering. Suppose I quit Cal Tech, we move away, and I finish the book somewhere else where there are no earthquakes. Afterwards Olivia and I could both do computer work from wherever we are, contract style."

Al: "It's a little risky, isn't it, George. I mean I know we both hate working for Cal Tech, but we get pretty hefty pay and benefits, also. I wouldn't rush into this."

Natalie: "What happens to me in this scenario?"

Juliet: "You can live with us!" laughing with joy.

Al: "Let's talk about that another time, Juliet," with cold anger written all over his face.

Doing things slowly is certainly not Karamazov style. By the next day Olivia had a realtor over to work on selling the house.

"You have to realize, Mrs.McNamara, that because of the quake this house is now worth $100,000 less than it would go for last week!"

"I don't care. Put it on the market immediately. We gotta get out of here fast."

These plans motivated me to put through a call to the Dean of Liberal

Arts at Franciscan University of Steubenville.

Tangent: Some 15 years ago, a small Franciscan College in Ohio was taken over by charismatic leaders: Laymen and Franciscan Friars. They turned it from being a "football" school to a model institution with students, mostly kids of charismatics, living in dorms in groups with prayers instead of partying being the norm. Some of my favorite students from Ignatius U., having earned Ph.D.'s in philosophy in the meantime, where teaching there. I had always wished I could be part of that faculty but what with Reuben's asthma problems, we couldn't even consider moving back to the cold winters of the Eastern part of the US.

After praying about it, I soon put through the call: "Hello, dear James. Guess what, I am thinking of quitting Ignatius U. and applying to teach at Franciscan. Can you get me hired?"

"Oh, Natalie, that's super. I'll start the wheels turning."

Two months later saw the McNamara's in their SUV with a U-Haul attached on the way to Sedona, Arizona.

"Sedona, Arizona?" Cassandra called me when she heard the news. "How come?"

"A month ago Olivia and George got in the SUV with the children and started going East looking for a beautiful place to move to. You remember, George has that contract for a book, so they could live anywhere."

"I've heard of Sedona. That's the place with the red rocks, famous, a tourist attraction. So that's where they're moving?" Cassandra's seemed excited.

I bet she's already planning trips to visit them, I thought.

"They put a down on a large adobe type house." I added.

"But you work here in Los Angeles. What are you going to do?"

"Oh, with all the confusion here I forget to tell you. I was hired at Franciscan University of Steubenville to teach there."

"Where would you live?"

"They said I could live in a room in the dorm, like a Dorm Mom, until I have time to look around for my own place."

"Hmmmmm!" Cassandra sounded sad. "Part of the reason I agreed to move to California from NYC was to be closer to you and the family. Now there's only Juliet left."

I realized that I had so many difficulties with Cassandra about church matters that I hadn't even thought about this part of my move.

LXXXVIII

Planning the move from the McNamara house in Los Angeles to one room at Franciscan University in Ohio led to other decisions.

The idea of becoming a Consecrated Widow went on the back burner with the earthquake. Or, did I really not act upon it because I was still dreaming of perfect second husbands?

Packing boxes for the move, looking at my colorful Hawaiian Muu-Muus hanging in the closet, I found I didn't want to bring them after all. In the rule of life I had sketched out for Natalie Karamazov Klein, Consecrated Widow, with a view to showing the plan to the Archbishop, there was a part about dressing simply, wearing only secondhand clothing. Now, cutting loose from most of my possessions, an image flashed through my mind of the cheap blue denim jumpers that so many home-school teenaged girls wore. You could buy them at the thrift shops for $5 a piece!

One of my last trips in the car I would give to Juliet when I left Los Angeles was to the local Good Will. There I bought 3 blue jumpers with different styles, 3 white blouses, and 3 blue sweaters. The next day I loaded the car with most of my previous garments and donated them to the same Good Will. When I got to Franciscan, my former students thought I looked like an Amish grandma.

Just before leaving on the plane for Ohio, I happened to run into a former spiritual director of mine in the faculty dining room at Ignatius U. This Jesuit priest had been away for 5 years getting an STL in Rome.

I asked him about world-wide developments on Consecrated Widows in the Church after that hiatus of so many centuries.

"It's slow going, Natalie. I know the canon-lawyer working on it at the Vatican. There are several reasons why they are bringing it back only gradually. One is the issue of women deaconesses."

"Oh, women deaconesses! I could be interested in that."

"No, you don't understand. The women who are dreaming of being deaconesses think that these women were like deacons, preaching to the people. Deaconesses in the early Church helped take care of orphans, like the consecrated widows, but basically they were there to minister only to women. For example, in baptismal rites the converts were dipped nude into the large fonts. The deaconesses held the women behind curtains and the priest reached his hand in between the flaps of the curtains to pour water over the nude women!"

"I see. I am sure no one wants to bring that back!" I laughed.

"So Rome is hoping that starting a ritual for Consecrated Widows won't encourage those petitioning to be deaconesses."

"So, just the same, if I feel called to be a Consecrated Widow, I would go to the Bishop?" I asked, after sketching out for him my experience with the El Greco Veronica's Veil picture of Jesus and His seeming desire to be my second Bridegroom.

"I suggest you wait awhile. Once you get to Franciscan, why don't you make up a rule of life and bring it to a priest and try it for a while. You could call yourself a dedicated widow in the meantime."

Juliet wanted to take me out for a farewell dinner before my leave-taking.

"But, Mom, please don't wear one of those awful blue jumpers with your big crucifix around your neck. It makes me look like the illegitimate daughter of a monk-ess!"

As you can see, my plan engendered little enthusiasm in the family.

And so, for the first time all the generations living of Sisters Karamazov's soon would be scattered: Steubenville, Ohio; San Francisco, California; Sedona, Arizona and Juliet left in Los Angeles.

It took a long time for any of us to see how radical this break would be for us. Symptoms there were, but their cause was not recognized for a long time. For example, both Olivia and Juliet, in effect, put much more pressure on their husbands to become surrogate twins, even with a life-style resembling twins in the womb!

How so?

When I came back at Christmas to visit Juliet and her family, I found Juliet and Al spending most of their time in their large bed together. Al had since also quit Cal Tech. He was doing computer work on contract out of the home. Juliet was also working computer from home. They both had lap tops set up on the bed. They sat up side by side, their backs supported by many large pillows. Hanging from the ceiling was a large TV screen on which they watched their favorite shows intermittently while doing their programming jobs. Little Clark would play on the bed, protected by a net draped over the four pillars holding up a canopy! When Debbie came home each day on the school bus she would join them at a desk with her computer set up for homework.

The surrogate twin set-up of Olivia and George was less dramatic but just as tight. They sat at computer desks side by side with baby Bobby suckling at Olivia's breast as she worked. In this way George was rarely out of sight of his "twin" Olivia.

I was very happy that my daughters, and many other women, through the computer industry, had found a way to do interesting work and still be home-mothers!

Both my daughters wore casual short flimsy clothes at home, but when guests came, especially male guests of any age, or when on the rare times they emerged from the "wombs" they had set up into the outside world, they would dress glamorously with high, high heels, tons of make-up, and revealing tight blouses. Even though I disapproved of such attire, I had to admit that the contrast between their home look and their public look, would make most on-lookers vote for the public look.

And I, Natalie? Even though Cassandra and I were never as close as Juliet and Olivia, I was always trying to make new women friends I met at Franciscan into surrogate twins. They had to agree with me about ev-erything, from simplicity of life to militant proclamation of Catholic truth. One candidate who seemed ideal, a charismatic psychotherapist, teaching at the University, in her final rejection speech said:

"Natalie, I really love you, but I don't want to be your 24/7 twin. Suppose we just meet at lunch once a month."

I had arrived at Franciscan late the evening on a dark August night. My 6 boxes of possessions were waiting for me outside my dorm room. My former student, now Dean, Jim and his wife, Cathy, helped me unpack.

"See you at the Mass tomorrow at noon, Natalie."

I had purposely left the drapes open to let the sunrise greet me so I woke up at 7 AM. On the way to the cafeteria for breakfast, I passed the round church building. Spontaneously I lifted my arm in praise and sang the joyful charismatic song, "Let the Fire Fall."

At noon, even though it was not Saturday evening or Sunday when good Catholics always go to Mass, the church was packed. That service lasted a good hour with joyful praise and worship songs, a dynamic pas-sionate sermon, climaxing with raised arms and thunderous praise at the Consecration of the bread and wine into the Body and Blood of Christ. Before and after, folks lined the walls waiting for confession administered by Franciscan Friars.

It felt as if I was in heaven. Here I was with my second bridegroom, Jesus, at a place where He was clearly the King. I was loyal to the teach-ings of the Church, charismatic, and relatively poor.

Relatively poor? Even though there were no fancy dwellings and the male students wore jeans, with most of the females wearing, guess what?, blue denim skirts or jumpers, still the students paid a whopping $15,000 a year for tuition, room and board. This usually mounted up to some $60,000 in student loan debts upon graduation!

Looking back, I would have to say that my first day at Franciscan was the peak, followed by a slow descent from heaven to purgatory until I left a year and a half later.

LXXXIX

Each time I go back to that time at Franciscan when I was a recent widow, 59 years old, I see the reasons it didn't work differently.

At this point in my life I see that the failure was God check-mating me on the idea that it was Reuben and child-raising that made me unhappy. I always thought that if I could just go to Holy Mass, pray, and do my teaching, writing, and speaking, I would be happy.

When my middle-aged friends at Franciscan talked about their marital and family problems, I would joke "You know, I have found since becoming a widow, that the absence of frustration is not joy!"

Now I had none of the annoyances of dealing with a personality as opposite to mine as Reuben's was. I had none of the burden of housewifery. I had no children, little or adult, to worry about. And, instead of being happy, I was mostly lonely and miserable!

Someone explained it this way: When your spouse is alive you have to cope with his or her faults which victimize you in little and/or big ways. But when they are gone you miss all the virtues you took for granted!

In this case what I missed the most of Reuben and Olivia and Juliet was their love of life. Even groaning under the cross of asthma, as I used to tell those who never met him, he could get excited just about walking into Denny's! Bubbling delight in their children was manifest each day in the lives of Juliet and Olivia.

My love of truth and of my work, and even my joy in receiving the love of Jesus in a new way as a dedicated widow, didn't quite fill the hole in my heart from the absence of my family. But, at the time, I would never, ever, have admitted that this was the problem. I was too proud of my independent new identity to think I needed anyone but Jesus!

"You don't sound so happy, Mom," said Olivia, eyes full of empathy, on my visit to their new house in Sedona, Arizona, during the first Christmas break after my move to Franciscan.

"It is such a joy to be with you all who knew Reuben and Dmitri."

It hadn't occurred to me before, that Olivia and Juliet's faces being so similar to Dmitri's made him seem still alive for me.

On the last evening before returning to Ohio, Olivia got me alone in their guest room:

"You could always move in with us, Mom. I'd love it."

"Thanks, darling, but I couldn't think of that. Don't you need to be alone with your husband after all these years of extended family?"

By the following Christmas I was back living with them, contributing my widow social security to their income. George was happy about that, since living on the royalties from his book and contract computer work brought in much less money than he had thought it would.

Now, in the bosom of the family, all cozy, how I missed teaching. True, Pastor in the parish was very happy to have someone with all my credentials to help with initiation of converts and to do workshops on the saints, and on prayer in daily life. But this was not the same at all, as the teaching students who were required to read the books I chose and to talk about them in class. Any hopes I had that Olivia would want to come back to the Catholic Church were squashed living with her again and finding her even more unwilling to come with me to Holy Mass except at Christmas and Easter. Both Richy and Bobbie were baptized and came with me on

Sundays because, as she put it:

"Even though I don't want to go, I want them to have the experience of the magical feeling of something beyond that you get as a child if you are Catholic." This attitude caused me much grief. I couldn't see why anyone would not want to know Jesus in the ways He had "invented" to be close to us such as by giving us His Body and Blood in Holy Communion.

Besides, the atmosphere in Sedona was strange. Even though most of the people who own homes in this town were retired main-line Christians, every weekend the motels were filled with New-Age tourists. This was because it had become the center of those convinced that it was the end of civilization as known in the West for 2,000 years. This was all to be replaced by a mystical way of life that some thought would be brought to us by aliens from outer-space. Such folk had actually built a landing strip on the top of one of the red rock plateaus for the touchdown of rockets from other planets!

Sedona was also the headquarters of the Satanist movement. The highways in and out of Sedona were lined with shops selling tarot cards, hexes, hosting workshops on new-age techniques and welcoming tourists to séances!

It was not uncommon for tourists to fall in love with the beauty of the red rocks, buy a house, move, and then, after a few years, find the atmosphere heavy and unbearable. Walking with little Richard, now 4-years old, on the trails up and down between the rock formations, we would see piles of sticks and ashes and dead birds or rodents, used for Satanic rituals.

Meanwhile, George was drinking more and more. Because he never acted like a drunk none of us paid much attention. Only in hand-sight did we see that the alcohol covered over his problems so that his happy-go-lucky calm exterior was paid for at quite price.

"Natalie, you won't believe this," a Catholic friend told me during a visit to her home in Sedona. "My son is a priest who runs a small college in Texas. Their philosophy professor was diagnosed with cancer and has to give up teaching, at least temporarily. My son happens to have read some of your books. When I told him we went to the same church here in Sedona he said, "How I wish we could get such a professor to replace the one whose leaving!"

"Why don't you call him this minute? I might want to try," I exclaimed.

A month later Natalie Karamazov De Toledo Klein was on the plane going to Austin, Texas, as a substitute philosophy teacher.

Tangent: When married I had always thought Reuben was the adventurous unstable one because he had been a seaman, then a book salesman, and loved to travel. But now I came to realize that his need for my stable income after he became disabled with asthma had held me down from a much more extreme form of ditziness.

Basically, if you have social security and you like best to live in one room, there is no incentive to put down roots anywhere. As soon as the negatives begin to outweigh the positives, you can just pick up and try something that sounds better.

XC

When I decided to write this semi-fictional autobiography I was thinking there would be many funny chapters about all the groups I tried to belong to after I left Los Angeles, detailing the foibles, defects of character … of the members of each of these religious communities.

But, now that I am up to writing about this part of my life, still on-going, it seems as if the Holy Spirit is telling me not to recount the story of each attempt and its end. Sorry, dear reader, you won't get to read such juicy stories!

Instead I need to just pull out of my memory what I learned from these experiences about my own foibles and defects of character from mentors along the way. Some of these were spiritual directors others were psychological counselors.

I always witness to how much such counselors, throughout my life, have helped me. This is because there are some Catholics who think that all counselors are crazed and dangerous people! I have found that even atheist psychologists can give me good insights and advice. No one would say that if they pray more, they don't need to go to a doctor for a broken leg. By analogy, we should not think, in my opinion, that when we are emotionally broken we only need to pray more but never go for professional help!

So, what was some of this good advice?

"You have such a great need to belong that you desperately try to fit into communities, but you are not suited for immersion in groups... even the Church documents say that to be called to consecrated communal means to put community above your work. But you give so much energy to your work that you don't belong in community."

When I heard this I thought of Alyosha Karamazov. If you read the book he starts off as a star novice in a monastery, but Dostoevsky brings him out to minister to others in a unique type of leadership.

"Because you are Jewish, but living in a Catholic cultural milieu you are always anxious. Most Jews like to openly debate and express their emotions bluntly. The Irish Catholics running many of the groups you look into come from a culture of "behind the hedge where the English can't know what you are thinking and doing." Not knowing what they are thinking makes you anxious."

"Remedy?" I asked.

"Be close to friends in sub-groups, and don't try to pry out the motives of the leaders. Be closer to Christ, your bridegroom, so that He can give you trust in the midst of inevitable uncertainty."

"So, maybe I am supposed to start my own school or community?" I would ask from time to time after another failure to fit in with one of 10 groups I tried.

"You could be such a leader if you didn't want everyone to be your clone!"

"Ah, the twin thing?"

"Yes. But also you are not very authoritative. Authoritarian is bad, but authoritative is absolutely necessary."

"Oh, because I am always needing to lean on men since my father left when I was so young?"

"Probably."

My own best insight into what made my life so stressful and kept me gyrating from manic-like joy to angry desperation I have already mentioned, but I am going to put it down again. It is universal enough that many people laugh with recognition when I talk about it:

Karamazov, drama-queen style, I want to be the heroine of the drama of my life. You others must agree to be secondary characters or walk-on cameos to enhance my role. If you neglect or refuse to do this I will show my anger, or reject you by fleeing from your company!

Remedy? Jesus seems to tell me I need to let Him be the hero of the drama.

(Note to editor, remove above dark line and this next one which I can't seem to remove.)

If I am humble enough to be the child of the hero, Him, I can be happy in a new, deeper, Christian way.

I will now put in here shorter advice I have taken with me over these years:

"Speculating all the time about the future and scheming to avoid suffering is ego-centric. It's as if what you do could control the future. The best is to trust in God for what you can't change and expect His plans of love will get you through no matter what."

A related piece of advice from another mentor: "Don't exaggerate about how you were so angry at Reuben that you wanted to kill him, proven by your fantasies about putting a knife into his throat when he was sleeping but you wouldn't try because he would have woken up and killed you instead. If you had really wanted to kill him you could have done it with pills in his coffee! Don't say your marriage was a failure since you are sure you helped Reuben get to heaven!"

(About fear for my children and blaming myself about Dmitri's suicide) "Did you think you could exempt your children from suffering? Could Mary, the mother of Jesus?"

"Instead of trying to psychoanalyze everyone you meet, a defense mechanism, go into each situation naively asking simply to be an instrument of God's love!"

"In your quiet prayer time over and over again say 'I surrender my whole self to You, my Jesus,' 'Into Your heart I surrender my future,' 'Into Your heart I surrender everyone in my family.'"

"If you love St. Teresa of Avila's famous words 'God alone is enough!' why do you get upset at the thought of losing anything in this world?"

XCI

Help with the pain and stress of my life during this period after Reuben's death also came from a group I joined to deal with anger and fear called Recovery, International. Not 12 Step, it was founded in the 1940's before 12-Step took that name. You can google it to find out the whole history of this extraordinary method for group-therapy founded by Dr. Abraham Low, a Jewish psychiatrist practicing in Chicago throughout the mid-20th century.

We meet face-to-face, once or more each week, or on conference calls, or on-line. Readings from the brilliant insights of the founder are followed by a tight rule for sharings of how we handled problems between meetings using specific phrases developed in this program, similar to 12 Step sentences such as "Let go, let God."

I belonged to Recovery, International as a participant or a leader for more than 20 years, finally stopping when I had managed to cut down 5 angry fits a day to 1 a week! The family loves that I got this help!

Here are some of the phrases we use with short explanations by me:

Accepting the average vs. exceptionality
We want to be exceptionally great, successful, holy, but we would

be better to accept that we are average in our attempts and failures. Not to have no higher goals but to forgive ourselves and keep going vs. giving up in self-disgust.

Comfort is a want, not a need

We have to plug along even when things aren't perfect.

Distressing but not dangerous

Frustration doesn't mean danger. We shouldn't make mountains out of molehills. Everything isn't a 911 as hysterical Karamazov women tend to think it is!

Don't take our dear selves too seriously – humor is your best friend.

How contrary to Karamazov drama-queen is this.

Excuse vs. accuse

How like Christian forgiveness this is. We should be happy to excuse vs. exalting in accusations.

Expect frustrations every five minutes and you won't be disappointed

Easiest to remember this pithy, humorous, slogan. Repeating it keeps us from imagining perfect days and relationships and then being disappointed.

Feelings should be expressed but temper should be suppressed

We learn how to speak the truth with love as the New Testament also teaches vs. raging.

Mental health is a business, not a game

We can't just rush through the agenda of our day and think that anger, fear and depression don't matter as long as we succeed. We need to work hard at mental health.

Take a secure thought

For members of the group who are not religious this could be something like all things pass away. For the religious ones trust in God is the best secure thought as in "God has gotten me through a lot worse, I should trust him about this problem.

The most important one for me of these phrases from Recovery International was avoiding what Low called symbolic victory. It is a subtle concept, but with a good example I think you will get it.

When I think I can't win in a battle of any kind from waiting on a line or in traffic to forcing my spouse and kids to do things "my way," I feel weak and powerless. But when I yell, I feel strong, on top, putting them down.

But it is not a real victory. Nothing changes except I feel terrible and the victims resent me.

Example: I can't get my daughters to come back to the Church. I feel weak in the face of their rebellion against the best thing I ever gave them. Then I yell at them, as in "Heh, look at the word Christmas. Does it mean the commercial holiday you love indulging in, or Christ-Mass, so why don't you go to Mass with me?"

This is not a victory, because instead of making them want to go to Holy Mass it just makes them defensive. So, we need to avoid symbolic victories in favor or accepting when we can't win, and praying in hope for good outcomes in the future.

In talks I give about anger-management I like to give this even more common example:

"You are driving down the highway. Another car is doing 75 miles an hour in a 60 mph zone. Even though it is winter and your windows are closed, you curse the other driver as you try to pass ahead of him…How is this curse a win? It is no real victory at all. But it is a symbolic victory. That is because when you curse you are the seeming superior one damning another person to hell."

Now learning to avoid symbolic victories is not a matter of a one-time insight into this mechanism. It takes years of practice to overcome such a habit.

Whenever I lapse into sarcasm, symbolic victory style, I try to stop and think: what is the fear underneath the anger? Harking back to the previous examples, do I fear that my adult children will wind up in hell for flauting the desire of Jesus that they be with Him in Church? Shouldn't I trust that since they are such incredibly loving women Jesus will apply to them the same words He uttered to another woman: "Love covers a multitude of sins"?

What fear underlies cursing a speeding driver? Of course, I am afraid he will cause an accident and others will be killed. Even if nothing I can do will stop him, are the lives of the others in his path not in the hands of God? Why not pray he slows down or gets off at the next ramp instead of cursing him?

XCII

"The ambulance just came to take Allan to the hospital," sobbed Cassandra calling me from San Francisco.

"If you need me I'll come on the next plane," I reassured her.

Alan was on the last month of chemo for lung cancer, probably caused by many former decades of smoking, even though he had given cigarettes up 5 years ago.

"Thanks, Natalie. I'll keep you posted. You might like to know that he told me that after years of doubt about whether the resurrection of Jesus was literal or just some kind of Jungian archetype, he had some kind of mystical experience, and he now feels peace about dying."

"I'll pray incessantly, dear Cassandra. How are you doing?"

"I'm shaking all over…goodbye, my ride to the ER just drew up to the curb."

A few days later came the call.

"He's gone, Natalie. Can you come?"

It was ten years after the death of Reuben, but flash-backs of that fatal evening came back on the plane trip from Texas to California, opening my heart to my twin in a special way.

Juliet was already with Cassandra having flown in from Los Angeles to help her with all the details.

"Alan wanted to be cremated, Mom," Juliet told me on the way from the airport to the Drury house. "Of course, Cassandra's parish friends and those from Allan's Episcopal parish are planning to be at the funeral and maybe even at the crematory before."

"How is Cassandra taking it?" I asked.

"Every now and then she pauses in her constant activity and goes to a kind of altar she made on the mantelpiece with photos of Allan, candles lit round the clock there also...and cries. I hold her..."

"Yes, she brings in beauty to the worst moments, Juliet."

It was good to be with my twin, as a comforting presence, at her the worst time of her life.

The most horrific moment came at the crematory. None of the close family members, and friends had ever been inside such a place. Usually the funeral home takes care of all this and then presents the vase with the ashes to the church. But Cassandra thought that seeing Allan's body laid out would be a good time for a circle dance honoring this body for the last time, before turning to celebrating his soul at the Episcopal funeral the next day.

I looked at the still body of Allan, usually thought of as my 'enemy,' and felt sadness that he was no longer leaping about in the manic way he exhibited when he was still a heavy drinker. This sight I hadn't had for a while since, after giving up smoking, he had diminished alcohol intake and was more sober when we visited them.

Seated around the body laid out on a table in a white shroud, New-Age friends of Allan intoned "Om" in mantra fashion. An Episcopalian read the passage from St. Paul about the resurrected body that would be all light and agility. Then Cassandra led us in a circle around Allan's body.

An employee of the crematory came in and announced:

"Now we will be wheeling the body into the room with the furnace. Most families leave at this point, but if you want to, you can follow the stretcher into that room."

It Cassandra had known what it would be like, she would never have opted to process dancing with the body to the furnace room. But she was gearing herself up to face the last time she would see that beloved body of her husband, and just followed the attendants waving the rest of us to join her.

Both of us Karamazov twins gasped when we entered the inner sanctum of the crematory. It looked like something from the Holocaust. Auschwitz? I grabbed Cassandra who looked as if she would collapse with horror. Everyone else in the group surrounded the two of us, closely entwined in each other's arms.

Abruptly, an attendant opened the door of a huge black oven. Then two of them shoved Allan's body in and

"Clank" went the door.

We rushed back to the room where we had left our coats.

"It's awful to end this way! Why don't we sit down quietly for a few more minutes and anyone who wants to could share a memory of Allan."

A neighbor delighted us with this story:

"One night I heard a knock at the door. It was already 1 AM, but my wife and I were up late watching an old film on TV. Before opening the door, you know it's not that good an area we live in, I called out to see who it was. Seeing Allan's face through the peep hole on the door, I opened to let him in. There was Allan stark naked with a bottle of vodka in his hand and a big smile on his face."

Even Cassandra had to laugh at this image.

Then Juliet read the famous poem of John Donne 'Death be not Proud', she had planned to recite at the funeral.

An unexpected conflict broke out on the way back to the house. I was in a van with Cassandra and Juliet. The driver was the man from Allan's church who had read St. Paul to the group around Allan's body.

"I wanted to affirm you for reading that New Testament description of the resurrected body. That could help the New Agers there to see the treasury of hope Christianity holds out to us."

Cassandra turned toward me in the back seat. "Natalie, why did you say that? It sounds as if you think that New Age people are going to hell and need us to save them!"

She pursed her lips and turned her head toward the window.

I muttered, "When people say it doesn't matter what you believe since all roads lead to heaven, I always say "How can you know Jesus and not want everyone to know Him?" Trying to get a symbolic victory?

By dinnertime Cassandra was her sweet peace-maker self again, making sure Juliet served me seconds on my favorite foods.

XCIII

Exit: George McNamara from the Home of Olivia and the Children

Olivia and George always seemed to me to get along much better than Juliet and Al, what with Al's passion for baseball leaving Juliet alone a lot of the time.

This all changed between Olivia and George shortly after the birth of the twin boys, Leonard and Vince.

Away teaching in Canada at the time of their birth, when I came for a visit to admire my darling new grandbabies, already six-months old, I heard this conversation.

"Olivia, this thing with working contract at home just doesn't cut it. We're maxed out on the credit cards and, without medical benefits, all we need is one more emergency and we'll be in the poor house."

"What's the alternative, George," Olivia asked.

"I've been offered a job at a big Hotel in town. They want to build a miniature golf course in the back of the hotel and triple their income from guests and tourists passing through."

"So they want a literal rocket scientist to do this?" Olivia mocked.

"They do. And this is why. They came up with a plan to build the scenes around the holes to be exact replicas of the red rock formations people come to Sedona to see! For this they want scientific accuracy."

"What do they pay?"

"A whopping $75,000 for the year of the construction, and then a big commission on profits."

The next day the minute George went off to the interview, Olivia grabbed me.

"Mom! If he takes that job I'll be alone all day! I can't stand it. He mustn't take it."

"Well, sweetie, if you'd pray more you'd have Jesus and you wouldn't be alone...besides you have the darling babies."

George took the job and the solution Olivia took for her loneliness was alarming. You'll see why.

The next summer when I came, besides the twin babies hitched to her breasts most of the day, Olivia had another appendage: a cell phone glued to her ear.

"Say hello to Thomas in England, Mom."

"Hello! I'm Olivia's mom, Natalie. Who are you?"

"I'm a friend from her poetry board...on-line..." came a voice with a mellifluous English accent, "and you must be Natalie Karamazov De Toledo Klein."

"Olivia told you our story?"

"Yes. We talk a lot."

Olivia grabbed the phone. "Tom, call ya back later."

Eyes blazing with excitement, Olivia settled the twins comfortably for their nap on her chest, and informed me:

"He's wonderful. He's the only poet ever to understand my poems!"

"So what does he do, just write poems and talk to you?" I asked curious and increasingly wary."

"He works part time at night. His father is a military caterer and he goes in at night and sorts out the provisions so he can write poetry during the day..."

"Religious? Catholic? Married?"

"He's very spiritual in the kind of way I am, but he's a former Catholic in terms of going to church, like me. He's single, younger, 30."

After putting the sleeping baby boys in their cribs, Olivia made us coffee and continued her narrative:

"Now, here's the problem. George hates this. Last night he laid down the gauntlet:

"It's him or me. I will always love you, Olivia, but I'm not going to that damned hotel working my ass off with my wife flirting with some man she's never met on the phone all day. Make up your mind. Drop him or I'm divorcing you."

"So what did you say to that?"

"I called Juliet. She says that it's a known thing that when people who get close on e-mail or the phone actually meet they hate each other. I want to figure out a way to meet him."

To my amazement, George agreed. "Borrow money from Juliet and visit this bastard, but don't you dare sleep with him. I'll know if you do, don't kid yourself."

An hour after meeting Thomas Petersham at London/Heathrow airport, I got a call.

"Juliet was right. I don't like him at all."

I rushed to call George at the hotel.

But, then, when she called again after 3 days of touring England, it was different.

"We really love each other, Mom. I don't know what to do."

Well, George certainly knew what he wanted to do. Before Olivia could get off the bus from the Phoenix airport to Sedona, he left me with the boys and moved into a suite at the Motel.

"Tell her the lawyer will be in touch with her tomorrow, Natalie."

XCIV

Enter: Tom Petersham

Once Olivia called Tom in England to tell him that George had left and wanted a divorce, it didn't take this long-distance suitor more than a week to arrive in Sedona.

What was I thinking during the interval? I was torn. On the one hand, even though Olivia and George were not married in the Catholic Church and didn't believe that divorce was wrong, they still seemed very married to me. After all, the 4 boys were there to "make the love the parents for each other visible," as Von Hildebrand liked to put it. On the other hand I had to believe her when Olivia told me, eyes beseeching for understanding:

"I never loved him the way I love Tom; never the way you loved Dad or he loved you, or even the way Juliet loves Al even though they fight so much."

"How will a 30-year-old single man take on 4 sons, 2 of them only babies? And what are you going to live on?" Even a romantic Karamazov grandmother would have to be worried about these practicalities.

The answer was not long in coming. The minute I spied Thomas Petersham walking off the airport shuttle toward the front door of the Mc-

Namara house, I thought, he may be 10 years younger than Olivia, at 40, but he looked 10 years older. Slightly stooped this medium height English-man with long brown hair and a beard looked more like an old poet than like a young roue who had just seduced my daughter.

Now, George was all-father in the sense of loving each of his sons passionately and be willing to take care of them hand and foot. But he was also very disorganized, probably because of drinking so much. The house was always a mess with toys and clothing and unwashed dishes strewn about.

When Cassandra called to see what was happening I could tell her:

"It's not as bad as you might think. Tom, brought up by conventional English parents, loves order! The entire house is now neat and clean, with Richy and Bobbie scheduled on laundry and dishwashing on a rotation basis!"

"Do they like their new...step-father?...do they call him father ...I mean Olivia and Tom aren't married yet? And what about money? I can contribute if they are very poor. Allan had lots of stocks and bonds I didn't know about."

"That's another thing that's better than I thought it would be, Cas-sandra. As I told you last month, I was sure George would try to get full custody of the children and live with them and a nanny in a new house, leaving Olivia to shift for herself. Instead, he decided to take a little vaca-tion from marriage and child-care. He handed custody over to Olivia, with weekend visitation, and agreed to give her the house and half his salary. This Olivia is augmenting by computer contract work plus income from Tom who got a job working part-time at a bar in one of the many dives for tourists flocking the streets of Sedona."

"Richy and Bobby love going to the Motel pool on the weekends and Olivia and Tom take a night out once a week with George coming and sitting the twin babies. They are on bottles now."

The worst part of this transition was the decline of George. Grieving

at the break from living without Olivia and his sons, and free every evening at the Hotel where he worked during the day, his alcoholic tendencies
increased by leaps and bounds. Every evening he spent at the Hotel bar or
at the pool table, drinking, now, not only beer but whiskey.

I didn't visit again for a whole year, going to Juliet's for Christmas
from my teaching job in Texas. Even though I liked Tom as a personality,
he seemed to want to keep a distance. Olivia was the usual former Catholic
who just didn't like Church, but Tom was a militant anti-Catholic and my
daily Mass and frequent visitors from other strong believers was annoying
to him. Tom was too well-brought up to argue with me or my friends, but
the look of joy on his face whenever he saw me walking out the door for
any reason was proof enough that he would be happy if I came less often.

One day, I got this call from Juliet.

"Mom, where are you?"

"Driving in Texas between the University and a concert."

"Pull off to the side of the road immediately."

"Something terrible happened. The manager of the hotel where
George lives made Olivia come over there. He told her that "I'm sorry to
tell you this, Mrs... sorry I forgot your new name...but George was found
dead on the floor of his suite this morning."

I took the first plane I could get a ticket on and rushed to Sedona.
Juliet picked me up from Phoenix airport. "One of George's drinking buddies told me that 6 months ago the manager insisted that George go into a
re-hab because his drinking was getting out of hand and guests were com-
plaining. He refused to go. Then he got pneumonia. They thought he was
just in his room recuperating, but when he stopped ordering room-service
they went to see and found him dead on the floor."

"So terrible, Juliet. When is the funeral?"

"They found George's will and he wrote in it that he didn't want any
religious funeral. You know his parents are long gone, so there was only
Olivia and Tom to bury him."

"The boys must be devastated."

"Well, the twins are too young to know what's happening, but Richy and Bobbie don't want to talk about it. They're just looking sad."

"On the bright side, though Mom, George had lots of insurance. Each boy gets $50,000 to be meted out by his lawyer to them over the years for anything they need."

That Sunday I took Richy and Bobbie with me to Mass on Sunday as I usually did when I was in Sedona. In the car on the way I told them, "Look dear boys. God created your father. God loved Him. You need to always remain Catholic and pray for his soul, so that one day you have a chance of being with him in heaven. I know your Dad wasn't a believer, but he might have gotten a big surprise when his soul left his body."

At the time of writing this story of the Sisters Karamazov, Bobbie, now 21, still goes to Mass every Sunday. I like to think God used my words that day to make a difference.

And a month later:

Enter: Marlena Petersham, the 5th baby to the womb of Olivia Karamazov De Toledo McNamara Petersham!

XCV

Fast Foward: 2015

I have a bittersweet feeling reading Epilogues. On the one hand, I don't want to say goodbye to a story I lived in vicariously as a reader. On the other hand, I want to know what happened later to the characters I grew to care about!

2015 finds me still a dedicated widow still in Austin, Texas. I tried applying to different Bishops to be an official consecrated widow. None of the 3 seemed interested in that vocation or in starting it up with me. When other widows call me to ask about the progress of this new possibility in the church I sometimes say:

"You can try with your Bishop. I have the feeling that even if a Bishop wanted to experiment he would be looking for warm, nurturing, practical women who like to help in the parish, not strange Hebrew-Catholic militant-magisterial, charismatic leaders like me!"

Without starting a community myself, God has surrounded me at the university where I teach with wonderful, spiritual, close women-friends, one also a dedicated widow inspired by my example. My interior life has blossomed with deep, personal, words that seem to come to me as from my Bridegroom. Here are 2 samples to give you the flavor of such consoling messages:

Jesus: In your language it is the shadow side of maternal instinct to be anxious for your children. Would you rather have no anxiety, but not those incredible children? It wouldn't be bad at all to right now spend the rest of your prayer-time with enfolding each one in My heart. "When you've been there 10,000 years, bright shining in the sun" will you regret the pangs of empathy for them?"

"Instead of trying to frantically dog-paddle through the waves of each day, why not let Me, Jesus, float you to the shores of eternity."

And here is what recently came to my mind as a response:

> "Hide me in Your Heart"
> "Make me an instrument of Your love…"
>
> From mantra-like repetition
> These phrases can seem no more than a tranquillizer.
>
> Until suddenly You, our Jesus
> seize and throw us into Your heart
>
> that the abandoned
> drawn to our small hearts,
> are led into Your heart…
> finally safe and sound."

God even sent me someone like the Abbot Zossima, of the Brothers Karamazov, an old, wise, fatherly man to guide me.

The Sisters Karamazov, Juliet and Olivia decided to throw Cassandra and I a family party for our 75th birthday. Everyone came from different States to Juliet and Al's house with the big garden and swimming pool.

Olivia, the poet, thought of this hilarious name for the gathering: The

Twintinabulation of the Belles. "Tintinabulation" is a word Edgar Allen Poe made up about the ringing of bells. So this title for us is punny to the max.

In another fun initiative, Juliet bought plain wooden dolls, 6 inches high, and dressed them up to look like us. For me, she made a tiny blue denim jumper and got hold of a small crown of thorns from Jerusalem on e-bay to place on my head of messy grey hair. The Cassandra doll has many layers of flowing gauze for a dancer's look.

Richy, age 22, figured out how to get both of us onto Wikipedia. This he surprised us all by projecting onto a large screen for all to see.

Tangent: Richy came to have a special place in the Sisters Karamazov scenario by dint of the fact that as a high school student he grew his hair long and, with his beard and Jewish ancestry, he looked so much like Jim Carviezel in The Passion that students started calling him Jesus. They carried on this joke all through his senior year when on Christmas Day his friends wished him a happy birthday!

Leonard, Olivia's third, is now a pianist and composer, so he played for us a composition called The Twintinabulation of the Belles.

Even the grandchildren who didn't do something spectacular at this gala had such loving smiles on their faces that Cassandra and I were practically in tears for much of the day.

Olivia wrote me a letter:

"You think you were a bad mother because you were always so angry at us. But I attribute all my love for truth and beauty and my new love for Jesus, to you. You were a good mother!"

Tangent: Olivia was stricken with a dread disease just before our 75th birthday. She wrote this graphic poem about what it felt like:

> It isn't what it is to be
> hairless, poisoned,
> crawling through

one dark tunnel to another
searching for somebody you
used to be. It isn't terror:

not of death or living like
<u>this</u> forever; nothing so
puzzling or mousy. It is more
this sense of distance
and a lack of door.

To be exact, the way your children, who
will forever
not now ever
want to grow up just like you,

linger, but will never ask you why
again tonight their Mama has to cry,
are captured by a camera's thoughtless eye:
arrested, and you see the way they try

to satisfy a space that once held you
which now has scraps, remainders and
each day, a bit more room.

Even though Olivia never goes to Holy Mass, she sees an interior vision of Jesus in the image of the famous Agemian Christ, based on the Shroud of Turin. In the interior visions, that have lasted many months, He spoke many words of comfort to her.

Her Sister Karamazov twin, Juliet, agreed to be the donor for a transplant if her twin needed it.

Olivia wrote this e-mail to family and close friends:

"I realize it's difficult to be forced by your love of me to undergo this unpleasant voyage from the sidelines: I wanted to say again that I so appreciate the love and support that is constant and surely makes it possible for me to survive these rocky waters. I know that the doctors may have twice saved my life, but that life would not be worth saving if it weren't for all of you. You are the reason I am able to push through. I love you all more than I can say, but more, I am filled with admiration for you... I know what it's like to so fear for someone you love and to have nothing you can do to help besides just continuing to be a presence despite your own spoken or unspoken fears.

"Here's to life getting slowly better!!! Here's to the day I can take my rightful place back as Mother of the family instead of being an invalid. Here's to a dinner I can almost taste at a vacation house on the beach or in the woods where we will all raise our glasses and shout for joy because all the terror, pain, and horror is long in the past, defeated, and unable to prod us with its dark fingers anymore. That day will come."

As of finishing this book, Olivia is courageously struggling to live on.

Back to the Twintinabulation: Even the son-in-laws got into the act. Tom and Al bought copies of leather-bound, gold leaf paged volumes of *The Brothers Karamazov* to give to each of the adults.

Present was my granddaughter Debbie, newly married to a convert to the Catholic Church from atheism. How's that for full-circle!

"I have a secret to tell you, Grandma Natalie," my beautiful long-haired blond granddaughter Debbie whispered in my ear. "You are going to be a great grandmother 7 months from now...And when she is baptized I am coming back into the Church also."

My cup runneth over!

After enjoying food and drink displayed on picnic tables, we put on a disc of Israeli dance music.

Cassandra and I joined hands in the center of the circle doing the traditional hora. And she cajoled even the son-in-laws to join in an outer circle round and round.

EXIT: The Sisters Karamazov! There are many brothers in the younger generation but only Debbie of Juliet's family and Marlena of Olivia's family. No more sisters, no more twin girls? If Debbie's baby is a girl, will she have another one? Who knows?

I am thinking, the Brothers Karamazov is universal? Every man is Fyodor, the father, Dmitri, Ivan, Aloysha, Smerdyakov, and when sanctified Zossima? And every woman is Grushenka and Katerina and Madame Hohlakov and, when sanctified, Mary?

That night, praying before going to sleep, Jesus seemed to say to me:
"I suffered, died and rose so that if you follow Me, you can be
"TOGETHER FOREVER."